The right of Shane O'Neill to
be identified as author of this work has
been asserted.

Paperback First Edition 2016

Published By:
Alternative Fiction,
Waterford, Ireland.
Publisher's ISBN: 978-0-9934247

Printed & Bound By:
IngramSpark,
La Vergne,
Tennessee,
America.

ISBN-13: 978-0-9934247-1-7

For Monica

*Beyond the passion for vengeance
lies discarded reason;
a trap orchestrated by the Devil
for the captives to mindless rage.*

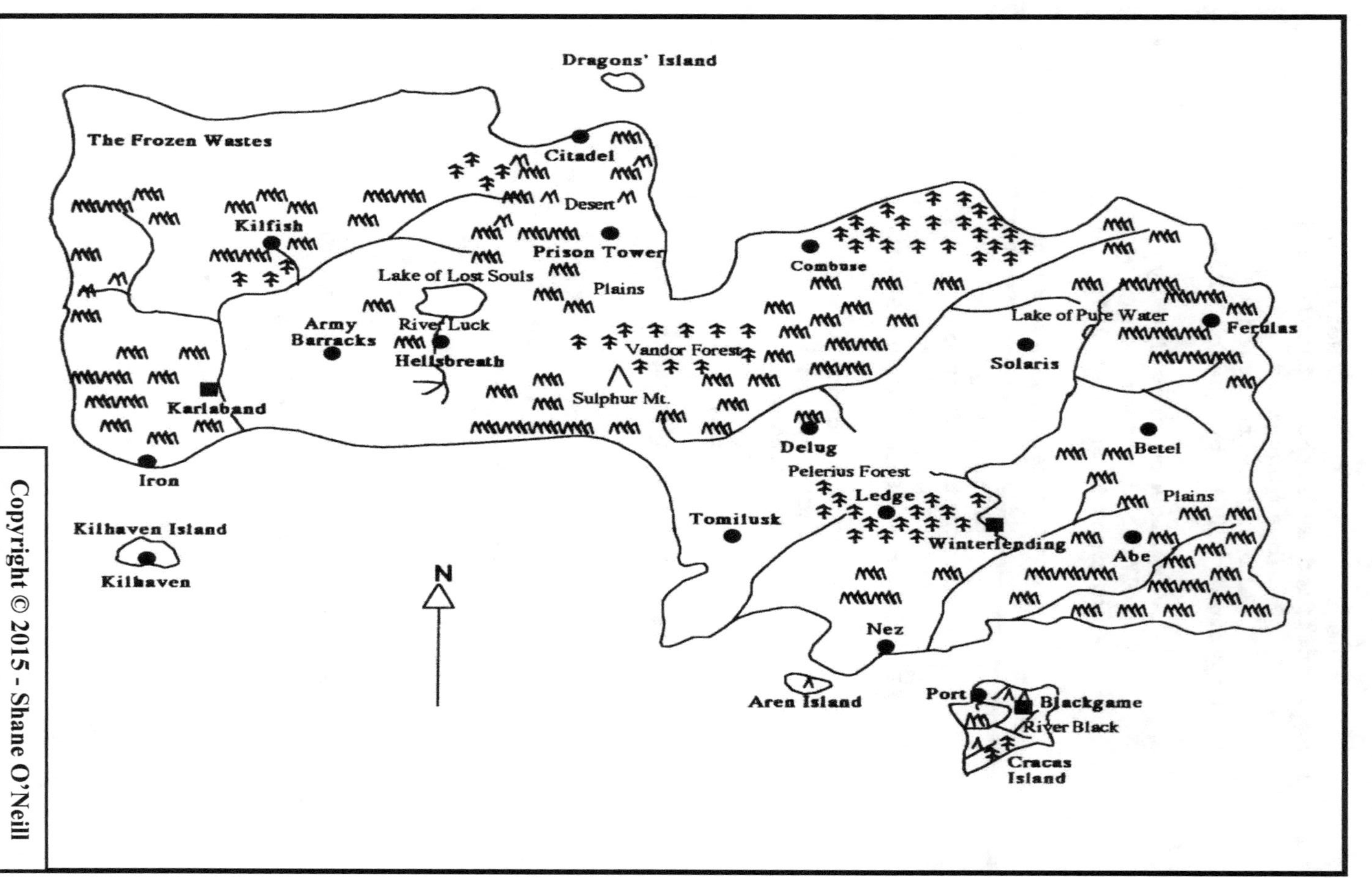
Dragons' Island
The Frozen Wastes
Citadel
Desert
Kilfish
Prison Tower
Combuse
Lake of Lost Souls
Plains
Lake of Pure Water
Army
Barracks
River Luck
Vandor Forest
Solaris
Ferulas
Hellsbreath
Sulphur Mt.
Karlaband
Delug
Betel
Iron
Pelerius Forest
Ledge
Plains
Kilhaven Island
Tomilusk
Winterlending
Abe
Kilhaven
N
Nez
Aren Island
Port
Blackgame
River Black
Cracas
Island

PROLOGUE

I remember only too clearly the night my wife was murdered. And if I knew then what I know now, I would have wished my life had ended also. I would have spared myself the anguish of dead friends and comrades-in-arms, of blood-soaked battlefields of the dead and the screaming dying, of nightmares consuming my sleepless nights. But I would have been denied bearing witness to magical times, of magnificent heroes and evil enemies, of incredible events that shaped a nation...of a simple sailor becoming legend.

A seemingly endless coastline filled his aching vision from the deck of the tiny ketch, creeping its way slowly inland. The bells of nearby trawlers rang out intermittently, making their way in to the harbour, examining the day's catch, sailors complaining about tomorrow's weather.

Storm glanced down, admiring the boat. The girl was old, too elderly to be riding waves such as these. But she was strong enough to fulfil her final voyage, carry her two passengers to land, for the last time. He reached a hand into his jerkin-pocket to once more check its valuable contents. The coins found his trembling hand as he sighed with relief. Sixty gold pieces, not much for his father's house and land. Though maybe enough to sustain them for a while in Karlaband, the giant city whose lights now beckoned them towards the distant pier.

The settlement Kilfish was to be their final destination, a far cry from the town Iron which he was once proud enough to call home. But the town had changed since his father's time; once a place of safety, now a settlement of fear and death. The capital city Karlaband was no different, perhaps even worse if half the foul tales he had heard were true. Karlaband, City of Lies; City of Dreams, centre of the 'civilised' world, a place known by many names. He would have preferred not to stop there at all, but halt there they must, for supplies were running low.

Nereid saw her husband's worried face and smiled. Fretting was his chief hobby; he had perfected it almost to an art form.

"I'd prefer not to stop at the capital," he muttered softly.

"Don't worry, we won't be there long. Besides, if we do meet with trouble, I'll protect you," she laughed, placing a giant crossbow across her lap.

He smiled, but did not laugh. It was a sore point with him that he had never taken the time to learn how to fight; sailing was his profession, not swordplay. He turned away and glanced at the map. Karlaband stuck out like an ugly thorn on the country, surrounded by mountains to the north and west, always prepared for any possible attack from its neighbours. But it had no enemies worth attention, a nearby army barracks made sure of that. The giant area of land called The Frozen Wastes lay to the north, a region hostile to life. The only other place of interest was the Lake of Lost Souls, a large pool believed to be haunted by the poor travellers who had drowned in it over the centuries.

The pier finally came into sight as they entered the city via the gap adjacent to the east tower. Three lightly-armoured soldiers quickly approached the ketch and came on board without invitation where they proceeded to search the boat for hidden stores of weapons or stowaways.

"Wher' you headin'?" barked the largest of the three.

"To Kilfish," Nereid retorted, casting a glance at the guard, wondering if the soldiers were as devious as the robbers in this city.

They searched the small vessel from bow to stern, yet found nothing. They departed from the boat, cursing. The weapons they would have confiscated might have fetched a high price on the black-market that ran throughout the capital.

Storm watched them leave, glad to see the back of them. However, he waved to them all the same, but they did not return the gesture. They decided to find a tavern that might provide them with a bed for the night before leaving the capital the following morning. They entered the main street and began to search until Nereid noticed a small inn down a side-alley. The street was dark and stank of dead fish and rubbish, but both were too tired to argue.

They had just entered the alley when Storm suddenly heard noises above him on the roof of a nearby house. He shouted a warning as five shadows leapt down to the street, surrounding them. He didn't have time to prepare himself before two of the men knocked him to the ground. One of the men, who Storm presumed was the leader, revealed a baton which he struck across his head. Just before blackness claimed him, he turned to see his young wife reveal her crossbow and shoot his attacker in the shoulder, hearing him cry out in pain and rage. But the wounded robber managed to get to his feet, draw his sword and cut the now unarmed woman down.

The dawn was several hours old before he awoke, stunned and shocked, unable to comprehend what had happened, wondering if it had only been a nightmare. But he knew it wasn't, especially when he took stock of his surroundings. His vision gradually progressed from being just a blur until he could see grey featureless walls around him. He glanced down and noticed that he lay in a small bed, seemingly the only piece of furniture in the otherwise humble room. Standing above him, staring down at his captive was a grey-haired balding old man. Storm knew he should have felt fear, or at least some puzzlement and confusion at his predicament, but strangely he felt only curiosity at his foreign surroundings.

"I found you in an alley last night," he said. "You were unconscious so I carried you here to my home. And you are..?"

"Storm," he stuttered, "and my wife?"

The old man sat on the edge of the bed with a sigh. "The City-Guards have her down at the morgue. They would have left you there in the alley to die also."

Storm stared at the old man in shock, not wanting to hear the words, but the memory of the previous night quickly shattered his disbelief. The tears began to flow down his cheeks and soon became a flood. The elderly man embraced him and held him close for several minutes.

Storm broke the tight hug and stared intently into the eyes of his rescuer. "I thank you for your compassion," Storm said. "But from this moment there is no room in my heart for mourning, only revenge. By the soul of my beloved, I swear they will pay dearly with every last drop of their blood. I will not rest until I have put an end to their miserable lives. Nothing else matters."

"Calm down, that can wait. I'm Kassier," the old man retorted. "You've also been robbed, as you might have expected. Though the City-Guards might have done that, their reputation is far from laudable."

"What am I going to do now?" Storm stuttered in despair.

"Can you fight?"

"I've never had training in any sort of weaponry," he replied with a sigh. "All I have known is sailing."

"Then I will teach you. Get out of bed."

"Why are you helping me?" Storm asked in puzzlement.

"Let's just say I've seen too many bad things happen in this city. I want to put a stop to at least some of it."

After he had dressed, the old man led him from the room down a hallway and into a small kitchen where lay a table lined with meat, bread and wine.

"Eat," Kassier stated. "There is plenty more from where that came."

"I saw one of the men before I blacked out. He was tall, had a slight limp and had a large scar running down his left cheek."

Kassier stared back in anger. "Kanaka," he declared. "It has to be him. He always goes with a well-known gang, a very dangerous group I might add. You'd find him in 'The Sinking Tavern' every night, the old drunk."

"Then that's where I'm going," Storm replied and rose to his feet.

"You're not ready to go there yet! Give me one week," Kassier retorted sharply. "Just seven days and I'll knock you into shape."

"Thanks for everything, but I'll manage."

"Now you listen here," the old man shouted. "You wouldn't last one second against Kanaka. He isn't even the leader."

"How do you know that?" Storm snapped.

"Because he's too stupid, like you if you go after him without weapons or the proper training. I can teach you the rudimentary skills and some tricks to keep you alive as regards swordsmanship and archery."

"All right, one week." Storm replied. "But no more than that."

"I hope for your sake it will be enough," Kassier replied. "Let me tell you some background history to the gang who attacked you. Hemlock is the leader of four men; Kanaka, Jacinth, Kail and Flax. Kanaka is a coward and will be the easiest to coerce, his whole life has been to follow Hemlock like a lost puppy from fetching his boots to wiping his arse if he so commanded. Jacinth and Kail were homeless orphans whom Hemlock befriended, starving children living on the scraps from bakeries on the dirty streets of Karlaband. They have known only poverty and violence their entire lives and a deep hatred of the upper classes who spat on them. Flax is somewhat different, he was born into a wealthy family and is well educated. His parents doted on him and gave him everything he asked for; it was this lack of discipline which caused him to nightly frequent every tavern and brothel in the city, much to their dismay. Finally they threw him out and this resentment brought him to the open arms of their leader. Hemlock is something of an enigma; he is highly intelligent and from an early age displayed powerful latent magickal abilities. He and his brother Kava as teenagers used to perform acts of illusion for laughing children for a few coins. That was before a heated argument between them about whose powers were superior drove them apart. Hemlock is insanely jealous of all wizards and their high position in society, and I suspect he has ambitions far greater than being a simple thief and murderer. You would be wise not to underestimate him, he is a skilled swordsman and very dangerous, many victims falling prey to his violent temper. He delights in suffering, which he learned from an early age torturing defenceless animals and flaying them as they screamed in agony." Kassier declared. "Come now, let us begin your training."

The old man led his new apprentice from the kitchen into the hallway and down a long flight of stairs until they had entered the cellar.

Storm turned to his teacher in puzzlement. "There's nothing here."

"There's me!" Kassier shouted as he snatched a sword off a rack on the far wall and suddenly attacked him.

Storm dived out of the way just in time to avoid the blow and grabbed a broadsword off the wall. Kassier came at him again with incredible speed, despite his elder years. The old man was full of surprises. He managed to block the blows for several moments until Kassier easily knocked the sword from Storm's hand. Before the blade had even hit the ground the old man had his weapon at his opponent's unguarded throat, with a smile on his wrinkled face.

In the long week that followed, Storm quickly learned the fine art of swordplay and found to his surprise that he was becoming quite fond of the old man. When Kassier was finally satisfied at his pupil's performance, he led him from the cellar back upstairs and into a small side-room. It was similar to the room he had awoken in one week earlier in that it was also almost completely bare of furniture. One small square table lay in the centre of the chamber upon which lay a lit red candle and a long item Storm couldn't quite make out. As he approached the desk he let out a gasp of astonishment upon seeing the object clearly. A large sword lay on the table and as Storm studied the weapon he noticed various designs and words on both the shining blade and the ornamented handle, a language he had never seen before. He picked up the weapon in his trembling hands and marvelled at how light and sharp it was. He felt he had to use it, like it was made for his hand, for no-one but him.

"May I?" he inquired, tapping the tip of the blade on the table.

"Of course," the old man replied with a smile.

Storm raised the sword high over his head and brought it down onto the table, splitting the desk in two, and sending bits of wood flying across the room. It had cut through the table like a hot knife through butter. Not a mark lay on the blade after the blow.

"Where did you find this sword?" he asked in astonishment.

"Let's just say I acquired it, and leave it at that," Kassier replied with a light laugh, "but the blade is now yours."

"I can't accept such a weapon as this," Storm said.

"You must. My fighting days are long gone, but yours my friend, are just beginning," the old man added. "Besides, you insult me if you reject my gift."

"In that case, I have no choice. Thank you friend, you have done me a great service, one I feel I cannot possibly repay."

"Just make sure you find Kanaka and his gang, and make yourself worthy of the ownership of that blade. It thirsts for nourishment, and I can no longer feed it or do it justice by hiding it."

"Then this is good-bye, friend," Storm stated as he slid the blade into its scabbard and strapped it to his waist.

"Perhaps, for I have a feeling you and I will meet again," Kassier smiled. "One final word of advice before you leave, Storm. Make sure your desire for revenge does not cloud your reason. I'd hate to see you dead for the sake of a wife who would have much preferred you alive and well, even though her murderers still ran free."

"Thanks. I'll try and keep that in mind," Storm said before he left the house for the tavern.

Dusk was approaching as Storm made his way to 'The Sinking Tavern,' a well-known drinking-spot for the cut-throats and thieves of Karlaband. It was easy to find, one had just to follow the sound of laughing drunken men who were falling out of its door and into the street. Storm pushed his way past them and into the tavern. The inn was packed to claustrophobic capacity with the smell of ale and vomit heavy in the air. Dozens of men of various dress, both poor and those moderately well-off were either drinking or fighting throughout the giant chamber.

He struggled through the crowd until he managed to find a vacant seat at one of the smaller tables by the far corner of the room and ordered a beer. As he began to drink, he wondered if Kanaka would come to the tavern this night. He could be ill, or have left the city, or anything. Storm was trying hard not to panic. As if in answer however, the tall robber entered the inn and approached the bar. Storm could see the scar on his cheek, and when he sat down at a nearby table, Storm rose and suddenly sat next to him.

"Can I buy you a drink?" Storm asked.

The man turned and looked at Storm for several moments in puzzlement, then his mouth dropped open in fear and astonishment as recognition dawned. He instantly reached for the hilt of his sword, but Storm was quicker and he grabbed the man's hand, holding it fast. Storm then slammed his other fist into Kanaka's face, splitting his lower lip. Before he could react, Storm had him up against the wall with a knife at his throat. The other patrons did not pay any attention to this commotion, they were too interested in their own petty feuds.

"Don't hurt me," Kanaka stuttered.

"Tell me where the rest of your gang are!" Storm shouted.

"I can't. They'd kill me."

"I'll kill you if you don't," Storm replied and stabbed the man in the right thigh. The robber let out a scream as blood flowed freely from his leg onto the floor. Storm returned the short blade to the man's trembling neck.

"Hey, I'll have none of that!" the barkeeper shouted. "I'll tolerate unarmed combat in this establishment, but any blood spilt will have to be done out on the street. My barmaid only works one hour a day and moans incessantly about mopping vomit, sweeping up shattered teeth and sticking her hand down the toilet!"

"Shut-up," Storm snapped. "Tell your story to someone who cares."

The barman began to wonder if he should pursue the matter further when a man cried for a drink and he turned away. The issue was really none of his business. Men had died in this bar before, what was one more?

Storm returned his attention to his captive. "Where are they?" he repeated. "In the city?"

"No, they've left."

"Without you?"

"I didn't want to go," Kanaka said.

Storm laughed. "More likely they left without you."

"They've gone to Vandor Forest." Kanaka said, trembling with fear.

"Why should they want to go there?"

"Hemlock wants to get some magical herbs that grow there to heal the wound your woman inflicted. He's coming back to steal a sword that's in the city somewhere."

"What sword? Why is it so important?"

"I don't know," the robber replied flatly.

"You're lying," Storm snarled.

"It's the truth," Kanaka declared. "Now let me go."

"You killed my wife, for the sake of sixty coins."

"That wasn't me. Hemlock killed her. You and your wife were simply in the wrong place at the wrong time, it was nothing personal. We only wanted the money, not your lives, if your woman had not fired her weapon she would still be alive.”

“How dare you blame her. You were there, you were part of it, you had the power to stop your leader but for your cowardice.” Storm retorted.

“No, don’t do it,” Kanaka sobbed. “Please don’t kill me!”

“Save it for the Devil,” Storm snapped as he stabbed the robber in the stomach.

The man uttered a cry before Storm let his lifeless body fall to the ground. Nobody in the inn seemed to take any notice of the incident, leaving Storm to depart the tavern unmolested. He entered a side-alley and looked at Kanaka’s blood on his hands. Storm took out a cloth and began to vigorously scrub the blood off. He gazed skywards and wondered at what he was becoming, he was no longer a simple sailor, but now a fighter…a killer.

Storm decided it would be wiser if he followed Hemlock to Vandor Forest, rather than wait for his return. He could find out his plans before Hemlock returned to the city.

The killing had only just begun.

PART ONE

CHAPTER ONE

The giant forest greeted the four men like old friends, welcoming them into its clutches, uncaring of their reason for intrusion. The thick undergrowth hid their passage into this hidden realm of shadows and tall trees. By noon they had come to a small clearing where stood in the centre a single signpost. It pointed the way back to the capital, as if requesting that all trespassers should leave immediately.

"The plant I require is quite unusual," Hemlock declared. "It has a blue stalk giving rise to fiery red flowers and a sweet aromatic smell reminiscent of strawberries."

"We might still be searching for days," groaned Flax.

"They like a lot of light so a clearing like this would be a good place to commence a search." Hemlock said. "I would advise you three get busy. The woods are unwelcome at night and monsters that crave human flesh are not uncommon."

Nearly three hours had passed when Jacinth let out a cry and all came running to investigate the commotion. The swordsman pointed at a nearby bush and their leader smiled.

"Well done, Jacinth." Hemlock grinned. "You have found one of the rarest and most sought after herbs in existence, the plant Sunstar."

Hemlock reached down and quickly pocketed the precious plant, while carefully avoiding the nearby poison-ivy and thorn-covered brambles.

"Is this all we came for?" moaned Flax.

"We travelled all over this stinking country for a pile of herbs?" snapped Jacinth, close to losing his temper.

"You're going to be travelling all over this stinking country again," laughed their leader.

"What?" shouted Flax in disbelief.

"We're going back to Karlaband, to the Temple of the Sacred Sword," announced Hemlock, still smiling. "I plan to steal the priceless sword their twisted religion is based upon and with it, we'll be rich. Security at the Temple will be lax in a couple of days because they'll all be away praying. That's why we couldn't have got it last week. I decided we could use this spare time to travel and get the herbs and heal my injury I got from that sailor bitch!"

"And just how will we become rich?" laughed Flax.

"By raising the demon of the sword through using an ancient manuscript I obtained from a lone mage who was passing through the capital," Hemlock retorted. "The demon will give us a mountain of gold in exchange for freeing it."

"How did you get the manuscript from him?"

"I 'persuaded' him to part with it," Hemlock laughed.

None of the three men questioned what he meant by that, it was perfectly clear. But Kail was not amused. "Fool, you don't know what you're messing around with."

Both Jacinth and Flax took a step back from Kail at this remark. Past experience told them it was not wise to insult Hemlock.

"The demon will make us rich, Kail," Hemlock stated and began to play with his dagger, flicking the short blade between his fingers. "But you don't have to come."

"Damn right I don't, I'll stay behind with Kanaka and find another way of getting rich," snapped Kail and began to walk away from the group, back towards the clearing and Karlaband.

He had hardly walked ten feet when Hemlock called out. He turned around, thinking their leader had changed his mind, but instead was hit by Hemlock's dagger which caught him in the throat. He took one feeble step back before falling to the ground.

"I forgot to mention one thing," Hemlock said as he approached the body. "I also need human blood to raise the demon. I'm sure you won't mind," he added as he retrieved his knife, and began filling a small bottle with Kail's blood.

Flax and Jacinth stared first at this, and then at each other in speechless astonishment. Even Jacinth, with his strong stomach, felt total repulsion at the scene before him. Flax began searching for somewhere to empty his unsteady stomach. Hemlock rose and turned to his two remaining employees in crime.

"Don't fret over him," Hemlock said coldly. "He was more useful in death than he was in life. Now, anybody else want to argue with me?"

Neither of the two men spoke.

"Right then, let's go."

But before any of the men had taken a single step back towards the clearing, an arrow hit the fallen oak tree next to them, not three feet from where Flax stood. The arrow was firmly lodged in the tree and supported a brilliant blaze of colours on its tail. All three men instantly drew their blades and prepared for battle.

Then they heard a voice suddenly cry out from the bushes in front of them. "Drop your weapons, or die."

Hemlock hesitated for several moments before throwing his blade to the ground and ordering the other two to do the same. After they had done so, from out of the bushes came two fat dwarfs, with bows aimed at the men. The two dwarves could have been twins. They were dressed in filthy ripped clothes and both supporting beards. One of the dwarfs approached the men with great trepidation and collected the weapons before quickly returning to the safety of his companion.

"You are trespassers," announced the one with the bow. "We will take you to the Elder for punishment."

The three prisoners were escorted through the forest for several long hours before they finally reached a giant clearing where stood the dwarfs' village. Excited dwarf-children crowded around them and goaded them on with small spears towards a circular straw hut in the centre of the village. Outside the hut sat an obese dwarf upon a makeshift throne of straw and mud. This grotesque creature they surmised had to be their chief; their Elder. The fat dwarf stared coldly at the intruders before him.

"Bunch of savages," Hemlock said. "They don't know who they're dealing with."

The fat chief turned to the two dwarves who had captured these trespassers. "Kill them," he roared.

"Sire," interjected one of the two dwarfs. "It would be more amusing if they fought each other."

"Yes," screamed the now excited self-appointed King. "Tomorrow at midday. Take them away."

Flax awoke with the rising sun and glanced out of the large cage and wondered if the weather would be fine on his last day of life. He cast a glance at Hemlock as if to ask what their beloved leader was going to do now. Hemlock did not look back, but instead called one of the dwarfs over to the cage.

"I want a cup of water."

The dwarf stared at him before going off and returned a few moments later with a mug. He then left the vicinity of the cage in a hurry.

"What are you up to?" asked Flax in despair.

"These stupid savages didn't take my herbs and left no guard by the cage," replied Hemlock slyly.

With that, he began to stuff some of the plant into the cup and poured some of Kail's blood from the small flask into the mug. He then placed his right hand over the cup and began to mutter some words Flax couldn't quite make out. But in less than a minute, the water suddenly began to boil and to Flax's amazement, a tiny red ball jumped out of the mug. The ball started to expand until it had reached the size of an orange. Flax and Jacinth stared fixedly at it in complete fascination as dozens of small mouths appeared all over the surface of the ball, each possessing lines of razor-sharp fangs. Hemlock then picked up the ball and pocketed it.

They waited until noon when five dwarfs appeared and dragged them out of the cage towards the centre of the village where a large congregation had gathered around their chief. Placed on the ground in front of them were their swords. Suddenly Hemlock produced the ball and flung it at the chief upon his throne. Panic reigned as the magical ball with its many mouths began to devour their king, its fangs digging deep into his fat neck. Dwarfs fled in every direction as their chief screamed in terror and pain. In the confusion, the three prisoners took back their weapons and made good their escape, fleeing back into the forest. They ran until they could no longer hear the screams of the chief or the cries of panic from his subjects.

"That was an amazing trick," said the astonished Flax.

"The spell will have worn off by now and they'll be sending a search party after us," panted Hemlock, "but I'd say their chief is dead," he added and laughed.

They sprinted for a further hour before deciding to rest by a small stream. They drank quickly before moving off again, and by nightfall on the following day were out of the giant forest. They began to make their way to the town Hellsbreath. Living off the land while travelling for three days, they eventually sighted the small trading town, but realised they had arrived at a bad time. New troops from the nearby Army Barracks had relieved the old soldiers at the town. Security would be tightened and Hemlock knew he would be thoroughly searched and the herbs would be confiscated. He decided it would be wiser to chance crossing the River Luck instead.

The River Luck ran through the town of Hellsbreath and possessed some of the most treacherous currents known. Flax and Jacinth didn't like the sound of trying to cross the river, but dared not argue with Hemlock. Flax's previous feelings of loyalty were rapidly turning to hatred for their leader, especially after the incident with Kail.

That night they made camp on the shore of the river and cooked two rabbits they had snared earlier. By noon the next day they felt they were ready. The river at this point was shallow and the currents would not be as strong. But still each carried a large rock on their shoulder to prevent the waters carrying them away. The river was freezing to the touch and Flax thought he might faint with the cold before he reached the opposite bank. But the three travellers eventually made it to the other side safely.

In just a few days they would reach the capital and Hemlock could begin preparations for the next stage in his evil plan, thought Flax. "And that's if he doesn't kill us all in the process," he whispered to himself, lest Hemlock hear.

CHAPTER TWO

Leaving the ketch at Karlaband, Storm decided to make the journey to the forest on foot. He was two days from the capital and close to exhaustion. But he couldn't stop, not even to rest. The rage wouldn't let him. The anger and hate felt like heavy baggage on his back that he could not remove, at least not until he caught up with Hemlock.

He was nearing the town of Hellsbreath where he could pass through in order to cross the River Luck, though unknown to him, Hemlock and his two fellow thieves were presently crossing the very same river a short distance downstream. In three days he reckoned he should be within sight of the forest. But one thing plagued his mind. Why should Hemlock travel all the way here for herbs and then return to the capital for a sword? It didn't make sense, at least not to a sane mind it didn't. He finally decided to make camp that night close to the west-bank of the River Luck, and head towards the wood at first light.

It was nearing nightfall on the third day when Storm finally sighted the giant forest. He possessed very little knowledge of this great woodland, except that it was home to several varied types of life, and all unpleasant. He knew of a tribe of dwarfs that had little or no contact with the outside world. They were widely regarded as simple savages. He hoped they had not found Hemlock and disposed of him. Storm wanted that exclusive pleasure.

He made camp at the edge of the forest and sat close to the fire, for the wind had picked up and the nearby trees gave no shelter from the icy-cold breeze. He was just about to open his shoulder-bag to pull out his rations for the day, when he suddenly heard a sharp crack, as if something large, maybe human, had accidentally stepped on a dry twig. Storm instinctively grabbed hold of his precious blade and rose to his feet.

He wondered if it might be Hemlock, making his way back. He considered if he was ready, if he was prepared enough to face him this soon. But from behind the trees came not his deadly enemy, but a small boy dressed in torn clothes and filthy bare feet. He stood at about four foot five by Storm's reckoning, possessing a great bush of fiery red hair and light freckles on his pale cheeks. Strapped to the left side of his waist was an old shortsword in a ragged leather scabbard and an abundant quiver of arrows over his left shoulder, one of which was positioned on a long-bow and aimed for Storm's heart. The small intruder approached until he stood no more than six feet away from his frozen captive and Storm realised he had no alternative but to relinquish his sword. He let the slender blade fall to the ground, but the boy did not move.

"Who are you, and what are you doing here in my forest?"

Storm realised he had to thread carefully. The child obviously believed he was the sole king of his own little realm, with little knowledge of the outside world. "I beg your forgiveness, my name is Storm. I came here because I seek someone."

"I am called Suzerain," the boy replied. "This someone you speak of, was he one of three men?"

Storm nodded as Suzerain relaxed and removed the arrow from his bow and returned it to the quiver on his back.

"They have left the forest," Suzerain declared, and Storm's head sank in despair. "But they left something behind."

Storm's head rose and he moved towards the boy in sudden excitement. "What did they leave?"

"A dead man," he added. "I know where he is."

"Will you show me?" Storm asked and Suzerain nodded.

As they travelled through the forest, Storm was amazed Suzerain could find his way through the woodland in the pitch blackness of night. Storm could hardly see ten feet in front of him. He decided to make friendly conversation with the boy. "Were you born in the forest?"

"No," Suzerain retorted. "My parents and I came here about two summers ago, but they caught fever and died soon after. I found an old hut and decided to stay here. My father had been teaching me tracking and hunting skills, so I used them to survive."

"It can't have been easy."

"No, but sometimes it was fun," he laughed.

Storm quickly realised he was hearing the world through a child's eyes, and one who had managed to make an adventure out of staying alive. "You speak well for someone so young."

"I keep up my schooling by reading my father's old books," Suzerain replied. "Ah, we're almost there," he added as they entered a large clearing.

Storm caught sight of the form of a lying body and ran on ahead, his heart beating fast, hoping it wasn't Hemlock. But upon reaching the corpse he abruptly stopped and turned away, retching. Wolves had got to the body, and there wasn't much left to see. He grabbed hold of the boy and led him away.

"Was it the man you wanted?" Suzerain asked.

"I don't know. The wolves attacked him," Storm replied. "But I don't think it was. It might have been one of his friends, they would have buried their leader."

Suzerain stared at Storm confused, not knowing what he meant. Storm saw the look and decided to tell him the real reason why he came to the forest. Several moments passed before he turned to Storm, full of questions, some of which only a child would ask.

"Is the man you seek evil?" Suzerain inquired.

"I believe so. He killed my wife, and she was with child," Storm retorted in anger, "another five months and I might have had a son."

"Do you know what the men look like that killed her?"

"I only knew the face of one, and he is now dead," Storm said simply. "But I have a feeling I'll know him and his pals when I see them."

Then he suddenly remembered the dead man's sword. There might be some identification of the man's name on the blade's handle. He ran back, and while avoiding looking at the body, snatched hold of the weapon. He quickly examined the handle and cried out in joy. There was a name carved into the metal and it was not Hemlock's. It belonged to Kail. He returned to Suzerain.

"It's not him," Storm said excitedly. "It was one of his friends."

"Then the man you seek is still alive," Suzerain added and he grabbed hold of Storm's hand. "Come on, I'll show you my hut."

Storm smiled and followed his young guide. He knew once he arrived at the boy's hut, it would be time to say good-bye. It was probably for the best since the child would only slow him down, and yet, he was becoming fond of him. His own son might have turned out like Suzerain, and that would have made him proud.

After about an hour of travelling through the dense forest Suzerain told him the hut was near. They entered a small clearing and the boy ran on ahead. Dawn was fast approaching and Storm watched the sun begin to rise when his train of thought was broken by a sudden shout from Suzerain. Storm drew his sword and ran towards the boy, hacking his way through the bushes that blocked his path. He caught sight of Suzerain, kneeling before a blackened ruin, crying. He approached as the boy rose and wiped his eyes and nose with his sleeve.

"There are footprints of dwarves around here. They must have been looking for someone," Suzerain stated. "It was probably Hemlock they were seeking. I can find him for you."

"I don't know if I should take you along," Storm mused.

"It can't be anymore dangerous than what I face in this hellish forest every day," Suzerain snapped. "Besides, I can't survive now that the hut is gone. Everything was in it. What dwarfs don't steal, they burn."

"All right, all right," Storm shouted in reply, and the boy smiled.

Two days later they were out of Vandor Forest and were making their way to the River Luck for Suzerain had tracked Hemlock to that location. Storm was amazed at how he could track Hemlock even though he was many days journey away from where they stood. By noon that same day they had crossed the treacherous river, employing the same method that Hemlock and his men had used to cross the dangerous waterway.

"We'll go south-west to the capital by using a short-cut my parents and I travelled on," stated Suzerain.

"What's the catch?" interjected Storm, not very familiar with the land.

"It's quite rough country with wolves and bandits abound, but it will save us valuable time."

"All right then, we'll use it."

The travellers had an uneventful journey until the late afternoon of the following day when Suzerain noticed suspicious shadows by the trees and bushes all around them. He told Storm, but the swordsman did not think much of it, believing it to be a simple trick of the light. But Suzerain was not convinced. His fears were confirmed when two large men in rough attire suddenly jumped from behind the bushes and onto the path directly ahead of them. They drew their swords as they advanced on the travellers. Both possessed black curly hair and beards to match.

Suzerain took aim at the larger of the two men. Before he could fire however, the bandit revealed a small knife and threw the short blade, hitting the boy in the left arm, sending his arrow wide off its target. Suzerain screamed in pain as his arrow imbedded itself in a tree. Storm remembered his own bow which he had purchased just before he left the capital, and the skills in archery Kassier had so relentlessly taught him.

The larger bandit advanced fearlessly, though received for his bravery not the blood of his enemy, but instead an arrow in his chest that pierced his heart and shattered several ribs before coming to rest out through his back. The man collapsed without a sound, but his companion seemed not to be intimidated by the man's death and ran towards Storm, waving his sword around in front of him. Storm realised he hadn't enough time to notch another arrow and so dropped his bow in favour of his sword.

The bandit swung his sword down, intending to plant the blade in his opponent's chest. Storm dared not dodge the robber for Suzerain lay nearby, vulnerable and unarmed. He instead decided to block the blow, and realising the man had let himself open, swung his blade in an arc and caught the bandit in his left side. The robber let out a scream before falling to the ground where he lay dying in a pool of his own blood. Storm stared down at his vanquished enemy as the bandit released his final breath to the wind. Storm sighed, it appeared the killing had become easier.

He knelt by Suzerain to inspect his injury. The dagger had only grazed the boy's arm, and he quickly bandaged it before helping Suzerain to his feet. "We'll camp soon and I'll then re-bandage your arm," Storm declared. "Can you manage?"

"Yes, I think so."

They left the bandits where they lay, food for the wolves that would soon come once nightfall approached. They journeyed for a further hour before making camp and resting for the night. Storm helped Suzerain to sit down near the fire and removed the old bandage. He carefully examined the wound and was satisfied it was healing before placing on the new bandage. Suzerain insisted he was fine and ran off to catch a rabbit for both of them were starving. He arrived back less than an hour later and the two travellers settled down to eat.

They left at first light and continued their journey to the capital, the only signs they left behind of their passing were the charred remains of the fire and the chewed bones of the rabbit.

CHAPTER THREE

Once inside the city via the heavily guarded steel-gates, the travellers instinctively made for the nearest tavern. The soldiers paid them no heed, more interested in the arrival of unwelcome barbarians or battle-crazy dwarfs.

Hemlock glanced at their fine broadswords and dreamed of the great blade he was about to steal. It was a weapon widely regarded as the most powerful of all ancient magical items; an object lusted after by men down through the centuries, and therefore closely guarded by the priests of the Temple of the Sacred Sword. Forged when the land was young, and recognised as more powerful than any weapon created by the dark-elves or any of the seven swords of power, it was prophesied that if the blade should be wielded in battle again, a terrible cataclysm would occur, plunging the land into an Ice Age after being washed away by an uncontrollable flood.

Hemlock had heard rumours that the prophecy of doom was being fulfilled, and that the great flood was approaching. If he could only steal the precious blade he might become the instrument to fulfil the final stages of the prophecy and bring about the cataclysm. He laughed to himself. The present security at the temple was so lax, that to steal the sword would take little effort. The majority of the priests had already left the city and entered the nearby countryside to pray, leaving only a skeleton-staff of unarmed clerics in charge. Believing no threat was possible, they would be completely surprised and Hemlock could enter, steal the blade and leave, even before they had realised anything was amiss. They could then be out of the city within hours.

The resulting cataclysm would leave the people weak, defenceless and very open to suggestion. It would not take much, with the help of the sword, to proclaim himself a King and lead the people into a new era, created by their monarch, after the brief Ice Age. His sons would rule this land for centuries to come, the sword easily dispatching any visible enemies. Once the blade was in his grasp, there could be no stopping him.

The three travellers entered the inn, ordered ales and meals, sat down and relaxed. Once they were comfortable, Hemlock whispered his plan, drawing them near. "Later tonight, we will sneak into the temple and steal the sword, before leaving the city and travelling north into the hills by the Prison Tower."

"They'll hunt us down," Flax interjected fearfully.

"We'll be long gone before they realise anything is wrong," Hemlock grinned. "We can raise an army who will be only too willing to fight in the company of the sword, if they try to follow us."

"What's up in the hills?" asked Jacinth.

"In the citadel north of the Tower lies a table; an altar used centuries ago for ritual sacrifices to a great demon," Hemlock declared. "If I perform a sacrifice using the herbs I collected and Kail's blood and saying the spell that is inscribed on the manuscript I stole, the god of the sword will appear and give us anything we want."

"What is this manuscript?" asked Flax.

"The sword is useless without it. That's why no-one decided to steal the sword before, they would need the manuscript also. It was fortunate the holder of the parchment happened to be travelling through the city recently, and I managed to find him and kill him," Hemlock said. "The manuscript had been protected by his family for generations, handed down from father to son."

"And what is this sword anyway?" Flax asked their leader.

"When the land was young, there was a great war between human and demon," Hemlock stated. "The demons were led by the God of Shape-Shifters Proteus, who also possessed powers over distance and time. When he and his minions were defeated, the soldiers forced him to shape-shift again, for a final time into a permanent form. They chose a sword for him to be trapped in for all time. If the blade should break however, the demon would die and a vast amount of energy would be released. But if certain rites are performed at the alter in the citadel, the demon of the sword could escape and will be able to finally rule this land!"

The journey to the temple was brief and without event, the streets deserted. The three thieves gazed up at the giant building, situated close to the west tower; the exit to the surrounding range of mountains and the outside world. Half a dozen marble pillars flanked the entrance, the columns decorated with the emblem of the Temple of the Sacred Sword, supporting a triangular-timber arch overlooking the doors. Ten-foot wooden double-doors barred entry to the four-storey structure, the walls painted black, hiding whatever dark deeds took place within.

They crept closer, noticing several guards at the entrance, the sentries cloaked in shadow, making their nightly patrol. Flax glanced at Hemlock, wondering how their leader planned to gain entry to one of the most fortified, not to mention the most dangerous building in the capital city.

The thief's question was answered as Hemlock pointed to the open window two storeys up, situated on the left side of the temple. Keeping close to the walls of nearby houses and taking advantage of the darkness, they made their way to the side of the enormous building. The soldiers appeared to be more interested in idly chatting about the day's events than watching out for any possible intruders. They figured only a madman would want to enter the temple, especially at night.

Jacinth threw up a grapnel into the open window and slowly began to pull himself up the dark wall. Momentarily halting his climb to peer into the window, he gave the all-clear to his two fellow robbers waiting below. Hemlock clambered up next, with Flax in close pursuit. Once all three were inside, they observed their surroundings. The thieves found themselves in a corridor, a winding staircase leading downstairs lay to their right ending in darkness, while directly ahead of them were a series of closed doors. This particular level of the temple appeared to be deserted of both sentries and priests.

The men proceeded to carefully open each door in their path, swords drawn. The rooms revealed no life, an assortment of furniture mixed with odd decorations adorned the chambers. Nothing of value, even for a common thief was present. The door at the end of the corridor revealed another staircase, this one leading upstairs. The intruders cautiously made their way up the staircase to the third storey, puzzled by the lack of security in the temple, even though the majority of the soldiers and priests were outside of the city praying.

Only two doors lay before them at the top of the stairs, one to the right and the other directly ahead. Like downstairs, lit candles adorned the walls, guiding the way. Jacinth pulled one off a ledge and glanced at their leader. Muffled sounds of what appeared to be chanting was coming from the plain wooden door to their right. The other door was decorated with the emblem of the temple and inscribed with abstract writing; a language none of the men could decipher. Although Hemlock did not understand the strange words, he recognised the significance of the language and the reason for its placing upon the door. The sword of Proteus lay beyond this door.

The thieves crept up to the door, swords at the ready. The sounds from the door to their right kept up a steady pace and the men could make out words being chanted; it appeared a number of priests were praying in a strange language. Hemlock examined the door which hid their prize. Four separate locks adorned the wooden door, but not so complicated as to elude the expertise of three highly-trained thieves. Hemlock removed a slender dagger from its scabbard at his hip and gently placed the blade into the first lock. It opened without much trouble, and the other three quickly followed.

Flax kept a careful watch on the other door, ready to cut down the first priest or soldier that might emerge and challenge them. But from the door came no victims for his blade.

Hemlock carefully opened the door of locks and peered inside. The room beyond was devoid of sentries and furniture. Only a single object graced the interior of the small chamber - placed at the far end of the room was a four-foot pedestal on which lay a plain-looking broadsword. The wooden pedestal was circular in shape with a smooth round two-foot diameter surface supporting the naked blade which balanced delicately on this makeshift altar.

Jacinth entered the chamber first, puzzled by the apparent lack of security and booby-traps. Stone windowless walls matched the equally bland cold wooden floor. If traps were present, they were almost impossible to detect. Apparently the priests and soldiers of the temple figured only the foolish or insane would enter this room and wish to steal the sword on which their entire twisted religion and culture was built.

Hemlock approached the weapon, but hesitated in touching the blade. The thief feared the sword might simply be a worthless copy and the real artefact lay hidden elsewhere deep within the temple. However, similar abstract markings adorned the blade like that on the door of the chamber, and Hemlock smiled. If it were a replica, the man responsible for creating such a copy was almost certainly a genius and would have charged highly for such work. Weapons were part of a thief's trade, and first glance told Hemlock that the blade before him was too old to be anything but the true sword of Proteus.

The leader of the group glanced behind at the other door that led to the priests before reaching out for the sword. Hemlock grasped hold of the handle of the weapon with a trembling hand, and received the greatest shock and thrill of his young life.

As if by magick, the blazing flames of the torches on the walls of the chamber and the corridor behind them dimmed instantly to a flicker. The three men felt their mouths drop open in astonishment as the sword in Hemlock's shaking hand seemed to take on a life of its own.

The blade appeared to be actually devouring all light and creating darkness instead. Hemlock pointed the sword at a nearby dying torch on the wall and the remaining flame perished instantly into smoke. The weapon seemed to be glowing, exuding darkness and the other two thieves found it difficult to distinguish their leader, even though he stood only a few feet from them. Hemlock let out a light laugh as he felt tremendous power enter his body.

Further surprise greeted the thieves as the other door in the corridor abruptly flew open to reveal half a dozen armed soldiers, followed closely behind by several priests, dressed in the familiar black robes of their dark religion. Jacinth and Flax moved to intercept them, but it was clear that they were out-numbered. Crossbows aimed at their unprotected heads quickly convinced the intruders to lay down their blades.

Hemlock took a step back, ready to strike out at the first guard that might be foolish enough to confront him. More than a dozen soldiers now occupied the chamber, four of which held daggers to the nervous throats of two kneeling bound thieves. The men-at-arms stood in silence as an elderly priest forced his way through them to face the thief who should dare to steal the symbol and foundation of their religion.

Hemlock gazed at this old man, intrigued by his appearance. A jet-black robe hung over his shoulders and flowed down to reach the ground. He was almost completely bald but for the few strands of pure white hair that criss-crossed his skull. However, he smiled at the intruder before him and Hemlock frowned in confusion.

"Welcome to the Temple of the Sacred Sword, my young friend," the old priest announced, his surprisingly strong voice echoing throughout the chamber. "I've been expecting you and your two companions for quite some time."

"Not again with that spiritual rubbish, priest," a voice roared and all eyes turned as a young man dressed in full battle-armour barged through the crowd of soldiers and priests.

Jacinth cursed under his breath at the approach of this new arrival. Any chance of tricking their way out of their dire situation was lost as this impressive guard stood alongside the elderly priest. The captive thief recognised the markings of a Captain on the soldier's shoulder and around his waist hung the sword of Commander of the military forces of the temple. Jacinth groaned, knowing they would not leave this building alive.

"You forget your place, Captain," the old man snapped. "I have authority in all matters magical."

The young man-at-arms faced the priest with a stern look. "And I have authority when it concerns the security of the temple. You waste your time entertaining spiritual philosophy with heathens such as these," the Captain sneered, "these common thieves will discover the true nature of spirituality soon enough."

"Hold your sword, soldier," the priest ordered. "I will tell you the time and place for the execution of these men. It is not for you to say."

The man-at-arms stared at the old man in angry silence and Jacinth let out a sigh of relief. It appeared the Captain had a superior in this ageing priest. They yet might live to see the dawn.

The old man turned to Hemlock. "I believe I should explain my delight in your presence after all these years of anticipation," the priest said and Hemlock stared at him in puzzlement, believing the old man to be insane. "I am the High-Priest and Leader of the Temple of the Sacred Sword. I command thousands of priests, the military side of the temple is overseen by the Captain, but he takes his orders from me, however sometimes grudgingly," he smiled and the officer alongside him sneered in reply.

"For over ten years I have had visions concerning your arrival and the attempted theft of the sword of Proteus, though I was never quite sure of the exact time of your coming, that is however until you stole the sacred manuscript and killed its owner," the High-Priest stated and Hemlock took another step back in suspicion. "I understand your mistrust, but do not doubt my magical powers. These are not the ravings of a senile old man; no other man alive, not even I can activate the power of the demon like you have just done," he said and Hemlock glanced down at the stolen sword in his hand which continued to glow and absorb all light in the room.

"The God of Shape-Shifters Proteus has chosen you for a reason, at last my people have an opportunity to wage a holy war and rid ourselves of the Temple of the Dragon," the old man laughed, "you will lead our forces against our enemies and crush them on the battlefield."

"And you will have my resignation by the morning," the Captain roared and prepared to leave the room. "This is preposterous, the man is a common robber and idiot, he couldn't lead a cow to the city market."

"I believe it would be most unwise to leave the temple, Captain," the High-Priest replied sharply. "Do not forget the Knights Order has a substantial reward for your capture, you would find it difficult to hide from the military-government anywhere in this entire land."

The soldier let out a growl. "I'm willing to take the chance, I would rather never work again and suffer the humiliating death of starvation than be the pawn for a thief."

"You will do my bidding, or your death will be upon you sooner than you planned," the High-Priest retorted, but then smiled and laid a friendly hand on the shoulder of the guard. "Come, my friend, you know I respect your judgement and leadership. This position is temporary and will not affect your reputation within this temple," the old man said softly, "besides, consider how much fun you and your soldiers will have after all these years of tolerating the Temple of the Dragon's existence to finally destroy their army on the battlefield and raze their buildings to the ground."

The Captain smiled in reply. "This is true, my soldiers tire of practice and seek to break their swords on the skulls of those priests of the Dragon. However, we should remember the Temple of the Dragon has an alliance with the Knights Order, their army will be difficult to defeat."

"Then perhaps it is time to consider a pact with the dark-elves of Sulphur Mountain, those blood-thirsty lunatics despise the Knights with a passion," the old man said and turned back to Hemlock. "Replace the sword on the pedestal and we will talk of your future."

"I'd rather hang on to it for the present moment," Hemlock said, still suspicious of these men. "I feel safer in the possession of your holy relic."

The High-Priest let out a laugh. "My friend, if I wanted you dead, not even the awesome powers of the sword would protect you from half a dozen soldiers with crossbows, which even now are still pointed at your head," the Leader retorted. "You would not have wished to steal the sword of Proteus if you didn't have ambitions to rule this land. I can help you to achieve that goal and promise you a future that you have only dreamed of."

Hemlock smiled as his two fellow thieves were released and had their weapons returned. "Then priest, why are we wasting time talking and not planning this great battle of ours?" Hemlock laughed and the High-Priest nodded in approval.

"Come, and let us begin the preparations for a war the like of which this world has never seen," the old man shouted, "and likely never to witness again."

Hemlock was led out of the crowded chamber, still steadfastly clutching onto his magical prize. His two fellow thieves kept close to his back, untrusting of the armed guards behind them. They all watched in awe as the blazing torches in the corridor before them dimmed instantly at Hemlock's approach, the sword of Proteus devouring all light, while simultaneously allowing fiery life to return to the torches in the room behind.

The High-Priest was not perturbed by this unusual disturbance, except for the fact that it distracted the soldiers from their duties. The old man turned to the thief with a smile which to Hemlock seemed to resemble more like a sneer. "Might I suggest if you are unwilling to relinquish the blade for even a moment, to at least allow it to be sheathed and so would keep hidden its powers."

Hemlock nodded in reply and was quickly handed an empty scabbard into which he shoved the magical weapon. The torches on the walls immediately burst into life once more as their predator was abruptly robbed of its abilities.

As the elderly priest led the thieves into the chamber of praying and deeper into the heart of the temple, he began to explain the plans for the preparations of the coming battle. "The Knights Order maintains intensive observation of our activities, especially in the capital," he said, drawing Hemlock near. "However, their surveillance becomes lax during the period of our annual time of fasting and praying, believing our priests are too busy on their knees worshipping to occupy their minds with thoughts of rebellion against the government," the High-Priest said. "Their over-confidence will be their undoing. I will send out covert orders to our priests and soldiers to cut short the period of religious observance and make immediate preparations for war. We will have approximately one week to gather our forces and begin marching north-east towards the Prison Tower before the Knights realise our intentions and send an army to intercept us."

"Why head for the Prison Tower?" asked Hemlock. "Would it not be better to attack the Army Barracks near Hellsbreath and take them by surprise, for surely that must be the greatest threat?"

The High-Priest shook his head in reply. "The Army Barracks are too heavily fortified, we would lose too many men taking it, and additional Knights from Hellsbreath and Karlaband would arrive to finish off whatever remained of our weakened army," the old cleric said sharply, "besides, we need the extra men we can free from the prison who will only be too eager to join our forces rather than starve out in the wilderness or be massacred by the priests from the Temple of the Dragon, for most of the criminals housed in the tower are incarcerated there for either treason against the government, or for unspeakable crimes against members of their religious order."

Hemlock let out a laugh. "I would never have believed it possible for thieves and murderers to fight alongside clerics of any religion."

"Aren't they all the same?" laughed Jacinth.

The old man led the company of thieves, soldiers and priests through a large oak door and into the great library of the temple. Shelves of books of various sizes and coloured covers adorned all four walls of the immense chamber and stretched to the ceiling. Hemlock and his two followers let out a gasp of awe at such a spectacle of literature.

The Captain drew near and said. "I'll bet eyes as ignorant as yours never feasted on such a sight, a book in your hands would suffer an undignified fate as a cleaning-tool for your bottom."

Hemlock reached for his sword, but the elderly priest laid a hand on his shoulder. "Ignore my number-one's jibes, if you have a desire for education, then in the coming week I will only be too glad to dramatically increase your knowledge of language and literature."

Hemlock nodded in approval of this idea and the Captain sighed in dismay. "You would be better spending your time asleep than attempt to transform a thief into a scholar."

The High-Priest snapped at the soldier in reply. "I believe our friend here is destined for great things, perhaps even the future leader of this land, given the proper guidance."

The Captain said nothing more but stared at the old cleric in disbelief at his remarks as the chief priest returned his attention to Hemlock.

"I'm afraid I won't be joining you for the battle," the old man announced, "my place is here in the temple, guarding this building from our enemies once they learn of my army's absence," he sighed in disappointment. "However, I will eagerly await your victorious return to the capital city when we can finally put an end to this totalitarian regime the Knights have forced upon us and their unholy alliance with the priests of the Dragon," the High-Priest smiled as he turned to his followers. "My friends, I present to you the saviour of our blessed order and the future leader of this nation!" he roared as Hemlock laughed and the assembly of priests began to cheer, their voices growing ever louder, reverberating around the chamber to the astonishment of Flax and Jacinth, and to the concern of the Captain.

The officer turned to Flax in nervousness; an emotion the thief suspected was previously unknown to the Captain. "I believe this world will be in ruins before your friend will even come close to realising his twisted dreams of power."

CHAPTER FOUR

Leaving the great forest far behind them, the travellers finally sighted the capital of the civilised world, Karlaband. But Storm sensed something was wrong, even for the City of Death. There seemed to be an awful lot of soldiers about with the insignia of the Temple of the Dragon on their shields and breastplates. He had not seen that emblem for years, not since he was a child. Something was definitely up. The sooner they made it to Kassier's house the better, maybe he could shed some light on what was going on.

They entered the city only after several heavily-armed guards had thoroughly questioned them. But none would answer any of Storm's questions as to what was the commotion. They walked quickly to the house and Storm knocked on the old man's steel door. Kassier came to the door and upon recognising Storm, yanked the two in before they could open their mouths.

"Thanks be to the gods you're safe," whispered Kassier to a puzzled Storm.

"What's going on?" Storm shouted. "There are soldiers everywhere."

"A couple of weeks ago a well-known mage was murdered and a manuscript concerning the sword of the demon Proteus was stolen," Kassier declared.

"You mean the sword of the Temple of the Sacred Sword?" Storm retorted.

"The very same," Kassier replied flatly. "Furthermore, the sword of the temple has been stolen by Hemlock, and I now know it was he who killed the mage to obtain the ancient parchment."

"Hemlock?" Storm roared.

"Keep your voice down," the old man said. "He's planning to raise the demon Proteus himself, and the temple of the Sword are supporting him."

"But he *stole* their sword," Storm retorted in confusion.

"Those damn priests are all crazy," Kassier declared. "They've acknowledged him as their long-awaited Messiah; the one who will free them from the unwanted existence of the Temple of the Dragon, and bring back their glorious god. They believe it was prophesied that Hemlock would come and steal the sword."

"But how will he raise this god of theirs?" Storm asked.

"There is an altar protected by soldiers of the Temple of the Dragon in a citadel north up in the hills," Kassier said softly. "He can use that to raise that foul demon. We can't allow that to happen, it would bring about a new dark-age, possibly even the prophesied cataclysm. Things are therefore hotting up around here. There is even talk of war."

"War?" replied Storm, perplexed. "I didn't think priests could fight."

"These ones do," Kassier retorted. "And there's an awful lot of them about, they have temples all over the land. They were just looking for an excuse to go to war against the Temple of the Dragon, and now it appears they've got it. I always said that those lunatics should have been put to the sword years ago. Already preparations for war have begun, with armies gathering from all over the land. The Temple of the Dragon will meet Hemlock and his *holy* army near the great Prison Tower, affectionately nicknamed 'The Tower of Hell' by the prisoners incarcerated there."

"Could Hemlock succeed?"

"With the sword in his possession, he just might," Kassier said. "I suggest you visit the Temple of the Dragon and tell them what you know about Hemlock."

It was then that Kassier noticed Suzerain. Storm introduced his young friend and quickly related their meeting in the forest to his old teacher. Since they were both exhausted from their long journey, Kassier suggested they stay the night and Storm visit the temple alone the following day. Suzerain gratefully accepted the invitation.

Early the following morning Storm rose and made his way to the city-centre. The Temple of the Dragon was easy to find. It stood right in the very centre of the capital, an impressive building of stone. Eight massive stone pillars stood, guarding the entrance, decorated with half-eroded engravings adoring the many gods, and of course the dragon.

Storm approached the giant double-doors and was instantly hailed by three men-at-arms. Storm stated his business and was escorted into the temple by two large soldiers, armed to the teeth. He noticed each man possessed an impressive broadsword, dagger, bow, quiver of steel-tipped arrows and a spear. Several guards and priests passed them, all heavily-armed. They were ready for battle at a moment's notice.

Tapestries adorned the walls depicting the great battle between the father of Dragons Zelerius and the demon Proteus centuries ago, and how Zelerius was mortally wounded by the God of Shape-Shifters, but still managed to make sure with his final act that the demon was imprisoned in steel. Because of that act, men still worship the dragon, even though these days the dragons hunt humans for food and sport. Storm remembered Kassier had said that these priests were not much different than their enemies, the priests of the Sword, just as strange and dangerous.

The three of them entered a small side-door which opened into a further corridor away from the main part of the giant temple. The corridor ended in a seven-foot door of bolted steel where twelve armed soldiers stood guard. One of his escorts approached the guards and whispered something to an impressive soldier carrying a shield with the Dragon's insignia. The soldier left the group and entered the chamber beyond the door from where he appeared again moments later, approached Storm and escorted him through the guards and into the room. Storm gasped. Before him was a giant chamber where stood a thirty-foot rectangular table upon which were strewn papers, maps and books of every possible description. The ceiling lay at least forty feet away with walls approximately a hundred apart. The room was decorated with fine furniture including small polished tables, velvet-lined chairs and sofas. Tapestries and pictures adorned every available space on the walls, praising past battles and the Gods. Bent over the giant polished centre-table were a dozen priests and soldiers of high rank. An elderly cleric dressed in fine robes approached their visitor.

"Yes?" the High-Priest snapped. "What is it? Why has Kassier sent you?"

"I'm a friend of his," Storm said. "I know about Hemlock."

The priest glanced at him in annoyance, but then dismissed the escort and beckoned Storm to follow him to the table. An elderly soldier with gold-inscriptions on his breastplate and a jewelled broadsword at his side glared at Storm. "What business has a peasant in this?"

"I've come to offer my help," Storm replied. "I know what Hemlock is up to."

"You do, eh?" the officer snapped. "We already know what he's up to."

"I believe we need every bit of help we can get in this matter," the High-Priest interjected. "If we lose this war, the Temple of the Sacred Sword will overrun the land and put everybody to the sword."

Another soldier, a robust man armed with only a sword stood up and silenced them. "It is time to formulate our plans," he boomed. "We know Hemlock has an army of at least five thousand men and are marching towards the tower. He plans to free the criminals and lunatics that reside there to cause confusion. I've warned the guards of his arrival, but they have not the men to defend the tower for long. Every scum and filth in the land is joining Hemlock's army," Commander Hartal declared. "In two days we will march and attempt to meet him before he destroys the tower. I will lead the first charge to eliminate his army. This meeting is adjourned. Good-day, gentlemen."

Commander Hartal sat down and began to gather up his papers and prepared to leave. But the High-Priest stopped him. "Just a second," he roared. "I have also called upon a new organisation of men from the island of Kilhaven who have agreed to help us. They are experts in armed and unarmed combat and are deadly swordsmen and knife-throwers. They plan to send a hundred men to the battle. Now you can leave, gentlemen."

The men shuffled out of the room and into the main temple, to carry out their individual preparations for battle. Storm watched them leave, seemingly oblivious to his presence, before leaving the temple himself. He was soon back at Kassier's house and upon entering, sat down by the warm fire.

Kassier approached him. "Well, what news at the temple?"

"He already has a force in excess of five thousand, while we have only time to gather six thousand, and of course, Hemlock has the sword."

"He'll use the blade to influence the scum from every corner of the land to join him, and who knows how many that could amount to."

"And all for money and power," added Storm.

"The two greatest forces that can grip a man," declared Kassier. "But you knew yourself that it had to happen sooner or later, the heat between the two temples was approaching a climax. Many innocent people are going to die two days from now. I've asked help from every white mage there is, but they say their magick is useless against the sword."

"So what now?"

"Hemlock will try to form an alliance with the dark-elves that reside in a giant cavern in the largest mountain in the land - Sulphur Mountain, so called for it is one of the most volcanic mountains in the land," said Kassier. "The dark-elves throw human children as sacrifices into the lava to get their dark powers. Hemlock has promised them land for the sulphur is poisoning them and any amount of children they want, if they would only join him. There are well over five thousand elves in that mountain. If he succeeds in an alliance, it will be the end of us. That alliance must be stopped, at all costs."

Kassier joined Storm by the fire. "Before a battle, the elves sacrifice a dozen children and pour the blood into a magical cauldron to give them power and morale before they fight. Twenty of our best soldiers are marching there to destroy the cauldron, for without it, the elves will lose heart and refuse to fight. I want you to go with them and help. The men plan to leave in two hours and intend to meet Hemlock's alliance-treaty party before they reach the mountain. I cannot over-stress the importance of this mission. I and Suzerain will hopefully meet you at the tower before the battle in two days. Go now."

Storm rose and prepared to leave, but Kassier snatched hold of his arm. "Good luck, my friend," he said before the young swordsman left.

He made his way to the eastern gate out of the city where the small army would be preparing for their dangerous journey. The men were already there, tending to their horses while nervously chatting about weapons and tactics. Storm approached the group and explained who he was. The Captain of the party, a large man by the name of Socerak, was grateful for the added presence of another trained swordsman and welcomed Storm into the group. A horse was fetched for the young swordsman and extra provisions obtained.

The day passed into night without event, and the Captain was beginning to worry that they might have missed Hemlock's party or his group might have already made it to the cavern. However, just as he was about to order they stop for the night, he noticed several men on horseback about three hundred metres ahead of them. It could be no-one other than them. He signalled to his Lieutenant to charge Hemlock's fifteen-man party from behind. The second-in-command let out a roar and the group swept into Hemlock's party, taking them completely by surprise.

The priests of the Sword were excellent fighters, but they were no match for Socerak and his soldiers. Hemlock's men lay dead or dying with a loss of only three guards to Socerak's group. The men let out a loud cheer before advancing towards the cavern of the elves. Half of their mission had been performed, even if it was the easier half. This part of the mission Socerak told Storm, was suicide.

The group of eighteen men made their camp at the base of Sulphur Mountain, out of sight of any elf-sentinels. At the break of dawn they awoke and stealthily entered the cavern, silencing the five elf-guards that lay at its entrance. They travelled deep into the cavern, unmolested until they were about mid-way to the main-chamber, creeping down a wide tunnel in groups of two, when they came across a force of ten elves. The dark creatures were arguing and gambling over their favourite in a rat-fight, the two rodents ripping each other to the death cheered on by the shouting elves. The elves intermittently shoved their bets to a fat elf standing in the far corner. The elf glanced over the elves, checking his rodents and examining their performance. It was he who noticed the group of humans, hiding behind a rock at the far end of the room.

"What the-?" the fat elf muttered before the Lieutenant's arrow caught him in the throat, silencing him while scattering his beloved coins across the room.

The group of elves stopped their frantic cheering and glanced over in curiosity at their bookie, thinking he was throwing a fit, and whether this was a prime opportunity to rid the elf of his coins. The rats continued to fight, their sharpened claws and teeth ripping flesh off each other. The elves had only just begun to draw their blades when Socerak and his men attacked. Most of the elves were already highly-intoxicated and unable to put up much of a fight, and thus the party had not much difficulty in massacring them where they stood. In a matter of moments, all that remained of the elves were broken bodies and the sound of the rats fighting. The Lieutenant approached the rodents and ended their torturous lives, stabbing them with his sword. Storm felt proud to be in the company of these men, their skill in swordplay had to be admired. They entered another tunnel out of the chamber and suddenly found themselves in the main chamber. The giant room was devoid of any furniture and Storm could clearly see the cauldron of war standing in the centre of the chamber. However, the chamber was also packed to capacity with approximately forty heavily-armed dark-elves, surrounding the cauldron and a dozen unarmed elderly elves. Storm surmised that they were the High-Council, protected by their many servants. This was an added bonus. They could rid the land of not only the cauldron, but also of the elves' leaders, perhaps finishing the dark-elves altogether.

"There she be," shouted Socerak. "Charge!"

The men swept into the elves. Surprise was still to their advantage, but they were heavily outnumbered. There was a terrific crash of metal as sword met sword. Storm stayed behind the party and fired arrows at elves who were preparing spells. In the total confusion as the elves tried to defend themselves and protect their vulnerable leaders, they forgot about the cauldron, believing the High-Council to be the intended target. Storm ran through the crowd, dodging both the blades of elves and humans, and seized hold of the cauldron. The giant pot was surprisingly quite light and Storm managed to make it to the opposite tunnel, leading deeper into the cavern. He turned around to the main fray to see Socerak go down under the attacking blades of a dozen elves. His men appeared to be suffering the same fate, the numbers against them too great for even them to handle.

Storm was amazed. Close to thirty elves, including several of the High-Council lay dead or dying compared to Socerak's eighteen, a tribute to a group of great men; of brilliant swordsmen. It was now however up to Storm to complete the mission and make sure their deaths were not in vain, he had to somehow destroy the cauldron.

Storm heard one elf near him cry out in a language he could not decipher, but understood its meaning, as the elves turned their attention to him. A giant door blocked the tunnel he was about to enter, and possible freedom. He frantically opened the door and quickly closed it behind him, just as the elves slammed into it. Storm glanced around the room he was in, and grabbed any bit of furniture he could find, which included a small table and several old chairs and shoved them up against the door, as the elves began hacking at the door with their swords. There was suddenly silence; an eerie quietness Storm found even more unnerving than the cheering, and abruptly realised its meaning. An elf was preparing a spell, the other elves backing away from the door. He noticed the door had changed from a dusty filthy brown to red, bright red. The large door then suddenly burst into flames, setting the furniture he had barricaded against the entrance alight. In dire sickening panic, Storm glanced around the room. There was an entrance to a wide tunnel at the other side of the room, leading down to a giant chamber where Storm could see a great dark chasm, crossable only by a slender unstable-looking wooden bridge.

Storm ran down the tunnel and across the bridge, lugging the cauldron on his right shoulder. He waited at the other side of the bridge for the elves. The door was pushed inwards by sheer force of bodies, and in rushed hundreds of armed elves, dogs at their sides, and all screaming in rage at their intruder. Storm hesitated for a few moments, before raising the great cauldron above his head and suddenly flinging the pot at the bridge. The elves stopped dead in their tracks and cries of rage now abruptly turned to fear and despair.

The old bridge collapsed with the blow, and both the bridge and cauldron fell into the chasm, never to be seen again. The effect of this action was both amazing and instantaneous. At the loss of their holy relic, the elves lost heart and lowered their bows which were aimed at Storm. Storm gazed at the elves and sighed in relief. He then noticed one tall impressive young elf stand out from his brothers and stare at Storm across the chasm. He appeared to be one of the surviving High-Council.

"Another time, swordsman," the elf cried out. "Another time!"

Storm glanced at the strange elf for a few moments more before disappearing down the tunnel. The passage began to go upwards and become wider, and soon with a cheer Storm saw light. He ran out of the tunnel and found himself not far from the entrance where they had first entered the cavern. He soon managed to find the horses, and momentarily pausing to set them free bar his own, he was quickly out of sight of Sulphur Mountain. Judging by the location of the sun Storm estimated he was at least twelve hours behind time, and possibly late for the battle. Storm pushed the horse to the limit, the beast collapsing one mile away from his meeting-point with Kassier. He was forced to now travel on foot, but quickly found the camp, the sounds of steel upon steel as men practised beckoning him on. Storm however stopped short when he arrived at the outskirts of the camp whereupon a glorious sight greeted him. Banners and flags of every description, most notably those of the Temple of the Dragon, filled his vision. He glanced over the massive crowd that had gathered for the common purpose of war, and guessed he was gazing at an army of upwards to ten thousand men. Commander Hartal and the priests had been busy.

A sentry approached him and quickly guided him to the main tent where the council of priests and soldiers were in session. As he entered, he saw Commander Hartal, his personal Lieutenant, Kassier, the High-Priest and his personal assistant and a strange man dressed all in black were bent over a large rectangular table lined with maps. Kassier immediately greeted him and directed him out of the tent and quickly explained the situation. Storm sighed in despair when Kassier told him the great Prison Tower had fallen and the prisoners had joined Hemlock and marched onto the plains to await the army of the Dragon. The old man was relieved however when the young swordsman told him the fate of the elves' cauldron and his lucky escape. But he was sad to hear the fate of Socerak and his men, a man like him would be sorely missed. Kassier quickly told him the outline of the battle-plan. Several hundred archers would fire a volley of arrows into Hemlock's charging army before Commander Hartal would advance with the main bulk of their forces while close to one thousand men would remain in reserve and block any gaps that should develop as the army marches. The total of men in the army came to just under eleven thousand.

"I believe however that Hemlock may have much more," Kassier said. "Maybe as much as over twelve thousand."

Storm sighed in dismay.

"But our men are trained," Kassier declared. "Unlike much of Hemlock's."

"Then we can win?"

"Maybe. Remember he has the sword," Kassier replied. "If we win, I want you to find Hemlock as he tries to escape, and kill him."

"You don't have to ask me for that," Storm smiled. "That I will do anyway. No way is he going to live."

CHAPTER FIVE

Commander Hemlock gazed out across the plains, full of confidence about the coming battle. At dawn two days from now, both sides would finally clash, and the Temple of the Dragon would die, he laughed to himself. He turned and glanced at the map which lay strewn on the table in his tent behind him, and laughed at the thought of how many troops and priests the Temple of the Sacred Sword had donated to their *Messiah*. He had promised them power and glory in the new age that was to come, but the demon would kill them all upon its release.

Intelligence reports from his spies had told him that the enemy had very few troops on horseback - another bonus, as if he needed one. Hemlock was confident his army was the superior one. However, he was angry that no response from the elves had been heard, he thought he could rely on those blood-thirsty freaks. Above all others, Kassier, Commander Hartal, the High-Priest and their Lieutenants had to die. Without their guidance, the army would fall into disarray.

He returned his attention to the map and the list of his army. Almost one thousand archers, ten thousand soldiers and priests of the Temple of the Sacred Sword and over one thousand unstable prisoners of the Tower, amounted to the population of his army. Hemlock turned away from the table, went outside and hailed one of the sentries. "Get me the Captain."

Ten minutes later the Captain; Commander of the Temple of the Sword appeared. "What do you want now?" the officer growled.

"I want you to notify the guild of assassins and have their best operative sent here by nightfall. The guild is located on the northern outskirts of Vandor Forest," Hemlock stated.

The Captain left immediately to fetch a soldier and sent a rider to the forest. Flax watched their great leader, now the omnipotent Commander, dish out his orders and said. "You still plan to go through with this insane battle?" asked Flax as he approached Hemlock. "You still intend to kill all those men?"

Hemlock stared fixedly at Flax. "Life is cheap, Flax," he declared. "Don't you forget it."

Hemlock turned away from his former number-one and once again gazed out across the plains and smiled. A month ago he was but a common thief and murderer, now he was famous; now he was a somebody, and soon to be all-powerful and rich. He turned to his army. Jacinth stood nearby, training the prisoners in swordplay and archery, clashes of steel as the men practised. The majority of the others sat idly around, nervously talking while shining their already gleaming blades. If Hemlock felt any remorse for the wives and children of these men who were about to die, he did not show it. Instead he let out a roar of laughter to himself as his thoughts turned again to money and power, and how they would soon be his.

The Captain returned to Hemlock, his Commander, after sending off the rider, ready to receive any further orders.

"I want you to send five hundred men to the citadel that holds the altar," ordered Hemlock, "and clear it of any obstructions."

The Captain stared back at his Commander, perplexed. "Obstructions?"

"Kill everyone inside the citadel, every soldier and priest of the Temple of the Dragon that guards the altar," said Hemlock coldly. "It will take about a week to get there. The journey is highly dangerous; some of that land is very treacherous, but I want that alter free of the soldiers before I arrive."

The Captain left and hid his displeasure at this order. The loss of five hundred men would be felt in the ranks, and for what? They were sure to win the battle, and then the entire army itself could march to the citadel. The idea was ludicrous, some of that land was home to the most dangerous and foulest of creatures to be found in the entire world. Just the thought of what those men might face sent shivers down his spine, but he dare not disobey the command, for Hemlock would surely have a fate in store for him to match theirs. The Captain sighed in anger, but nevertheless approached his Lieutenant to organise the party of men that would march to an obscure fort in the middle of nowhere.

The assassin arrived as ordered before dusk and was escorted to the Commander's tent. He entered the tent as Hemlock turned to face him and the assassin bowed in respect to his rank. The man before the assassin possessed short brown hair and a rough face, old before his time. He was dressed in fine clothes, a flowing black robe that hovered just above the grass and a peculiar blade strapped to his left side, the handle jewelled in gold and precious stones. The assassin blinked, for a brief moment, he thought he had seen the sword glow with a vibrant red radiance. His attention was however broken by the Commander who abruptly spoke. "How much?"

The assassin blinked again. "What-?"

"How much for the task?" Hemlock snapped and the assassin saw anger and frustration in his trained eye.

"Twenty gold pieces," the man declared.

He watched nervously as the strange Commander reached a gloved hand into his jerkin-pocket and threw a number of shiny coins across the table. The assassin carefully, but quickly picked up the coins, saying nothing. Hemlock then took out a small parchment, the size of his hand and threw it onto the table. On the paper was the rough drawing of an old man with white hair. The assassin wondered what possible threat a frail old man like this could pose to such an obviously powerful individual. But it was not his place or job to ask questions, only carry out the task appointed to him, collect the money and get out fast. Carved into the parchment above the picture was a name and rank - Kassier, Chief-Adviser to Commander Hartal. He stared back at the man with the mysterious blade.

"Find him, and kill him," Hemlock stated flatly. "The Lieutenant outside will tell you where the enemy camp lies."

The assassin left the tent and was immediately approached by a soldier who directed him towards the location of the camp. After the Lieutenant had left, the hired-killer glanced at the banners and flags of this great army and wondered if he should interfere in the fate of this land. The coming battle would decide the destiny of the world, and the killing of this man, Kassier, might throw the balance in favour of the Temple of the Sacred Sword. But his reputation and possibly his life would be at risk if he failed to complete the task, so he headed for the camp.

It was nearing the midnight hour when the assassin finally sighted the camp after travelling silently through the fauna, bearing the single weapon of his profession - a slender dagger. He was regarded by his comrades in the guild as the finest assassin amongst them, with almost fifty kills to his credit. He feared no man, bar perhaps the men from Kilhaven whose art excelled even his. But their home was far from this place, there was nothing to fear here.

He gazed across the camp and observed the many banners of the army of the Dragon waving wildly about in the breeze. He counted hundreds of tents and began to wonder how in hell he was going to be able to search all for his target without being observed. Just then to his delight, the old man strolled out of a nearby tent and halted, breathing in the clean night air, far healthier than the smog-filled air of the capital. The assassin unsheathed the short blade and prepared to take aim when a small boy appeared, muttered something to the target, before heading off for the warmth of a nearby fire, one of many which lay all around the camp.

This was his chance. He stood to his feet and threw the blade. The knife hit Kassier in the chest and the old man screamed briefly before he fell. The assassin prepared to leave when he realised his mistake. Too late he saw the familiar men in black, dozens of which approached him immediately. Stealth was now out of the question, he began to flee blindly into the night. Seven six-inch daggers flew and instantly took the assassin's life, halting his flight.

Healing priests, Commander Hartal, Suzerain and Storm ran through the camp upon hearing the commotion and approached the fallen man, but it was too late. He was beyond their help. Commander Hartal after some discussion with the High-Priest appointed Storm to Kassier's status and command, citing the knowledge Storm had acquired of military-strategy through conversations with the old man. At first light the following morning the body of Kassier was laid to rest, surrounded by priests praying for the man's soul and its journey to the world of the dead, while Storm stared on in anger for the brutal murder of a noble man who had saved his life.

Commander Hartal approached Storm. "My deepest regrets for your loss. Kassier was a fine swordsman and brilliant strategist. In his younger days he was a mercenary and in business for himself. Rumour is he fled Sulphur Mountain being chased by a large party of elf soldiers led by a powerful and very dangerous elf sorcerer called Ucein. The eleven wizard appeared to have been somewhat annoyed by Kassier stealing a magical artefact of great power, the same weapon I believe you now possess."

"Then it is a fitting legacy to a great man," added Storm.

Dawn the following day saw great commotion around the camp and it was this that awoke Storm and Suzerain from their deep slumber. The noise shattered Storm's dream - a vision of the battlefield littered with the dead and the screaming dying, adjacent to a fast-flowing river, once blue, now crimson with the blood of fallen warriors. He was grateful to have been suddenly awoken and spared further horrors, the nightmare being all too frighteningly real.

Storm and his young companion quickly dressed and armed themselves. This was the day to shed blood and take lives, and even perhaps lose theirs. The day of the battle was finally upon them. Outside their tent the camp was alive with soldiers and priests preparing for combat. Within the hour, all were ready and began to march out of the camp, leaving behind a field littered with empty tents.

"We'll come back for the tents," Commander Hartal whispered to Storm. "If there's anybody left to collect them."

Within a further two hours they had travelled around the nearby mountains and sighted the field. Before them lay the grass-lined plains that was to be the battlefield, the ruins of the Prison Tower lying off in the distance, though even from where they stood, all could clearly see the great destruction that had been caused by Hemlock. Off to the east lay the vast army of the man in question, the edge of the great field marked with hundreds of tents and several flags waving wildly about the camp, but no soldiers or priests could they see.

Then from the tents came first dozens, then hundreds of men, all bearing arms. Archers moved quickly to the front of the army and notched arrows, preparing to fire in their direction. They were backed by thousands of soldiers and priests, some on horseback. In a matter of a few minutes, the army had become organised and ready for battle. Yet there was no sign of their leader. After the sudden noise of Hemlock's army organising themselves, there was complete silence. All stood motionless, seemingly afraid to move, lest it provoke the start of the battle. Commander Hartal broke this stance by ordering his archers to the front of his army, though this did not cause movement on their opponent's side.

Then from the midst of Hemlock's army appeared the Captain of the Temple of the Sacred Sword, dressed in full battle-armour on horseback. Suddenly his arm rose and the surrounding army let out a roar which was reciprocated across the plains in their enemy's army as Commander Hartal gave the long-awaited signal to fire. The battle that followed was short and furious. The archers of both armies let fly their arrows and a rain of death fell to strike flesh. Dozens of men on both sides fell as steel-tipped arrows pierced chainmail and armour. Commander Hartal's archers had no time to notch a second volley before the bulk of Hemlock's army charged towards them, roaring their battle-cry to the sky. The Commander quickly shouted several orders as he rallied his army together and prepared to charge. There followed a terrific clash of metal and flesh as armies collided. To Storm, the sight was frightening and yet amazing, as men stood alone from their comrades, each fighting desperately for his own life.

The riders from Hemlock's army used their lances to deadly effect, easily cutting down the helpless foot-soldiers and whatever remained of the archers. Commander Hartal replied by gathering approximately seven hundred of his men together, traversed around the main fray to Hemlock's rear and massacred his archers. Not one of Hemlock's archers escaped the Commander's blood-thirsty soldiers, extracting revenge for fallen comrades. He then returned to the centre of the battle, striking unwary soldiers from behind. Soldiers and priests of both sides fell everywhere as the battle raged on.

Storm stood at the edge of the battle, surrounded by Suzerain and a dozen men-at-arms. He gave an order and they entered the battle. As they entered the fray, one lone soldier from Hemlock's army advanced on Storm dressed in full battle-armour and waving a broadsword wildly about his head. Storm bore no protection, but had the advantage of being on horseback, towering over his approaching opponent. He spurred the beast into action and charged as he drew his blade. The soldier however nimbly avoided the blow and struck at the horse. The sword severed the stirrup, leaving the horse unharmed. Storm fell heavily to the ground as the horse bolted in fright. The soldier quickly moved above Storm and heaving the giant blade above his head, brought it down on his vulnerable victim. Storm moved his sword in front of himself, grasping the flat of the blade in both hands, blocking the fatal blow. He then rolled out of the way and rose to his feet to face the soldier.

In rage and increasing frustration, the soldier charged, his sword wielded above his left shoulder in a striking motion. Storm side-stepped to his right and as the soldier was about to pass him, swung his blade across the man's belly. The soldier halted and looked down at his stomach in amazement. The armour should have protected him, even from a blow stronger than this one, yet the sword seemed to have sliced both the armour, chainmail and his stomach open without much effort as if he wore none. The soldier stumbled before falling to the grass with a low groan.

The battle appeared to be weighing heavily in Hemlock's favour. His soldiers had killed most of Commander Hartal's main army and now moved on to strike at the reserves. The Commander realised what was happening, and quickly rallying his remaining force of approximately two thousand men around him, charged into Hemlock's approaching army. The reserve which consisted of nearly eight hundred veterans and the elite garrison of men from Kilhaven, ran to cover the gap in their forces, but in vain. Hemlock's party smashed into this futile resistance and massacred the veterans with little cost to their army.

Then they charged towards the men from the island of Kilhaven, confident of eradicating them also with little effort. However, they were to find out that these men were not so easy to dispose of. The elite squad stood motionless, seemingly unafraid of the oncoming army screaming their battle-cry to the sky. Suddenly they acted. With a combined roar, they charged and the air was filled with the sound of a hundred daggers thrown into the approaching army of the Sword. All knives reached their intended targets with deadly accuracy as a hundred horsemen fell to the ground. If any had survived the assault of the daggers, they were quickly killed under the horses of their brothers who cared not whether they were alive or dead in their great desire to kill the men from Kilhaven. The elite garrison then drew their swords and swept into Hemlock's army. Blades removed heads from shoulders, cleaving through armour and flesh seemingly with little effort as they rushed into the army of the Sword.

Soldiers were dropping like flies and Storm cried out in triumph, believing that these men alone would win the battle for them. However he quickly began to realise in growing despair that this was not to be the case. The men were brilliant fighters, surely the best Storm had ever seen, but the odds were simply against them. Perhaps against a lesser force they might have won. But there was just too many men for them to handle and eventually they fell, though they took many a soldier down with them.

The sounds of battle began to finally fade, yet there still remained over three hundred soldiers from Hemlock's army. Storm looked around the battlefield in panic, searching for any soldiers or priests from the Temple of the Dragon, but all he saw were the dead and the dying. Barely a hundred metres away from where he stood lay the lifeless body of Commander Hartal, a spear sticking out of his chest. Alongside him lay the High-Priest surrounded by his aides, their advice lost with their rotting carcasses. Around the High-Priest's cold neck shined a gold medallion, the symbol of the Temple of the Dragon engraved in silver and gold. This would surely be taken from his lifeless body by the ghouls who now stared at Storm. There was also no sign of Suzerain. Storm hoped his body did not lie somewhere on the battlefield, yet it mattered not, for it appeared he was soon to join him. The horsemen began to approach him, laughing.

Storm started to run in blind fear and tripped over one of the blood-soaked bodies. He looked to find it was the High-Priest he had fallen over. He began to rise and his gaze once again fell on the medallion. The craftsmanship was superb, engraved with ancient symbols Storm could not decipher. Yet it suddenly occurred to Storm that the medallion's function was more than just for the purpose of being an ornament. He removed it and began to wonder if he could trade it for his life. But the soldiers would simply take the medallion and then his life, so he flung it at them instead in anger, hoping that at least it might be lost and they would not have it.

One horseman moved in front of the others and began to wave his sword about, meaning to cut

Storm down. In his left hand he held a magnificent round shield, the coat of arms of the Temple of the Sacred Sword engraved in gold upon it. Neither Storm nor the soldier saw or heard the medallion hit the shield with an odd sound quite unlike metal against metal. The medallion seemed to have been absorbed into the shield as it disappeared. The soldier halted abruptly as he noticed that his shield seemed to be glowing red, and then began to melt. Frantically he tried to drop it as he screamed in pain as it began to burn his arm. Suddenly both he and his horse were enveloped in a light red glow and his comrades gathered around him in curiosity and puzzlement. Too late they realised this was a mistake. Within moments, all the horsemen were glowing while Storm could only stare on in awe. It appeared the High-Priest had specially prepared the medallion for such a purpose as this, but was killed before he had the chance to use it. Storm had carried out the task for him. Suddenly there was a blinding flash and a terrific bang that made Storm cover his eyes and ears in pain. Faintly he heard horrible screams, before there was eventually silence.

He opened his eyes and was shocked by the over-powering smell of the dead which almost made him throw-up. Ravens now feasted themselves on the dead before the wolves would shortly arrive and rob them of their meal. He gazed across the battlefield to where the charging army had been. All that remained of them was a black pit which was still smoking. Storm gazed into the pit and doubted whether anything would ever grow in there again. He then turned his attention back to the battlefield and wondered whether either temple would survive after the majority of their priests lay dead. But he had a feeling that they probably would somehow, and perhaps in another ten years, the land might very well see another battle such as this. A detachment of men from the capital would arrive within the next week to secure the tower once news of the battle's outcome had reached them. Hemlock and his group of thieves had probably fled in the direction of the citadel and Storm did not have the exact location of the fortress, believing that his mission would end here; that he would not have to travel again to get his vengeance.

There was still no sign of Suzerain, perhaps he was indeed dead and his body lay nearby. Suddenly he heard a faint noise behind him and turned to find the boy making his way through the maze of bodies to reach him. Storm let out a light laugh of joy and ran and embraced him. They sat on a nearby rock and rested.

"What do we do now?" Suzerain sighed.

"Kassier told me that whether Hemlock lost or won the battle, he would head for the citadel," Storm replied. "But the citadel is guarded, so he will probably enlist the help of a friend reputed to own a castle somewhere in the desert. But I don't know where the castle is or the exact location of the citadel itself for all that land is unmapped."

"So, how do we find Hemlock?" Suzerain retorted. "Beyond these plains lie desert for miles around, I can't track him through sand."

"I don't know," Storm sighed. "Perhaps the remains of the Prison Tower will offer some clues. I'm interested in finding out the identity of this friend of Hemlock's, for I would like to know how any man could build a house, never mind a castle on foundations of sand."

"He might be a mage."

"I think you may be right," Storm echoed. "Someone interested in the sword."

The two survivors made their way to the blackened ruins of the tower. All that remained of the prison was one intact room on the bottom-floor. The small chamber offered no clues. In fact, it offered nothing at all for the room was completely bare, devoid of furniture or ornaments of any kind; anything to indicate this was once a prison for dangerous criminals was amiss. They turned to leave in frustration when Storm heard moaning coming from just outside the tower. They travelled around the perimeter of the prison until they came upon a lone soldier with an out-stretched hand towards them. On his chest-armour he bore the emblem of the Temple of the Sacred Sword which was barely recognisable under a thick coating of blood. Storm lifted the injured soldier and placed him against the prison-wall. The man sneered in feigned gratitude when he realised Storm and Suzerain were not from his army.

"Where is he?" Storm demanded.

"Who?" the soldier retorted weakly.

"Your Commander, Hemlock," Storm snapped.

"Go to hell."

It suddenly occurred to Storm that he had gone through this routine before, back in the capital with Kanaka. However, he did not think it wise to cold-bloodily kill this man also in front of Suzerain. Perhaps he might not have to, but if it was required, he would harm the man. He had to have that information. "If you don't tell me," Storm stated coldly. "You'll be joining your comrades there sooner than you planned, and I'll make sure the path is most *uncomfortable* for you."

"All right, all right, I'll tell you," the soldier barked. "The castle where he is journeying to lies due north seven miles from here. Now leave me to die."

The travellers left the man to his dying and headed for the desert. Behind them the wolves had arrived onto the bloody field of battle, their meals laid out like headless chickens for the taking. But they did not look back. Their path into the seemingly endless sea of sand lay before them, with a madman orchestrating their journey in his wake, and Storm had a feeling that there would be much to settle before he would find him and have his revenge.

CHAPTER SIX

Flax brushed back his thick black hair from his face in frustration and anger. He cursed the oppressive heat and the sand which perpetually filled his shoes every time his feet sank deep into the hot desert-sand. In rage he turned to Hemlock, who seemed to be unaffected by the heat. "What happened back there?" Flax roared. "We were winning! I counted over three hundred survivors of ours, and then suddenly there was a flash, and they were gone. And now here we are, trudging through this baking hot desert to a castle built on sand. Where are the men you sent to the citadel? They should have met us here."

Hemlock did not reply. He knew now that he should have heeded the words of his late Captain and not sent the five hundred men to the citadel. The fact that they were not here meant they obviously fell foul of something on the way to the citadel or else were killed in the assault on the fortress, either way they were dead. They should have returned by now. He had sent those men to their deaths as surely as if he had killed them by his own hand.

Flax turned away from their leader in frustration and disgust. He began to wonder if he should have remained in Karlaband with Kanaka, at least back there if you encountered danger, it was something you could understand and fight. Instead here he stood following a certified lunatic with a glowing sword. He glanced over at the other member of their seemingly fast decreasing company - Jacinth; a man whose only pleasure is to kill, and he even looked like death. His face was pale and vacant; a face seemingly devoid of emotion with cold piercing eyes of stone. The man called Jacinth who had once been his friend was a changed person, ever since the time in the forest when Hemlock had killed Kail. Flax felt he was the only sane man left in the group; a gang who had once been composed of cowardly common thieves, but now had become mass-murderers following a crazy pretender to the vacant throne of this land. Flax's thoughts were abruptly broken by a sudden shout from Hemlock.

"We're here."

Flax looked in the direction where Hemlock was pointing and he gasped. He felt his heart would jump out of his chest and so placed a hand to his flesh in awe. In a sea of sand stood an enormous castle displaying three towers stretching into the clouds. The castle appeared to have been painted black surrounded by a twelve-foot wall of thick black stone. Flax noticed something odd; something which had caught his gaze. Then it suddenly hit him what he had seen. In several places on the tower-walls from hooks swung severed human heads, the walls below them shining in the blazing sun from blood that ran down the dark towers into the sand. The castle itself seemed to rise magically out of the sand, and Flax guessed that the building had indeed been built by dark forces. There appeared to be no windows, making sure no light entered the castle or accompanying towers.

"By all the gods," he screamed. "What sadistic maniac lives in this place?"

"Gulag," Hemlock retorted simply.

"What-?"

"The mage Gulag lives here. In fact, he's the only living thing in the castle."

"Living?" Flax said. "What do you mean *living?*"

"You'll see, Flax," Hemlock laughed. "You'll see."

The travellers approached the giant black steel double gates which barred their entry to the courtyard and the castle beyond. Flax wondered what they should do next, for both the gates and the walls were unclimbable. An answer was provided as the gates suddenly began to slowly swing open as if by silent command, allowing them free access to the courtyard. As Flax passed into the yard of black flat stone he was amazed that there appeared to be no sign of sand in the yard itself, though there were small heaps surrounding the castle-walls. It was as if the stones had devoured the desert, yet allowed some sand to accumulate around the castle outer-walls, giving the impression that the entire fortress had indeed risen out of the desert. Flax began to feel great dread about this building. Here was a place of diabolical evil, this castle was home to dark unknown forces.

Before they had even reached the ten-foot steel double-doors, they like the gates, began to inexplicably open without touch. They moved to the sound of mad creaking, as if they had not been opened in decades. Flax guessed that would be appropriate. Whoever held rule in this place had not seen the outside world for a long time, perhaps never. The doors opened to reveal a hallway hidden in darkness, however it did not hide what greeted them at the entrance to the castle. A five-foot figure hidden completely under a black robe with hood waited for them. Flax gasped when he noticed the creature was hovering several inches from the floor with no sign of feet to be seen. As they approached, he noticed it was breathing heavily as if in distress. Then he suddenly coughed with nausea for the creature stank of rotting long-dead flesh and now realised what Hemlock had told him about the castle's occupants was true. Everything in the castle was dead, perhaps the owner was also. Flax again began to wish he had remained in the capital.

It was Hemlock who broke the silence. "We've come to see the sorcerer Gulag."

"Who shall I say is here?" it whispered in a coarse tone.

Hemlock smiled. "His brother," he laughed.

"What-?" Flax stuttered, and even Jacinth looked up in puzzlement.

The sentinel turned about and disappeared down the hallway to give the message.

"Is this true?" said Flax, surprised. "I always thought you were an only child."

Hemlock smiled in amusement. "Both I and Kava wanted it to be known like that. It appears my educated brother has an extreme dislike for me. He even changed his name to disassociate himself from me."

Flax smiled. Not surprising, he thought to himself, especially after Hemlock's recent performance.

The demonic butler returned shortly and escorted the three men in. The floating creature led them down dimly lit corridors and Flax could barely make out tapestries and paintings of long-forgotten heroes and battles which lined the walls. However, they appeared to be free of dust and surprisingly in good condition. Eventually the creature halted at an unimpressive wooden door, reached out a fleshless skeletal hand and made a single knock, before leaving the group and disappeared into the darkness of the corridor. Hemlock hesitated momentarily before opening the door and the three entered the chamber beyond. Unlike the corridor they had just left, this small room offered no furniture or ornaments bar shelves of books and volumes which lined every available space on the walls, a single large rectangular-shaped crude table and a small chair. However, the room was similar to the corridor in that it too was cloaked in darkness, as if the castle itself was afraid to reveal its occupants to the outside world. Flax wondered who feared who the most; whether the master of the castle was more afraid of the ruthless ignorant world than it were of him, or was it the other way around. Being Hemlock's brother, Flax guessed it was probably the latter, the populace most likely feared and despised this mysterious sorcerer for his dark powers and ambitious intellect.

The chair was occupied by a medium-build tall man displaying a crop of short brown hair and beard. He was dressed in a fine black silk robe and held a seven-foot staff in his left hand which was extensively decorated in various magical symbols. Strapped to his waist by a thick brown leather belt was a slender kriss knife. But Flax guessed such a man required no weapons. The wizard rose and approached Hemlock and Flax noticed with some surprise that the mage had a slight limp in his left leg. He was using the staff not for any magical purpose, though rather for support.

"Well, what brings you here, brother?" the mage said in a tone of voice that was almost musical. "I doubt it is a social visit."

"You're right," Hemlock stated flatly. "It isn't."

"I thought as much."

"I need your help."

"You need my help?" the mage remarked softly in a tone that was almost sarcastic.

"Listen Kava, I-"

"Don't call me that," the warlock roared. "My name's Gulag. In twenty years you did not visit me since our parents died, and now suddenly you turn up asking for help. Well, you can go to hell."

"I always meant to visit, but something always turned up."

"Save your excuses," Kava interjected. "You're an uneducated common thief, you always were, and you always will be. You had potential; you could have been someone, perhaps even a mage. But you don't have the patience. You want everything the easy way and you want it now. But you'll get nothing from me, now get out."

"You're going to give me what I want, or else-"

"Or else what?" Kava snapped. "Don't make me laugh. There's nothing you can do to me, my power is beyond your feeble comprehension."

"Or else this," Hemlock shouted and drew his sword.

What little light the room offered was seemingly absorbed into the glowing blade and reflected out as blackness which darkened the chamber further until Flax could only make out the three men as dark shapes, though could not distinguish between them.

"Where did you get that?" Kava muttered softly in unmistakable fear.

"I stole it," Hemlock retorted. "Oh Kava, you really are a prisoner in your own castle with no information of the going-ons of the outside world."

"What do you want?" the mage asked timidly.

"You're going to travel with us to the citadel of the Temple of the Dragon. You know the land from here to the sea, and you have the power to blast that fort from here to the island of Kilhaven."

"I can't-"

"You can," Hemlock interjected, "and you will, brother."

The sorcerer collected his three most important books and placing them in a small bag, followed his brother out of the castle with Flax and Jacinth close behind.

"Oh, and one more thing Kava, leave that kriss-knife behind," Hemlock whispered. "We wouldn't like you to have the temptation to put it between my shoulder-blades some dark night, now would we?"

The mage let the slender blade fall into the sand and prepared to march into the desert when an arrow flew suddenly through the air and pierced Flax's shoulder. All turned and ran for the safety of the castle as a second arrow ricocheted off the stones of the yard.

"Who the hell-?" Flax roared in pain and pulled the arrow from his shoulder with a loud shout.

"It can't be anyone from the battle, they're all dead," Hemlock snarled as Kava picked up the arrow and began to examine it closely.

"This arrow did not come from any of the nearby tribes," Kava remarked. "The feathers come from a bird only to be found in the capital, as far as I remember. What do you suggest we do?"

"Kill them," Hemlock snapped in rage.

The mage reached into a jerkin-pocket and pulled out two small pouches, removed brown dust from each and threw it onto the stones while muttering words the other men did not recognise. The ground began to shift until the courtyard broke open and something huge; something dark started to crawl its way seemingly out of the stones. Flax gasped in shock as a giant hound rose to the surface. It was as large as a donkey with thick black fur, blood-red eyes with no pupils and two-inch long fangs protruding from a frothing mouth. It was followed close behind by two more until three enormous hounds stood before their creator and master, awaiting his command. The mage pointed to the desert and the three dogs instantly took off, baying; a sound which made Flax shiver in sudden fear. Hemlock decided they should remain in the castle until they were sure the monsters had completed their task, lest they return and attack them when Kava's back was appropriately turned.

Storm and Suzerain thought it was an earthquake as the three hounds ran across the wasteland towards them as they hid behind a nearby dune. Storm put down his bow and glanced around, but could see nothing. However, he gasped when he saw what approached them. He notched an arrow and fired, hitting one of the hounds in the neck. It fell dead to the sand and seemed to dissolve into the desert to Storm's amazement. The other two dogs did not seem to notice their companion falling and carried on without him. Suzerain notched an arrow and prepared to fire, but screamed when he saw their attackers and his arrow missed and flew harmlessly into the sand. Storm pulled the boy back behind the dune and drew his knife. The hounds leapt over the dune and the travellers with little effort and without knowing they were there. As the dogs leaped over their heads, Storm reached up and stabbed one in the stomach. It stumbled and fell alongside him and Storm pulled the blade up, disembowelling the beast, and scattering its intestines to the desert. It dissolved into the sand as the third hound attacked. Storm attempted to stab the beast in the head, but with one quick movement, the hound snatched the knife from his hand and to his astonishment, broke the dagger in two before swallowing it. The knife did not appear to taste nice, and the hound wanted something much more tasty - human flesh. The beast approached them, breathing heavily. Storm coughed and Suzerain abruptly fainted, for the creature's breath stank of rotting flesh. Storm believed he would pass out soon also. The hound opened its mouth to reveal dagger-like teeth and a dark throat he feared must lead to hell itself. It now stood mere inches from his face and he realised he had only one chance. He couldn't reach his sword and Suzerain was still unconscious, but the boy's knife was near and he snatched hold of that instead.

He hesitated, before suddenly shoving his hand and the short blade into the gaping mouth and sank his arm almost to the shoulder. He then began to twist and turn the dagger inside the creature. The hound started to panic and began to first bite, then chew at Storm's arm. Storm cried out with the pain and thought he wouldn't be able to hold on when the beast suddenly collapsed, unconscious. Storm released his arm from out of the hound's mouth and with his free hand, cut the beast open with his sword. The creature dissolved into the desert as he tore a piece of cloth from his jerkin and bandaged his arm.

Suzerain appeared to be unharmed and Storm shook him awake before helping him to his feet. He gave the boy some water from his flask though they had little left. Storm hoped they would find some soon once they entered the castle. He needed Suzerain's help in entering the building for the boy could open any lock with a skill and speed he doubted even Hemlock could match. Storm heard the lock open and carefully pushed in one of the doors before the two crept inside. There was no sign of the men or the mysterious master of the castle who had tried to kill them. Storm thought it unwise for them to search along the main hallway and so suggested a small corridor cloaked in darkness to their left which appeared to run deep into the building. Suzerain did not like the look of the corridor, but feared the master of the castle more and did not wish to run into him without warning, and so agreed.

Drawing his sword, Storm led the boy into the darkness of the castle and towards whatever other surprises the dark mage kept hidden in a fortress built on sand.

CHAPTER SEVEN

"I hope your hounds killed those bastards," roared Flax as he rubbed his shoulder in pain.

The four men sat before a twenty-foot long rectangular varnished oak table in the great dinning chamber of the castle, eating a feast created by the demonic guards. Hemlock watched these sentinels go about their duties with great suspicion, wary for any hidden daggers meant for their backs.

"You yourself heard the screams," Kava replied sharply. "Those dogs would complete their task, or die in the attempt."

"But they didn't return," interjected Hemlock.

"Naturally, *dearest* brother," said the mage. "They would disappear back into the desert after their mission was completed. Besides, nothing could survive an attack from those hounds of hell."

Hemlock sneered at his reply, his answer was obviously sarcastic. Kava always was one to rub salt into the wound of ignorance of his brother the common thief. But this ordinary robber, Hemlock vowed, would bring this land to its knees; something Kava would never do, for all his bold words. He glanced down at the sword. It began to glow as if reading his dark thoughts. He had forgot to mention to Flax and Jacinth that he required one final ingredient for the altar in the citadel if he was to raise Proteus. He needed a virgin.

However, a virgin was something difficult to come by in this age. Still, if he could not find one in time, anyone would have to do, and he was keeping an eye on Flax as a likely victim. He knew Jacinth would have no scruples in killing his friend. Jacinth had acquired a taste for violence recently that almost matched his; a man after his own heart. Unfortunately, he would probably cut out that same heart if the opportunity arose, Hemlock realised he could no longer trust anyone.

Once they had finished their grand meal and the rotting butlers had cleared the table, Kava brought in a map and a giant leather-bound book which was several inches thick. The sorcerer passed the volume across to Hemlock and spread the map across the length of the table. He pointed to a spot on the parchment which was near the north edge of the map. The three men rose and bent over the table to examine it closer.

"There's the citadel," said Kava as he glanced at his brother, but Hemlock ignored him and was studying the book.

"What's that?" asked Flax.

"It's a spell book," the mage replied. "My best magick book, and-"

"What's this?" interrupted Hemlock, throwing a square torn parchment onto the table which he had removed from the volume.

"A detailed map of the castle," retorted the wizard. "It shows the tunnels, dungeons, secret entrances and the homes of the other creatures in the fortress. Part of the building goes underground, but there…"

"What creatures?" Hemlock interjected sharply, remembering the hounds.

"The guards, other beasts like hydras, skeleton-guardians, dwarfs, trolls, great quantities of massive snakes and spiders and even a few werewolves around."

"Werewolves," Hemlock screamed. "You say you have werewolves in here, where?"

"Near the dungeons," answered Kava, perplexed. "Why?"

Hemlock did not reply. He did not want them to know of his only fear - that of werewolves. Shortly after Kava had left home when he was a child, his friend and himself were attacked by a werewolf one dark night in winter. They had been fortunate for the beast was injured, yet it managed to scratch his companion on the arm as they escaped. The following night, the friend broke out in hairs and Hemlock was forced to behead his friend to save his immortal soul, though mostly because the beast was about to eat him. He did not wish to run into another one of those creatures. Spilling blood did not bother Hemlock, drinking it did. There was a time and place for everything, even that.

He returned his attention to the book and quickly began to memorise a few of the shorter spells. They might come in handy in the near future, smiled Hemlock.

The light from the blazing torches on the walls guided their way into the castle as they ventured deeper into the ground, below the very foundations of the building itself. They abruptly came to a dead-end in the tunnel. There was a wall of stone blocking their path, there was no way to go but back up into the castle.

"Where do we go now-?" Suzerain said in dismay, but was interrupted by a deep rumble that shook the tunnel and the ground beneath their feet began to cave in. "Run," he shouted in panic.

It was too late. The stone below their feet gave way and the travellers fell ten feet to another level and more sturdy ground. They rose to find impassable stone all around them bar directly ahead where stood a seven foot door of steel. Engraved on the door in blood were the words 'No Trespassers allowed beyond this point on pain of death'. Storm noticed the blood was fresh and ran down the door into a pool on the ground. He looked up from where they had fallen and realised there was no way they could get back, they had no choice but to enter whatever lay beyond the door. He wondered what manner of man or creature would go to the trouble of writing the chilling message when nobody had seen this side of the door since the castle had been built. If they had not fallen, they would not have found the door and be in this predicament.

Suzerain drew his blade and Storm readied his as he pushed in the door. What lay beyond the door was a nightmare neither of them could ever have imagined. The large chamber or wide cavern they had entered was devoid of any furniture leading to another similar single door directly across the room. However, scattered over every conceivable space on the ground were the various rotting and fresh remains of other creatures that lived in the castle. Storm noticed something that looked similar to a wolf, another that of a large man, all missing limbs. Dozens of rats were gorging themselves on the great abundance of food that decorated the chamber. Their speechless disgust and astonishment was broken as a large shadow jumped down from somewhere on the ceiling and confronted them. The creature which stood at over eight feet was almost beyond description and certainly defied nature. It was basically humanoid in shape, though it possessed eight pairs of arms and two pairs of legs. Storm now realised why so many opponents lay dead, the creature must be virtually undefeatable in battle for in each hand it held a broadsword, already heavily stained with blood.

"You read the words on the door?" it smiled from a perfect human head with wild eyes that Storm recognised as madness in its purest form. It seemed to be unconcerned as to how the travellers had found the door.

"Yes," Suzerain said.

"You should have heeded the warning," it laughed, as the beast attacked, waving the sixteen swords about wildly.

It had no skill in swordplay, but simply waved the swords around at random, knowing it had to eventually hit something with sixteen blades. It moved towards Storm first, realising he was the greater opponent and the boy would be easy to dispatch once his companion had fallen. Eight left arms bearing swords lunged at him, but Storm simply side-stepped out of the way and as the beast passed him by, pushed the creature on the back, sending him crashing into the door. The beast quickly recovered from the blow and prepared to attack Storm again. However, five out of the eight swords on his left had pierced the door and appeared to be stuck.

It was pondering on whether it should relinquish its hold on the blades and recover them later when Storm suddenly ran the creature through the back and his own blade pierced the door after exiting the beast through the chest. The many-armed warrior let out a moan as Storm retrieved his sword and fell to the ground, dead, leaving a legacy of five blades impaled in the steel door.

Suzerain abruptly burst into laughter at the manner in which the seemingly undefeatable monster had died, to have vanquished all the enemies whose bones littered the chamber and then die by getting stuck in a door leading nowhere. Storm began to make his way through the labyrinth of dead and rotting carcasses towards the second door which he hoped lead to somewhere, and not another dead-end. Suzerain stopped laughing and quickly followed him. Storm opened the door and the two found themselves in another tunnel of stone leading deeper into the earth. The tunnel turned left and ended in another door, a wooden one this time. The travellers halted for there were sounds of laughing mixed with screams coming from beyond the door. Storm bent down and looked through the keyhole, but could see nothing. Slowly and carefully he opened the door and peeked in. Scattered around the small chamber were various instruments of torture - an Iron Maiden, cages of all sizes, thumb-screws which hung by chains from the ceiling and a rack. Light for the room was coming from the blazing fire in the hearth on the far right wall. The sounds they had heard came from the far end of the chamber where two dwarfs dressed in torn jerkins were stretching a human on the rack, his screams for mercy going unanswered.

Storm fired an arrow, hitting one of the dwarfs in the back and he slumped forward onto the rack without a sound. His companion instantly halted his activities and drew a shortsword. He glanced all around the chamber, searching for the source of the attack, expecting another dwarf jealous of this entertainment and wanting it all for himself. He was surprised when he saw Storm cowering behind the door, but smiled; another human for the rack would be nice, since the one he had was already near to death. He advanced on

Storm and took an arrow in the chest, dropping him where he stood.

Suzerain checked the dwarfs to make sure they were indeed dead while Storm untied the man on the rack, though he need not have bothered for the man was dying. He grabbed Storm by the sleeve and thrust something into his hand which Storm saw was a large iron key. "It will open the door to the second level of the castle," he gasped hoarsely. "But beware the werewolves and the traps-"

The man had breathed his last, he was dead. Storm frowned for he had meant to say more as he laid the corpse back on the rack, his body no longer in torment. But death had robbed him of more words that might have helped the travellers escape this foul castle and find Hemlock. Storm pocketed the key and they left the torture-chamber via another small wooden door set in the far wall. Beyond the door lay yet another long winding tunnel which ended in a huge eight-foot steel door. Suzerain reckoned even a dragon could not break this door down and hoped the key they had was the right one for the door, otherwise they were stuck. Storm apprehensively placed the key in the giant lock and the two travellers held their breath in nervousness. However, Storm let out a light laugh as they heard an audible click and the giant door swung open to reveal a tunnel with steps cut into the very stone leading upwards.

Beyond the stairs the ground levelled out and the tunnel began to widen. On their left they came across a large wooden door inscribed on which was the word 'Dungeons'. They ignored the door and came across another at the end of the tunnel bearing the word 'Stairs'. Suzerain ran ahead and was about to open the door when Storm suddenly stopped him. "The last door leading to a stairs was unmarked, larger than this one and required a special key to open."

Storm walked past the boy and kicked the door in. Beyond lay not stairs but a twenty-foot drop into a pit where five-foot wooden sharpened stakes lined the floor for the unwary traveller. "This must be the trap the man on the rack was trying to tell us about," Storm whispered.

They went back to the other entrance leading to the dungeons and after a small flight of stairs and through another door, they found themselves in the very centre of the dungeons where cells lined the walls to their left and right, the cages still containing the rancid remains of long-forgotten prisoners, still chained to the floor, ceiling or rotting beds. The travellers now broke into a run and approached the other door leading out of the dungeons. However, a surprise awaited them. Storm opened the door and gasped in alarm. At the end of the short tunnel was another familiar giant steel door, leading to the next level and into the heart of the castle.

Next to the door was a small wooden casket which had to contain the key for the door. However, lying on the ground blocking their way to both the box and the door was a seven foot robust stone golem guardian. With a heavy sigh, Storm remembered what Kassier had told him about stone golems, that they could not be harmed by edged weapons like swords, knives or arrows. They would have to break him up, piece by piece by using something blunt like a rock. Hence, they were perfect guardians, being virtually indestructible.

"I'll keep it busy," Storm whispered. "While you get the box," hoping he would survive that long.

Suzerain nodded as Storm picked up a large rock and threw it at the huge creature. His shot was true and hit the stone golem in the chest. The beast of stone which seemed to have been sleeping, suddenly came to life. It slowly rose and moved first its left foot and then its right, inching its way towards the travellers. When it was nearly three feet from Storm, Suzerain seized his chance and made a leap, hoping to pass it and get the box. However, though the golem was slow when walking because of its bulk, it could move its arms very quickly. It snatched hold of Suzerain's jerkin at the collar as he attempted to jump past the creature. Storm realised if he was to save the boy's life, he would have to act fast. Moving quickly, Storm picked up another rock and with a shout, flung it at the golem's hand that was holding Suzerain.

He had thrown the rock with such force that it shattered the wrist upon impact and the boy fell to the ground with a heavy stone hand still clutching his jerkin. He ripped the hand off and made a mad dive for the small chest at the door, while the golem with its one remaining hand made a grab for Storm. Storm rolled out of the way as the golem's fist smashed into the ground, leaving in its wake a small hole. As it tried another attack at Storm, Suzerain opened the box by picking at it with his knife and unlocked the giant steel door with the large iron key he removed from the wooden casket.

The Goddess of Luck Storm reckoned must have been looking favourably upon him as he made a dive and jumped between the stone creature's open legs and raced through the door, locking it behind them. They both collapsed on the floor in exhaustion as they heard the golem bang on the door in anger and frustration. But it could not break down the door for all its great strength. They were safe from its wrath.

"That was a close one," said Storm with a laugh.

"Almost too close," added Suzerain.

"Come on," shouted Storm, rising to his feet and grabbing the boy's hand.

He pulled Suzerain to his feet and they ran up the flight of stairs, leaving the tunnels of the castle behind.

"I've been hearing strange noises," Kava said as he entered the grand sitting-room on the fourth floor of the castle.

"Well, what noises?" Hemlock retorted in annoyance at being disturbed.

"I don't know exactly," the mage replied. "Sort of odd crashing noises and doors being slammed."

"Is that all?" Hemlock snapped. "You said yourself that there were many other creatures in this castle. Get out and leave me alone."

Kava cursed under his breath at his brother as he left the room. He knew the sounds his guardians made, these were something else. Something was wrong, perhaps the archers in the desert had survived his hounds after all, and had managed to make it into the castle. He was determined to find these intruders and prove their existence to his ignorant brother. The travellers found themselves before another giant steel door, blocking their path. Engraved to the right of the door at chest-height on the wall was a rough outline of the fortress, showing levels and rooms to be found in the castle and the adjoining towers. There appeared to a fifth floor devoted exclusively to bedrooms high above them. The first, second and third levels as they had found out with much effort were underground; under the very castle itself.

"How do we get past this door?" inquired Suzerain. "Where is the key?"

"I don't know," Storm retorted in dismay, kicking the door in frustration.

Suddenly to their amazement and joy, the door began to open. However, their delight was short-lived. The door opened fully to reveal a tall man dressed in the all-too-familiar robes of a black mage, bearing a long staff in his left hand. As he began to approach the travellers, Suzerain noticed the wizard had a slight limp. He sneered down on the trespassers into his private kingdom.

"Greetings good sir," Storm stuttered. "We're lost."

"Lost, eh?" Kava laughed. "What do you take me for? The nearest civilisation is Hellsbreath."

The travellers turned and made a run for it back down to the tunnels. The sorcerer watched them flee with great amusement for several moments before raising his right hand towards them, muttered a few words and two streaks of lightening shot from his fingertips and lit up the corridor. The flashes hit them squarely in the back, sending them flying to the ground with a thud. They did not even hear the dark mage laugh behind them, his laughter echoing throughout the castle.

CHAPTER EIGHT

Storm awoke suddenly, shivering with the cold. He rose up onto his elbows and gazed into the darkness of the chamber, the only light reaching this room through a small crack in the ceiling. He noticed he lay on a badly water-stained mattress and as his eyes became accustomed to the blackness, he could see Suzerain lay unconscious on a similar bed not three feet alongside his. However, he let out a gasp of shock and dismay when he noticed the rust-coloured iron bars not seven feet directly in front of him. He and the boy were in the dungeons. Storm felt despair enter his mind at the thought that they were at the mercy of Hemlock, a man without remorse. The mage they had earlier encountered, considered Storm, must be the master of the castle and the mysterious friend of Hemlock's. A formidable foe, one he hoped he would never have to fight.

Storm began to wonder how long his captors would leave them in silence when the door on the right wall abruptly swung open and four men entered the dungeons. Storm instantly recognised the dark mage, though did not know the other three. He did not have time to see the faces of his wife's murderers in the darkness of the alley. But he knew Hemlock would have the sword of Proteus. Kassier had told him the sword was unmistakable, it would visibly glow with power. One of the men held a blazing torch as they approached the cell. The wizard jammed a large iron key into the lock and it turned with a loud click. Storm could feel his heart racing. He was finally about to come face to face with his mortal enemy, though under circumstances he wished were more to his advantage.

Storm watched one of the men step forward and stared at the blade strapped to his waist, heavily jewelled both on the handle and the scabbard. He could see a light glow surround the hilt and sneered at the man as he approached, looking down at his vulnerable prisoner. Hemlock glanced first at Storm, then at Suzerain before returning his full attention to Storm.

"Do I know you?" Hemlock said, staring down at Storm. "You look familiar."

Storm did not reply, his identity could wait until circumstances had improved in his favour.

"So, my brother was right, there were intruders," Hemlock smiled. "Good, we can use the boy as the sacrifice," he laughed. "Lucky for you, Flax."

Flax turned to Hemlock, perplexed. "What do you mean?"

But Hemlock just burst into laughter in reply. Flax put a hand to his blade. Hemlock stopped laughing. He instead stared fixedly at Flax with a blank expression. Flax hesitated for several moments before removing his hand from the handle of his sword and Hemlock smiled. Flax cursed under his breath at his own cowardice, but it would be wiser to attack their leader when he was unarmed. He was far too dangerous while in possession of that magical blade, though his brother Kava might protect Flax if he did attack Hemlock for Flax could see the mad desire in his eyes every time he looked at the sword, which was frequent. He also knew the mage hated being servant to his brother because of his fear of the sword.

"What do you mean a sacrifice?" Storm said with a growing feeling of apprehension.

"You'll find out," Hemlock laughed and the four men left the cell, the mage locking it behind them with a loud clang.

The sound woke Suzerain and he moaned. "What hit me?" Then he realised his surroundings. "Oh no," he whispered in dismay.

"After all that hunting, tracking and fighting to end up being captured by the very man I came to kill," Storm cursed in anger.

"Don't worry," Suzerain smiled. "We'll get out of this."

"I admire your optimism," Storm retorted. "But how? We're finished."

"Easy. They may have taken our weapons," Suzerain laughed. "But they forgot this."

From out of a hidden pocket inside his jerkin he removed a slender broken three-inch sliver of metal which once must have belonged to a dagger, though had now become the perfect lock-opener. He jumped off the bed and kneeling before the cell-door, proceeded to insert it into the rusty lock the sliver, turned this way and that way for several moments before there was a click and Suzerain smiled as he pushed the door open. Their weapons lay next to the door, their captors confident nobody could escape the dungeons. They opened the door and moaned in despair. Before them was the stone golem with its missing hand, though it did not notice them. It appeared to once again be deep in slumber. They began to ponder on how to get past the creature a second time when they heard voices coming from behind the golem, beyond the great steel door into the castle. Hemlock and the others were coming back. The travellers fled back into the dungeon and through the other door leading deeper into the tunnels under the fortress. On their left they noticed the false door marked stairs that offered the pit instead.

They raced down through the second floor and found a junction, one tunnel stretching on, the other leading to a dead-end marked by a large nest of dried mud and straw for whatever creature roamed this level.

"Where now?" Suzerain said in panic.

"Wait, I have an idea," Storm replied and led the boy down the short tunnel to the dead-end.

They came to the bare wall and Storm glanced at the nest on the ground. He made the boy lie down and quickly poured leaves and straw over him until he was completely hidden. Then he laid down himself and began to cover his body, first his legs, followed by his torso and finally his head until he could feel nothing but straw all around him, blocking his vision. He held his breath in nervousness.

The four men entered the dungeons and Jacinth observed the rotting remains of old prisoners with much relish. They approached the cell of their captives and stopped short with a gasp.

"What the hell?" Kava stuttered. "They're gone, it's not possible."

"Find them," Hemlock screamed.

They raced out of the dungeons and into the second floor of tunnels. Hemlock drew up alongside his two fellow thieves and brother.

"Flax and Kava, search the dead-end," Hemlock ordered. "Jacinth and I will check down this tunnel."

The two men glanced at the bare impassable wall and nest for several moments before returning to the junction in frustration. Hemlock and his silent partner returned after only a few brief moments, Hemlock cursing loudly in anger. "They can't have got past the steel door on the first floor," roared Hemlock in blind rage. "Search again!"

The four men searched every corner and crevice, but in vain. There was no sign of their prisoners. Kava began to wonder if they had been mages, though quickly dismissed the thought. He would have known if they were. Yet, they had seemingly disappeared into thin air without a trace.

"Maybe something got them?" Flax said.

"What a pity for you if something did indeed get them," replied Hemlock with a sneer.

"Yes, a great pity," Jacinth echoed suddenly, finally breaking his apparently religious silence.

For the first time in his life, Flax knew with conviction that he was alone; alone in a dark evil castle with three men who wanted him dead, three men who cared for nobody but themselves. Flax didn't know how, but he had to get away from these people before he lost his sanity like Jacinth or be murdered by Hemlock.

The men gave up their hunt, exhausted, and returned to the upper levels of the castle which promised luxury and safety.

The travellers waited for a further hour before brushing away the dust, leaves and straw and made their way to the junction.

"That was close," Suzerain breathed. "What do we do now?"

"We'll hide in one of the three towers in the courtyard," Storm replied as they proceeded to the first floor where a welcoming committee greeted them.

Storm opened the giant door into the first floor to reveal a gathering of guardians for this level. Suzerain let out a gasp as he gazed upon a group of human-skeleton-warriors, six in all. Each of the creatures brandished a broadsword in front of their bony bodies and instantly upon spotting the two intruders, began to move towards them in quick jerky movements. Storm groaned as he remembered what Kassier had told him about these deadly fleshless creatures. Created by mages to guard rooms or corridors, these beasts had to be maimed to be stopped, and would fight on even after the loss of limbs. Kassier had mentioned one man who had once hunted such creatures for a living, searching endless castles and caves for the beasts. He learned that their only weakness was the neck; separate the skull from the torso and they would be helpless, losing the ability of their limbs. They could then be dispatched quite easily. However, until that happened, they were formidable foes. It was ironic that the man was known to have killed hundreds of the fleshless beasts, surviving the encounters without a scratch and yet choked to death on a fish-bone telling the tales of his valour before an astonished crowd over a meal in the capital city.

Storm moved in front of Suzerain as the creatures advanced. He drew his blade and attacked the leader. Storm could not believe the speed of the beasts of magick as they swung their blades at him. He removed his long-bow from his back and attempted to use it as a stick in his left-hand to keep them at bay, but one skeleton-warrior simply cut the bow in half as it approached him. Storm began to fear they had met their match and would die here in this tunnel. The sword was knocked from his hand by the quick movement of a blade from one of the beasts and sliced his right shoulder with the same motion. Storm screamed in pain as blood flowed freely down his side. He prepared himself for the death blow.

Suddenly the door leading to the room of bodies they had encountered earlier at the opposite end of the tunnel flew open to reveal the dark mage. The creatures instantly halted their attack at the sight of their master and moved back to allow him to reach the intruders. Storm sighed in despair and abruptly fainted.

He awoke hours later to the familiar sight of the dungeons with Suzerain who had bandaged his shoulder. Standing outside the cell with a vacant expression was Jacinth, guarding them lest they attempt to escape again, his cold eyes never leaving the travellers. Suzerain could not bear to look upon the thief, his emotionless face frightened him more than the skeleton-warriors. Jacinth rose as Hemlock entered, carrying a large two-headed stone hammer in his hand. He approached the cell and smiled; an evil grin that sent shivers down their spines. "Greetings, Storm," he laughed to Storm's fear and surprise. "Yes, I know who you are. To think you travelled all this way to kill me, and now I am going to kill you. Especially after all the trouble you caused me at the battle. But no matter, I shall still triumph."

"I always knew you were a bastard," Storm snarled. "But now I know you're a *crazy* bastard."

Hemlock burst into laughter in reply. He walked over to where their weapons had been placed, and one by one, smashed them with the hammer. Heaving the large stone-hammer over his shoulder, he broke the arrows, knives, Suzerain's bow and shortsword. He brought it down onto

Storm's sword with a dreadful crash of metal and let out a scream as the blow sent shudders throughout his body. He stared down at the blade in astonishment for there was no sign of a crack in the metal, not even a scratch. "Well, well, well. What do we have here?" he roared, as he picked up the weapon and carefully studied it. "Where did you steal this? This is too good a blade to waste, especially on a poor swordsman like you," Hemlock laughed and passed the blade to Jacinth, his silent partner. He approached the cell once more and smiled down at his prisoners. "We leave the castle at dawn for the citadel and there you will see the fate that awaits you."

Then he left them to the silent company of Jacinth, who sat watching them while admiring his new-found weapon.

Light from the crack in the ceiling had barely begun to enter the cell when the travellers were impolitely awoken and forced up through the dark tunnels by the silent thief, who frequently pushed them into the rough stone walls, cutting their faces and making them stumble, much to his amusement. They eventually reached their destination in the dinning-room on the fourth floor; the level the travellers had struggled so hard to reach and failed. Storm was taken aback in awe at the size and luxury of the chamber; huge tapestries lined the walls above velvet-covered furniture and shining empty suits of armour of Knights, vanquished in a battle long ago. A large polished table surrounded by chairs and decorated with silver lay in the centre of the chamber.

Seats were pulled out for them and the two prisoners were forced to sit. Around them sat the three thieves and the mage, watching their every move. Meals on silver plates had been placed before them, though no cutlery was present. Jacinth sat two chairs down from Hemlock across the table and sneered at Storm as he looked down on the foul-smelling food before him.

"Last meals for the condemned," Jacinth laughed, his voice echoing around the giant chamber, hammering into Storm's skull.

Storm looked up from the table and stared across at the thief in silent rage before picking up the plate of food that reminded him of putrefying dog's vomit and suddenly threw it at the laughing lunatic. The meal exploded onto the thief's face and chest, sending pieces of meat flying. With a speed that even the skeleton-warriors could not match, Jacinth was off his seat in moments, had dived across the table and drawn his dagger to reach his attacker. Storm had barely risen from his seat, when Jacinth was upon him and had the knife at his throat. Storm snatched the dagger from Jacinth's hand in time to save his life, and bringing the slender blade around in an arc, shoved it into Jacinth's stomach. He placed his free left hand around the astonished man's neck and while embracing him, withdrew the blade only to shove it back in, again and again, Jacinth letting out a moan as the life left him. The thief collapsed to the floor in a heap, the dagger sticking out of his stomach like an ugly thorn. All this had happened in a few brief moments. Hemlock, Flax and Kava had barely risen from their seats in speechless awe to find it was all over. Jacinth, their fellow thief, was dead.

"Three down," Storm said flatly as Suzerain stared on in astonishment. "Three to go."

"Storm, you are becoming a bit of a pain," Hemlock snarled as he approached Storm. "You're very foolish. I could have killed you quickly, but now I promise you'll die on your knees, screaming in pain."

Before Storm could act, Hemlock brought his foot up and kicked him squarely between the legs. Storm fell to the floor with a groan.

"Lock them up," the thief boomed and two of the ghostly sentinels in black cloaks approached and picking up the helpless travellers, dragged them off to the dungeons.

"You're letting them live after what they've done?" shouted Flax in rage.

"Yes, I have something special in mind for them," he laughed in reply.

"He had something special for Jacinth, and you're keeping them alive so you can torture them for fun in your spare time," Flax said. "You're crazy."

"You're beginning to irritate me also, Flax," Hemlock roared as his hands reached out and grabbed Flax by the throat, intent on strangling him.

He was close to breaking the thief's neck when Kava stopped him. "We'll need all the men we can get to take the citadel."

"Yes, you're right," Hemlock said and relaxed his hold. "Just make sure you're ready for it with your sorcery, Kava," he roared, letting Flax fall to the floor. "Pack your bags, we're leaving at noon. Oh, and one last thing," he said, turning once more to Flax. "You can have Jacinth's sword, but try using it to cut me and I'll leave you headless."

Flax hesitated before removing the blade from the corpse and left the room quickly in fear.

The hot desert sun had reached its zenith in the clear sky when they left the safety of the castle and ventured onto the baking sand. They travelled due north for several hours when a wind arose and blew sand into their faces and eyes. But the end of the desert was in sight and all cried out in relief. The mage shook the reins of his horse and rode ahead to the front of the group. He drew up alongside his brother and lowered the cloth covering his mouth and nose from the sand. "About two miles from here lie the mountains," he whispered, "we'll have to climb, leaving the horses and most of the supplies behind. The citadel lies on a small mountain near the coast and the altar lies in the very centre of the fortress."

"You said there were dangerous tribes around here," Hemlock said. "Where are they?"

"All around, especially in the valley," Kava replied. "Some of them have perfected cannibalism almost to an art."

"Could we pass through under cover of nightfall?"

"Impossible. Last time I was here years ago there were five tribes and three of those hunted at night. Dragon knows how many there are now!"

"Could you make a magical shield around us that nothing can penetrate, protecting us from their spears and arrows?"

"No use," the mage sighed. "We'd have to move very slowly to use the shield, and the savages would simply barricade themselves around us so we could not move and wait for the spell to fade."

"So if they attack, we'll just have to run for it?"

"Yes, I'm afraid so," Kava stated flatly.

The travellers could now see the mountains clearly, a giant wall of barren stone rising high into the clouds, blocking their path. They rode to the foot of the mountains and dismounted. It had quite suddenly began to rain heavily, drenching them to the skin. Hemlock cursed, the weather would probably get even worse the further they travelled up the mountain. They each took on an equal load of the supplies, Hemlock even forcing his two prisoners to carry a share. Hemlock decided he should travel first, closely followed by Kava, the prisoners and Flax, all bonded together by a thick rope which was wound around their waists. The mountain appeared almost completely vertical with very little evidence of nooks and cracks in the rock-face for hand-holds.

Hemlock had only begun to climb and was barely two feet off the ground when he noticed something in the rock-face to his right near the ground. It appeared to be a cave, cutting into the mountain, perhaps offering easier entry into the valley beyond. The mage glanced up at him in confusion, not understanding the reason for his sudden cessation.

"Hey, look," Hemlock roared above the noise of the rain, pointing.

All glanced over, seeing nothing at first bar rock, but then noticed a dark shadow on the mountain-face. They ran to the spot, Kava pushing Storm and Suzerain in front of them. They quickly discarded the rope and Hemlock was the first to reach the large cave and glanced inside. He could see nothing bar utter darkness, though it seemed to be deep and perhaps indeed led to the other side of the mountain. Hemlock was willing to give it a go, anything was better than scaling the mountain in the lashing rain. Even now, the wind began to pick up to accompany the heavy rain, maybe even promising a hurricane.

"Flax, get the torches," Hemlock ordered as he turned to his brother. "Have you seen this cave before?"

"No, Never," Kava replied. "But I don't like the look of it, it doesn't appear natural."

Hemlock ignored his comment. "Can we bring the horses with us?"

"We'll soon have to crawl in there," the mage moaned. "It's far too small," he snapped, noticing the cave was barely six feet in height. "Bringing the horses is out of the question."

"But it might bring us out at the other side," Hemlock said as Flax returned with three unlit torches. "It would save us having to hike up the mountain."

"Maybe," Kava whispered, his eyes watching Flax light the torches and how the flame danced in the wind and the rain. "And then again, maybe not."

Hemlock and Flax entered together, shortly followed by the mage, shoving their prisoners in front of him. As they walked, they noticed the walls and floor were not rough but smooth, every bit of jutting rock had been eroded away by some unseen force.

"It's all very smooth," Flax said, perplexed. "Why?"

"Occasionally the valley fills with sea-water from an inlet in the coast, or when it rains heavily the water collects and probably flows through here, eroding away the rock," Kava explained.

"That means there is a way out," Hemlock shouted, glancing back at his brother to confirm that he was right, and the mage had been wrong.

Kava did not reply, he felt talking to his feeble-minded younger brother was a waste of time and breath. The travellers walked slowly through the passage, the mage and Flax's head bent, sometimes even needing to crawl as the cave-ceiling dropped sharply, though opened again soon after. Eventually they sighted light and Hemlock broke into a run, free of the constricted tunnel. A giant though barren U-shaped valley stretched before them, mountains all around, blocking their escape and directly ahead far off in the distance, a hill whereupon lay the citadel.

Flax began to walk around, stretching his aching back after the cave and then halted. He looked skywards and then all around in apparent confusion. He knelt to the surprise of the others, his long black hair blowing about his face in the rain and wind. He placed an ear to the ground for a few brief moments before slowly rising and turned towards Hemlock.

"What's wrong?" asked Kava.

"Can you hear something?" Flax replied sharply.

All stopped and listened attentively, but all they could hear was the rushing wind and rain.

"I can hear something," Storm suddenly uttered, speaking for the first time since they had left the castle. "A sort of roaring sound."

The sorcerer stared at Storm fixedly and Storm saw in his eyes the look of absolute fear as the colour drained from the mage's face. Storm wondered what could make a man such as the warlock fear anything so intently when the roaring became suddenly stronger and all eyes turned, gazing across the valley floor. Hemlock now knew why the altar had been built on a hill. For a moment nobody said anything. Their legs had become frozen to the spot, their eyes fixed on what fast approached them.

"By all the gods," Kava stuttered. "Flash flood!" he screamed as a ten-foot wall of water which stretched right across the valley-floor engulfed them.

All went under as the giant wave slammed into the mountain behind them, filling the cave in an instant, rushing out the other side. There was a terrific crash as rocks and boulders carried by the raging torrent smashed into the mountain-face, tearing chunks out of the mountain. As suddenly as it came, the flood disappeared. The water subsided after draining through the cave and drew back like the tide, leaving a mess of mud and debris in its wake.

For what seemed like hours of silence in the valley was abruptly broken as a hand pushed its way up through the mud and emerged like a severed limb, separated from its owner. It was soon followed by a second hand and a filthy face lined with cuts broke the surface. The seemingly unrecognisable survivor rose to his feet, glanced all around him before falling to the ground and began digging at the mud, searching for other survivors. As he worked, he wiped the mud from his face with water from nearby puddles and scooped mud from his black hair and moustache. Flax suddenly shoved his hand into a deep puddle and pulled up the battered cut face of Hemlock. He pulled his injured leader to the surface and laid him on the ground before beginning to search again for the others. Hemlock appeared to be breathing, though it was coarse. In the heat of the moment, it did not occur to him to halt the breathing altogether while he was vulnerable.

Within moments, he had found Storm and Suzerain, also alive, but there was no sign of the mage. Hemlock had recovered consciousness and crawling over to Flax, grabbed his saviour by the collars of his jerkin. "Where is Kava?" he screamed. "Where is my brother?"

Flax did not reply, his strength had left him and he fell to the ground, exhausted. Hemlock turned in desperation to Storm. "Help me find him!"

"Go to hell," Storm snarled in reply.

Hemlock staggered over to his prisoner and drew his dagger. He placed the slender blade at Storm's throat in rage. "Do it," he roared.

Storm was tempted to spit in his face, but Suzerain grabbed hold of the sleeve of his jerkin in fear and Storm realised he couldn't leave the boy alone to the mercy of this madman. He got up and began to move debris and dig at the dirt. Within the hour, they had found the dark mage, lifting the last rock off him, revealing his face. His entire face was awash with blood and all knew he had to be dead. Nobody, not even a mage could have survived injuries like his. His eyes were wide open, staring skywards, but Hemlock felt they were staring at him. For one of the few times in his wild and fearless brutal life, Hemlock felt a chill run up his spine. He thought he could hear his dead brother talking, cursing Hemlock like he had done in life.

'Why didn't you climb the mountain instead of going through the cave?' he seemed to say. 'I would still be alive. You always want to take the easy way, don't you? It shall be your undoing, brother. I'll wait in hell for you, whatever path of madness you take will surely lead you there.'

Hemlock turned away from the corpse as Flax approached him and placed a hand of sympathy on his leader's shoulder.

"I'm sorry," Flax said, looking down at the crushed body.

"What for? He was no loss," Hemlock retorted flatly, astonishing Flax. "The only thing I'm sorry about is that without his sorcery, I don't know how to destroy the citadel."

Flax staggered away from his leader in shock and began to make his way through the mud towards the distant mountain of the citadel. A few moments later he was joined by Hemlock and his two prisoners, pushing them towards the citadel and whatever fate he promised them at the altar.

CHAPTER NINE

The Lieutenant carefully entered the warm room and sighed in relief as he left the cold corridor behind. He slowly approached the single bed which stood in the very centre of the room, casting a brief glance at the blazing hearth set into the wall not five feet from the bed. His quarters did not benefit from such luxury, but he did not really miss them all that much. He was a soldier, trained for hardship and he would not have it any other way. The walls were adorned with pictures of ancient battles and long-dead nobles in between windows revealing a wilderness of sea and barren rock.

He shook the motionless form in the bed until its occupant awoke with a groan of protest. The man in the bed looked up and yawned. The Lieutenant smiled. In all the years he had known his superior, he could not get over the size of the man. Captain Falgar, Commander of the Citadel of the Temple of the Dragon, was a Knight who stood at a massive six foot four inches, displaying an enormous though hairless head and face, his puffy cheeks red from fatigue below eyes as blue as the great sea that greeted them from the north. His large and muscular chest was almost hidden under a thick bushy covering of black hair accompanying arms and legs that bulged with muscle and noticeable sinew. The Lieutenant always wondered how the man managed to get into the tight-fitting suit of armour and chainmail. Even though the armour had been custom-made for the soldier, it must still be terribly uncomfortable.

The robust Captain commanded just fifty soldiers and one hundred and fifty priests, the citadel being more akin to a temple than a fortress; not much to protect the unholy piece of rock in the small courtyard, thought the Lieutenant. Lying across a chair adjacent to the bed were a dozen or more varied medals for bravery beyond the call of duty, one Lieutenant Ionfield noticed was earned in the notorious Winterlending battle over ten years ago when a pretender to the vacant throne attacked the capital city, hoping to establish the land's first monarchy, but failed and lost his life, though his sons survived and were reported to be still in hiding and planning their revenge. It had been a particularly brutal long battle in which there had been heavy loss of life on both sides. He hoped never to see its like again. The wealthy and influential Winterlending family had suffered a great defeat and he knew that they would not rise again, and least not in his lifetime, he was certain of that.

The Lieutenant rubbed his lean face with his right hand while he waited for his only superior this side of the world to rise and dress himself. The Captain sat up and glanced at his number-one. Dressed in a light chainmail, the young man was gaunt and appeared feeble. Yet he knew the Lieutenant was a brilliant swordsman and possessed a mind that almost matched his own when it came to battle-strategy. The young soldier was barely thirty unlike his own fifty years, possessing a wavy crop of bright red hair, moustache and beard. He might have been handsome but for the ugly deep scar running from the side of his left eye to his mouth. A memento from a drunken brawl several years ago in Hellsbreath that robbed him of any chance with women, though there was nothing bar rock and water for miles around.

"A messenger from the capital has arrived," the Lieutenant suddenly said, waving a parchment in front of his superior.

The Captain snatched the note from the soldier's hand and as his eyes ran down the paper, his face became cold and drained of blood. He looked up at the Lieutenant in concern. "It comes from the High-Council in the capital," he said simply. "It appears the outcome of the battle at the Prison Tower is uncertain for there are no survivors. Commander Hartal and the High-Priest are both dead, but they cannot find Hemlock's body. It seems he may have survived and will be heading this way, intending to claim the altar. We are to be put on a war-footing until further orders arrive."

"And if Hemlock does arrive," the young soldier replied. "What do we do?"

"My orders are to stop him taking the citadel at all costs," the Captain retorted. "But say nothing to the men, their morale is low enough already, we don't want a mutiny. I will tell them of this when the time comes."

The Lieutenant nodded and left the room, leaving the big man to finish dressing himself. The Commander left his comfortable bedroom behind and entered the courtyard, casting a glance at the men on the battlements with their crossbows. He approached the centre of the small yard and placed a gloved hand on the altar. The stone platform was waist-high, supported by two thick pillars and was heavily decorated with symbols the meaning of which the Captain knew had been lost in time, though he did not doubt that Hemlock would understand them. All this killing, just to get to this table, the Captain pondered. Although he did not know the altar's ancient language, he knew its terrible history, an era thousands of years in the past when demons had walked freely under the command of Proteus; a God who shape-shifted into the form of your worst nightmare just before he took both your life and soul. Sacrifices had been carried out on this altar less than a century ago in its name, but without the correct spell and the sword, they could not raise the demon, until now.

"Devil-worshippers," he whispered to himself. "Dirty devil-worshippers."

He turned away from the altar towards the battlements when he noticed one soldier appeared to be in some state of agitation. He was shouting something incomprehensible, but acted as if he was trying to get the Captain's attention. The soldier ran down the short stone steps that led into the courtyard and approached the Commander.

"What appears to be the matter, Corporal?"

"Sire," he said. "Approximately half a dozen dragons are heading this way, and their leader appears to be a Gold-Dragon."

"By all the Gods," the Captain roared. "Sound the alarm, quickly man."

The Commander began to return to his chamber and fetch his sword while he cursed in anger and fear. A Gold-Dragon, I haven't seen one of those bastards since I was a child. Thanks be to the Gods the priests worship the father of Dragons and not also its descendants, or they might not fight. I should find the Lieutenant, knowledge of dragons was his speciality.

His chain of thought was broken by shouting above him and the sudden ringing of the alarm-bell in the yard. Soldiers and priests ran past him, frantically strapping on blades and armour as they headed for the courtyard. He entered his room and snatched up his giant blade. He unsheathed the sword. The metre-long blade felt comfortable in his hand, the shining metal decorated with various symbols of the Knights Order accompanying a jewelled handle.

Unfortunately the sword possessed no magical properties, something that would be of great use at this time. It was next to useless against the skin of a dragon, they would require the special arrows in the armoury; arrows with diamond-heads specially designed to pierce their tough pelt. No blade fashioned by man could harm the reptiles, though the sword of Proteus that Hemlock carried could easily not only slice through their skin, but stone and steel also. No weapon of any nature was protection against the sword of Proteus, the Captain remembered, bar the fabled lost seven swords of power created aeons ago which had not been seen by man for centuries. Though it was rumoured a dark-elf had created two weapons - a sword and spear, that were a match for the sword of Proteus and the seven swords. But these were tales told only by drunks of weapons never seen by human eyes, and perhaps never would. The elves kept their secrets hidden from prying human eyes, fearing their discovery and theft; any great magical weapon man could not fashion, he would steal from those that could.

He returned to the corridor and grabbed by the sleeve the first man that passed him, brought him and several others already dressed for combat down through the citadel to the armoury. In sealed wooden boxes heaped against the north wall were the arrows in their hundreds. They set to smashing open the boxes with their swords and carried their contents to the men above on the battlements watching the flying monsters approach closer with every passing moment. The archers eagerly took the arrows and prepared to fire across the sea.

They waited nervously for several minutes as the beasts approached and the Captain cursed aloud as the Lieutenant drew alongside him. "Why couldn't the evil bastards stay on that infernal island of theirs, instead of bothering us?" But the Lieutenant did not reply, he could now hear the beating of their giant wings and waited for them to scratch a spark from the two bones which criss-crossed in their throat and ignite the fumes which arose from their second stomach that would release their hell-fire.

"Prepare to fire," the Captain roared as the huge creatures began to circle the mountain, preparing to dive and breathe down on the citadel's vulnerable occupants.

A Red-Dragon swooped down, breathed in and blew out a fine golden stream of flames that engulfed two priests. They stumbled and fell over the battlement-walls, their screams sending chills up the backs of their companions until it was abruptly cut off by the rocks below. The Captain let out a roar in reply and the sky became filled with arrows, some going wide, but most hit their intended target. The giant beast let out a screech of both rage and pain as the diamond-tipped arrows pierced its flesh and entered vital organs. It let out one more final roar before falling down into the sea with a dreadful crash. The dragon's companions did not seem to be affected by the fate of their fallen comrade and attacked in its absence.

The Gold-Dragon began to screech at the other beasts to halt their attack, but the blood-lust was upon them and they ignored the warning of their leader and dived in towards the citadel, preparing to engulf the structure in flames. The men lay hidden behind the battlement-walls as the fiery creatures flew into the trap. Lieutenant Ionfield gave the order and another volley of arrows flew for the scaly-heads of the dragons. Even the tough resilient skin and bone of their skulls was not protection enough from the slender weapons which pierced their brains, ending their brutal lives. They fell silently from the sky into the sea below leaving their leader to the mercy of the humans.

The men let out a roar of triumph that was short-lived when they gazed upon the last beast hovering just out of range of the bows. All knew the dark stories concerning Gold-Dragons; they were considered the most cruel, evil and intelligent of their species, renowned for killing other dragons and even their own relatives when competition arose in the mating-season without a trace of remorse. Its breath might be white-hot, but its heart was as cold as the dark waters of the sea that lapped against the citadel-walls.

The beast continued to hover silently above the waters and out of their range, its black eyes staring fixedly at the murderers of its brethren. The Captain noticed his men were quickly becoming nervous, the bows shaking in their unsteady gloved-hands and wished the evil creature would do something soon, even kill them just to put the men out of their misery. His answer came as the dragon approached and suddenly began to blow a fine golden stream of fire not at the men but at the north battlement-wall several feet below them. The beast continued to blow, keeping up a steady pace until some of the men on the battlements noticed the wall beneath their feet was beginning to crack, then shatter under the weight and heat.

Panic reigned as the men realised the wall was about to collapse at any moment and they would be either devoured by the dragon as they fell or be smashed off the rocks below. The men began to run down into the courtyard though halted abruptly upon noticing the tower was beginning to shudder. The Gold-Dragon finally stopped blowing and flew instead at great speed towards the citadel. Its huge head hit the crumbling wall with a dreadful thud, making some of the men fall to their knees as the entire fortress shook with the impact. The tower began to sway as the north-wall collapsed from the blow of the dragon, leaving a giant gap in its wake.

The fire-reptile appeared above the gap, its head cut, blood streaming freely down its scaly gold skin, but it was otherwise unhurt. The beast let out a deafening roar as it peered in at its vulnerable victims. It hovered just outside the shattered wall in silence, as if the creature were contemplating what fate it should decree upon the helpless mortals before it. The dragon moved closer and suddenly stuck its huge head into the courtyard and with one quick motion, snatched up three soldiers and a priest into its open fang-lined mouth. The men let out screams of pain and fear that echoed all over the mountain before they disappeared down the beast's throat.

Some soldiers on the battlements had found their courage and picking up bows, fired point-blank at the reptile. But the beast shrugged off the arrows with little concern and continued with its ready-made meal, grabbing three fleeing priests and snapping them in two before devouring their broken bodies. The men resorted to their blades, but the swords simply bounced harmlessly off the creature's tough skin. The Captain moaned in despair and began to wonder if he would have any men left to defend the citadel against Hemlock. The madman would be able to enter the courtyard and reach the altar unmolested.

The Lieutenant drew up alongside his superior and gestured for him to move back towards the other side of the citadel, away from the dragon and the noise. "I have an idea," he whispered, drawing the Commander close. The Captain looked at him in puzzlement, and the Lieutenant smiled. "With his next meal, I'm going to give him something a little harder to swallow."

The Gold-Dragon continued its assault in earnest, snatching up screaming priests and swallowing them whole. It seemed the creature had not two stomachs, but a dozen, for its appetite had not slackened since the attack had begun though it had devoured more than ten priests and soldiers already. The Lieutenant had returned from below and approached the beast as it attempted to grab a fleeing soldier. The Captain watched his number-one anxiously, holding his breath, not knowing what the soldier intended. The dragon saw the man approach in confusion, his meals usually didn't come to their deaths this willingly. But it shrugged in apathy and reached its head forward, ready to snap the gaunt Knight in two.

Just as the fiery beast was about to snatch the soldier from the courtyard, the Lieutenant abruptly hefted a small open bag at the dragon. The creature swallowed it without a thought and moved on to the bigger meal before it. Suddenly to everyone's amazement, the beast stopped and began to first cough, then frantically claw at its throat with its fore-legs. It rose off the courtyard in panic, now tearing scales and strips of flesh off its head and neck. The dragon seemed to lose its balance as it left the citadel via the shattered north-wall and fell down the mountain. At the last moment it attempted to right itself, but it was too late. The creature fell onto the rocks and there was an audible snap as both its spine and neck broke. It slipped off the rocks and into the sea, as dozens of toads seeped out of its lifeless mouth and dived into the water.

The Captain and the Lieutenant joined the company of men at the shattered wall, watching the dead beast slide into the sea.

"Toads?" the Commander asked, perplexed. "I don't understand."

The Lieutenant smiled. "When a toad is swallowed, it inflates itself and sticks in its attacker's throat. I put several dozen into a loose bag which I knew were in the kitchen."

"That was a good trick!"

"I'm not just a pretty face," the Lieutenant laughed.

You're certainly not that, the Captain smiled to himself.

CHAPTER TEN

It was approaching midday as Hemlock and his three prisoners traversed over a small hill to see their destination; the citadel of the Temple of the Dragon barely a mile distant. However, they were interrupted in the final part of their journey.

From behind nearby rocks appeared approximately twenty men, if they could be called such. The strange bandits were bare-chested with various designs decorating their torso, arms and face and their ripped pants were hidden under a thick covering of mud above bare-feet. Each possessed a crude though effective bow which was aimed at the travellers' throats. Hemlock remembered what Kava had told him about the tribes that occupied much of this region, they would almost certainly be cannibals.

Two natives relaxed their bows and approached the travellers to relieve them of their weapons. Steel was a rarity among the tribes, a sword would give them an extra edge over other clans when conflict arose, which was frequent. The natives had an old habit of not eating their own and preferred the taste of other tribes.

However, they found relieving Hemlock of his blade quite difficult. As the savage prepared to strip his prisoner of his glowing sword, Hemlock suddenly struck the man in the face, a hollow crack sounding as the native's nose was shattered. He then drew the sword of power and deftly removed the screaming man's head from his shoulders. The other natives responded by firing at this mysterious attacker, but before their open-mouthed speechless faces, their arrows abruptly disappeared after seemingly been drawn in and absorbed by the shining blade. The strange sword appeared to have gained energy from the arrows as its glowing increased in brilliance, dazzling the astonished savages.

Hemlock let out a laugh at their mystified expressions and pointed the sword of Proteus in their direction. "Here, have them back," he roared as the arrows returned. The slender shafts shot out of the tip of the blade and struck their original owners, dropping the natives where they stood.

Four savages remained, but before Hemlock could dispose of them, they went to their knees and began calling him names in a language none of the travellers could decipher. However, it appeared to their amazement that they now considered Hemlock a god. Within moments several more primitives had arrived and set to worshipping the thief also. Before long the travellers were surrounded by natives, all having a similar appearance of dirt and ripped clothing. Five of the primitives suddenly lifted up Hemlock and carried him off into the wasteland, while the others followed close behind, pushing Flax, Storm and Suzerain in front of them.

The village of the tribe lay west of the valley deep in a wood, leading them away from the citadel. Hemlock cursed in frustration, he could do without this time-wasting. But these savages before me might come in useful, pondered the thief. The village composed of a gathering of mud-houses thatched with straw and sticks on a foundation of water-logged dirt. Naked children appeared from every direction and with their confused parents crowded around the intruders. The natives appeared not able to speak Common, but pointed at the travellers with a series of grunts and gestures. They gathered around Hemlock in awe, despite the fact that he had just killed almost twenty of their kinsmen. Make-shift thrones of straw and wood were hastily erected and the trespassers were carefully sat while others presented their god with various fruits and brown-tinged water. Several of the savages were amazed at Flax's moustache and couldn't understand why he didn't have a beard like the majority of their tribesmen.

However, one native did not come to worship. A bare-chested though clean robust man appeared from the largest of the huts, curious about the commotion. Around his neck hung various necklaces made of stone and bone which seemed to identify him as a sort of shaman; the tribal medicine-man, a man of some authority. Both Hemlock and Flax reached for their blades, fearing this scene might turn nasty.

"You," the man suddenly roared, pointing at Hemlock who was amazed the savage could speak Common when the others could not. The shaman turned to his subjects in anger, cursing their stupidity. "He has the sword of Proteus," he screamed. "He is evil."

A crowd of confused natives had already gathered around their shaman, fearing his anger more than whatever dark powers Hemlock had at his disposal. However, many still remained at the side of their new-found deity, unprepared to forsake their god and his reign. It appeared to the travellers that although the majority of the natives could not speak Common, they could somehow understand it. Flax let out a curse under his breath, it seemed they had just provoked a tribal civil war which could very well get them killed, and as usual it was Hemlock's fault.

The travellers and their traitor-natives fled from the clearing to the safety of the nearby wood to hide.

"What now, my Lord?" Storm laughed.

"Shut up," Hemlock snapped, hitting his prisoner across the face with the back of his fist, sending Storm flying to the leaf-covered ground.

After a brief speech of encouragement by the medicine-man, a crowd approximately one hundred and thirty men strong began to approach the travellers and the other savages. They were led by the shaman who wielded a lit torch.

"They mean to burn us out into the open and massacre us," Flax said, turning to Hemlock. "And it's all your fault."

Hemlock ignored him and turned instead to Suzerain. "You lived in Vandor Forest, you know the language of these people. Tell them to climb into the cover of the trees so we can ambush the other natives."

"Go to hell," Suzerain replied flatly.

"Do it," Hemlock retorted, grabbing Storm by the collar of his jerkin and placing the tip of his blade to the prisoner's throat. "Or else..."

Suzerain sneered at the thief in anger and disgust, but nodded. "All right, I'll do it."

"Don't," Storm said.

"Nobody asked for your opinion," the thief snapped, placing the magical blade further on his throat, forcing Storm's head back.

Suzerain approached the savages and through a series of grunts told them to climb the trees whereupon they were shortly followed by Flax, Storm and Hemlock. Flax had to help Storm up the tree for he was still bound with ropes. The shaman arrived at the start of the wood, but then hesitated. He looked back at the village and cursed, the fire would spread to the huts and they would have lost the only source of wood for miles around and so would be unable to replace their homes. He would have to flush out the trespassers and the traitors another way. He turned to his subjects and told them to ready their bows while he revealed a rusty sword.

Hemlock waited for the right moment and then gave the order. Suzerain related the command to the natives and they let fly a wooden rain of death on their fellow kinsmen. Within moments, forty savages lay dead. The shaman and the remainder of the tribe fled, though this process cost them another twenty men as arrows pierced the backs of the helpless natives.

Although the medicine-man's force now numbered less than seventy, he knew exactly where to strike. He let out a yell and his army fired into the trees. A broad smile lined his fat face when he heard the echoes of many screams from within the wood. Hemlock gasped at the accuracy of the primitive archers, years of hunting had trained their skill with the bow to perfection. Out of the original forty men force he had, thirty-three fell from the trees. Many had sustained only minor injuries from the arrows, but had lost their balance on the branches as a result and fallen the twenty feet to their deaths. The travellers had been fortunate, the thick branches and foliage surrounding them had protected them, though all around them the tree was marked by arrows with bright red feathers on their tails. The remaining nervous seven natives looked to Hemlock for guidance, but he could give them none. To leave the cover of the trees would be suicide, and yet they were pinned up in the tree at the mercy of the medicine-man and his force.

The shaman's army came charging into the wood, firing at the same time high into the trees. Once again they were successful. Their arrows struck home as the last seven natives fell from the branches. One arrow hit Suzerain in the right arm above the elbow and pinned him to the tree. He let out a scream which echoed throughout the entire wood, giving away their exact location to the shaman below. Hemlock heard the fat savage let out a roar of laughter and triumph, and decided it was time to use sorcery.

He muttered a few words and to the astonishment of the others, let fly a small fist-sized fireball from his out-stretched right hand which flew down the tree towards the advancing tribe. It seemed to swerve as it descended, avoiding the branches and hit a native close to the shaman. The savage let out a cry as he was blown five feet back across the ground, until he finally came to rest whereupon his kinsmen gathered around the smoking battered body in awe. They began to wonder if they should change sides.

Hemlock smiled in satisfaction, though realised he could not eradicate the entire tribe one by one by these means. The shaman ordered the tree to be felled and the thief knew if he was going to do something to save their lives, he would have to act fast. He looked down at the sword of Proteus and suddenly smiled. He could use the power of the sword, it was time to find out just what dark powerful forces the blade possessed.

He fired another fireball, but this time sent it down the flat of the blade and directed the tip at the army below which stood barely twenty feet from the base of the tree.

The result was devastating.

The explosion caused by the medallion Storm flung at the army of the Sword at the great Prison Tower was dwarfed in comparison to the firebrand which consumed the tribe below. Great shudders ripped through the tree as the travellers hugged the branches in terror. A wave of bright golden flame rose up and nearly roasted them, setting fire to most of the branches surrounding them. Below, most of the surrounding area was ablaze as they quickly descended the blazing tree, singeing their faces and hands. All that remained of the attacking tribe and their leader the shaman was a wide circular region of blackened earth and a few charred corpses which were no longer recognisable as human for they were all fused together into a large black heap. The smell of smoke and burnt flesh was overpowering and the travellers fled from the wood back into the valley, ignoring the blazing flora which burnt their clothes and legs.

Hemlock looked towards the distant mountain of the citadel and cursed his bad luck. The citadel would now know he was close after witnessing the explosion which could have been only his doing. But at least he now knew some of the sword's awesome power, perhaps he wouldn't have needed his brother's help after all.

Storm bandaged Suzerain's arm before the travellers moved off again, scanning the wasteland, wary for other tribes that might hinder their journey. Hemlock looked skywards, it would soon be dawn. But the weather worried him, first a heavy rain and then a mysterious flood, and there were signs there was worse to come. It had also become very cold, nearby puddles already freezing over as they passed. Perhaps the great flood Kava prophesied was really on its way, the weather certainly seemed to indicate that some great catastrophe could very well be coming. If that was true, then he was running out of time, taking the citadel quickly was imperative. At least its high altitude would protect them for a short while from the flood waters, down here in this valley they would drown within minutes. But it was not the flood that troubled him, a great Ice Age which could last for centuries was prophesied to come directly after the flood. Hemlock sneered, he never did really like the cold, and supplies in the citadel would not last long. He hoped the god Proteus had some means to make sure his servant avoided the ice and water, once he raised him using the sword and altar.

He was certain some good times lay ahead whatever occurred, though perhaps not for Flax and their prisoners, he thought and laughed; his voice echoing throughout the valley and beyond, sending chills through the citadel's occupants who gazed south-wards in puzzlement at the sound.

CHAPTER ELEVEN

The Captain awoke early, restless after a troubled sleep filled with dreams of Hemlock and ancient ceremonies carried out around the altar in the centre of the courtyard. Nightmares of an era when priests dressed in black danced around the table, singing their praises to Proteus and other long-forgotten demons while performing bloody acts beyond description upon an unfortunate man bound to the altar; a man whose screams had awoken the Commander in a bath of sweat.

He turned over and put his bare feet on the wooden floor, welcoming the cold, knowing the dream was over and he was in the safety of his room, his broadsword within easy reach. He reached over and snatched hold of the blade, hugging it to his chest as if it were a lover. The Captain of the citadel sighed, the only sound his ears heard in the silence of the chamber. Dawn was fast approaching, he could just make out the outline of the great wasteland that stretched south-wards as far as the eye could see from the small window directly in front of him. It appeared a fine day was promised, he hoped it would not be his last.

The large man rose to his feet and approached the window. A barren sea of cold rock and surrounding mountains greeted his vision. But it was always not so, once this land had the richest soil for miles, perfect for crops and grazing, and the citadel was a lighthouse for fishing-boats which made their way into the booming town that lay in the valley. This was even once the capital for the entire land before the war; the great war between the two emerging temples which destroyed the town and gave birth to the altar where black magick created by the dark priests of Proteus drained the land of its vitality to feed the ever-hungry demon in its endless quest to make humans extinct. The foul god almost succeeded, and now another madman comes to light the fires of battle again, with hopes that the reborn demon will bequeath to him a kingdom, though rather his body will be the first to be slaughtered before the beast extracts its vengeance for imprisonment with a passion.

He then noticed what appeared to be small forms in the valley making their way north towards the citadel. The Captain gasped in shock as the shapes became distinct, revealing four trespassers approaching with some haste. Almost tripping twice in panic, he grabbed the rope which hung from the ceiling on the far wall of his chamber. As he yanked the thick rope with all his might, he smiled in relief as the bell in the tower rang out. He cast a glance out the window and saw the four shapes halt as if in confusion before now taking to running towards the citadel.

The Captain quickly donned his armour as he heard great activity coming from the corridor beyond his door. He vaguely heard the Lieutenant shout battle-stations above the noise of feet and armour. They didn't need to ask their Commander the reason for the bell, all knew Hemlock, holder of the sword of Proteus was fast approaching.

By the time the travellers had reached the point where they were just out of range of the archers of the citadel, the priests and soldiers on the battlements were ready for them. It would be suicide to come any closer, the archers could pick them off at leisure. Hemlock threw his two prisoners to the rocky ground and the Commander could see that there really were only two men in the man's army.

"We need not have worried," Lieutenant Ionfield smiled. "What can two men do against a fort containing nearly two hundred men?"

"Don't underestimate the bastard," his superior replied sharply.

Flax turned to Hemlock in anger and frustration. "What now, oh great leader?"

"Shut it," Hemlock snapped, turning away from the last member of his gang of thieves and began running his hands through his brown hair in contemplation. Suddenly he turned to face Flax, a smile lining his rough face. "I have an idea," he laughed. "I'm going to give those soldiers a present from the past."

The three travellers watched in curiosity as Hemlock unsheathed the great sword and suddenly threw it several feet into the air. The heavy blade quickly returned, implanting itself about a foot into the wet earth. It stayed upright and began to glow with a red brilliance, as if sensing what was coming and knowing it was soon going to taste human blood again.

Hemlock stretched both hands into the air and started to shout at the top of his voice, the strange words clearly heard by all occupants of the citadel, the priests gasping with shock as they understood their meaning and realised what was about to happen. They began to mutter counter-spells, but to little avail, the sword of the demon was too strong and they had to admit defeat as they quickly became exhausted.

"Rise, rise, rise," Hemlock roared. "Selah Briah Proteus. Rise, you ancient human-hating creatures of the darkness. Come, and serve your master."

Flax gasped in shock and awe as the whites of Hemlock's eyes disappeared and his eyes turned completely black as night, yet he appeared able to see. The sword's power was changing him, both physically and mentally; shaping him to its will. Hemlock began to cackle like an old woman and Flax realised any taint of sanity his leader might have had was being extinguished, and he drew back from him in abject fear. Near him, Storm's mouth dropped open in shock and Suzerain fainted. Hemlock was now laughing aloud, the mad sound of a lunatic that made even Captain Falgar shiver in sudden nervousness.

Before the witnesses to this awesome spectacle could recover, a shudder ran through the earth that made the soldiers sway and some grabbed onto the battlements for support. All looked to where Hemlock stood in confusion, but quickly realised the reason for the mysterious arrival of this minor earthquake. Before their open-mouthed faces, small hands shortly followed by earth-caked heads began to break through the surface of the dirt. Within moments, an assortment of rotting creatures had risen all over the valley. A three hundred men army of long-dead beasts quickly gathered around Hemlock, grunting and groaning as they approached their creator.

The Commander of the citadel saw before him a mixture of orcs and goblins, most missing a limb or more, shambling or crawling towards their master. All however carried a weapon, an assortment of swords, knives or spears filled their maggot-ridden hands. Large numbers of the undead creatures bore grievous injuries which probably were the original cause of their demise, though all now seemed quite lively and enthusiastic to continue on blood-letting from the moment they had stopped years ago.

"By all the gods, they died decades ago," the Lieutenant stuttered. "They shouldn't be alive!"

"But they are," his superior moaned, echoing the feeling of despair that was rapidly running through the ranks of his soldiers who stared on in fear at the spectacle.

Hemlock called together his unholy army before him as Flax and his two prisoners drew back in disgust, wanting no part of this gruesome scene. The army of the dead stank of putrefying flesh and many crawled with maggots, eagerly feeding on the creatures, uncaring that their meals had mysteriously taken on some sort of life, though their bodies were still quite dead.

"Hear me, my servants and obey. Before you are the descendants of the men that drove you to your deaths," Hemlock boomed, laughing and pointing at the fortress. "Now you have a second chance for revenge. Kill them, kill them all."

The Commander and his number-one gazed on in disgust and nervousness.

"Life in The Frozen Wastes would have been better than this," the Lieutenant moaned. "I should have applied for a transfer to there."

"So should have I," his superior sighed in reply.

CHAPTER TWELVE

Hemlock gazed upon his make-shift army of rotting orcs and goblins and smiled in satisfaction while Flax and their prisoners cowered behind him in despair. The necromancer ordered a dozen of the orcs and several hobgoblins to traverse back to the wood and return with a felled oak tree which would be used as a battering-ram and long thick branches which would be chopped and converted into ladders.

By noon the undead creatures had returned as their creator explained the simple, yet effective battle-plan. A dozen orcs would attack the citadel double-doors while the rest of the army would either follow close behind or climb up the ladders placed against the wall and enter the battlements.

The orcs immediately set to work, constructing the ladders, using knives to attach the branches together. All this was overseen by Hemlock and the citadel's occupants with a somewhat nervous morbid fascination as the madman orchestrated their deaths. Storm stared on in awe, amazed the orcs could understand the thief, though most of their brains had long since been devoured by the eager servants of the Worm-God.

Once Hemlock was satisfied with the instruments of destruction, the army advanced on the citadel. Flax and the two prisoners stayed behind in the valley, his services were no longer required, and that frightened Flax more than the undead monsters the madman had awoken. The orcs at the front of the army carried the battering-ram, running up the mountainside towards the wooden double-doors, while their unholy companions screamed their battle-cry in encouragement as they followed close behind; an inhuman screech that shattered the calm thoughts of the soldiers.

Captain Falgar gave a sudden order and the mountainside became filled with arrows as the goblins began placing the ladders against the citadel wall and the orcs prepared to smash the doors. He feared that since the creatures were already dead, further injuries, even fatal ones under ordinary circumstances, would be next to useless. However, whatever dark powers Hemlock had used to reanimate the monsters, it was not enough to protect them from further attacks. Arrows struck rotting chests and heads, and the undead beasts fell, and did not rise again.

Hemlock roared in anger, believing the sword would had given these creatures not just a new lease of life, but an immortal and invulnerable one also. Still, he smiled, there were plenty left to carry out the task before he sent them back to the earth. He let out a string of curses as the ladders which at one moment were placed on the wall of the fortress were at another moment pushed back by soldiers and priests on the battlements, hampering the advancement of the blood-thirsty hobgoblins on the ground. However, eventually some goblins managed to keep the ladders against the wall long enough for some of them to climb onto the battlements whereupon the soldiers quickly felt the receiving end of their rusty shortswords and axes. Many of their companions followed close behind, using this diversion to safely climb the ladders.

"Use the oil!" the Captain shouted through the noise to several soldiers positioned above the doors.

A large cauldron of boiling-oil soon appeared on the battlements and was quickly poured over the wall and onto the orcs with the battering-ram far below. Goblins and orcs fled away from the cracked doors, screaming in pain and began to trip and stumble down the mountainside in their panic, several of whom were killed after smashing their rotting skulls on jutting rocks.

Hemlock let out a roar at the sight, realising the battle was being lost. He drew the great sword of power and proceeded to climb one of the ladders, his undead army screeching in joy, their failing morale restored. Flax did not attempt to stop him, if the madman got himself killed, so much the better, he smiled.

The necromancer raced up the ladder and was soon on the battlements. He ran along the narrow path towards the steps leading down to the courtyard and the altar, cutting down soldiers that rose to meet him with little concern, the magical blade slicing through swords and armour with little effort. He momentarily halted and glanced at the block of stone in the courtyard and let out a laugh of delight. He had finally made it after all this time, his prize stood waiting to be claimed. The altar seemed to glow with a red shimmering light as if sensing his approach and anticipated the reunion of the sword where its ancient master lay imprisoned.

Priests and soldiers ran past him, seemingly unaware of his presence as they were completely occupied with the advancing army of the dead, and Hemlock was able to enter the yard and approach the table unmolested. He drew alongside the altar which stood at waist-height and apprehensively placed his left hand on the cold stone, attempting to feel the power which ran through it. He lifted his hand just in time to avoid it being severed at the wrist, as a sword came flying down upon the table with a crash of metal.

It was Lieutenant Ionfield. He grinned at Hemlock, the scar on his cheek moving across his face like a snake. "So we meet at last, warlock." the soldier said, eager for a fight.

But Hemlock simply laughed in reply.

The two men moved away from the altar, giving themselves space to do battle. It was the gaunt Lieutenant who started the fray. He swung his slender blade towards Hemlock's left hip, but was quickly blocked with a clang of metal. Hemlock retaliated by striking at the soldier's head which was likewise blocked. For over ten minutes they exchanged blows without injury to either party until the Lieutenant suddenly managed to strike Hemlock across the left thigh, causing him to stumble and fall on his back. He grunted in pain and rose to his knees before the Lieutenant, and brought the sword of Proteus around and gripped the handle with both hands, intending to bring it down on the soldier's chest with all his strength behind the blade.

The blow was easy to defend. The gaunt Lieutenant prepared to block the attack by holding his sword in both hands in front of him, but the magical blade sliced the soldier's sword in two as if it were not there and struck him in the centre of the chest, cutting through his armour with a sickening crunch of metal and bone, killing him instantly. Lieutenant Ionfield died in silence, his mouth agape in astonishment. Hemlock did not hear Captain Falgar scream in rage at the sight of his deputy, lying in a growing pool of blood and bone. The Commander began to make his way through the crowd towards the warlock.

Hemlock was about to rise to his feet when the Captain of the citadel attacked, bringing his giant broadsword down on the kneeling murderer of his deputy. Hemlock moved out of the way just in time, but dropped the sword of Proteus. He reached over to retrieve it and the Commander swung his sword down to prevent Hemlock obtaining the dangerous weapon. Hemlock figured he was faster and grasped hold of the handle, but the Captain was the better swordsman. He had spent long years training as a Knight and fought in more battles than he could readily count. He struck Hemlock's hand, severing his smallest finger at the knuckle. The warlock let out a scream, but managed to retain his precious hold on the sword. He quickly rose to his feet only to be sent back to his knees by a sharp kick to the stomach.

For the second time in his short though brutal life, Hemlock feared he was finished; this giant soldier before him was faster in battle than he would have believed possible. He began to pray under his breath to the deaf god Proteus to save him as Captain Falgar raised his massive blade and prepared to behead his kneeling enemy, when he was interrupted by an orc who punched the Commander in the centre of the back. The Captain turned in rage and struck the weaponless orc in the face with his free left fist with all his strength, smashing the monster's jaw and snapping his neck, killing the beast. He pushed the dead creature away and returned his attention to Hemlock.

But the injured warlock had used the diversion to escape and stood against the battered north wall, nervously bandaging his bleeding mutilated hand. The Captain advanced towards the weary swordsman and Hemlock in a last futile act of desperation, threw the sword of power at the approaching soldier in despair. The Commander let out a short laugh and moved to avoid the flight of the blade. However, it also moved; changing its projected flight-path, once again travelling through the air in his direction. He gasped in shock and awe as each time he moved out of the way, it too changed its course in his direction, seemingly taking on a life of its own, all the time heading towards him.

He decided the death of Hemlock could wait, saving his own life was the first priority. He turned and took to running back towards the tower, its walls would protect him from this magical weapon. But the sword moved faster than his legs and struck him in the centre of the back, piercing armour and flesh, the tip exiting out his chest. He grunted in astonishment and reached out a hand. He did not realise his hand touched the altar as he fell to his knees, the sword protruding from his back like an ugly thorn. Captain Falgar felt no pain, just an odd tickling sensation that brought a brief smile to his face before his head hit the ground.

The soldiers and priests after witnessing the brutal fate of their two superiors lost heart and most fled from the citadel in fear, those that remained were rapidly massacred by the undead army of orcs and goblins that poured eagerly in through the shattered doors. When the monsters were satisfied none of their enemy remained, they stumbled out of the citadel and back towards the valley. Flax watched on in speechless amazement as did his two prisoners as the creatures returned to their unmarked graves, pushing themselves back into the ground; tunnelling into the earth like worms avoiding hungry birds. Within minutes, the army that had vanquished the citadel's occupants was no more, their task completed, they had seemingly lost all desire for life and returned to the unmoving rotting carcasses they originally were. The sword of Proteus had taken back its borrowed gift.

Hemlock watched them leave the courtyard in apparent apathy, he no longer needed their services. The altar of the God of Shape-Shifters stood motionless before him, patiently awaiting the warlock's words that would free its ancient creator from his prison. The lifeless Captain of the citadel lay at its feet, the instrument of destruction impaling him before the table's foundations; the one place in the entire land he would have most wanted not to have given up his life. Hemlock knew with a smile that his was but the first to be taken before this night ended.

CHAPTER THIRTEEN

Hemlock was still staring in morbid fascination at the blood-soaked bandage that covered his left hand, when Flax and their prisoners finally wandered up the steep mountainside and entered the body-littered courtyard via the shattered double-doors. The battle finally over, Flax safely pushed the two travellers towards the crumbling north-wall where their executioner awaited. Complete silence saturated the citadel bar the occasional screech from the large gathering of ravens that had amassed over the blood-streaked bodies.

Suzerain could not bear to look at them feasting, his heart beating fast, contemplating what terrible possible fate awaited him at the warlock's merciless hands. Storm's mind was also not on the dead soldiers that decorated the courtyard, his eyes were fixed unblinking at Hemlock, casting an occasional glance at the blade strapped to Flax's waist; the sword bestowed to him by the late Kassier. He began to regret never stopping to ask concerning the mysterious origin of the weapon and how the old man came to obtain the blade. Strange designs adorned the metal and hilt Storm knew were not engraved by human hands, and certainly not by Kassier. But those questions could wait, first priority was to recover the sword from the feeble-minded thief beside him, and finish Hemlock.

Flax's thoughts also focused on that same weapon and the semi-conscious warlock who lay heaped against the wall, oblivious to their presence. It would be so easy, Flax smiled, looking down at the dazed thief turned mage turned self-proclaimed

King. Then his gaze caught sight of the sword of Proteus at his side, glowing with a dazzling green light as if sensing the fear of the thief, and so Flax forced thoughts of murder from his mind. He would have to find another, perhaps safer method, to escape the devious clutches of Hemlock.

The warlock eventually managed to force himself to his trembling feet and the familiar wily grin began to line his pain-wracked face. He ambled towards the altar and with shaking hands placed the sword of power upon the smooth table. Both seemed to hum at the touch after so many centuries and impatiently awaited the words from the stolen scroll that would awaken and free their god.

"Stay away until I'm ready," Hemlock said to Flax as he began to prepare the altar.

Flax and their captives moved to a far corner of the courtyard and watched the preparations. Hemlock removed a small flask from his jerkin and to their disgust poured the blood of the late Kail whom the warlock had murdered for treason back in the great Vandor Forest. Then he revealed the manuscript he had plucked from the battered hands of the old mage from the capital and immediately started to shout to the heavens in a tongue unknown to his captive audience.

After some time Hemlock called to his one remaining fellow thief to bring Suzerain to him, while Storm stared fixedly at Flax in hatred. The warlock continued the incantation, roaring ancient words to the sky while Flax placed the bound prisoner on the table and Suzerain spat at him in reply. He returned to his other prisoner in silence while Hemlock prepared the boy as a sacrifice; the final catalyst for the violent awakening of the God of Shape-Shifters. Flax ran a trembling hand through his sweat-streaked black hair in nervousness and knew he could no longer stand back and watch his insane leader plan the destruction of the world. He could wait no longer, if he was to act at all, it would have to be now. But he would not be the instrument of the warlock's death, that would be another's task.

He knelt before his prisoner and to Storm's astonishment, released him of his bonds.

Storm stared at him in confusion as Flax undid his belt and handed back the sword. He feared it was a trick; a ploy to give him false hope only to take it away again just as quickly as it was given. But the thief was now unarmed and at his mercy. "What are you doing?"

"Hemlock's completely mad," Flax whispered. "He'll kill everybody, including me."

"So what?" Storm retorted. "Why don't you kill him?"

"I can't," the thief said. "Despite his madness, he's still my leader. Besides, I just don't have the courage."

"Why should I help you? Your gang killed my wife."

"Hemlock killed your wife, I didn't. On his shoulder is a scar where her crossbolt hit him, that's why he murdered her. It was all his doing, you've got to believe me, I was a new member to their gang. Surely you realise that when you see that I don't possess their lust for blood-letting."

From Storm came no reply. This cowardly thief before him was still part of the gang that killed Nereid and should by all rights die for his crimes. He stared at Flax in anger and disgust and rose to his feet. But the thief was right, he had suffered enough at Hemlock's hands, more punishment for his involvement in her murder than he could ever enforce, and so he decided to let him live. Besides, Storm sighed, he feared the prophesied flood was indeed on its way, and nobody would leave the citadel alive.

CHAPTER FOURTEEN

It was nearing nightfall when Hemlock felt he was ready to complete the incantation, one final task remained to be performed before the God of Shape-Shifters, who also had powers over time and space could be released; the sacrifice. He lifted the sword of power and raised it high as Suzerain looked up at the madman in speechless fear. However, before the warlock could bring the glowing blade down on his helpless captive, he suddenly felt a sharp pain in his right side that sent him to his knees. He rolled several feet from the altar fearing the descent of a sword upon his unprotected back, and looked up in surprise to see his would-be assassin Storm who had just delivered the punch and in further astonishment, Flax standing calmly behind him, making no effort to hinder this assault.

Hemlock rose to his knees and watched in speechless amazement as Storm released Suzerain from the sacrificial altar while Flax stared on, motionless. The warlock knew it did not take a genius to realise he had been betrayed at this crucial moment and his prize was slipping from his grasp, though he knew who was going to suffer most dearly for it.

Storm took the boy aside and laid his hands squarely on Suzerain's shoulders. "The time has finally come for me to claim my revenge," Storm said. "This battle is between me and Hemlock, you have to leave this place."

"Leave?" Suzerain stuttered, perplexed. "I don't understand. I want to stay here with you."

"You can't. Listen to me Suzerain, time is short," Storm said simply. "The flood is coming. If you want to live, you have to leave. Go back to the valley and find a high cave, it should protect you from the flood. When the water subsides, return quickly to the capital before the ice comes."

"What about you, aren't you coming after you've killed him?"

Storm sighed. "I don't believe either one of us will leave this courtyard, there's just not enough time before the flood arrives. Already the weather is changing drastically."

Suzerain glanced skywards before turning back to him. "So this is it? This is how it ends?"

"This is how it ends," Storm echoed and suddenly embraced the boy. "Go, now!"

Suzerain ran from the courtyard, but stopped momentarily at the shattered doors and glanced back at Storm one final time, before disappearing down the mountain. He watched the boy leave with a heavy heart before returning his full attention to the warlock.

Hemlock rose to his feet and stared at Storm in disgust. "That was touching," he said before turning to Flax. "So, traitor, it has come to this?"

Flax could not bear to look at him and decided it was time to leave also. This fight was now between Storm and the madman, it no longer concerned him. Hemlock however had other ideas. Flax ran for the other side of the yard, but was halted abruptly in his tracks by a fireball shot from the right hand of his leader which hit the thief squarely in the back. Flax's whole body burst into flames and he ran from the citadel and down the mountainside, screaming at the top of his voice before his screech was suddenly cut off as he tripped and smashed his head in off a nearby rock. Storm watched all this with little remorse, though the cowardly thief had released him, he still had been part of Hemlock's old gang of bandits and had forfeited his life when he joined the group. Storm promised a worse fate for the warlock, Hemlock he vowed, would die screaming on his knees in unspeakable agony. This, above all other things, he would most surely do with the greatest of pleasure, before he finally joined Nereid in whatever world lay beyond this hell.

It unnerved the warlock to see a smile line Storm's face as he confronted him, despite his massive powers and the superior blade the thief possessed. Storm drew his sword and advanced on the madman. However, Hemlock's gaze turned suddenly away from Storm in apparent apathy to his dangerous predicament and looked instead towards the sea. The waters had become violent and frequently crashed off the crumbling north-wall, sending a wave of froth high up into the air and even into the courtyard itself. Neither of the two men had ever seen the ocean so rough and began to fear the worst. They momentarily halted their argument to wander towards the wall and gazed across the sea and the wasteland surrounding the citadel to the south.

Both men gasped at the sight before them. Sea level had risen several metres in as many minutes, the valley-floor was already submerged under frothy waters, smashing against the steep mountains on both sides as the sea made its way further inland. Within the hour, the citadel would disappear under a maelstrom of salt-water. It appeared the great flood had indeed come to wash away their lives after all and leave the land reborn.

The two-hundred year Ice Age was sure to follow soon after the water subsided. Storm sighed in despair, he had been right, neither of them would leave the citadel alive. But, he promised, of all the terrible fates he would decide for the warlock, simple drowning was not one of them. The thief would die by Kassier's blade as it was always meant to be.

Hemlock glared at the swordsman who stood barely ten feet from him. The boy was gone, probably drowned, this assassin would have to be the sacrifice. If not, then he would die in agony for destroying his plans. Either way he would be joining his wife sooner than he expected.

The warlock suddenly struck out at Storm, all of his strength behind the attack. Storm brought Kassier's sword up and blocked the blow, resulting in an almighty crash of metal. Hemlock was amazed. The sword of Proteus should have cleaved the blade in two and finished this fight quickly. The sword Storm held appeared to be unmarked by the terrific blow. No matter, Hemlock smiled, this battle is completely one-sided and no contest.

Storm retaliated by striking at his opponent's knees and then at his head. Hemlock easily defended off both blows, but the blade struck his shoulder, ripping open his jerkin. Storm snarled in rage as a dark scar was revealed which could have only been inflicted by a crossbolt shot at close range. He struck out at the thief in blind fury, his anger increasing his courage in swordplay. Such an attack would have killed a lesser able-bodied swordsman, but Hemlock was a mercenary and thief by trade, his skill honed to near perfection by years of swordplay. Storm hadn't received enough practice or training to effectively fight such an opponent.

Hemlock struck Storm's sword-hand and with a cry of pain, sent the blade flying across the yard of the citadel, well out of his reach. Recovering the weapon would be impossible, staying alive was the next priority. He started to avoid Hemlock's blows, ducking and moving out of the way, yet Storm knew he could only keep this up for so long, the warlock was sure to hit him a fatal blow at any moment. Hemlock forced him back towards the altar, meaning to have his precious sacrifice.

Hemlock began to swing the sword in all directions and forced Storm onto the edge of the table. However, the warlock left himself open and Storm suddenly punched him squarely in the face, breaking his nose with an audible crack. Blood flowed freely down the thief's face and into his mouth, driving him insane. He struck out in blind rage, his anger robbing him of his skill in swordplay. However, he was now an even deadlier foe. In his efforts to dodge the blows, Storm slipped and hit the back of his head off the edge of the table and was momentarily dazed.

In his fury, Hemlock had forgotten about the sacrifice. He just wanted Storm dead. He brought the sword of Proteus up and swung down towards his helpless enemy, all of his strength behind the blow. Storm managed to roll out of the way in time and Hemlock watched him move. But the momentum behind the sword was too great for the blade to change in direction in order for him to strike Storm down. Instead the magical weapon struck hard stone, sending a shudder up Hemlock's arms. He realised he had struck the edge of the altar, yet thought nothing of it.

Then he looked down, and his jaw dropped open in a mixture of shock, fear and confusion at what he had done. The great altar which had withstood the onslaught of time and erosion, now cracked and fell in on itself, crumbling into dust. He let out a long loud moan when he gazed down at the sword of Proteus. The tip of the blade, the top three inches had been broken off and was missing, and was nowhere to be seen. The sword was already ceasing to glow so brightly and was growing cold.

Hemlock abruptly turned for he thought he heard a high-pitched inhuman scream echo briefly around the mountain and knew what it meant. The demon Proteus; God of Shape-Shifters, time and space was dead. Its altar and prison destroyed, it too died with them as if they had supported the demon and gave the god life. Hemlock's dream of a kingdom built on foundations of human bodies had died with the destruction of the sword.

The blade's powers were fading fast. But Hemlock was wrong, his god was not yet dead, and had one last spell for its faithful servant. It would not leave the warlock to the mercy of the approaching sea, which even now lapped at the shattered double-doors of the citadel. There was a blinding flash, a scream, and Hemlock disappeared.

Storm slowly rose to his feet and searched the courtyard in panic before fully realising the warlock was gone, he had somehow escaped the flood and his wrath. He retrieved his sword and prepared to leave when he suddenly saw water flowing into the yard, lapping at the bodies of the soldiers. Bar a few mountain-tops, land was nowhere to be seen. He was stranded. He sat down at the shattered altar in despair when he noticed something small, glowing near him.

It was the missing tip of the sword of power. Storm smiled, there might still be a chance to get his revenge. He just hoped the dying god did not realise it was helping the enemy of its servant, yet Storm had no choice but to try. No available other paths lay open to him. Storm glanced once more at the incoming sea before grasping hold of the sharp metal and grimaced as it cut into his hand.

There was a second blinding flash, Storm screamed with the sudden pain and fell unconscious to the ground.

Outside what remained of the citadel, the water continued to rise and already it was becoming cold, heralding the arrival of the two-hundred-year Ice Age. Inside the crumbling fortress, Storm lay in a motionless heap, though before the water reached him, he was gone.

PART TWO

CHAPTER FIFTEEN

Palcial shuffled his way through the flora of the forest which scratched and pulled at his frail ankles. He let out a sigh of exertion and frequently stopped momentarily to catch his wheezing breath, clutching at his chest, fearing his weak heart would burst. Palcial cursed, he was too old to be wandering this forest for food. "Should have moved to the capital long ago," he pondered. "But it's too late now. My old bones won't carry me that far, this is my home now and this is where I will die, no matter how soon it comes."

Palcial liked to consider himself a hermit, living out his remaining life in a small cottage deep within the forest, though many was the time he had led lost travellers less knowledgeable than he of the forest's paths back to the neighbouring capital city. Yet those incidents were many years past, he had not seen another human soul for a long time, and he did not miss their company. He had longed for solitude ever since he left the mountain which had been his home since birth. Palcial had seen enough bloodshed and barbarism encouraged there to last him a lifetime.

Wood for the fire seemed scarce today and the old man was forced to venture deeper into the forest. The nights were still too cold though the ice had left, for him to forsake his search. He entered a familiar small clearing of dense grass and flowers and walked more briskly now, making for the other side and the trees. He suddenly halted upon noticing something odd. The grass began to turn black and die before him as if they were on fire. Palcial glanced around in panic, fearing a forest fire that would spread through the clearing within moments and finish him before he had even time to draw breath. But no smoke or flames could he see, yet the grass and flowers continued to wilt, as if some strange dark force was draining the clearing of its vitality.

The old hermit continued to stare in puzzlement and amazement when a sudden dazzling flash of white light and strong wind blew him off his feet and he fell to the ground with a thud, the air forced from his lungs. He fortunately slumped onto a cushion of dead grass and rose to his knees in fear. Palcial peered over the few standing blackened clumps of grass in curiosity and in shock, saw the still form of what appeared to be a man in his early thirties. Nobody, not even an elf could have moved that fast and entered the clearing without him seeing, the hermit mused, it could only have been an act of magick. The strange bright light added further weight to that conclusion.

The trespasser's clothes were torn and ripped and he appeared to be bereft of any weapons bar a sword strapped to his left hip. Palcial cautiously approached the stranger and noticed a small object fall out of his hand. The old man bent down and examined the item, though unwilling to touch it. It appeared to be a three-inch rusty piece of metal, a type of ore he was quite unfamiliar with, despite the great knowledge of metallurgy he had gained deep within the bowels of Sulphur Mountain. Intrigued, he stroked the object and watched in fascination as it disintegrated into fine dust at his touch. He apprehensively opened the stranger's hand and saw a deep, bloody-scar in the centre of his palm.

Palcial might have been old, but he was not weak; years of hardship in the mountain and in this forest gave him strength beyond what would have been expected at his age, though at the expense of his heart. He lifted the unconscious man over his right shoulder and halting momentarily to catch his breath, slowly carried the stranger out of the clearing.

The hermit's solitary log-cabin lay in the centre of a meadow deep within the forest. A brook ran near the hut and seemed to be the only source of noise in the otherwise silent clearing. He pushed the wooden door in to reveal sparse possessions. A single torn blanket covered a rough wooden bed adjacent to the left wall accompanying a bare waist-high table and a stool; the apparently only visible furniture in the one-roomed cabin. A lone wolf in the far right corner of the hut instantly rose to attention at their entrance, though relaxed upon recognising its ageing master.

Palcial carefully placed the unconscious man on the bed and reaching under the table revealed a flask of red wine. The old man slapped his patient once on each cheek, yet got no reply. He then put the tip of the opened bottle to the stranger's lips and gently poured, watching the liquid flow over the still man's face. The cracked lips did not move at once, but after some time opened and gradually accepted the wine. The man let out a series of groans, though did not try to open his eyes; they were for the moment too sore to venture restoring the power of sight to their frail owner.

The hermit's patient began to mumble, before shouting as if he were in the grip of a fever or trance. "The water, the water. You'll not escape me, warlock. Suzerain." Then he became silent once more and did not speak again for several days.

He awoke in a sweat, eyes wide open, feeling as if he were on fire. He rose from the bed and stumbled out of the cabin in a daze. However, he stopped short when a wolf greeted him at the door and growled up at him. It was this that attracted the old man's attention from chopping wood at the side of the stream and he turned with a smile to greet his patient.

"Kassier?" Storm stuttered, rubbing his eyes in fatigue. But then sighed, it was not the old teacher he once knew.

He moved towards the hermit and fell into the old man's arms. Palcial returned him to bed and gave him more wine. Storm drank the liquid gratefully as he gradually regained his senses, though at the expense of a splitting headache. "What is this place?"

"You're in Pelerius forest."

"Pelerius forest?" Storm screamed in confusion.

"Yes," Palcial said. "Where did you think you were?"

"At the citadel of the temple, of course."

"What citadel?" the old man replied. Palcial reached under the bed and revealed a map of the land and laid it over the blanket.

Storm glanced at it and turned to the old man in shock and confusion. "The capital city is Winterlending! What is 'Winterlending'?"

"He is the King."

"King?" Storm stuttered. "There is no King. The Knights Order rules the land."

"Knights Order?" the old man inquired, puzzled. "The military have not ruled this land in almost two hundred and sixty years. It appears you're suffering from a loss of memory."

"The hell I am," the patient retorted. "What about the two temples?"

"Temples? I don't know what you mean."

Storm sat up, his face red with rage. "This is ridiculous, what do you take me for? I suppose you'll tell me you've never heard of Hemlock?"

Palcial smiled, but there was a taint of anger and disgust in his tone at the mention of the name. "That's a name I haven't heard in many years," he said. "That evil man was the root of all our problems, yet thankfully he died nearly three centuries ago."

The patient smirked. "Ever heard of another man, by the name of Storm?"

The old man frowned. "I vaguely remember that name. He was involved in the battle at the old Prison Tower and is reputed to have been the one who killed Hemlock."

"Do you have a picture of this man?" Storm asked, almost laughing.

"Yes," he replied, perplexed. "I think I have a book somewhere from the library of the capital around here," he smiled. "Always meant to put it back, but I confess I took a liking to it."

The old man revealed a large black volume, its cover and binding ripped and worn. He flicked through it and eventually paused at one page. It was a picture of Hemlock, wielding the sword of Proteus. Though the sketch was crude, it was accurate. Storm glared at the picture in hatred, yet said nothing. He was not about to give away the surprise. Palcial flicked through the book again and finally found the page he wanted. He placed the tome upon the bed facing his patient and frowned in confusion. Then he glanced up at Storm and his mouth dropped open in shock and disbelief. He couldn't believe his eyes. "It's not possible," Palcial screamed, rising to his feet, fearful of this apparition. "You're somebody dressed up, playing a cruel joke on old Palcial."

"I'm real," Storm said flatly. "Now, tell me, how did I get here?"

"I found you in the forest. There was a bright light and-"

"Did you say a flash of light?" Storm interjected.

"Yes, why?"

But the hermit's patient did not reply for several moments before suddenly looking up at the old man who now cringed in nervousness, fearing his death would come by a means more painful and even less dignifying than old age. "Do you know your history?"

"I spent more years in Sulphur Mountain reading what books we managed to rescue from the flood to cure the chronic boredom than I care to remember."

"Good," Storm replied. "Sit, and tell me everything you know of the last three centuries."

The hermit hesitated before eventually sitting down on the edge of the bed and related his ancestors' history to a two hundred and sixty year old living, breathing corpse. He removed from a jerkin pocket an old wooden pipe and settled down for a long chat. "The flood waters subsided after three days but left a wasteland in its wake. The majority of our population survived by hiding out in the mountains or filling every available boat to capacity. The land was devastated, our agriculture and towns destroyed. However, the worst was still to come; the great Ice Age swiftly arrived and we were forced to flee the towns to find sanctuary and warmth in Sulphur Mountain."

"We were led by a man called Phyfifus who five years later was crowned the first King of this land. He led the Knights into battle against the dark-elves in the mountain and massacred them. However, it is believed some survived by making themselves look human and mingling with the murderers of their families. We used their immense food reserves to sustain ourselves through the two-hundred year Ice Age, though our population decreased greatly due to pestilence and malnutrition in the later years as the reserves ran out. Another two or three years and we would have starved had the ice not left our land."

"Ten years after the flood the two temples, what remained of them, were disbanded by the King before he died some forty years later. A new King by the name of Abacus was crowned until he was executed after a short battle led by the sons of the old Winterlending brothers. The eldest, a despicable young man, was crowned King and a man of the same name and equally evil nature still rules this land, though it is rumoured his idealistic young daughter may be planning to overthrow him."

"After the Ice Age ended we had to face the enormous task of rebuilding our land and towns, and here we are, sixty years later," Palcial paused for breath. "Don't tell me Hemlock has returned like you?"

"I'm afraid it's quite possible," Storm said. "If I appeared, then so will he. But my rage and hatred hasn't calmed down, even after almost three centuries," Storm looked up at the old man. "Tell me, in Sulphur Mountain, did you hear of someone called Suzerain?"

Palcial paused and frowned. "Yes, I believe there was a Lieutenant Knight by that name who fought under King Phyfifus."

Storm smiled in satisfaction. So, he survived the flood, he pondered, at least that is good news.

"Although it sounds like bad advice," Palcial suddenly said. "You should go to the King and warn him of Hemlock."

"I thought you said he was a ruthless tyrant?"

"He is," Palcial retorted sharply. "But he's still in charge of this land and evil as he is, the blackness of his crimes will not match Hemlock's if he tries to seize power."

"All right, I'll go see him."

"You must leave no later than tomorrow," Palcial said flatly. "Time is of the essence."

Storm smiled at the hermit. "You're as bossy as another old man I once knew."

CHAPTER SIXTEEN

"Bring me more drink slave, and be quick about it," the big man roared to one of the many nervous young men gathered at his feet in abject fear.

The obese King; seventh ruling monarch of the entire land was in that fragile state between drunk and unconscious and enjoying the process immensely, when a guard entered the great throne room and momentarily broke the drunken silence.

"Sire, I apologise for the interruption," the soldier said timidly, fearing the large man's uncontrollable temper. "But a serf is here to make a complaint."

"I'm in no mood for a peasant's moaning," his superior snapped.

"He says it's important," the guard interjected, moving back a step. "He talks of witchcraft."

The monarch sighed. "It's probably our court-mage Sacrais up to his old tricks, making fun of the peasants. Tell him to go away and leave me alone, or I'll have his skull on a spike."

"Very well, my Lord," the soldier replied, bowing.

The guard was about to leave the giant chamber when the tyrant called him back. "Wait," he shouted. "Let's see what it's all about, let the fool in. If it is Sacrais up to his tricks again, I'll have his head, and it'll take more than mere spells to keep me back."

The officer left as the frightened slave appeared with the giant flask of wine which was instantly snatched from his hand. The Chief of

Guards quickly returned with the peasant who was visibly shaking with nervousness as they approached the King. The serf came forward and knelt before his master in forced servitude, still trembling and rapidly regretting his hasty decision in coming here. Nevertheless, it was too late now and he decided he had better make the best of it.

"Well sire, it happened on this fine summer day in the middle of-"

"Cut it short you fool," the King roared. "Or I'll cut you short."

"Sire, I...I-" the quaking farmer stuttered, almost out of his mind with terror.

While the serf desperately attempted to explain his predicament, the fat ruler began to tap his fingers upon the arm-rests of the huge throne in silent anger and growing frustration, contemplating the headman's axe.

"I...Ah, it happened when I was walking through my fields when I did see a flash of light and...an explosion that near did blow me off me feet," the serf said quickly, recovering his speech. "Then before my eyes, a man appeared. He was tall and had brown hair, but did not have a weapon. Yet when I did go up to him, I saw his eyes were as black as night. I thought he was blind, but he could see as he knocked me down and stole my wood-axe before running off."

"Give the officer a description of the man," the King replied, sighing in boredom and frustration.

The serf and the Chief of Guards conversed closely for several minutes as the soldier drew a rough sketch.

Suddenly the peasant nodded to the guard. "Yeah, that's him."

The soldier frowned at the picture. He knew he had seen the man before, though could not put a name to the face. He handed the piece of skin to his monarch who recognised the man immediately and growled in anger. "Take this joker to the headman and tell him he's got a customer."

The Chief of Guards frowned in confusion, though nevertheless dragged the screaming peasant from the chamber and headed for the dungeons. It was not wise to question the fat ruler, former officers that had protested had met a horrible fate deep within the bowels of the palace.

King Winterlending the fifth leaned over and threw the picture into the blazing fire adjacent his throne. Yet before the sketch had become completely consumed by the hungry flames, the monarch could still make out the unmistakable face of Hemlock.

CHAPTER SEVENTEEN

After receiving a copy of the map of the land from the hermit, Storm took his leave. Before he left the meadow, he cast one final glance back at the old cottage. It was unlikely he would return to this place, and even if he did, the period of his absence would likely see the old man in the grave. He opened the map. It would take him two days walk to reach Ledge. In that small town, he could purchase a horse to make travel less laborious to reach the capital city. He wondered if the King would release to him any information concerning Hemlock's location, though Storm feared if he was the man Palcial said he was, he would not give it freely, if at all.

The old hermit had relinquished to Storm a crossbow. He had refused the large weapon at first for it reminded him of Nereid's fate, yet realised he would probably need it, and gratefully took it. Palcial also gave him a small backpack containing some spare clothes, food and space for nine steel-tipped crossbolts.

It was just after midday on the second day of his journey that Storm finally sighted the town of Ledge; the nearest civilised settlement to the capital. After buying a horse, Storm headed for a nearby tavern. He placed the steed in adjacent stables and entered the inn. He approached the barkeeper and ordered an ale. A small balding man next to Storm looked up in momentary puzzlement, swearing that he recognised the swordsman from somewhere, but quickly dismissed the foolish thought and returned to his drink.

Storm lifted the mug to his mouth and drained almost half its contents in a single gulp, such was his thirst from the journey. He glanced around the room and gasped in surprise upon noticing a hooded man staring fixedly at him from across the bar. Storm looked behind to see if he was mistaken, but realised there was no error, the mysterious figure was indeed gazing directly at him. The hooded stranger rose from his seat and approached him. Storm noticed the tall man wore a light chainmail coat under the dark cloak and a shortsword at his left side. However, it was what the stranger held in his right hand that caught Storm's attention. He carried the most magnificent spear Storm had ever seen. Two metres in length, the handle made of varnished hazel and engraved in strange designs with a ten-inch blade at the top that Storm suspected was magical. The symbols on the wood puzzled Storm, knowing he had seen them somewhere before, yet could not place their origin exactly.

He sat on a stool facing Storm and removed the hood. Storm noticed he was handsome, possessing jet-black hair and striking green-eyes. There was something uncanny about the man's eyes. Storm knew this was no ordinary warrior. Here was a man who might hunt Gold-Dragons for a living, or something even worse. His skill with the spear could not be doubted from one glance at the man, he gave the impression he was anything but incompetent with the huge weapon.

"I see you are a stranger, like me," he said softly in a tone of voice one might expect from a mage or musician. "Are you on your way to the capital?"

Storm remembered what Palcial had told him about why everyone called Winterlending the 'capital' and not by its real name, because of the great hatred for the King and his crushing taxes. Storm glanced at the spear again and with a gasp recognised the symbols and now knew why this man was striking up a conversation with him. The same designs were engraved on his blade; the same mysterious sword Kassier had given him. The weapons were a pair, Storm realised. He began to suspect this stranger wished him ill and wanted to steal his sword, yet decided to give the hooded-man the benefit of the doubt and trust him. Besides, Storm mused, he was probably deadly with the weapon and a sword or crossbow were no match for a spear in a capable man's hands.

The silence bothered the stranger and he suddenly thought he was talking to a mute, but Storm did finally speak. "Yes, I am."

"Like some company?"

"Sure," Storm replied, intrigued as to the man's identity and the circumstances as to how he came across the spear. But the mystery of the weapon could wait.

"I'm Cairn. They call me Cairn of the Spear," he said. "The reason as you see is obvious."

"Yes, it is," Storm smiled. "I'm Storm."

If Cairn recognised the name, he did not let it show. "When do you plan to leave?"

"As soon as I finish my drink," Storm replied with a smile which made Cairn burst into laughter.

CHAPTER EIGHTEEN

He had been walking without cessation for over two days and was convinced his legs were finally about to fail him in exhaustion. A lone traveller he had encountered earlier that same day with some gentle persuasion had imparted strange information concerning his unfamiliar location and the date. The terrified man also generously donated a comprehensive map of the land before Hemlock let the traveller flee into the countryside. The town Nez seemed the nearest spot of civilisation in which he could get his bearings and consider his next move.

Though he was alone and bar a blunt wood-axe virtually weaponless, Hemlock was not worried. The 'long-sleep' had seemingly not only restored his personal powers, but also increased their potential for destruction to a frightening degree. Yet he would require much more strength now the sword of Proteus was gone if he were to survive in this hostile land and destroy his new political opponents. The map indicated he should travel to the distant volcanic Aren Island. The tiny isle was completely devoid of all life and uninhabited, except for one particular person; the one man who could survive the treacherous conditions on the island and with whose stolen magical abilities he could still rise to power and unseat the King.

Hemlock thought back to the incident at the now destroyed citadel, as if it all happened just yesterday. Damn that Storm, he cursed, the man caused me many problems, but at least I know he drowned. No way could he have escaped the flood-waters. He remembered gripping the shattered sword of power one moment, and then suddenly felt a great surge of energy rip through his body. There was a blinding flash followed by a feeling of excruciating pain, and Hemlock believed he was dying.

However, next moment he found himself in a neck-high field of corn with a strange man running towards him, roaring various curses concerning Hemlock's dubious parentage while waving about a large wood-axe. Disconcerted, he snatched the weapon from the astonished peasant and wandered out of the field and into open moor. Unknown to Hemlock, he was fortunate, for unlike Storm, Hemlock felt stronger after his transition and able to travel almost immediately. As he began to walk, he noticed small lizards began to flock and gather at his feet, though did not attack. As he kicked the infuriating creatures from his path, he wondered if this had something to do with Proteus killing the father of dragons and pondered on how he might be received by their larger cousins. However, that question could wait. He presently needed his full attention on reaching Aren Island and the man there who likely foresees his impending arrival.

The warlock sighted the town of Nez shortly before nightfall and was surprised to find its entrance unguarded. Excited children ran past him while their apathetic parents stood nearby, eagerly drinking themselves into a stupor. It appeared some festival was underway. Hemlock cursed, it was sure to make obtaining sea-transport that much harder.

"What's going on?" Hemlock asked a nearby merry-maker who was waving about an overflowing mug of ale, the majority of which was all over his once-white jerkin.

The man stopped momentarily to gaze at Hemlock in confusion, blaming the drink for thinking this stranger before him had no whites in his eyes. "What do you mean?" he laughed. "Have you been asleep for the last fifty years?"

Hemlock suddenly grabbed the drunk by the collars of his drenched jerkin and shoved him up against the wall. "Listen my friend," he growled. "If you don't tell me, I'll shove that mug so far down your throat you'll think you were born with it there."

The drunk ceased his laughing and stared fixedly at Hemlock in terror. "It's The Game," he said timidly.

"What Game?"

"The grand combat which is held annually on Cracas Island, men and women fight each other to the death and the sole winner gets a large sum of money. The King oversees it and awards the prize."

Hemlock glared at the nervous drunk before finally letting him go. The man continued to stare at his mysterious oppressor for several moments before he was dragged off by the crowd. Hemlock resumed his journey through the noise-filled streets, the drunken gathering ignorant of the madman in their midst and his intense hatred for them. However, he had forgotten about his eyes until he caught his reflection in a puddle and shielding them with his hands, ran through the town towards the waterfront. He began to wonder if people would consider him even more of an outcast now because of his eyes before he cursed his own stupidity and sudden fear. He was really not ashamed of his solitude and great powers. These idiotic morons, he vowed, would all bow before him in time, or die like their ancestors for defying him.

Hemlock eventually reached the harbour and noticed only one trawler stood in the calm waters with its lanterns alight. He instantly ran on board and began searching for the ferryman.

The Captain of the boat was celebrating The Game in his own way. He had little time in which to get satisfactorily intoxicated before he would have to ferry tourists to Cracas, business being brisk during that time and content in the knowledge that he could charge extravagant prices to the blood-thirsty cowards. He was in the process of draining his eighth mug when he heard sounds above him. "Those stupid kids again," he cursed. "I'll break their legs!" He rushed up the small flight of stairs, stick in hand. However, he was confronted not by excited children, but by a tall man in torn clothes, holding his hands to his face.

"Who the devil are you?" the Captain roared in anger at the intruder before him.

"I want to go to Aren," the stranger retorted.

"You must be out of your mind," the ferryman snapped. "The Game begins in two days and I want to get some rest before then. Get off my boat before I throw you to the sharks."

"I won't tell you again," Hemlock said.

"You what-?" the Captain laughed. "Nobody, not even that fat fool the King gives me orders."

The ferryman however abruptly halted his laugher when Hemlock removed his hands to reveal his unnatural eyes. He began to wonder if he had drank too much, but those dark eyes seemed real. This was no ordinary peasant before him, he knew with dire certainty that the man had to be a mage. "Are you the sorcerer Agouti?" he stuttered, trembling in sudden terror.

Hemlock hesitated before answering, recognising the name of the Arch-Mage from the map, but then smiled. "Yes, I am," he said proudly, knowing he would shortly assume the rank and status of the man.

The Captain nodded in terror and respect to Hemlock, knowing he was gazing upon the most powerful and feared wizard in the land, a sorcerer never before seen by human eyes. He let up the sails and casted off the moorings before heading out towards open sea.

Hemlock stared up at the starless night sky and smiled in satisfaction. In two days he would be on Aren Island and with the knowledge stored in the Arch-Mage Agouti's library, in a matter of weeks he could rise to become King. Almost three centuries ago my plans failed, Hemlock pondered, this time I will not fail.

CHAPTER NINETEEN

The travellers arrived at the capital city-gates shortly after noon, a day before The Game was scheduled to commence. They approached the giant double-doors of the palace one hour later after Cairn had led his less street-wise companion through the densely crowded alleys.

"Well," Storm said as he dismounted and prepared to place his steed in the nearby stables, "this is where we must part."

"Why?" Cairn replied.

"Because I'm going in to have an audience with the King," Storm retorted. "I have an important message to give him."

"But I'm going in also. I am participating in The Game."

Storm stared fixedly at his friend. He remembered what Palcial had told him about the grand combat held every year on Cracas Island, a barbaric ritual which involved killing your fellow man or woman in the name of greed. He thought the warrior with the spear before him was destined for greater things, it appeared he had misjudged him. He was no different than Hemlock.

"But Cracas lies several days journey away," Storm said, perplexed. "The Game begins tomorrow!"

"True. However, the King has several giant eagles behind the palace which can ferry special contestants," Cairn replied. "They can cross great stretches of land and water in a matter of hours."

Storm stared at him in confusion. "Special contestants?"

Cairn smiled. "I am the King's champion. If I win, he does not need to pay out the large sum to anyone, and I only get paid a much smaller fee."

Storm sneered. It seemed his majesty's greed knew no bounds, he was rapidly regretting his decision to warn him of Hemlock, he should leave the tyrant to his fate. However, perhaps he had been right all along about Cairn, maybe he was being forced to participate in The Game, and he was really after all a good-natured man. Yet only time would tell when the warrior told his tale. "All right, let's go in," Storm said, glad this powerful fighter might indeed be on his side.

As they approached the doors Storm noticed the dozen or so heavily-armed guards which surrounded the entrance. He began to wonder how they would get in if they were refused entry. But he gasped in surprise as the sentries instantly stood to attention upon recognising Cairn.

"Tell his majesty his servant, Captain of the Guard at Tomilusk is here and requests an audience."

Storm watched on in speechless astonishment and confusion as the sentry bowed before disappearing behind the doors. It seemed Cairn had indeed quite a tale to tell, being in charge of an army reaffirmed his belief that the man was no ordinary warrior.

The guard returned some time later and escorted the two men in. As they walked down endless grand corridors Storm was taken aback by the sheer luxury and extravagance of the building. The Temple of the Dragon in Karlaband could not match such rich beauty, the halls decorated with all manner of tapestries, pictures and other ornaments including suits of armour shined to gleaming. A fortune in gold had been lavished on the palace; money Storm knew from Palcial had been ruthlessly and mercilessly stripped from starving peasants with the King's high taxes. Palcial had said revolution was in the air, Storm could not doubt it when he gazed upon such greed.

Eventually they entered a giant chamber which appeared to be the throne-room, devoid of any kind of furniture bar a great royal-sofa whereupon an obese man sat, lazing on this huge velvet covered chair, heavily decorated in gold and engraved above his head the seal of the family of Winterlending. The chamber displayed similar tapestries and wall to wall paintings, and Storm's eyes now ached from gazing upon such objects that seemed to demand his attention.

The King of the mapped world sighed in boredom at his entertainment. Several men ambled around the room before him, fighting with various weapons, proving their right to enter The Game and travel to Cracas. Only five would be allowed transport on the King's great eagles and one of those was always the monarch's long-standing champion. Close to his highness was a tall gaunt man taking notes of the warriors' progress until it came down to five men. The contestants gave a combined cheer for there were no other visible challengers and therefore their place in The Game had been assured.

The fights had been decided so swiftly that by the time the two travellers and their escort had reached the King, the contestants had been chosen. Each of the five warriors possessed a different weapon and method of combat from his opponent; some using their skill in swordplay or archery, others simply using their brute strength to defeat their enemy by barging into him and knocking the challenger to the floor where he could be easily dispatched.

Cairn introduced himself even though he was the champion and had been for the last three years. He like the others would nevertheless have to prove his worth and fight one of the competitors. The five warriors before him groaned in nervousness, knowing that whoever was chosen would surely fall at the soldier's feet within moments; Cairn's skill was known all over the land and could not be equalled.

Storm stepped in front of his companion and bowed more out of ceremony than respect before the obese monarch. "I have come to warn you, your majesty."

"Warn me of what?" the man snapped. "I am in no danger."

"No, but you soon will be," Storm replied. "From a maniac who wants your throne."

"Who doesn't want my crown?" the King laughed. "Especially that treacherous daughter of mine and my brother on Cracas."

"It is difficult to explain, but you've got to believe me."

"Why should I?" the monarch growled. "And who the devil are you?"

Storm quickly related his tale of the short battle at the citadel in a lost age and the incredible fate of himself and Hemlock, much to the complete astonishment of the King, Cairn and the scribe.

The obese ruler glared down at Storm in rage and disbelief. "You expect me to believe such a fantastic story? You must take me for a fool, or are at least one yourself."

"My presence in this throne-room this very day is my proof," Storm said.

"Faces can be altered by sorcery," the scribe interjected, and the King nodded in agreement.

"Then I ask you this - how do you explain my knowledge of Hemlock?"

"By studying a history book," the fat monarch growled in anger, rapidly tiring of this charade and fondly began to think of the ever-restless axe-man.

"All right, I'll give you proof," Storm said. "Before the great battle at the Prison Tower, I took over from Chief-Adviser Kassier after his death on orders from Commander Hartal and signed a manuscript to authorise this promotion. Do you have this paper?"

The King instructed the scribe to fetch the ancient parchment from the great palace library while a second clerk handed Storm another paper on which he wrote his signature. He wrote his autograph quickly so there could be little chance of an accusation of forgery while being closely observed by the scribe lest he write the name from memory from a copy of the parchment. The clerk handed the article to his ruler and the King studied the two documents intensely. His mouth dropped open in disbelief, either this swordsman before him was a brilliant forger or he was a warrior who should have been dead for almost three centuries.

"This is impossible," the monarch said.

"I am living proof to the contrary," Storm retorted.

"What am I to do?"

"I need information to the likely whereabouts of Hemlock."

"Like you, I have no knowledge of his exact location," the King said. "Yet I have a good idea where he's heading. It would be insanity even for him to come directly here and steal my throne."

"Then tell me," Storm demanded.

"A favour for a favour," the monarch laughed, recovering his cunning. "Fight in The Game for my amusement and I will give you your information."

Storm cursed under his breath at this delay, not to mention his concern regarding his doubtful survival in the grand combat, yet he knew he had no choice but to entertain this fat freak before him, though he vowed the King would meet a nasty end for his evil ways.

Cairn swiftly disposed of his challenger who reluctantly volunteered to fight the undefeatable master-warrior, and Storm had to choose one of the four remaining men to contest against. All appeared highly-experienced, would give no mercy and expected none. Storm couldn't be sure which of the men might be the weakest. Suddenly they broke into a furious argument about who should have the pleasure of killing this stranger before them, until one abruptly moved forward and threw a two headed axe at Storm's feet in challenge.

The warrior was a huge robust man of six foot three with bulging arms the size of the King's chubby thighs and stank of something terrible. He began to slobber and froth at the mouth in anticipation of killing this stranger while the King and Cairn watched on in interest, wishing to see the combat-expertise of a man who would go up against Hemlock alone. Storm cursed under his breath a second time as one of the scribes handed him a large round shield.

With a deafening roar, the contestant picked up his axe and advanced on Storm, swinging the weapon back and forth across Storm's shield, each blow causing great dents to appear on the light armour. The fight would be over in moments unless Storm did something. In rage, he suddenly threw the battered shield at his attacker. The large round object struck the contestant in the face, breaking his nose with an audible turkey-bone sounding snap. The colossal warrior began to shout in anger as blood flowed into his open mouth, driving him into an intense fury. Storm saw the giant man had let himself wide open and punched him in the stomach with his left hand, before upper-cutting him to the chin with his right, felling the huge contestant. He crashed to the floor as the King burst into laughter.

"You certainly have an unusual method of combat," the obese monarch laughed as guards dragged the unconscious challenger away, before throwing him into the street.

"I second that," Cairn said. "It appears I have a companion for The Game. Come, let us prepare, we leave within the hour."

Cairn led him to the armoury where he persuaded Storm to try on a light chainmail coat and gave him another dagger, several more crossbolts and a large round black shield. Storm began to complain at the extra weight until Cairn silenced him. "You can never have enough weapons or protection," he said. "I however only need my spear."

Before he could argue, a bell sounded throughout the palace which brought Storm sharply to his senses and the matter at hand.

"The eagles are about to leave," Cairn said. "We must hurry."

Storm caught his sleeve and stared at the warrior coldly. "How many survived last year's Game and how many compete?" Though Storm already knew the answer, he felt he just had to ask the grim question all the same.

"About a hundred compete," he retorted.

"How many survive?"

"Just one," Cairn replied flatly. "But do not worry my friend, you're in The Game for information, not money. The organiser on Cracas might allow you to live while I collect the prize. Just stay close to me and I'll see you right," Cairn said, though he doubted this would be the case.

Cairn's answer did nothing to calm his nervousness, though Storm did not doubt his safety in the company of such a brilliant warrior. However, he also wished he knew for certain Cairn was being a friend because he longed for company, and not the ownership of his sword.

They entered the courtyard of the palace where the other contestants waited anxiously. A giant eagle stood in the centre of the yard, only one of a dozen such beasts in the entire land. Standing at a massive twenty-five feet with wingspans the length of the courtyard, its huge black eyes watched the men with great interest. A waist-high wooden box was strapped to its back above its wings with just enough room for the contestants for The Game. Storm wondered what sorcery or strange breeding-method had been used to create such monsters, he knew nothing of such creatures before the flood.

He noticed the other men who gathered around the pilot of the beast were all heavily-armed as they prepared to board the giant animal. He wondered if the weapons would be of any use to them when they reached the island. Cairn stared on in silence as if mentally preparing himself for the lives he must take on Cracas. Storm also decided to keep silence for the entire journey, unwilling to talk to men who were in essence already dead, content instead to stare down at the countryside as it passed beneath him as they travelled over land and water at great speed, the island looming closer with every passing moment.

CHAPTER TWENTY

The great eagle flew across the land, leaving the capital city far behind. Storm glanced over the box to the distant countryside below and gasped, knowing they must now travel at an immense height, the clouds above appearing terrifyingly close. He could already see the coast as night began to fall. The contestants watched the coastline disappear as they flew across the ocean, the only sound the loud beating of the giant bird's wings. The sea seemed so vast and endless, and the voyagers knew it would be certain death to fall in.

They arrived at the harbour-town Port by dawn and were greeted by an escort of the King, the eagle landing in a special open region for the creatures adjacent to the busy pier. A soldier brought five horses and as they travelled to the aptly named capital of the island, Cairn told Storm a short account of the history of Cracas and the capital Blackgame.

"The ruler of the island is King Aliped, the brother of King Winterlending. They hate each other because Aliped rules a small isle in the middle of the ocean and wants his older brother's much larger kingdom. To keep his younger sibling amused and pacified, he allows Aliped to hold The Game every year on the island, which he has done for the last twenty years."

"I vaguely remember the old history of the Winterlending family," Storm said.

"In their arrogance, when the next in line takes the crown, he or she must change their name to Winterlending. That is why the King back in the great capital city on the mainland calls himself King Winterlending the fifth."

"What is his real name?" asked Storm. "And what part does his daughter play in all this?"

"His real name is Banock," stated Cairn. "His daughter Sobranie is rumoured to be planning a revolution to overthrow her tyrannical father and abolish his crushing taxes."

"Why doesn't he simply have her executed for treason?"

"He hopes he can change her views," Cairn replied. "Because he lacks a son and is unwilling to relinquish his throne to his greedy brother. Besides, he feels he really has nothing to fear from what he sees as a foolish idealistic young woman."

"Were all of the five Winterlending Kings tyrants?"

"Banock is the worst," Cairn retorted. "His taxes are killing the farmers, and if anybody contradicts his policies, they pay his headman a terminal visit."

"Why don't they overthrow him?"

"That's easier said than done," the warrior replied. "But his time is coming, my friend, I promise you."

"You should be quiet," Storm said sharply. "You openly speak eagerly of treason."

Cairn smiled. "I may be one of his many army Commanders, but that doesn't mean I support his reign. My loyalties lie elsewhere, and if you're wise, you'd do well not to trust the fat bastard."

By noon they sighted the city Blackgame, the capital of the largest island known neighbouring the mainland. Compared to the cities Winterlending and Karlaband, Blackgame was a tiny settlement with a population barely reaching ten thousand.

However, this total usually rose to as much as thirty thousand at the time of the grand combat, as huge crowds travelled from the mainland to witness the event and cheer the sole winner as he returned to the city to collect his well-earned blood-money.

Storm noticed the fortified wall which surrounded the entire settlement as they approached, hindering their entry and protecting the populace from sea-faring barbarians that occasionally attacked the small city. The gates were heavily guarded by two dozen soldiers, each brandishing spears which were instantly pointed in the contestants' direction, and only relaxed when their escort revealed their identities. Storm saw excited children gather around the horses, only to be swiftly dragged off in protest by fearful mothers into nearby houses with heavily barred doors.

They soon arrived at the palace of King Aliped and were confronted not by more wary troops, but rather by several other contestants, eager to tell their own story as they idly shined their blades and various other weapons. Such sociable conversations everyone knew would be soon replaced by harsh words and cold steel, though for now they would be content to talk like old friends. Storm was quick to note even from the outside, the general appearance of the palace was crumbling and run-down, King Winterlending making sure his younger brother lived in less comfortable surroundings than he, keeping the majority of the money even on this tiny island to himself. He knew there could be no love between the two distant siblings, only pure and untainted hatred.

One man out of the gathering of competitors approached the company and hailed them, dressed in the familiar armour of the guards of Cracas. "My name is Aphis, Commander of the armed forces on Cracas and the organiser of The Game," he said. "You may dismount and greet the others. In one hour, a meeting of all this year's contestants will take place which will demand your attendance."

He then left as they placed their steeds in the adjacent palace stables, already densely crowded with horses, all of which bar one would never gaze upon their owners again. Storm glanced around at the competitors, chatting with other contestants they would soon wish death upon. About one third of the fighters Storm noticed with great surprise were women; shield-maidens and mercenaries who had come from every corner of the land to do battle, to kill men who on another day might have been lovers, but were now only enemies; an obstacle like any other that had to be removed to claim the prize. Storm did not doubt these contestants would fight as viciously as their male counterparts and would despite their gender, also kill without mercy.

After what seemed like hours, a bell rang throughout the town which brought the group to their feet and they were quickly ushered into the palace. They were escorted by dozens of guards, wary hands on their sword-handles as they led the competitors down undecorated dusty corridors. They entered a large empty chamber not unlike the throne room Storm saw in Winterlending, though it was devoid of both decoration and royalty. Storm could not say he was sorry the monarch was absent, unwilling to greet the King of Cracas, despite his hatred for his older brother.

They were made to sit on the cold marbled floor as Aphis, the organiser of The Game appeared and called a halt to their anxious chatter. He briefly glanced over the gathering with little interest, knowing he was gazing upon men and women who would soon be no-more. "We begin at six this evening at the city-gates," he roared, his voice echoing throughout the chamber. "One contestant shall leave the settlement followed by another two minutes later until all have left. The rules are simple: to kill your opponents by fair means or foul. However, you have just exactly two days to dispatch all other competitors and the sole winner to return to Blackgame."

"No contestant is allowed to leave the island until the grand combat ends, but may travel anywhere on Cracas outside of the capital. Any man or woman found trying to flee the isle or hiding in the town Port will answer to the royal executioner. You will each be given adequate supplies of water, food and medical provisions for The Game. The actual combat-festival will commence exactly three and a half hours after six," he said and sneered at the amassed gathering. "Remember, only one competitor may return here. Good luck!"

Then the Commander left the room and the excited contestants were escorted once more out of the palace and given provisions before shoved into the street. All drifted into the main part of the city, eager to spend their remaining money on drink and wenching before it was time to die.

"Well, what do we do now?" asked Storm, eager to get through this ridiculous Game and return to the mainland to obtain information about Hemlock.

Cairn looked at him, as if in disbelief. "We have some fun," he said, walking quickly towards the nearest tavern. "Do not worry my friend, if I am called before you at the gates, I will simply wait outside for you," he smiled. "I would hate to see you die before you had planted that fancy blade of yours in Hemlock's chest."

Eventually the time came for The Game to begin and they gathered with the others at the gates, anxiously awaiting their turn to leave the city and prepare for battle. Finally they were called and Storm met Cairn outside the settlement's walls, before heading off into the countryside towards the forest that lay in the southern part of the island where they could safely hide and wait out the two days, leaving the majority of the killing to more bloodthirsty impatient contestants.

They had just reached the north bank of the River Black when bells rang out from all over the island, signalling the commencement of the great grand combat and the end for most of the foolish greedy competitors.

CHAPTER TWENTY-ONE

It was nearing midday on the second day of his sea journey when Hemlock sighted Aren Island, its one single though highly unstable volcanic mountain the first thing he saw seemingly jutting out of the ocean. He came out onto the deck as the Captain let go the anchor. The bow-shaped metal abruptly halted the boat's motion with a jolt, almost sending its passenger overboard. Hemlock retaliated by giving the ferryman a glare that sent shivers up the man's spine. Hemlock lowered the small rowing boat at the rear of the vessel and moments later was joined by the Captain who positioned himself in the middle of the craft and took the oars. The entire island appeared completely devoid of life of any kind whatsoever due to the three hundred foot high volcano which even now spewed black smoke into the otherwise clear blue sky. The ferryman gave his passenger frequent nervous glances, anxious to leave this dark place and return to the mainland where better customers waited. Yet he dare not argue with this man with the black whiteless eyes, whether he was the true sole inhabitant of this vile isle or not. The wooden craft hit the rocky beach with a scrape and came to rest in the shallow water. The Captain wanted further payment for the trip, though decided against asking for it. He simply rowed away furiously from the hellish island, leaving Hemlock alone, whom appeared seemingly unperturbed that his only transport off the isle was departing and had no intention of returning. The warlock instead instantly took to frantically searching the tiny islet for any sign of habitation which might reveal the Arch-Mage who called this barren rock home. However, his hunt was in vain, revealing nothing. If the great sorcerer Agouti was indeed living on this island, he was hiding, perhaps even using his great magical powers to camouflage himself from the outside world.

Hemlock was about to scream in frustration when he noticed a small hole cut into the mountain. The cavity was barely the size of his fist, yet nevertheless he began to dig his nine digits at the soft earth. Within minutes he had widened it enough so he could crawl into the cave beyond. The opening revealed a tunnel which stretched on into the darkness, offering no clues to its eventual destination. Hemlock began to wonder if this might be the true domain of the mage when he caught sight of an unlit glass lamp attached to a metal hook on the ceiling just above his head. He reached up and snatched hold of the light-giver and after a few frustrating moments with his flint soon gave brightness to the gloomy shaft. The passage was constricting and led off in one direction only. Hemlock noticed the tunnel had not been made by lava or any other method of nature, but by man, probably by the Arch-Mage. The wall of earth he had been forced to demolish in order to gain entry to the shaft meant the wizard either had another exit or he had not left the mountain in some time. Both this and the frightening stories surrounding this mysterious man made Hemlock momentarily uneasy and he began to mentally prepare himself for the inevitable confrontation with the sorcerer.

The passage of smooth rock seemed to continue on forever and Hemlock knew he was now quite some distance below sea-level. Suddenly the shaft came to an abrupt end in the shape of a small wooden unmarked door, blocking his way. He crouched up against the portal and strained to hear, but could hear no sounds beyond the door, though he knew with dire certainty and excitement, that it would reveal the mage and creator of this tunnel. He feared time might have jammed the door shut and he would have to somehow smash his way in and give away the element of surprise. However, he let out a light laugh of delight and relief as the portal swayed inwards with little effort.

The warlock peered in, searching for the Arch-Wizard and saw before him a large cavern with another similar door set into the far opposite wall. The portal he had just pushed in though did not open without noise. The man in the chamber turned at the creaking and gazed in astonishment at his intruder. Before Agouti was a roughly attired brown-haired man in his mid twenties, bearing no weapons bar a small knife at his waist which was in the process of being removed from its scabbard by a hand with four fingers. But it was the trespasser's eyes which captivated his attention. Dark soulless eyes stared fixedly at him in hatred and mad desire. He had never seen eyes like that, black as night; eyes without any trace of compassion or mercy.

"What do you want?" the sorcerer shouted, knowing fully well what this intruder wanted: his great magical library.

"I need your help," Hemlock responded, climbing out of the shaft and into the cavern, facing the mage.

"I thought as much," Agouti said. "What is it that you require?"

"You must get very bored and lonely here;" Hemlock replied. "Doing nothing else but reading and carrying out experiments," he said, pointing to the various bottles and books that adorned every conceivable space in the chamber.

"What is it to you?" the sorcerer snarled, realising the man was only delaying the inevitable and suspecting he had seen the trespasser's face before.

"We could form a partnership, you and I."

"To do what?" Agouti said, perplexed.

"To take power."

"From who?" the mage said in puzzlement.

"The King, of course," Hemlock replied flatly, the knife now completely freed from its scabbard.

"How, and why?" Agouti inquired in feigned interest, stalling while he prepared a spell in his mind.

"The King's a tyrant, as you very well know," Hemlock said. "We could relieve him of the burden of royalty and live in comfort, ruling over the entire land."

"You're crazy," Agouti roared. "I've seen your ugly face before. Leave now, or I'll blow it off."

"That wasn't very pleasant," Hemlock laughed, throwing the knife at the Arch-Mage.

Hemlock had aimed for the heart, but a simple wave of his right hand from Agouti sent the weapon flying way off its intended target and instead implanted itself in the wall near the wizard. The sorcerer broke into laughter which echoed around the room, filling Hemlock's mind with sudden dread.

"You fool," the mage roared. "My powers are beyond your feeble comprehension."

With a movement of his hand, Agouti made a circle in the air before him while simultaneously whispering various words. To Hemlock's amazement, a transparent shield formed in front of the wizard. The thief in panic picked up any books and bottles that greeted his wandering fingers on the ground and threw them at the sorcerer, yet these simply bounced off the impenetrable wall, crashing to the floor at Agouti's feet. The shield appeared not to be only transparent, but also relatively soft.

The Arch-Mage ran towards him, smashing into his intruder, forcing him back into the opposite wall and began to crush him into the rock. Hemlock could feel the rock-face pushing into his spine, but could not move any part of his body. However, he managed to free a hand and remembering the fireball spell he had learned in Kava's book, fired one across the chamber.

Agouti watched the ball of fire leave his captive's hand in amusement and began to laugh loudly at this feeble attempt on his life, the shield protecting the front of his body. "What did you do that for?" the wizard laughed. "You cannot penetrate my shield."

"Remember the oldest rule of sorcery - any spell which does not hit its intended target, will return to its owner," Hemlock laughed, despite being crushed. "It's a pity you're in the way."

The Arch-Mage turned his head in terror and tried to move the shield to face the oncoming fireball. But it was too late. The ball of flame hit him full force in the back and Hemlock shut his eyes as the wall and he were sprayed with blood. Hemlock pushed the shield away and what remained of the sorcerer, while wiping the blood from his face.

He then set to searching through the wizard's extensive library, seemingly unaware

Agouti was using his fading powers to keep himself alive long enough to ask his murderer one question. He began to crawl on his stomach slowly towards Hemlock and the intruder turned at hearing the sound.

"Who are you?" he whispered, reaching out for the trespasser.

The thief knelt before him and smiled in amusement at the dying man's predicament. "You know who I am," he laughed and Agouti's eyes opened wide in realisation and shock.

"It can not be," he moaned briefly, before his pain-wracked face finally hit the floor with a thud.

He returned to the sorcerer's enormous library and sighed in dismay, it would take years to read and absorb all the knowledge before him. Nevertheless, he sat down amongst the mountain of books and began reading furiously, committing the contents to memory. However, before he could rise to power, he needed to do one thing first - to make sure no other mage could possibly compete with him, he therefore would need to kill all other wizards in the entire land, only then could he challenge the King in safety, comfortable in the knowledge no sorcerer could threaten his reign. He set about hunting for an incantation in earnest for the immediate elimination of all men with magical abilities, except himself. This time he was confident there would be no stopping him.

CHAPTER TWENTY-TWO

All occupants of the city bar the visiting spectators fled indoors when the time for the commencement of the grand combat arrived. Old women huddled close their young grandchildren behind iron-barred doors and talked nervously about the greed and savagery of men. But they also chatted excitedly about the contestants, their individual progress, and the mysterious and probably bloody circumstances of their deaths.

It was dawn and twelve hours had passed since The Game had begun. However, only fourteen men and four women had so far fallen foul of traps or ambushes, resulting in their unfortunate demise. The remainder searched out their quarry feverishly, eyes wary for unwelcome surprises.

Storm and Cairn finally reached the great forest of Cracas, and Storm wondered where in the vast undergrowth they might hide from their less than friendly fellow competitors. The King's champion soon directed him to a bush of brambles which hid a large hole cut into the base of a thick oak tree. Cairn had apparently used this same location over the years to hide from his jealous challengers. They packed close together, obscuring themselves from prying eyes. They then seized the opportunity to devour some of their rations and replenish their strength.

The two travellers had barely finished when they abruptly heard the sound of something heavy moving through the undergrowth. Carefully parting the bush, Cairn peered into the forest surroundings and watched a man clad in full armour run blindly through the gaps in the trees, obviously terrified of something which pursued him seemingly relentlessly. Both companions then suddenly heard a familiar low whistle as a crossbolt flew through the air and struck the man squarely in the back, impaling the soldier. Storm knew the crossbolt had to be fired at close range to pierce armour. The individual instantly halted in his tracks and crashed to the ground with a heavy thud of metal.

They stared on as another figure entered the area, bearing a large unloaded crossbow in his hands. He knelt before his dying victim and began to steal his rations and provisions. Storm watched all this happen in disgust, the ghoul robbing his helpless prey without remorse, ignoring the soldier's fading groans. Storm lifted his own crossbow and prepared to fire when Cairn laid a hand on the weapon, forcing it down to the ground. "Wait, he could have a partner nearby," the master-warrior said softly.

Several moments later another man arrived and approached the fallen contestant. This individual was slightly smaller than his friend, though was chubby, puffing and wheezing as he came upon his partner in crime. He also knelt and began to strip the man of his armour, hoping it might fare them better against other competitors.

Storm and Cairn waited for some time to make sure no other men were on the way before striking. Storm let fly a crossbolt a moment before his companion threw his spear, both weapons hitting their targets. The bolt struck the smaller of the two men in the chest and he fell silently to the grass, while Cairn's instrument struck the larger contestant in the lower back and he let out a short grunt before collapsing as the spear exited through his stomach. They waited for some moments before leaving their haven and retrieved their weapons. After hiding the bodies under debris of branches and leaves, they returned to the tree and waited for nightfall.

The weather that night was particularly cold, the dark clouds frequently sending down showers of rain and the travellers huddled close together into the heart of the base of the tree. Cairn whispered that come the dawn, they would journey out of the forest and attempt to inquire concerning The Game's progress and how many competitors remained.

Balata was your average contestant; possessing greed that would put even the King to shame, coupled with its close cousin - cowardice. Failing through sickness to participate in last year's combat, he had settled instead for observing some of the finer moments of the bloodthirsty event, witnessing the prowess of the Commander of Tomilusk as he disposed of less able challengers. He recalled the same warrior had entered for this year's Game also, which was peculiar, since the prize money for one year would be enough to set you up for life. However, this meant such a man could not be killed by fair means; a knife between the shoulder-blades might be more appropriate, and for a man like Balata, he knew his conscience would not suffer any shame for such a cowardly act.

He was just approaching what appeared to be a shallow river and decided to wade across. He succeeded in almost reaching half-way when he realised he was going to get more than just his waist wet. Balata was considering returning to the bank and searching for another method across when he heard the rustling of leaves and talking, heading towards him. He began to panic, realising he was completely vulnerable and his part in this contest was soon to be over. There was only one option. He knelt and let the freezing water pass over his head, hoping the competitors would not bother to closely inspect the river's depths.

Holding his breath behind trembling closed lips, he watched two men approach the bank moments later. He instantly recognised Cairn, the magnificent weapon he proudly held clearly identifying the warrior. This was an opportunity that could not be forsaken. He notched an arrow to his bow and let the tip of the shaft pierce the surface of the river so it would not miss its target due to bending through water.

Cairn and Storm set to talking on how they should proceed when Balata poked his head out of the river and fired. The Commander turned and before Storm realised what was happening, with a flick of his wrist, the warrior had let fly his spear. Both Storm and Balata knew even Cairn could not save himself in time, yet to their astonishment, the weapon struck the arrow in mid-flight and both instruments fell into the river. Master-warrior or not, Storm could not believe his companion was capable of such incredible skill, and his question was answered when Cairn extended out his hand and the spear rose out of the water and returned to his grasp.

Storm once again began to wonder where the weapon and his own sword had really come from, he knew Kassier for all his philosophy and metallurgy had not the skill nor knowledge to produce such an instrument. He feared the old man had rather stole the sword from a greater man than he. Perhaps Cairn had the answer to those questions, as Storm now suspected the reasons for his success in The Game over the years and why the King kept such a man close to hand. Maybe this soldier before him was not the great warrior he once thought, nor possessed the noble heart he hoped. However, time would tell.

Cairn raised the magical weapon to a striking position at the defenceless man who now stood waist-deep in the waterway.

"I beg of you, sire," Balata pleaded, trembling more from terror than the cold. "Spare my life, give me a chance."

"You didn't give me one," Cairn said. "An arrow in the back is what you promised me."

"But you're too good a warrior, what would you have done in my place?"

Cairn glared at him in disgust before turning about and walked away. Storm wondered without the spear would he truly perform such a cowardly act if their roles were reversed. He followed the departing soldier, leaving Balata to his fate at the hands of a passing more ruthless contestant.

To the north-east of the island at the base of a mountain-range a more serious predicament was currently taking place. Four shield-maidens stood over one of their own, protecting their injured companion from the violent and somewhat crude advances of four men. One of the male-competitors cursed when he realised they were unlikely to take the women alive as three of their own group had already fallen to their one. They had wished to have some amusement before sending these shield-maidens to the land of their forefathers, though it now seemed they would have to settle for their broken bodies with their virtue intact.

The leader of the women, a tall golden-haired plain female of thirty-something age, approached the largest of the four men, brandishing a broadsword. Her opponent grinned at her, displaying blackened scurvy-eaten teeth, while waving about an enormous two-handed double-headed battle-axe. Despite her gender, she defended off every wild blow until the contestant in desperation attempted to lop off her head, leaving himself wide open. Side-stepping out of the way, she struck at his unprotected stomach, slicing his abdomen open. He fell to his knees with a cry of shock and attempted to cling onto his escaping entrails as they slipped through trembling blood-soaked hands, before his body hit the ground.

In rage, the three remaining men attacked. One of the male-contestants struck the leading shield-maiden across the chest with his shield, breaking several ribs. The woman fell adjacent her injured groaning companion as the men advanced. The competitors dispatched the three remaining standing shield-maidens, though lost two of their own number for their trouble. Only one of the previous four men now stood and sneered down at the injured woman before him, her protectors lying motionless amongst her. He began to approach, sure of his victory and comfortable in the knowledge nothing would now deter him from his piece of amusement. He was barely three feet from the apparently defenceless shield-maiden when she revealed a loaded crossbow and fired at point blank range. The bolt hit him squarely in the stomach and severed his spinal cord on its exit. It was the woman's final act and she smiled briefly before the darkness claimed her sight forever. However, it was several hours before her victim finally died, unable to move and nobody in the vicinity to hear his pain-wracked cries.

It was nearing the midnight hour when the two travellers began to approach the north-east mountain-range of Cracas Island. Shortly after lighting their second batch of torches, Storm noticed the gleam of moonlight off something in the distance. They investigated further, only to discover the battered still bodies of the shield-maidens. After searching their killers for identification, Cairn cursed aloud upon realising their true identity; they were not contestants, but rather soldiers from King Winterlending's elite guard. These unfortunate women had been sought out not for their part in The Game, but for their ideals and participation in the preparation for the revolution to come. It appeared the fat tyrant was taking precautions in preventing an uprising by eliminating key figures. Cairn hoped the monarch did not suspect his part, or that the leader of the revolution was his own daughter. However, he knew even the King was not that stupid.

Storm discovered the leader of the shield-maidens who was semi-conscious, though was bleeding profusely from her shattered ribs which had pierced her skin. Neither men could do much for her except keep her warm until the Reaper finally came for her. As Storm attempted to make her more comfortable, she appeared to regain full consciousness and began to mumble. Cairn knelt alongside and strained to hear what could very well be the shield-maiden's dying words.

"Go to the town Abe," she whispered, "where the shield-maidens' control is strongest. Give this to their leader," she stuttered, shoving a plain brass ring into Storm's hand and sighed as the life left her, her other hand clutching his jerkin in sudden pain before relaxing and fell to the ground.

It was close to dawn when they had finished burying the shield-maidens, though left their murderers where they had fallen, meals for the wolves and birds that would arrive with the light. Cairn collapsed with exhaustion and was soon asleep, but Storm could not find peaceful slumber. His tormented mind was filled with the pain-lined face of the shield-maiden and wondered what the last moments of life of his own Nereid must have been, whether her death came quick or slow he would never know, and that ignorance made her loss all the more difficult to bear.

The dawn was several hours old when Cairn woke and found Storm's blanket empty. He glanced around the clearing until he caught sight of his companion sitting, facing away some ten metres from where he lay. He thought he was mistaken at first, but it appeared Storm was sobbing. Cairn sat up in puzzlement and stared at his friend's back, pondering whether he should intrude on the man's privacy and problems, and then decided not. Rumour and history held it his wife had died at the hands of Hemlock, it appeared almost three centuries had done nothing to improve the unfortunate man's grief or rage.

Cairn began to understand Storm's all-consuming lust for vengeance and how he would not rest until he personally had dispatched Hemlock. Cairn had hoped he might have persuaded his companion to relinquish ownership of his sword for he knew both Storm's blade and his own spear were a pair. He feared Storm did not know the true origin of the magical weapons and was unsure whether to tell him, afraid it might damage their friendship if he confessed his terrible crime. The time would come when the truth must out, and the Commander knew he would be unprepared for the consequences of that moment. He only hoped their friendship would be strong enough to survive, for he needed Storm's help in the revolution to come, for the man was a living legend and people would flock to him in their thousands. It was imperative he remained alive and well; Cairn would make sure he got his friend to their leader Sobranie in safety, knowing well she would convince him of the truth and his necessary part in the uprising.

Cairn laid back and pretending to be still asleep, made a few deliberate audible groans and listened attentively as Storm ceased his weeping, and moments later began to prepare breakfast as if nothing had happened. The master-warrior rose and they ate quickly, realising less than half a day remained in The Game and that they had to return to Blackgame, or be executed for lateness. Cairn hoped they would be the only contestants alive upon arrival at the capital, for any remaining challengers would have to be dispatched before entering the city. However, considering the recent pathetic performance of Balata, Cairn was confident other such competitors would be relatively easy to eliminate.

Balata was in no hurry to forget his encounter with the Commander of Tomilusk, though for the moment was prepared to let it pass. Other more immediate troubles took priority, such as the two contestants who were fast approaching and close to discovering his hiding-place. Like Cairn, Balata was using the convenient hollow of a nearby thick oak tree to crouch in and await the arrival of unwary passer-bys.

The competitors which neared the coward's haven were brothers; an unusual and rare match-up in The Game, for one must die at the city-gates or risk execution for breaking the rules. However, this predicament did not seem to bother them as they talked about what they might buy with the prize money. Once within range, Balata fired and hit the taller of the two men in the chest, piercing his heart, the brothers' choice of survival no longer a valid issue.

The second man dived out of the way to his right, hitting not solid ground, but the lightly covered surface of a pit. The brother instantly stood to his feet, shaken though unhurt, to discover himself at the muddy bottom of a twelve-foot high square hole. Balata approached the crater as his captive began to fire arrows in panic into the air, fearing his persecutor might fill in the gorge and bury him alive. But Balata had a better idea. He had recently snared a live cobra and retrieving the deadly reptile, threw the snake into the pit, staying some distance from the chasm in case his prisoner got lucky with his bow. He listened with amusement as his victim began screaming in fear and laughed as the shouts suddenly halted. Glancing into the hole, he smiled down at the still body of the contestant and the snake which seemingly observed its prize in satisfaction.

He strolled off through the trees, breaking into violent laughter. Tears rolled down his cheeks from mirth at the competitor's last moments in the pit and obstructed his vision, momentarily blocking from sight the second pit. Balata had earlier discovered the empty crater into which his captive had fallen, but did not for a moment consider the existence of a second nearby cavity. He fell headlong in, screaming in fright into the darkness. However, unlike the first hole, this pit was not empty; a dozen sharpened wooden stakes lined the floor and Balata screeched a second time as he was impaled in several places.

He gazed down at the ground in dismay, transfixed as he was two feet above the floor by a shaft entering both legs, left arm below the elbow and the stomach. In excruciating agony, he attempted to lift himself up and off the stakes, though in vain. He was helpless and sure to die from both pain and loss of blood before too long. He cursed in anger, knowing Cairn was now sure to escape his vengeance.

The two travellers arrived at Blackgame with one hour to spare. However, they were greeted at the city-gates by a furious Commander Aphis, the cheerless organiser of The Game. He glared at the two men in rage and frustration. As he began to curse, it rapidly became obvious the Commander was expecting only one contestant to return to the capital. Aphis refused all attempts by Storm to explain he was in the grand combat for no other reason but for the vile amusement of King Winterlending and thus felt he was not entitled to the prize money. The officer however was quick to point out this island was under the control of King Aliped and not his older brother, and the rules stated clearly that only one competitor can enter the city.

"I will apologise to the King of your unfortunate demise," the Commander laughed at Storm. "I am sure it will trouble him greatly, perhaps for even as long as two minutes."

"I refuse to kill my friend," Cairn said, "and if you attempt to force me, several dozen of your soldiers will die first."

"Then it appears we have reached a stalemate," Aphis replied. "We will wait out the hour to see if any other contestants return in time and then decide your fate, but I must warn you, your future looks dubious, very dubious indeed."

CHAPTER TWENTY-THREE

The wind-stricken lights of the capital city of Cracas Island revealed a steadily increasing gathering of heavily-armed soldiers surrounding two men at the gates. Cairn glared perpetually at Aphis as the hour dragged on and came to an end, with no other arriving competitors in sight. The organiser finally turned to them, his gaze full of spite and frustration at this inconvenience to his life.

"Since you persistently and quite ridiculously refuse to fight each other, I will make the choice for you," Aphis snarled. "Come morning, you will be sent back out and will shortly be followed by my men who will ruthlessly hunt you down, while they simultaneously search for any remaining contestants in hiding. Whoever survives until midnight tomorrow and returns here will be the winner. If neither of you return, I shall give your regrets to the King, I am sure you will be mourned for several seconds, at least," he laughed. "If both of you return, I will have to force myself, despite my nagging conscience, to execute you both immediately," he said and turned to a nearby soldier. "Now get these offensively ugly morons out of my sight."

The corporal escorted them to an adjacent tavern and allowed the two travellers to converse briefly before they would be put into guarded separate rooms. Cairn snatched hold of Storm's sleeve and drew him close. "Ignore that pig Aphis," Cairn growled. "Over the years he has become gradually more obnoxious as I returned alone and alive from The Game and collected the prize money; apart from his jealousy and insults he's relatively harmless, though do not doubt for a moment that he will not have us killed if we both return to the city tomorrow night," the master-warrior said. "I have a plan - in order for both of us to live, I will fake my death. I know the island better than anyone and can easily find a boat to the mainland, while you collect the prize and return to the King and get your information concerning Hemlock from the fat fool," he stated and suddenly embraced Storm, whispering in his ear. "Be careful my friend, the hunt Aphis plans for you is a far less treacherous danger than what the King may have in store."

Just before he was escorted away, Cairn turned briefly once more to Storm and raised a fist to the ceiling; in a symbol of solidarity. "Be sure my comrade, we will meet again soon." Then he was dragged away and Storm wondered whether he would truly see the warrior again, though he doubted such a man would so easily succumb to the Reaper. No, he assured himself, it would take something special to dispatch such a magnificent fighter and idealist.

Storm was abruptly awoken the following morning by shouts and was roughly dragged out of bed by a seven-foot muscular giant of a guard. He allowed Storm to dress quickly before shoving him out of the room. Moments later a small square-shaped chamber greeted his fatigued vision in which lay a tiny rectangular table decorated with an assortment of fruit, including oranges and wild berries. Adjacent to the table on the left wall hung on a single peg his weapons. After the hurried meal, he summoned the huge guard by kicking at the door, resulting in a crack appearing from handle to bottom. The soldier looked in, glanced once at Storm and then at the fractured door frame, before glaring at Storm in rage. He considered striking Storm, but then thought not, realising it might be unwise to kill a contestant before he could die at the eager hands of the hunt.

The giant soldier led him out of the tavern towards the city-gates where waited Aphis impatiently. There was no sign of Cairn, he had obviously been sent out earlier and had long since disappeared into the wilderness. Storm sneered at the Commander and he replied by staring back in hatred, seemingly barely restraining himself from drawing his blade and attacking the competitor before him.

"It is now the fourth hour after dawn, your friend left one hour earlier," Aphis said. "The hunt leaves in two hours, I look forward to personally redding my sword with your worthless carcass. Now go!"

Storm instantly fled the capital and soon left the city behind. The northern mountain-range would be the wisest route to take where a wide choice of deep caves would be available to hide in. He knew time was of the essence, the hunt would soon leave Blackgame in hot pursuit and were certain to have dogs; bloodhounds that would track a man's scent to the very gates of hell if necessary. These were canines that would not have been fed in several days and if they managed to catch their quarry, they would tear the unfortunate prey to pieces.

He collapsed at the sight of the mountains in relief and exhaustion just before midday. He spent several hours searching for a suitable cave, but in vain, the holes in the mountain-face he discovered were either too small or too noticeable from afar. As

Storm began to curse in frustration, he suddenly heard the distant barking of approaching dogs and knew the hunt could not be far behind. He could not afford to waste any more time scouring the hills for possible sanctuary and so decided instead to make for the nearby town Port to the north-west. Unfortunately to reach there, it would require climbing a mountain, crossing open plains and a river. However, as far as the populace of Port knew, The Game was officially over and would therefore not hinder the entrance of a stranger to their settlement and so finding temporary sanctuary might be relatively easy.

Storm cast one final glance behind him before dashing up the steep mountainside in fear while hoping feverishly Aphis and his diabolical posse would not notice his ascent.

Cairn was having similar problems with his escape from the island, having eventually reached the forest only to discover a search-party in close pursuit. It was then he stumbled upon an appropriate place in which he could fake his demise. Before him, blocking his path lay a large patch of quicksand and nearby a crop of strange sweet-scented flowers which seemed to actually flourish in such a soil-deprived area. Cairn knew the flowers would confuse the dogs' scent and hopefully put them off the trail his odour had left behind.

Unfastening his chainmail coat, he placed it on the ground before striking it several times with the tip of his spear. Usually such a fine chainmail jacket as Cairn possessed, would withstand dozens of blows from either sword or axe, but it instantly disintegrated at the blows of the spear. Pieces of the coat were relatively light and Cairn was able to place parts of the armour on the scum-surface of the quicksand, making them easily noticeable. He threw in the remainder of the jacket before finishing the job by casting in the spear. Stretching out a hand, he forced the magical weapon to the surface by force of will, and yet out of reach of the approaching soldiers who might wish to risk their lives to the quicksand in order to steal the spear.

The instrument stuck almost a foot out of the pool of sand and remained in its seemingly upright position. Cairn quickly scrambled up an adjacent tree and camouflaged himself with branches, forcing his body to remain absolutely still.

The hunt appeared moments later, consisting of almost a dozen heavily-armed soldiers from the city's elite guard and a pack of large hounds which slavered in hunger and excitement, knowing their meal was near. The troops stopped short of the quicksand and instantly noticed the familiar weapon of their quarry protruding from the lethal pool.

"It appears we have lost our amusement to one of the forest's traps."

"So it seems," a guard smiled. "But that doesn't mean we have to leave his weapon behind. It would look far better in my able hands than rather let nature claim it."

"You're mad, that quicksand is deadly."

"That's why my friend," the soldier replied. "I have no intention of touching it."

The first guard watched his comrade retrieve a rope from his pack and making a lasso, began to throw the rope at the tip of the spear which still protruded from the sand. His first few attempts were unsuccessful, but Cairn watched all this with horrified fascination, fearing his instrument might be lost to such ignorant men, though he could not reveal his position. Risking his very life, he outstretched a hand out of the branches and by force of mind, pushed the spear fully into the quicksand. As it sank under the surface, Cairn heard the soldier cry out in rage and growl to his friends who drew back in trepidation, recognising the guard's violent temper.

"Well, that's that," he snapped. "Let's return to Blackgame and inform that maniac Aphis he has one less head to put on a royal spike."

Cairn watched the men leave and waited several more minutes before climbing down from his haven and retrieved his weapon without even touching the deadly pool, the spear returning to his open hand with a single thought. He wiped the instrument clean before heading off deep into the countryside once again, making for the western coastline and transport back to the mainland.

Storm was rapidly becoming exhausted, having to frequently halt his panic-crazed climb up the mountainside, even though the hunt and its dogs were close behind. The soldiers increased their progress and with a roar suddenly let go the dozen or so hounds which now dashed off up the mountain-face in great leaps and bounds, forsaking the recklessness of their actions, such was the insane hunger and excitement that gripped them.

Storm cried out in dismay, knowing the monsters would be upon him in moments and their razor-sharp fangs at his throat. The top of the hill was within his reach, yet he feared he would not make the summit in time. Then it occurred to him there was one chance to rid himself of both the hunt and the dogs at his ankles. Managing to climb onto a stable ledge, he began to push nearby rocks and boulders down the mountainside. The rocks gathered speed as they descended and the soldiers below fled, screaming in fear. The hounds however had no such sense of reason, far too concerned with the meal that seemingly awaited them to worry about approaching boulders. The dogs were all swept aside by the giant rocks and Storm heard their sickening cries as they were crushed underneath or thrown several feet into the air, only to come crashing down onto the jagged edges of jutting stones. Despite the horrible manner of their deaths, Storm could not afford the creatures any sympathy. They would have shown him just as little mercy, had they reached him.

The remaining soldiers seemed temporarily unwilling to give chase and Storm was able to arrive at the harbour-town Port some time later without further event. Entry to the settlement was unguarded as Storm had guessed and he made for the nearest tavern that caught his eye. However, he knew the hunt would quickly recover and make for this town, knowing well this was his intended destination. Despite the settlement's dark corners and secluded houses, the troops would be sure to find him before long. If he were to survive The Game, he would have to backtrack to the mountains and begin searching once again for a suitable cave.

The hunt would scour the town, not suspecting for a moment that he would risk his life again by travelling through open land to evade capture. The hills would be his haven until it would be time to return to the capital and claim the prize in Cairn's place, and finally secure the knowledge from the King that would lead him to Hemlock, and vengeance.

CHAPTER TWENTY-FOUR

The very mountain itself seemed to shake more from the mad laughter that rang throughout its cavern than from its temperamental summit, all too eager to spew its fiery contents to the sky and across the sea. Deep within its bowels, a man consumed by greed and new-found powers pranced around a chamber in excitement; a wild dance only performed by the truly insane.

His fingers trembled in nervousness, impatient to use the serpent of sorcery that ran through his veins and boiled his blood; a desire greater than lust to let himself go. Hemlock smiled an insane grin, contemplating in the silence of the room the final expression of shock and surprise that would cross the faces of the unfortunate victims of his rage. But they were people that required elimination; to make certain of his safe path to the throne and the subsequent shaping of this land in his image. What did it matter if, Hemlock sneered, that great plan involved the deaths of a few hundred, or even thousand ignorant peasants?

"They all should be grateful and honoured to lay down their lives for their leader, and a cause that will continue to live on in the minds of their grandchildren," he roared to the un-replying mountain, satisfied its deep rumbles signified its acknowledgement of his ideals.

However, those same rumblings and groans that regularly shook the chamber had apparently increased in ferocity over the last few days and Hemlock feared the island's life was coming to an end, the unstable volcano was preparing to obliterate it and light up the night sky one last time. Whatever forces Agouti had been using to postpone this event had obviously died with him and Hemlock had been unable to discover those particular spells that kept the mountain stable. But no matter, he smiled, he had found what he came for, and it was better the library's contents were destroyed with the island rather than they fall into another's hands.

"Though before I leave," he said, as he cleared the table of books with a sweep of his hand. "I will rid this land of every sorcerer. It would be unwise to leave an opponent alive who might cause a dent in my plans."

Raising up his hands first to the ceiling and then to the open tunnel from whence he came, he began to spout quickly ancient words known previously only to the Arch-Mage Agouti. Power arose from deep within him and was unleashed out through his fingertips, and the room was suddenly engulfed in blinding orange light as fireballs, larger than the size of his head, left his hands and rushing up the tunnel into the outside world, broke off into separate directions, streaming across the night sky.

In the grand throne-chamber of King Winterlending the fifth, the court-mage Sacrais was performing a levitation spell to amuse the monarch, forcing the thirty-foot length rectangular-table in the centre of the room to rise several inches off the floor. Moments later a fireball flew in through the open side-window and struck the sorcerer in the chest. The King, fearing an assassination attempt was in progress, dived to the ground as his servant screamed in pain. Sacrais burst into flames as the table fell to the marbled-floor with a crash. The monarch was unhurt, though all that remained of his court-magician was a heap of dust amongst some unrecognisable blackened bones.

Likewise across the entire land, similar events were taking place. Witnesses reported back to the King that every sorcerer was being killed by a mysterious fireball. Winterlending quickly realised the connection and suspecting Hemlock's involvement, sent spies out to find and kill him. Though knowing the maniac's history, he feared Hemlock would be too cunning for them and evade capture. It was obvious he meant to seize the throne and the King groaned in frustration, as if his own daughter's and younger brother's attempts weren't enough to contend with.

Almost one hour after the spell had begun, it was all over. The charred remains of student-mages, teachers and sorcerers, whether powerful or amateur, littered the ground before amazed onlookers. The people feared the revolution was upon them, and gathering at the palace, badgered the King's guards into releasing information. The monarch sent out plain-clothes elite soldiers into the crowd to eliminate key trouble-makers and after some time, the populace gave up and returned to their homes, annoyed at being kept in the dark, but grateful for their lives, noticing some of their neighbours had inexplicably vanished near them and realised the cause.

The King watched from the safety of a high window in the central tower as the crowd dissipated and returned to their houses in ignorance. Banock cursed, uncertain what it would take to rid himself of Hemlock, and he had quite possibly sent the only man who could have stopped the lunatic to his death.

The soothsayers promised a fierce storm heralding devastation, and that is exactly what the populace of Cracas received. The wind appeared calm at first, yet within the hour had transformed into a great maelstrom; a raging mistral of driving rain that engulfed the island. Unwary travellers and farmers unfortunate enough to have been caught out in the open, were blown together with the buildings, crops and livestock that crossed the hurricane's undeterable path and were thrown across the countryside, only eventually coming to rest in an unrecognisable wilderness of mud and debris.

The island's rivers overflowed, washing away bodies, making the process of searching for survivors all the more difficult. By early morning the storm had passed and headed north for the mainland. However, it dispersed before reaching the coast, sparing the land of the hurricane's wrath. Once news of the destruction reached the palace in Blackgame, the house echoed with the curses of the King, knowing his older brother, safe from the ravages of the storm in the capital Winterlending, would offer no support or assistance.

Storm survived by managing to find after a long and frustrating search, a suitably deep enough cave to protect him from the gale. Several hours into the morning, peasants and soldiers scouring the devastated countryside for missing relatives, noticed a lone man come unharmed out of the wilderness and approach the island's battered capital. News quickly reached the ears of Aphis and he came running out to greet the mysterious survivor, surprised at Storm's clean appearance, despite the hurricane, yet pleased it was not Cairn; satisfied the master-warrior was indeed dead, unwilling to believe the earlier reports of the hunt.

"I could lie and say I'm pleased to see your ugly face back here, but I won't," Aphis said. "However, I am glad that arrogant bastard with the spear did not return instead of you, I prefer you to him any day," he laughed. "However, you're still late, I expected you last night at midnight."

"I believe the recent weather conditions allows some leniency," Storm snapped. "Even you have to admit that."

"That is true," the organiser of The Game said. "Though the lateness will only add to the King's fury, after receiving the news that his long-standing champion is dead," Aphis declared and turned to a soldier near him. "This guard will escort you to the town Port where you will receive transport back to the mainland. One final point before you leave swordsman, use your prize money wisely, do not make the same mistake of returning here next year; as you have seen, even brilliant warriors like Cairn fall eventually."

Storm nodded. "I hope never to set foot on this wretched island again," With that, the soldier escorted the winner of The Game out of the capital and began to make their way towards the harbour-town Port.

As they travelled, the destruction the hurricane had inflicted upon the land became clear. Farmers knelt weeping before ruined crops adjacent crumbling houses and barns. Trees which had witnessed the passing of centuries lay broken and twisted, occasionally blocking the road, forcing the horsemen to make a slight detour. The road itself had been torn up by the driving rain and the nearby overflowing river, and was now a sea of thick mud. The path to the town Port would be arduous and lengthy. The guard warned Storm this would add several hours onto their journey. Storm groaned in reply, it seemed the very weather itself was conspiring to keep him on the island.

However, this made him all the more determined to reach the mainland and return to the King. He began to fiddle with the ring in his jerkin pocket which the dying shield-maiden had given him and pondered on the voyage he would take to the settlement Abe, after leaving the capital and receiving from the fat tyrant his blood-money.

By early afternoon they finally arrived at the harbour-town Port, the blue ocean a refreshing sight after days of city smog and dense forests. Storm could already clearly smell the vile stink of rotting fish as they entered the gates, almost forgetting the violent stench of rancid fish carcasses the first time he had arrived in the settlement. The past few days had temporarily subdued the memory; the deaths of the contestants burned deeper in his mind than the odour of putrid fish, and they were memories that would haunt his dreams for years to come.

The familiar giant eagle immediately greeted his vision, the massive beast awaiting passengers it would ferry back to Winterlending. The pilot of the creature came forward upon noticing the approach of the travellers. The man was short, barely five foot and dressed in woolly garments, possessing no weapons bar a shortsword strapped to his left hip.

He shook the hands of both the travellers, before turning to the soldier. "A small delay, my friend," he said. "I must collect passengers at the town Abe before travelling on to Winterlending."

The escort-guard's mouth dropped open in shock. "My companion here is requested immediately in the capital on the mainland," he growled. "The King will have my head!"

"I apologise, my friend," he replied. "It is beyond my control."

Storm frowned in suspicion. His presence was required in Abe, and here was a man who would be stopping in the very town. It was too much of a coincidence for his liking. As the soldier turned away from the pilot in anger, Storm saw the short man wink at him and he gasped. He instantly realised the situation; Cairn had planned to make for Port after faking his death and was obviously either near or had already reached the mainland. The pilot before him was a member of the resistance against the King and had been ordered by Cairn to halt in Abe, so his passenger might meet the shield-maidens situated there and pass on his message. Storm smiled, it appeared spies for the princess Sobranie lay everywhere. The path to the revolution had been well planned. It also meant his friend the master-warrior was alive and well, their reunion would likely be imminent. Storm looked forward to such a meeting, he was already missing the soldier.

The escort-guard left the winner of The Game to the care of the pilot and left the town. The short man smiled at Storm briefly before quickly ushering him into the large basket on the eagle's back. Moments later the giant animal unfolded its tremendous wings and rose up into the sky, its one passenger gripping tightly to the basket in fear. The pilot looked behind at Storm and laughed at his pale face, clasping the reins that controlled the beast in one hand, while the other held onto the leather saddle that lay strapped three feet in front of the basket around the beginning of the creature's long neck.

Storm replied by collapsing back into the safety of the large straw box, grateful for its four-foot high walls which kept him inside. He prayed his uneasy stomach would hold out until they sighted the town Abe and the eager shield-maidens who would surely welcome him.

CHAPTER TWENTY-FIVE

On the battlements surrounding the fortified town waited a company of shield-maidens staring northwards, their tireless eyes scanning the darkening sky for the approach of a messenger bearing bad tidings. Their light armour glistened in the fading light of the day, above lay flowing hair tied behind chainmail and battle-weary faces; worn out from the endless fretting regarding the dangerous preparations for the coming uprising.

One of the five women sighed and pointed, her companions following her gaze skywards. From beyond the clouds approached a growing speck until it became clear, its massive wingspan gradually filling their vision. The giant bird landed twenty metres from the town walls, directly in front of the heavily guarded gates. The shield-maidens watched the sole passenger climb down from the eagle and salute the pilot before being quickly ushered into the settlement by a waiting soldier. The pilot of the creature nodded to the women on the battlements before they too disappeared into the town, eager to greet their famous guest.

The guard escorted the champion of The Game through crowded streets until they arrived at a small house situated down a back alley. The dwelling was dilapidated and crumbling, an odd rendezvous for such an important meeting, pondered Storm, yet necessary in its isolation for such dangerous times. He was brought inside the one room that occupied the building where stood a lone shield-maiden. The soldier briefly saluted her before leaving the chamber, taking up position as sentinel outside the door.

The woman before him was not unattractive with short dark wavy hair, dressed in the familiar attire of a shield-maiden; light chainmail under breastplate armour accompanying the single weapon at her side; a magnificent sword comprising of a jewel-encrusted helm and scabbard. Storm smiled, the fact that this officer before him openly displayed such a valuable weapon without fear of mugging, meant she was obviously a swordswoman of some skill. The escort guarding the door to the building Storm guessed, had the job of keeping watch for prying eyes, and not rather the occupation of bodyguard for this shield-maiden. Storm suspected she would be far more capable of dispatching him if he posed a threat to her safety, than the male soldier.

She stepped forward and smirked. "My name is Sotera, Commander of the shield-maidens here at Abe," she said. "And you are the famous Storm from the old capital Karlaband?" she laughed. "You look pretty healthy for a three hundred-year-old corpse," She extended a hand which he shook. "I expect the King will be annoyed at this lateness to welcome his new champion," she smiled. "Well, let him wait! For all the trouble he has given us, the least we can do is inconvenience his busy schedule," she announced. "I hope our pilot didn't frighten you too much on that monstrosity of his?"

"The speed at which we travelled was incredible," Storm said, agape. "The journey took just over eight hours so he could get me here as fast as possible."

"Word has it you have an important message for me?"

Storm reached into his jerkin and revealed the ring. "It appears the King knows of the coming revolution and is killing your operatives."

"That is not news," she replied grimly. "However, what worries me is how he discovered the shield-maidens' involvement in the resistance. What annoys the King most is not knowing who is loyal in his army, it seems his spies have become extremely accurate in finding who is not."

"What will you do?"

"I must warn Sobranie of this, and hope she can step up the plans for the uprising," she said. "I hope I can trust you with this knowledge?"

"I am a friend of Cairn from Tomilusk," Storm retorted. "He would not put his faith in a man who would easily betray you."

She smiled lightly. "Have you seen him?" she stuttered, clear anxiety in her trembling voice. "The fact that the pilot of the eagle knew of you, and sent on a message informing us of your impending arrival hints that he might well have escaped the island."

Storm's face dropped. "No, I have not. But I do not believe for a moment such a man as he would have found his grave on Cracas," he said. "Do you know him well?"

She began to fiddle with her gloves in nervousness, before turning to him and forcing a grin. "I am his fiancée," she sighed. "We plan to marry immediately after we put a Queen on the throne."

He gasped in momentary shock, not believing such an independent soldier as Cairn would settle down, but quickly recovered his composure. "I am sure that event will still take place," Storm replied sharply. "And I will be there at his side to see it."

She smiled in reply. "It seems Cairn placed his trust rightly in you," she said. "And you can return that trust by being my messenger to the princess Sobranie in the capital. She will be expecting you, eager like us to greet a living legend who might benefit our struggle," she declared and called for the guard before turning back to Storm. "All going well, Cairn should be back in Tomilusk within the week. Once the King's spies notice his miraculous return from the grave, the tyrant will order his immediate assassination, knowing then for sure his sympathy for the resistance, for he has always suspected it, yet could never prove it. Tell Sobranie if we are to save his life and many others, the revolution must take place very soon."

The soldier directed him towards the door as she turned to Storm one final time. "I hear that maniac Hemlock also still lives?" she asked, and he nodded. "Perhaps we may be of service to your quest once the King is dead?"

Storm nodded again, but hid a sneer. Help was offered on request he perform for their amusement and be a beacon for reluctant sympathisers for the revolution. Sotera and her band were not so removed from the policies of King Winterlending, just not as ruthless as he was when he made a similar offer; one which he was now about to finally collect.

The guard escorted him out of the house and back through the dirty streets of Abe until he once more sighted the familiar giant eagle, his transport to the capital city. The pilot smiled down at the swordsman before dropping the rope-ladder so he could climb up the beast's back and reach the basket.

"Final stop, the capital," the pilot said before pulling on the reins and the creature soared up into the night sky.

Storm glanced down at the fast disappearing town Abe and sighed. A tyrant and a revolutionary awaited his presence, both requiring his assistance in matters that really did not concern him; the King wishing to acknowledge him as the new champion and most likely replace Cairn in next year's Game, Sobranie probably offering a prestigious position in the new order if he would only further her plans for high-treason. He had become a tool for other people's ambitions, when all he ever wanted was to simply fulfil his vengeance. Storm growled under his breath in anger as he settled back into the basket to briefly relax, before it would be time for this jester to perform.

It was pitch black when the eagle arrived in the capital of the world and Storm was escorted to a bed-chamber to rest, before having an audience with his majesty come morning. He saluted the pilot and he waved in reply, before he too disappeared into the palace for his well-earned sleep. Storm guessed his next mode of transport would not be so grand, yet he welcomed the familiar soreness of a saddle to the dizziness of flying.

The bedroom was a sumptuous chamber of velvet and gold, the bed dressed in satin supported by varnished wood and gleaming silver. Surrounding the double-bed on brightly painted walls were tapestries of battles long forgotten above exotic plants more colourful than the rainbow. The guard departed, leaving the swordsman to his shock and awe of a lifestyle more extravagant than anything he had ever witnessed.

The morning came quickly after such a refreshing slumber, rough nights spent on Cracas a distant memory in the presence of such luxury. Storm had barely dressed when a soldier knocked on the door and peered in.

"Her majesty the princess Sobranie requires your presence," he said. "Before you visit her father."

Storm strapped on his sword and followed the guard out of the room. He led the swordsman out of the palace and into the royal garden. A majestic sea of inch-high grass broken by islands of brightly coloured flowers suddenly absorbed his vision, the sun occasionally obscured from sight by surrounding magnificent oak and chestnut trees proudly stretching their foliage to the sky. The soldier directed him behind a group of such trees which hid him from the palace where waited a single woman. The guard left as the leader of the resistance approached him.

Storm noticed she was quite plain, dressed in a flowing robe of silk, her shoulder-length dark hair dancing around her face in the light breeze. She appeared reasonably tall, barely under six foot by his reckoning, the only weapon she seemed to possess on her person was a dagger at her waist. Storm guessed the garden was being observed by several hidden troops loyal only to her, their eyes wary for any sudden movements that he might make, and which would most likely result in him suffering the fate of a well placed arrow in the back. Storm was surprised at her appearance, for she seemed somewhat shy and timid, not the strong revolutionary he expected. However, it was to she he would be answering to shortly, of that he had no doubt. Whether she was personally courageous enough to stand against her father did not matter, people like Cairn and Sotera would make sure she would not face the King alone.

"Welcome to Winterlending, Storm of Karlaband," she smiled, years of elocution-training evident in her voice. "Though I doubt this city is as splendid as the old capital was in its prime before the flood. 'City of Dreams' they called old Karlaband, now it is a dilapidated twin of this City of Nightmares," she sighed. "But I hope all that will change when my father is off the throne."

"I wish you luck in your crusade."

"Surely you will stay and fight alongside me?" she said. "Your name carries much weight."

"I regret I have business elsewhere with a man who could pose a far greater threat to this land than your father ever could."

She smiled in reply. "You seek Hemlock," she said, and he nodded. "Surely you realise I can offer you an army to hunt for the madman once I am Queen?"

"The fight is between Hemlock and I, it is the way it was meant to be," Storm declared. "Yet you are right, I should stay for the revolution. I owe you that much."

She smiled and suddenly embraced him, surprising him. She let go and appeared somewhat embarrassed, and so he quickly changed the subject back to politics.

"You will have a difficult job getting the people to accept another monarch, especially the first Queen to rule this land," he declared, and she nodded. "Perhaps it might be wiser to relinquish the throne back to the military and the then assisting Temple of the Dragon, like it was in my time?"

"Do not be so quick to praise the extinct Temple of the Dragon," she abruptly growled. "They put hundreds of innocent people to the sword for questioning their role in our society and the great influence they used to have in virtually every aspect of our lives," she said, much to his surprise. "They liked to see themselves as the almighty saviours of our souls, but in reality they were just a different breed of evil to the other temple."

"I had no idea that kind of corruption took place," Storm said. "Politics was never my strong point."

"It was never mine either," Sobranie announced, solemnly. "Until I realised what my father was doing to his subjects."

The soldier returned at that moment and informed them the King wished to see his new champion immediately.

Storm smiled. "I will see you directly afterwards?"

She nodded. "Be wary of my father," she said. "Don't underestimate him, too many others have, and paid the ultimate price."

They returned to the palace as the guard told Storm the King was in one of his many foul, possibly homicidal moods. Storm grinned in amusement, after what he had gone through over the last few days, dealing with this fat fool was quite trivial. However, he heeded Sobranie's warning, and placed one hand on the hilt of his sword. The soldier escorted him into the familiar giant throne room and left the swordsman alone to the mercy of the monarch.

"I've come for the information."

King Winterlending the fifth did not reply. He instead stared down at the champion in disgust and anger. But Storm was not going to be intimidated by this and glared back at him in defiance.

"The man you seek is on Aren Island," the King said. "Now, get out!"

Storm began to head back for the door when the monarch called out. "What about the prize money for The Game?"

"I'll be polite and not tell you where to shove that blood-money," Storm snapped in reply, moments before he slammed the door behind him.

Storm made his way to the garden, happy in the knowledge that it was doubtful he would ever gaze upon the bulbous face of the King again. Sobranie was waiting there for him, chatting to the Deputy Chief of Guards. It seemed the princess's influence was far reaching, even to the ears of men closest to her father. As he approached, the soldier departed after saluting her and disappeared back into the palace.

"How fared your conversation with my father?"

"It was brief," Storm replied. "And utterly unpleasant."

"The King has a habit of making all discussions distasteful," she said. "It is his speciality," She grasped hold of the sleeve of his jerkin and drew him out of view of the palace. "I have given orders that the final preparations for the revolution be undertaken, it will now be only a matter of days before the battle commences," she said. "However, before that happens, I have a special task which you can do to further those plans."

"I am at your disposal," he stated, and bowed. "I have no immediate designs other than my search for Hemlock, and you are after all soon to be Queen."

She smiled. "You need not be the obedient servant to my wishes, Storm of Karlaband. I can give no orders to a living legend, only make requests," she said softly. "I require your assistance in receiving the sympathy of the town Nez; a settlement reluctant to offer any of its able population to the uprising. The towns that do offer support to our cause are few, quite possibly too few to win us the war, but they number all we could acquire without alerting the spies of my father. So, you see our need is great," she declared. "I can only afford to give you an escort of twenty soldiers to guard your path to the settlement, convincing the populace of the urgency of their participation in the revolution will fall on you."

"Surely they must realise riding the land of the King can only be a benefit to their lives?"

"The common man wants freedom," Sobranie said. "But only if someone else fights and dies acquiring it for him."

"I know nothing of rhetoric, how can I possibly persuade a crowd of strangers to follow my lead into a war which could well mean the end of their lives?"

She smiled. "I have confidence in your hidden talents, they have kept you alive these last three centuries," she replied. "Go now, for I must go into hiding, far from this city. My father has regularly threatened me with a life of solitude in one of the seven towers, he will not hesitate in carrying out that promise once he hears of the uprising," she whispered. "By the time you return from Nez, we will have amassed our army deep within Pelerius forest. You can meet us there before we march on the capital."

"Well, this means I must bid you good-day, your majesty," Storm said, as she called a guard and give him her orders for the escort to be prepared. However, before Storm left with the soldier, he turned once more to her. "Though I dare say our paths will cross again in more pleasant times."

The princess Sobranie watched him walk back up the garden, her eyes never leaving him until he had vanished into the depths of the palace. "I sure hope so," she whispered. "Otherwise I firmly believe we will not meet again, except before the royal executioner."

CHAPTER TWENTY-SIX

Nearly three days had passed since the company had left behind the capital and ventured deep into the wilderness, before they finally sighted the harbour-town Nez. The journey was uneventful, the bandits who frequently attacked passing travellers had obviously heard the revolution was near and soldiers from all over would be hurrying to reach Winterlending City, thus the countryside would be crowded with battle-hungry guards, only too happy to relieve some of that tension on wandering robbers stupid enough to assault them. Storm smiled, he guessed Sobranie knew this, yet still insisted on the escort, if not to protect his life, then to add weight and some panache to his claim that he was indeed the swordsman who had fought Hemlock almost three hundred years ago.

The gates to the settlement were heavily guarded as one might expect with talk of war in the air, but they did not bar the company's path. The emblem of the Imperial Guard still counted, no matter who commanded them. Bored citizens gathered around the group, eager to hear any news of the impending revolution. The Captain of the company drew up alongside Storm and announced to the crowd that they should assemble the populace into the town-centre forthwith. They responded by staring at the soldiers in confusion, yet nevertheless quickly left their presence to inform curious relatives and neighbours of this strange order.

Within the hour, the four alleys which intersected at the town-centre were filled to capacity with excited people, eager to learn the reasons for such an urgent meeting. Their patience and attendance was rewarded as Storm moved beyond the band of troops and into the centre, drawing alongside the fountain, the only sounds to be heard in the tension-filled silence was the steady flow of running water hitting stone. Women reached down for small children, fearful for their safety as the crowd surged forward as Storm let his gaze fall on the three thousand-plus assembly. Their curious faces stared up at him in puzzlement and watched him catch his breath in nervousness.

"Citizens of Nez," Storm began, his fingers playing with the reins. "Your day of liberation is at hand," he roared, expecting some response of approval, but the gathering gazed at him in confusion; seemingly not comprehending his words, or realising his true identity. "I am Storm who fought Hemlock at the citadel, and I am here to bring you news of the uprising."

"How do we know you're not a fraud; a spy sent by the King to fool us?" a man not twelve feet from Storm shouted, and several others around him cheered in agreement. "We've heard vague rumours of Hemlock returning, yet that does not mean his hunter has returned also."

Storm watched them grumble amongst themselves and snarled in anger. "If it's proof you want, then I shall give it," he roared and with that, drew forth his blade. "Behold, the sword of Kassier from Karlaband, the Master-Smith," Storm leapt from his horse as several members of the crowd murmured 'fake' as he approached the fountain.

They watched on in curiosity and then in astonishment as Storm leaned over the basin of the fountain and struck the top of the waterspout. There was a great gush of water from the tip of the fountain as the three-inch stone top was slashed cleanly off, only to land before the feet of the amazed onlookers. They glanced at the sword, expecting it to be broken, but not a single scratch adorned the blade. Storm climbed up onto the rim of the basin which was quickly filling due to the great amount of water flowing freely from the shattered spout. He raised high the sword as the soldiers behind him gazed on in fascination, unwilling up to this point to believe that a living legend stood before them.

"March with me and the future Queen into battle," Storm screamed, "and I will give you a victory you can tell your grandchildren."

The Captain glanced at his number-one in speechless wonderment as the town of Nez roared in excitement and surged towards Storm, eager to touch him. The Lieutenant stared back at his superior in likewise awe, as several large men lifted the swordsman up onto their shoulders and carried him into the midst of the throng, so their wives and children might meet a legend who would grant glory to their town and finally rid their land of two madmen.

First light on the fifth day since Sobranie had sent Storm on his errant, did she finally see his return, though not to the capital city, but to the cover of Pelerius forest. It was here she had amassed her makeshift army of soldiers and serfs. It was here she would lay the final plans for her father's long-awaited abdication.

Cairn approached her and smiled. Storm had not come alone; he dragged behind him a giant rabble of lightly-armed farmers and peasants, being directed by a few dozen troops. Sotera groaned at the sight, training men like these whose only fighting experience was drunken brawls would take a lifetime, and all they had was a few days. However, such people were not alone. The majority of their army was composed of such frustrating inexperience. But these men were willing to fight and if necessary, die so their children might be free and not live a life of hunger under King Winterlending. They expected some measure of respect, and she would make sure they got it, and perhaps even save their lives with what combat-knowledge she could bestow.

Storm approached the cover of the forest and smiled at Cairn, glad to see the master-warrior had survived The Game on Cracas. Sobranie quickly walked towards him and embraced the swordsman, much to the surprise of both Cairn and Sotera. The princess led Storm deep into the wilderness until they arrived at a large clearing. Here a makeshift camp adorned the open forest floor, yet hidden from the nearby town Ledge; a settlement very much loyal to the King.

Storm noticed several shield-maidens and soldiers stood near the future Queen, nervous for her safety. "Is it wise making camp so close to Ledge?" he asked, as two troops brought forward a table and laid out a map of the land.

"My father would not suspect I would plan his downfall so close to one of the few towns still loyal to him," she replied, and directed him towards the map. Cairn, Sotera and several high-ranking soldiers gathered around the table, including the Deputy Chief of Guards. "We have an army of just over eight thousand troops and untrained peasants, while the King boasts a legion of nearly nine thousand guards. Most of his army will be heavily-armed and trained. However, we have been fortunate in that our situation could be a lot worse," Sobranie added. "The majority of the garrison at Karlaband is on training-exercises in The Frozen Wastes, and the northern towns are too far to send help in time to assist him."

"What about King Aliped on Cracas?" interjected Storm. "Could he not send assistance to your uprising? It would after all be in his best interests, since the hatred he has for his brother is great."

"I do not trust my beloved uncle," she said. "Although we could do with his soldiers, I fear the price for such an alliance would be too high. He is sure to pose a problem once I become Queen, just as he is a bane in the side of my father."

"We will have to manage with what we have," Cairn said. "I just hope it is enough."

"We have no choice, it is too late to change minds," Sotera declared. "Further delays will only strengthen the King's position and weaken ours, we have to strike while the fat bastard is relatively vulnerable."

Sobranie smiled at her remark, before bringing their senses back to the map. "We should have the element of surprise by attacking at night, and a special squad of guards inside the city have been given explicit instructions to cause confusion by means of mass arson, so the King might not realise we are laying siege to the capital before it is too late," she added. "However, it would be unwise to underestimate my father, he knows we are coming and the city will be crawling with troops."

Sotera took over to discuss the finer points of battle-strategy with the men as Sobranie snatched hold of Storm's sleeve and dragged him away from the table. Cairn watched them leave and smiled, it was about time his friend opened his heart to another woman, perhaps it might even cool his rage and lessen his obsession for vengeance.

She led him deeper into the forest beyond sight of the camp after dismissing her guardians. "You're not staying for the battle, are you?" Sobranie said, turning to face him.

"My search must continue," he retorted. "The men I led here will just as easily follow you as they would me. But I will return to see your coronation."

"I suppose you must have some motive to return."

"I have other reasons," Storm smiled.

She frowned in feigned puzzlement and did not try to stop him as he held her face in both hands and bending his head, lightly kissed her. She returned the gift, only more passionately as her arms wrapped themselves around his neck and his arms encircled her. They remained like that for several moments, tasting each other, until they finally broke the embrace.

She stared fixedly at him. "What about Nereid?"

"I think my late wife would approve," he smiled. "I have spent nearly three centuries mourning her loss, I don't intend spending the rest of my life in solitude."

"Then you can give up your desire for revenge?" Sobranie added excitedly.

"I still have a duty to avenge her and the friends I have lost to the maniac," Storm replied. "I will only be able to rest when my sword has put an end to him."

She lowered her gaze in despair, knowing she could not change his mind and free him of his obsession. Sobranie glanced over his shoulder and cursed under her breath. Soldiers were nearby, scouring the forest, worried for her safety. One of the guards spotted them and approached, and she quickly gave orders for a horse to be fetched. They made their way back to the camp and Storm shook both the hands of Sotera and Cairn, before approaching the steed.

The princess drew alongside him and grabbed hold of his jerkin. "You will return?" she stuttered.

"You have my word," he whispered before kissing her cheek, and mounted the horse.

The future Queen watched him guide the beast out of the clearing and into the depths of the forest, heading south for the coast and Aren Island. She remained motionless for some moments after he had left, staring at the trees, before turning her attention back to the camp where waited her loyal subjects, eager to fight and place her on a throne she wasn't sure she really wanted anymore.

PART THREE

CHAPTER TWENTY-SEVEN

Lights flickered into life all over the city, as the last rays of the day disappeared over the horizon on the capital city Winterlending, focal-point of the civilised world. Sentries strolled methodically around the battlements surrounding the settlement, sighing in the silence, frustrated from fatigue and boredom. The city-crier abruptly roared into the night the approach of the third hour before dawn, and the soldiers groaned, annoyed at the length of their watch. The guards, burdened with the mindless task of perpetual monotonous walking, did not notice the shadows dart amongst the alleys and silently break into houses that crossed their path, only to exit moments later, blood dripping from their daggers. The soldiers were unaware that friends and relatives were being murdered in their sleep, their military-service to the King had ended. When the assassins realised they could not kill any more troops in safety, they took to throwing lit torches into nearby houses, most especially those buildings that lined the inside of the battlements, hoping the heat of the flaming dwellings might cause cracks in the giant walls. The guards may not have noticed the assassins' murders, but their other handy-work was clearly visible. Alarm bells quickly began to ring throughout the city, waking those soldiers that had escaped the assassins' blades. However, by the time they became organised, the majority of the houses were either partially or completely being devoured by flames.

Terrified citizens, realising their homes were ablaze and crumbling around them, fled into the already crowded streets, blocking access for troops to reach the battlements. Half-dressed guards, knowing with certain fear that the promised rebellion was upon them, quickly strapped on blades and reported to their brigades. Despite the assassins' deadly handy-work, the army of the King swiftly and efficiently mobilised themselves and prepared for battle. Barely five hundred metres away in the darkness of the wilderness lay the amassed army of the princess Sobranie, her Lieutenants Cairn, Sotera and the Deputy Chief of Guards at her side, whispering advice.

"It appears your plan was successful," Sobranie smiled to Cairn, "your chosen troops have caused much disarray."

"Unfortunately not enough to grant us easy access to the capital, your majesty," the Commander replied sharply. "But perhaps they will have inflicted a sore wound in the over-confidence of your father," he added, betraying a sneer.

King Winterlending the fifth was less than pleased to be awoken at such an early hour and even less cheerful at the news that his estranged daughter was advancing on the city-gates, heralding the revolution and his death.

However, despite this burden on his conscience, he was swift to locate the arsons and assassins within the city-walls and even quicker to hang them from the battlements, their legs dangling feverishly in the darkness, acting as an eerie beacon for the approaching army.

Cairn drew near a group of thirty men and whispered sharp orders. They responded by revealing several wooden-ladders and followed closely by dozens of armed peasants and soldiers, advanced on the city-walls. Guards on the battlements were however quick to notice this attempted intrusion and reacted by firing arrows and large stones on their vulnerable victims.

Despite their numerous losses, several of the intruders finally managed to place the ladders against the city-walls and made the perilous journey up and onto the battlements. They were met with heavy resistance, the pitch-forks of the peasants little defence against the swords and axes of the guards of the King. Cairn cursed as the farmers were quickly eliminated and ordered fifty archers from his own barracks at Tomilusk to the front where they proceeded to even the odds by picking off the over-confident city-soldiers. Veterans from the town Nez scrambled up the ladders and using their enormous round shields in front of them ran into the guards. The slender path of the battlements measured barely four feet across, and the soldiers of the capital had to either retreat or risk losing their balance and fall the thirty feet into the courtyard below. This action bought precious time for the veterans' companions on the ground to follow them onto the battlements.

"I am tired of being a motionless witness to my men's destruction," Cairn declared aloud. "It is time to redden my spear with the blood of the King," he added, spurring his horse into action and headed for the capital-walls.

Sotera cried out after him, fearing her fiancé's rash behaviour, but knew however that it was hopeless to attempt to change his courageous though reckless nature.

The master-warrior approached one of the ladders and scrambling up, soon found himself in the centre of the revolution. Around him lay the battered bodies of peasants and soldiers, their differences now meaningless as their blood mingled. Cairn watched his comrades battle hopelessly against overwhelming odds and realised the capital was too well defended to fall to the invading army of the princess. Their only hope was to distract the majority of the City-Guards long enough to gain entry to the palace of the King and finally dispose of the tyrant. Cairn hoped the military's loyalty would change and they would accept the princess as the next ruling monarch once the King had fallen under the sword, otherwise this civil war promised to be both brief and for Sobranie and her supporters, ultimately tragic. Losses on the side of the princess on the battlements were quickly replaced by eager troops waiting outside the city-walls. However, they were being dispatched within moments of reaching the courtyard inside with little or no casualties to the King's army.

Sobranie groaned in both frustration and despair and leaned over to her Lieutenants, the Deputy Chief of Guards and the Commander of the shield-maidens Sotera from the town Abc. "Our losses are becoming too great, we cannot maintain this method of intrusion into the capital," the princess sighed.

"I suggest it is time to dispatch the battering-ram, your highness," the Deputy announced, "it may have some success now that your father's troops have their hands full with our men on the battlements."

Sotera nodded in agreement. "It is worth a try, your majesty," the shield-maiden added, "however, true success lies with the death of the King. I advise sending a small party of your elite with Cairn to infiltrate the palace and dispose of your father, his severed head hanging from the capital-gates will destroy the morale of the City-Guards and end this revolution with the minimum of bloodshed."

The princess nodded in approval of both plans while Sotera sighed in anxiety. Although it was both Cairn's and her idea and the best course of action, it was still a highly dangerous mission for her future husband to undertake. But she was confident of his abilities and his almost-miraculous luck in surviving battles that would kill other men. Nevertheless, this didn't make her fear of his safety any the less. Cairn awaited the arrival of his reinforcements and amused himself in the meantime by randomly killing guards of the King in the courtyard below with his spear, the magical weapon returning at his command after each impaling.

The elite soldiers from Tomilusk which Sotera had promised approached and announced their presence to their Commander on the battlements as the city-gates suddenly started to shudder with the impact of the battering-ram. Cairn greeted the twenty-strong force from his barracks and began to explain the straight-forward though dangerous plan of travel to the palace of King Winterlending the fifth. Keeping to the back-alleys, they hoped to evade the majority of the City-Guards who were already too occupied with the simultaneous attacks on the battlements and the gates to be bothered with such a small force. They would then make their way to the palace of the King, located in the very centre of the capital of the civilised world and extract justice on the tyrant within, finally bringing peace to a country which has known only strife for two centuries at the hands of the Winterlending sons. The Commander briefly embraced each of the twenty men, having served with them for many years and knowing few if any would survive the perilous mission, before they made their way into the courtyard below.

Cairn knew the journey from the yard to the relative sanctuary of the narrow alleys that criss-crossed the city would be the most hazardous part of the mission, bar gaining entry to the palace itself. Upon entering the courtyard, they were instantly confronted by a dozen armoured soldiers, intent on prohibiting further access to the city.

Several men on either side recognised each other, having trained together as brothers under the same flag of the monarchy, but now possessing opposing ideals. Past friendships would not hinder their actions or cause them for a moment to contradict their loyalties.

Cairn let out a laugh and his men responded by rushing into them. The battle that followed was short and furious. The master-warrior lost eight of his twenty men before the dozen soldiers of the King lay dead. They wasted no time, for a further two dozen guards ran to intercept them, eager to extract revenge for fallen comrades.

The back-alleys were close and they lost only another two men to arrows before reaching the sanctuary of the darkness. The guards however were quick to follow, failure under the King was not an option. They would rather face a relatively swift death at the hands of their enemies than the long torturous fate the monarch had planned for them.

Cairn cursed as their pursuers advanced, knowing they would not stop for anything. A further two of his men began to lag behind and the City-Guards were quick to dispatch them, losing only a few seconds to carry out the deed, before continuing the chase. The Commander knew their only chance of survival was to reach the palace and upon gaining entry, bolt the giant double-doors behind them, locking out the soldiers for at least a while. However, gaining access to the enormous building would not be easy, for it was sure to be heavily-defended. The City-Guards began to cry out in excitement as they closed on their prey, each one eager for the much sought-after prize of Cairn's spear. They hoped the King would be satisfied with the head of his traitorous former champion and not request the possession of the magical weapon.

Cairn for the first time in his life began to fear for his safety. Not even his spear or great swordsmanship would defend him for long against such overwhelming forces. However, he cried out in relief as they neared the end of the alley and the palace of King Winterlending came into sight. His joy was short-lived though when he saw their greeting-party which stood watch outside the doors of the building. Ten heavily-armed soldiers whom Cairn recognised as a detachment of the King's own personal bodyguard instantly spotted them and moved to intercept. Without stopping, Cairn let fly his spear and one of the sentinels was swept off his feet with a scream. The weapon returned to its owner, leaving its victim bleeding in the street, his cries for mercy going unanswered. The soldiers did not seem to notice the predicament of one of their own, their primary concern was the safety of the King; casualties were meaningless.

Cairn and his small party reached the end of the back-alley as the sentinels from the palace slowed and drew their blades. The master-warrior and his men however did not slow down but instead swept into the guards who were astonished by Cairn's courage and perhaps recklessness. The sentinels fell, but not before claiming a further five men from the Commander's group. The City-Guards from the alley behind them were now quite close and an arrow in the back removed yet another man from Cairn's already fast-diminishing brigade. The path to the palace though was now clear of any visible obstructions, and Cairn immediately with his remaining men made for the giant doors.

To their surprise and relief they found it was not locked and entered with much haste as the soldiers closed on them. Grabbing any available pieces of furniture, they quickly stacked them up against the double-doors. The palace seemed to be devoid of life and Cairn feared the King was not present, but rather safely hidden elsewhere. However, years of serving under the tyrant's rule convinced him of the King's arrogance and over-confidence. He believed he was invincible and none would dare confront or challenge him.

The Commander and his four-man squad made their way to the throne-room. They passed by luxury that made his soldiers gasp for they were used to purely a life of humble poverty. They entered the enormous throne-chamber and surrounded by his advisers was the fat monarch, comfortably sipping wine and laughing at the news of his daughter's approaching defeat.

King Winterlending glared as his former champion walked towards the throne. "So my friend, it has come to this," King Banock roared in anger, "I personally promoted you to a high rank beyond your young years, and you repay me with treachery!"

Cairn laughed in reply. "You forced me to compete in The Game each year to retain the prize, risking my life for your amusement," the Commander growled as he drew closer to the monarch. "But I am here to finally bestow justice on our battered land and place a Queen of fairness and honesty on the throne."

The King burst into laughter. "You entrust the country to my naïve daughter?" Banock said. "She is as without intelligence as she is lacking in experience, you will bring the world to its knees."

"You have done worse," Cairn declared, "she will learn from your mistakes and create a better future for all which you could never provide."

"I will see you in hell, Commander!" the King screamed and pushing aside his advisers, drew his sword and began to rise off the throne. However, the fat tyrant never did leave the seat.

Cairn raised high his spear and let fly the weapon. "It is likely I will meet you there, Banock, but you will be there first," the Commander roared as the spear struck the King in the stomach and exiting his back, punctured the seat behind and pinned him to the throne.

The monarch began to splutter blood onto his giant stomach as his advisers crowded around, not believing with their own eyes that their ruler was dying.

Cairn drew alongside one of his men. "Remove his head and throw it into the street, it is time to end this war," the Commander ordered and left the chamber.

Outside the battle continued, yet through the noise Cairn still heard the final scream of the monarch behind him as his soldier severed the King's skull from his shoulders. The man-at-arms returned a few moments later with the Commander's spear and the head of the former ruler, leaving a trail of blood in his wake. Cairn reclaimed his weapon as the doors of the palace were pushed in by sheer force of bodies as the soldiers from the alley poured into the building. However, they halted upon seeing the fate of their leader and all hostile intent within them vanished. The City-Guards did not hinder the soldier before them, but rather escorted him outside as he held the King's head high for all to see. The effect on the populace was both amazing and instantaneous. Upon witnessing the death of their King, the majority of the soldiers ceased to fight and began to welcome in the army of the princess. Any remaining guards still loyal to Banock were killed within minutes. Sobranie entered her capital city and was received by cheering crowds, eager for her coronation. The civil war and revolution were over. Cairn watched all this with a sense of apathy, as his mind now turned to thoughts of Storm. He feared his friend was facing a far greater and deadlier threat than any the former King could have unleashed.

CHAPTER TWENTY-EIGHT

It was the increasing shudders from the mountain above him that broke Hemlock's concentration and forced him to cease his furious studying. He had committed the majority of Agouti's library to memory, but now feared time had run out and he would never be able to finish the task. Cracks began to appear in the walls of the windowless chamber and he knew with dire certainty that the mountain's life was coming to an end. The unstable volcano that frequently acted as a lighthouse for passing trawlers was about to darken the sky.

Hemlock in panic grabbed hold of several of the most important magical volumes, and only hesitating momentarily to snatch a black-hooded robe off the former Arch-Mage's chair, ran for the entrance to the tunnel. The ceiling of the chamber began to collapse and Hemlock sighed in annoyance as the library was buried forever. He emerged on the mountainside to find a stream of lava already starting to flow down the volcano towards him. Dense black smoke and ash quickly began to cover the island and block the sun from view.

Hemlock made his way to the coast and was sent to his knees by a massive shake that ripped through the isle, creating crevices in the ground around him. The ferryman who earlier deposited the warlock on the small island was nowhere to be seen and Hemlock feared his plans for conquest were about to end here on this miserable isle.

In growing panic, he searched the few grimoires he saved from the Arch-Mage's extensive library for a spell which might ensure his escape from the dying island. Despair began to fill his mind however as the particular incantation he required eluded him.

The warlock's attention was drawn suddenly to the mountain towering above him which dramatically increased its deep rumblings, and Hemlock knew he had mere minutes to live as the volcano was about to finally explode and probably devour the entire island. He started to laugh at the absurdity of the notion that after all he had seen and lived through that he was going to meet his end here on this small barren isle.

Hemlock gazed skywards and watched the sun barely filter through the growing thick smoke and awaited the final shudder of the mountain, when something caught his attention. Breaking through the dark clouds was a long golden streak which as it drew nearer the island, Hemlock recognised the shape as a large Golden-Dragon. The necromancer sighed, it appeared he was going to suffer the fate of being devoured by a wandering dragon before the volcano had a chance to consume him.

However, the magical beast slowed and to Hemlock's amazement, landed on the small beach not thirty feet from where he stood. Its piercing cat-like eyes gazed fixedly at him and its scaly-head turned and pointed at its back as if requesting the warlock should mount him. The mountain's shudders now became constant and Hemlock feared the choice had been made for him. Snatching up the half-dozen grimoires, he climbed up the dragon's back and wrapped his legs around its neck. The beast reared up and spread its wings. The reptile glanced once more at the warlock before taking flight and left the dying island behind.

Hemlock looked back and watched as lava consumed the beach where he had previously stood and entered the sea, steam rising to greet the black smoke and ash. The dragon made for the mainland in the direction of the coastal-town Nez.

As they travelled north-east, Hemlock began to wonder why the dragon like all magical reptiles who despised humans should save him. He could only surmise that since he once held the sword of the demon Proteus who killed the father of dragons, the beasts might very well look on him as a master. Golden-Dragons were widely regarded as the most vicious and intelligent of all the reptiles, and Hemlock figured if one should serve him, then perhaps all the lesser dragons might also.

One dragon would be equal to a hundred armed troops, if he commanded all the magical reptiles in the land, he would have the equivalent of a large and extremely deadly army. Hemlock smiled, with those beasts under his control and the vast knowledge he had acquired from Agouti's library, he was sure nothing could possibly stop him from claiming the throne.

Storm had regrets about missing the opportunity to partake in the revolution and fight alongside Cairn and Sobranie, but his quest for Hemlock took precedence. He knew the war would succeed in his absence and Hemlock was a greater threat even if the King survived.

He made his way to the town Nez that was loyal to the princess to find transport to Aren Island. Storm journeyed up a small hill overlooking the town and the coast and stopped to admire the magnificent view. The whole world seemed to be before him, the great ocean stretching out into blue infinity. Trawlers rang out as they approached the pier while fishermen stood idle at the harbour awaiting their arrival, life here at the coast was free of the frantic activity that was so prominent in the capital.

Storm watched all this with some regret. Memories of his former life as a sailor came flooding back, the tranquil calm of the open sea and the gentle sounds of the waves crashing against his boat. He could almost picture himself back there with Nereid at his side, together singing some old song they had heard years before. Storm clenched his fists in silent rage, and cursed the man responsible for robbing him of that peaceful life and the chance for a family. He vowed Hemlock would die on his knees screaming in agony before Storm would feel any satisfaction that his wife had been adequately avenged.

His thoughts of vengeance were broken however by a mighty explosion on the horizon. A gush of orange flame and smoke spurted into the sky as the volcano on Aren Island unleashed its awesome fury. Fishermen and children began to crowd around the harbour, eager to catch a glimpse of this once-in-a-lifetime spectacle. Boats raced for shore, fearing a tidal wave as the explosion ripped apart the tiny isle. As the populace of Nez now started to run for cover, their excitement rapidly turning to blind terror, Storm could only watch on in speechless astonishment and anguish. It appeared nature had robbed him of his revenge, no man could have survived such fiery devastation. Storm began to turn away in dismay, when something caught his eye. Swooping down out of the dark clouds and across the mainland was a massive dragon, its spiny-tail waving in the sky. As the swordsman watched in fascination and a growing sense of joy, a distinct shape of a rider astride the beast came into view. Storm observed their course as they proceeded north-east towards the capital. He knew it was unlikely that Hemlock had intentions of directly attacking the city Winterlending in such fashion as a giant army was currently amassed there and not even a powerful creature like a Golden-Dragon would protect him for long against such a force. Storm figured he would continue further up the country, a destination beyond his reach and for the moment not of his knowledge. On horseback, he would not be able to follow for long for the reptile could fly at such a great speed that Storm would soon lose sight of his prey. Nevertheless, the swordsman decided to pursue, there was nothing else to be learned here. Storm turned his beast towards the path of the dragon and followed, as a fifty-foot wave of water rushed in for the coast, the population of the town Nez frantically bolting windows and doors to offer some minor protection against the approaching tsunami.

Hemlock gripped tightly onto his dangerous method of transport in nervousness, the world below appearing distant. He passed over hills and valleys in a few moments that would take days by foot. Farmers tending their fields and livestock began to run in fear, amazed to see a dragon this far south and away from home.

The warlock continued north-east, bypassing the capital until they came upon a range of mountains. Surrounded by hills was the town Ferulas, the population of this small district isolated and virtually cut-off from their neighbours. They considered themselves self-sufficient and not requiring the outside help or interference of the monarchy, the mountains that encircled their town they believed giving them both privacy and safety. They never pondered on the possibility of attack from the air.

Hemlock smiled, it almost seemed the reptile read his mind as it commenced its assault upon the defenceless region. The town's sixty-year peace was shattered as the dragon swooped down, its rider clinging on for dear life. Fireball upon fireball descended on Ferulas, the heat and flames obliterating several houses at once, though the beast avoided attacking the very centre of the town where resided the castle of the Alderman.

Arrows were no defence against the dragon, the slender shafts bouncing harmlessly off its tough skin. The majority of the population which survived the initial assaults fled into the surrounding mountains, where they would later decide to head for the capital and report the destruction of their homes. Burning houses prevented twenty of the populace from leaving their dying town, their exit blocked by overwhelming heat. They gazed fixedly in abject fear as the reptile began its descent and landed in the centre of Ferulas, adjacent to the residence of the now dead Alderman.

Once safely back on solid ground, Hemlock ordered the twenty remaining people to the castle, where later after the flames had died down, they could commence clearing the charred rubble of their former homes. They could do nothing, but comply. They were too terrified to protest or find the courage to kill their self-appointed dictator. Later they would have wished to have at least tried and died like men, instead of living like slaves.

The warlock approached the dragon that had saved his life and provided him with a new base of operations from where he could plan the downfall of the monarchy. The magical beast reared up its scaly-head and glanced skywards, and Hemlock followed its gaze, letting out a long laugh. From the north-west appeared tiny specks on the horizon that could only be dozens of dragons. As they drew nearer, the warlock could make out various distinct species of flying reptiles. It seemed his theory was correct, he at last had an invincible army.

Storm followed his prey as best he could, but the dragon and its elusive rider moved too swiftly and he let out a scream of curses as Hemlock and the reptile disappeared from view. He watched the warlock vanish in frustration before dismounting, for his horse was close to collapse from exhaustion. Storm began to kick the ground in anger, sending clumps of grass and earth into the air. He knew he did not have any choice but to now return to the capital and seek information concerning Hemlock's destination. Gossip and rumour would run through Winterlending like wildfire, for the warlock was sure to cause much devastation wherever he landed. Storm prayed the revolution had been successful, otherwise his stay in the capital promised to be both brief and unpleasant, for the King was now sure to know of his involvement in the uprising.

CHAPTER TWENTY-NINE

It was the sickening smell of death that hit Storm first, then he caught sight of the heaps of bodies which littered the outside of the city-gates. Two hundred metres from the capital lay a giant open pit where dozens of soldiers were depositing their fallen brethren. Women and young children knelt at the edge, crying into the enormous mass grave, their wailing sending a chill down Storm's spine.

Surrounded by this grief, Storm hurried to the gates and managed a smile as something grabbed his attention. Dangling from the battlements with a rope attached to his hair was the severed head of the King, his face bloodied and marked by stones thrown by passing guards, once loyal but now possessing only hatred for their former ruler. Maggots had already begun to feast, robbing the monarch of his eyes with which he had once counted his vast fortune at the expense of starving farmers. As Storm approached the gates, he was greeted by two soldiers who upon recognising him, escorted him through and directed him towards the palace. He passed by citizens busy sweeping blood from the streets and pavements, eager to return a sense of normality to the capital.

Storm followed the guards into the palace of the former King and through the familiar tapestry-lined corridors until they approached the double-doors which barred entry to the magnificent throne-room. Several heavily-armed soldiers stood impassively outside the decorated doors, seemingly unwilling to allow Storm entrance into the chamber.

The doors behind the City-Guards suddenly began to open and the Commander of Tomilusk emerged from the throne-room. The soldiers immediately saluted and moved, allowing their military-superior access to the corridor.

Cairn however stopped short upon recognising his companion and smiled. "So my friend, it appears you survived the destruction of Aren Island," the warrior declared and briefly embraced Storm, not caring whether their audience minded this tactile sign of affection.

"So did Hemlock," Storm said, "and escaped my wrath by riding north on a dragon."

"Yes," the Commander sighed, "your enemy has been busy, that same reptile razed Ferulas to the ground. We can only hope the library of the Alderman of the town was also destroyed."

Storm gazed at him in confusion, not knowing what he meant by that remark. Cairn placed a finger to his mouth, motioning for his friend to keep silence as they turned and entered the throne-room. Sobranie and Sotera were already inside the enormous chamber, surrounded by advisers discussing agriculture and the rebuilding of houses in the capital city. The leader of the civilised world smiled at their approach, and took her turn to embrace Storm and held onto the swordsman for several minutes.

"I prayed I would see your face again," Sobranie sighed, "I feared Hemlock had taken you from us."

"I didn't survive nearly three centuries to die so easily," Storm said.

"It is a pity you missed my coronation," the Queen declared, "it was necessary to place me on the throne quickly for the land was in turmoil after my father's death."

"I saw his head swinging from the battlements," Storm smiled, "the only thing which will give me greater joy will be to see Hemlock alongside him."

"That may be difficult to achieve," Cairn interjected, "he has amassed dozens of dragons at the ruins of Ferulas and he is sure to be studying the forbidden books in the library."

"What is so dangerous about a few volumes?" Storm asked, perplexed.

Sobranie sighed in anxiety. "Hemlock chose Ferulas for a specific reason, not only as an isolated haven from where he can formulate his plans for the throne, but also he would have learned of the library's existence from knowledge gained on Aren Island," the Queen groaned. "Hidden from the outside world in the castle of the Alderman are seven books of magick, each devoted exclusively to the Seven Swords of the Gods; weapons which are supposedly to have been used at the dawn of time to create the world."

"That is just a myth; a fairy-tale told by parents to their children at bedtime," Storm declared, "I remember my own father telling me that story when I was a child."

"Unfortunately those legends are quite true and have a basis in fact," Cairn said, "the location of the swords have been kept secret and known only to a few to prevent them falling into the wrong hands. With one blade, Hemlock will be a formidable foe, with all seven he will be invincible."

Storm gasped in shock. "If you always knew of their position, then why didn't you send a brigade of soldiers to retrieve or destroy them?"

"The swords display an immense aura associated with their individual properties, giving the appearance of natural disasters where they are located. To bring the blades to the capital would have invited destruction to our door and we could not risk placing them elsewhere for they would have been discovered," Cairn announced. "Destroying the weapons could be hazardous and could very well release an enormous amount of energy, laying waste to an entire region. On the other hand, like the sword of Proteus when it was broken, they might very well fade in strength and disintegrate. Unfortunately, the choice has now been made up for us and we are forced to conclude that the blades must be destroyed."

"Since Hemlock will be searching for the weapons almost immediately, it is imperative that we act fast and reach the swords before him," Sobranie said, "I have here our resident expert on the blades, a brilliant metallurgist by the name of Dryad who will further explain the individual nature of the swords and their location."

Storm watched as an elderly man forced his way through the royal-advisers to reach the swordsman. Dryad was almost completely bald but for a few strands of white hair that criss-crossed his wrinkled skull and he had to squint to see Storm though the swordsman was barely four feet from him. Storm glanced at Cairn in amusement at this odd character before him and the master-warrior smiled in reply. Dryad scratched his head once before beginning to flick through a small black notebook he removed from his jerkin. The Queen tapped the old man on the shoulder in impatience and Dryad responded by briefly glaring at her in annoyance. He finally turned to Storm and handed him the open volume. Scribbled in rough handwriting was the listing of seven swords and their reputed location. Storm recognised the names of towns and other regions as Dryad coughed and began to speak.

"The weapons according to legend were used by ancient mages to teach mankind about nature and using that force for good or evil. I believe they will shatter like any normal fragile blade and hopefully lose their powers quite quickly upon been broken," Dryad said gruffly and pointed to his notebook. "The first of the swords is called Land; a weapon which the owner can use to influence the ground and cause earthquakes," the old man announced and Storm gasped.

Dryad saw his reaction and sneered. "The Land blade is regarded as one of the less powerful of the seven swords, the others are much worse," the metallurgist declared and continued his listing of the weapons. "The second instrument is Fire which can be used to create giant fireballs or sct ablaze entire regions instantly. The next is Water with which the operator can create floods or bring about tidal waves. The fourth is Wind which can be used to control the air and perhaps even cause typhoons or tornadoes. The next blade is Day which has the properties of the sun, therefore the owner can use it to make dawn or dusk happen instantly at will and use that advantage in battle or simply bring about a heatwave which can sap the strength of an army. The sixth sword is Night which has powers over darkness and light," Dryad sighed and paused for breath. "Finally we come to the seventh sword of the gods, the most powerful and awesome weapon ever created, the blade Time," the metallurgist declared as his audience listened in nervousness, while Storm stared at the old man in curiosity, "the instrument Time can be used to cause the element of time to stop or increase at the will of the operator within a large region, and Hemlock will be able to annihilate an entire army instantly by making the men become old almost immediately. This weapon above all others must not fall into the warlock's hands and must be destroyed at all costs."

Sobranie turned to Storm in anxiety. "Hemlock has already killed every mage in the land and the destruction of Aren Island caused a tidal wave which inflicted much devastation and loss of life at the town Nez."

"We attempted hiring an assassin from the guild to infiltrate the ruins of Ferulas, but in vain," Sotera finally spoke, "they refused every high offer, knowing such a mission would be suicide."

Storm scratched his chin in contemplation for several moments before turning to the group. "Since I know Hemlock better than anyone, I therefore volunteer my services to this expedition," the swordsman smiled, knowing this would give him a further opportunity to meet the warlock. "Perhaps Cairn can accompany me on the voyage, his skill and knowledge of the land would be invaluable."

"Sadly that is impossible," the Commander sighed, "my military-expertise is required in the capital to reorganise the army and increase morale, thus preventing a new civil-war."

"We also can only bestow to you a few men as escort," Sotera announced, "a large force travelling north would attract suspicion, and the populace might deduce the nature of the mission and discover the swords, embarrassing the government."

"It appears as usual that I am on my own again," Storm said, grasping the handle of his blade, "but I prefer it that way, I believe it is better I meet Hemlock alone."

"We suspect the warlock will begin his search shortly," the Queen declared, "we have placed spies around Ferulas, they will send constant reports on the necromancer's movements and any visitors he may have."

"Do you predict any newcomers joining his cause?" Storm inquired.

"We believe it is very likely every scum and criminal who might have a grudge against the government will support him, despite his insane nature," Cairn said.

"I fear a new war may soon be upon us," Sobranie sighed in despair, "and it could very well be a campaign that will involve the entire land and leave the population devastated."

"Then it is my duty to prevent that outcome," Storm declared, making for the door and the outside world, as his audience gazed on in anxiety, fearing for his safety in the mission before him. "I will destroy the seven swords and return forthwith, and if I meet Hemlock on my travels, I promise he will find only a cold grave instead of the blades!"

CHAPTER THIRTY

A fresh horse and provisions awaited Storm upon leaving the palace and he was immediately greeted by a ten-man party of soldiers. He noticed the guards appeared nervousness, knowing the mission before them was hazardous and meeting the warlock on the journey was not a thought they wished to dwell on.

Storm opened Dryad's small notebook and observed his barely-legible scribblings. The nearest town from the capital which hid the location of one of the seven swords was Betel. This district that harboured the Night blade was two days journey north-east from Winterlending. Storm hoped he could destroy most of the weapons before the warlock had even begun his search. He knew Hemlock would have to study the library of Ferulas to first establish the reputed location of the swords. However, once the necromancer had that knowledge, he would make fast progress to the regions in question by travelling by dragon.

The Captain of the escort-party drew up alongside the swordsman and requested they should begin the trip. Storm gave his permission and they commenced their journey to Betel to destroy the first of the Seven Swords of the Gods.

The company arrived at the settlement just after noon on the second day of the voyage and observed the strange appearance of the region before them. Betel was a small trading settlement which sold its sole produce of weapons to the capital; blades being their only export for they had virtually no agriculture to speak of and thus required heavy imports of wheat and potatoes. Storm realised the significance of this economy upon sighting the district. The town Betel seemed to be enveloped by a permanent smog; a dense black fog that cloaked the region in a perpetual night. Crops stood no chance of growth in such an environment and only massive support from the government prevented starvation or immigration. Storm, unlike the unfortunate populace of Betel, knew the reason for such bizarre weather. It had to be the power of the Night sword which caused this strange malady.

As the company entered the town, they suddenly left daylight behind and embraced darkness instead. Gazing skywards, Storm could see no stars or other forms of light. The swordsman could barely distinguish the occasional passer-by going about their daily business, the only sounds that of several hammers beating out the shapes of blades.

Storm began to wonder if creatures such as vampires roamed these streets, for such an environment would be paradise for them. But he reckoned such wraiths would be fearful of feeding off a town that produced so many weapons. However, as the group entered deeper into Betel, Storm could make out several figures strolling around the outside of one particular grey building in the darkness. The swordsman sneered in disgust at these parasites of society as the wandering individuals began cheering, hoping to entice the company into the establishment. Storm recognised the house as a brothel, the women making brisk business in a town that suffered from intense depression from living in eternal night.

The swordsman gazed in disdain at these vampires, feeding off the pain and frustration of the weapon-smiths in the town. But he could really not blame their immoral nature, knowing starvation was worse than even what their employment entailed. He watched as these lines of lost women gathered on the dark street-corner, selling their virtues for a few bronze coins; living in a place overshadowed by desolation and despair where perpetually hungry children cry into the night for absent mothers and anonymous fathers.

Storm turned away from the scene and ventured down the main-street towards the residence of the town Alderman. The politician was easy to find and almost seemed to be waiting for the visitors, relaxing out on his front porch while sipping from a bottle of red wine. As they approached, the swordsman noticed the individual was quite drunk and appeared either unwilling, or more likely unable to stand and greet them.

The Alderman gazed up at the horsemen more in annoyance than in curiosity and Storm saw his eyes were bloodshot with alcohol. The swordsman glared at the politician in disgust.

"I will on my return to the capital, request your termination of employment immediately," Storm growled to the Alderman who glanced back in apathy.

"It matters not," the man responded, quite articulate despite his obvious drunken state, "I would rather starve than rule over this nightmare a day longer."

"How long has this darkness afflicted your town?" the Captain of the escort-party inquired.

"As long as I can remember," the Alderman replied, "we would have all left years ago but for the support of the monarchy towards our economy. Even to this day, I still cannot understand why first the King and now the Queen would cater for this miserable town, when it would be far cheaper to let Betel rot."

Storm glanced at the politician in momentary nervousness, fearing the man would discover the true nature of the settlement's distress and embarrass the government. The swordsman was therefore quick to change the subject. "What is the extent of the darkness; where do you believe it to be at its most severe?"

The drunken Alderman gazed at Storm briefly in suspicion before slowly rising to his feet. "Follow me," he declared, "and I will show you a place where no light dare thread."

The politician led the company out of the town and into the surrounding wilderness. Storm could no longer see the trail before him and so requested the guards should dismount and hold hands to keep contact. The swordsman grasped hold of the sleeve of the Alderman as they entered the wasteland. Storm considered it wise to keep conversation going to both avoid being lost and panic the soldiers following behind him.

"I saw no lights in Betel," Storm inquired, "would it not be sensible to keep many lanterns burning?"

"Perhaps," the politician replied, "but not practical. It would be far too expensive to keep torches alight continuously, we reserve the lanterns for the smiths to work."

The Alderman abruptly halted and the company barely avoided colliding into each other in the pitch blackness. Storm knew they had to be close and so with a few polite words of gratitude, dismissed the drunken ruler of Betel. He could not allow the man to witness the discovery of the Night sword and its subsequent destruction. The politician sneered in reply before promptly leaving, the group quickly losing sight of him in the darkness.

Storm waited for several moments to be certain the ruler had truly left before turning to the guards. "Remove the spades and pick a spot."

The soldiers revealed from their backpacks shovels with two-foot wooden handles and set to work, digging in separate areas about three feet apart from each other. Storm removed his own spade and followed suit. After an hour, there seemed to be no sight of the Night sword and the company began to groan in frustration when something caught the Captain's eye. He had dug four feet into the soft earth and saw what appeared to be a piece of metal sticking out from under a large rock. He hailed the rest of the group and Storm came running.

The eleven men gathered at the site as four guards congregated and continued the excavation. The company let out a cheer as a broadsword gradually became revealed. Storm ordered the men to keep a safe distance as he leapt into the small pit. Bending down, the swordsman cautiously touched the strange object. The blade seemed warm and was surprisingly free of rust though the weapon had probably been buried for decades. Storm commanded the company to return to Betel, for it was unwise to risk their safety as he prepared to destroy the Night sword.

The swordsman watched the men leave, holding hands in the darkness as they ventured back to the town. He waited for several minutes before rising to his feet and drawing his own weapon.

Glancing around once in every direction, he heaved his blade and brought it down on the Night sword. There was a resounding clang that seemed to echo throughout the wilderness and Storm gazed down.

At first, the Night instrument appeared unharmed, then Storm saw a crack develop which rapidly spread across the weapon. The ground around him started to shake and the swordsman believed it wiser to remove himself from the pit. He began to make for the safety of Betel and the awaiting company. The earth seemed to take upon the guise of quicksand as the rocks and dirt they had removed from the site slid down into the cavity. There was suddenly an explosion that sent Storm to his stomach, and he turned to see earth and what appeared to be shards of metal being thrown high into the air. The swordsman quickly became enveloped in the debris and a close examination of the pieces around him confirmed that the shards were from the Night blade. The first of the Seven Swords of the Gods had been destroyed.

Once Storm was certain the ground had become stable, he rose to his feet and cautiously approached the open pit. Gazing in, no sign of the Night weapon could be seen and daylight seemed to be returning to the region. Storm could now see the sun filtering through the fading darkness and the town of Betel became distinct in the distance. Already the settlement and surrounding wilderness became crowed as the populace gathered in excitement and disbelief. They could not believe the malady that had plagued their home for decades was finally disappearing from their lives.

The escort of soldiers approached the swordsman, leaving the confused crowd behind and the slaps of gratitude on their backs. Storm considered it wise they depart quickly from the district, knowing the Alderman would offer uncomfortable questions. They mounted their horses and swiftly left the revitalised town of Betel behind as the Captain turned to his superior.

"That was relatively easy," the officer declared, "perhaps the destruction of the other swords might be just as uncomplicated."

"Maybe," Storm echoed, "but I have a feeling the rest of the blades will be more difficult, and Hemlock is sure to begin his search shortly. We cannot allow the warlock to gain possession of even one of the weapons," the swordsman announced as the company left the region and moved west towards Delug and the Water sword. "Yet I believe the blades will elude Hemlock," Storm said firmly, "and I will be there to greet him!"

CHAPTER THIRTY-ONE

The darkness almost hid the passing of eight horsemen into the domain of Ferulas. The dozen spies of the Queen drew back in fear and astonishment as they observed the motion of these visitors towards the castle of the necromancer. Several soldiers began to mount their steeds in nervousness within moments, eager to leave the mountainous region and report back to the capital. Their companions remained transfixed in abject terror and fascination as the mysterious guests ventured into the ruins of the town.

The hooded horsemen approached the blackened gates and entered Ferulas. A large crowd of bandits and mercenaries who had gathered at the invitation of Hemlock moved aside to allow entrance for the dark robed visitors. The strangers dismounted and walked towards the building of the former Alderman. The leader of the group halted momentarily to admire the passing of dozens of dragons above their heads, the roars of the beasts echoing throughout the territory. The man revealed a seven-foot staff of engraved hazel which he used to bang once against the entrance to the castle. The double-doors opened without any visible sign of force and the men entered.

Before the strangers was a long corridor which stretched off into darkness. The dimly-lit hall revealed tapestry-lined walls and velvet-covered chairs shoved up against the pillars. Several doors lay at either side as the men entered and immediately approached the third one on the right, as if sensing the location of the warlock and not requiring exploration of the alternative entrances.

The leader of the hooded strangers pushed in the plain wooden door as his companions followed close behind. Inside the small chamber was a varnished rectangular-table surrounded by a dozen tall chairs. Seated at the head was a lone robed figure engrossed in a black volume, studying the contents to memory. Strewn across the table was a further six books the visitors recognised on the subject of the individual nature of the seven swords.

Hemlock glanced up from the volume in disbelief and rage at this intrusion, not believing the bandits outside would dare risk his wrath. "Who challenges my privacy?" the warlock growled and rose to his feet. "Your deaths will be long and painful for such impertinence."

The leader of the visitors approached the head of the table and said. "Sit down and be quiet, human."

Hemlock glared at the stranger in astonishment, believing the intruder to be either insane or a fool. The sorcerer did not suffer such idiots gladly and thus reached across for his axe. The man removed his hood and Hemlock gasped in amazement. Before him was an elderly dark-elf, his flowing white hair which touched his shoulders in stark contrast to his black skin. His piercing green eyes gazed at the warlock, as if sensing Hemlock's vulgar thoughts. The stranger's companions now also removed their hoods to reveal seven younger dark-elves who approached and pulling out the chairs, calmly sat themselves at the table.

"It's not possible," Hemlock gasped, "all the elves were killed by the Knights Order at the beginning of the Ice Age."

"Not all died in the massacre," the man replied, "a few of us disguised ourselves as humans and lived out a meagre existence amongst our enemies. We are here to extract revenge for our dying race and repay humanity for the deeds committed in Sulphur Mountain."

Hemlock stared at the elf in disbelief. "Who are you?"

The stranger briefly smiled, seemingly pleased at the warlock's ignorance of his identity. "I am Ucein of the High-Council," the man declared and Hemlock took a step back in shock, "I and my brethren are the last of the dark-elves," the visitor announced and leaned back against the edge of the table. "We were in discussion with you before the Ice Age at the Battle of the Temples formulating plans for our mutual benefit, but a swordsman wielding my possession destroyed our cauldron and robbed us of the opportunity to wage a holy war on the humans. I am here to rectify that situation and finally have vengeance for our fallen comrades."

Hemlock stared at the elf in anxiety. "I too am human, what plans do you have for me?"

Ucein glanced back at his companions who smiled in reply before turning to the warlock. "You will live as long as we share the same objectives, betray us and you will suffer an eternity of suffering," the visitor retorted coldly and Hemlock sighed in nervousness. "The fact I escaped your genocide spell for all mages proves my powers, I am the single most powerful sorcerer to have ever lived. I will use my extensive knowledge of magick to gain you victory in the almighty war to come, and establish an empire built on greed, fear and the blood of the innocent."

Hemlock let out a laugh. "What else is an empire built on?"

The company of elves sniggered in reply as their leader sat down at the table. Hemlock fetched a bottle of wine and nine tall glasses and began to pour. Once all had ample drink before them, the warlock too sat and smiled across the table at his new-found friends.

"You spoke of a swordsman in Sulphur Mountain," the thief inquired, "tell me about him, he sounds familiar."

"I remember that bastard clearly," Ucein retorted sharply, "he was of average build and height, possessing a crop of short brown hair and appeared to be in his early thirties."

Hemlock said in reply. "Indeed I know this man," the warlock growled, "he was appointed Chief-Adviser to Commander Hartal at the Battle of the Temples after I had Kassier eliminated, and this swordsman pursues me still, all for the sake of his bitch who I killed long ago in Karlaband."

Ucein and his gang of elves rose to their feet in surprise. "It begins to make sense," the leader of the group replied, "Kassier was the thief who sneaked into Sulphur Mountain and stole my magical sword, and so it seems he passed on the weapon to his apprentice. My other possession was stolen nearly three centuries later by a young soldier who now commands the army of the Queen, a position he could only have assured himself with the help of my magical spear."

"It appears we have common old enemies," Hemlock said, "it is wise we join forces and put all our energies into destroying these two men who have long been a bane on our lives."

The company of dark-elves nodded in agreement and retook their seats at the table. Ucein glanced across and saw the books. "You seek the seven swords," the sorcerer declared, "I know not just of their location, but also the resting-place of the great Shield of Protection; an object forged by the ancient mages to combat the seven blades. It is an instrument which will make you impervious to any weapon; be it sword, arrow, spear or axe created by humans and thus make you invincible."

Hemlock grinned. "I have a feeling this partnership will be of great benefit," he smiled, "I am eager to learn of the dark secrets of magick which you must have studied in Sulphur Mountain."

Ucein turned to the warlock and stared coldly at him, an emotionless expression that momentarily shocked Hemlock. "Any black knowledge you learned on Aren Island could not equal my foul deeds, to study such magick you would have to forfeit your soul and relish suffering. I once raised a King demon from a pit of dark blood and laughed as it spat fiery salvia onto naked human children, the heat and flames robbing them of their clothes and lives, leaving only charred bodies behind; the medium for eternal grieving mothers."

Hemlock gasped in disbelief at such savagery. "It is necessary in my occupation to kill the innocent, but I take no pleasure in the act. I do what sometimes needs to be done, yet I will not unnecessarily inflict grievous pain on my victims."

The assemblage of elves burst into laughter. "You by your actions sentenced thousands to die at the Battle of the Temples, I am certain you would not have committed such a deed if you thought for one moment of the widows of the men back home," Ucein grinned, "and what of the future plans you have for the world? I am sure hundreds of thousands will perish before they will allow you as King to rule over their pitiful lives."

"You mock me," Hemlock snarled.

"You insult yourself," the elf replied firmly, "you should be honest and true to your nature and rejoice in the victory which I promise and the deaths of our common enemies," Ucein declared and snatched hold of his glass, encouraging the group to do likewise, "So let us raise a toast to our partnership," the elf announced and Hemlock once again began to smile, "and forge an empire which will last a thousand years."

CHAPTER THIRTY-TWO

It was approaching dusk when Storm and his escort of soldiers reached Delug in pursuit of the Water sword. At first inspection, the settlement appeared unremarkable and seemingly unharmed by any maladies usually inflicted by the aura of one of the seven swords. It was the Captain however who pointed out the distinct sole form of agriculture which supported the town. Dozens of paddy-fields encircled the region, the populace knee-deep in muddy-water tending the rice. Storm knew such an overabundance of liquid was neither natural nor man-made, it was not possible to divert the flow of the nearby shallow river to produce such a constant flood of water.

The company approached a weary farmer, tired from the day's labour and considering abandoning his employment for the night. A brief conversation with the peasant alerted the group to the extent of the deluge and its likely source. The farmer directed the soldiers to a nearby small pond barely thirty feet in diameter. Storm and his companions traversed through the paddy-fields, taking care not to damage the fragile crops underfoot. Ten minutes journey led them up a mountain which levelled out and into the region surrounding the tiny lake.

The party dismounted and stared fixedly in fascination at the tarn before them. A constant stream flowed from the deep reservoir and down into the town, supporting the rice. What further amazed the group was the solitary tree standing in the very centre of the pond, apparently feeding off the water. Bright orange-coloured flowers budded off the many branches and drooped down to touch the liquid. Storm hoped this bizarre plant was the source of the unnatural tarn and hid the Water blade, otherwise the sword might lie at the bottom of the obviously deep lake.

The swordsman knew that the situation here in this district was drastically different to that of Betel. The settlement they had just left had lived in misery, scratching out a meagre existence in the perpetual darkness. This town actually depended upon the power of the Water sword and perhaps would be hostile to any thoughts of its impending destruction. A swift departure from the area might be advisable once they had discovered the weapon.

Storm discarded his shoes and any excess baggage before cautiously wading into the strange pond. A quick swim brought him to the tree which he proceeded to climb, removing himself from the cold water. Drawing his sword, Storm began to hack at the branches, sending splinters of wood onto the calm surface of the lake. The guards watched carefully for any change in the temperament of the liquid.

Once all the foliage had been severed, Storm moved onto the main part of the bizarre plant, hacking at the stem. The soldiers cringed in sudden fright as their superior's blade abruptly hit metal deep within the shattered tree. A shudder went through the arm of the swordsman and Storm narrowly avoided dropping his weapon, knowing the precious instrument would be lost forever in the dark depths of the tarn.

Gazing down as he balanced himself atop the broken peak of the plant, he could distinguish the glistening handle of a broadsword impaled in the very centre of the tree. Removing the blade would require the total destruction of the plant down as far as the water's edge, but such work was fortunately not necessary.

Storm cleaved further into the stem, revealing fully the handle and part of the actual blade of the Water sword. He was amazed at the nature of the tree, it was as if the wood had grown around the weapon and absorbed the instrument into its being, hiding it from the world and prying eyes.

Storm heaved his sword and struck the Water blade just below the hilt. His blow severed the top of the weapon and with a splash sent it into the pond. The effect was instantaneous. The remainder of the tree burst into flames and Storm fell off in sudden terror. The swordsman resurfaced and swiftly began to make his way ashore as the company watched on in astonishment. Still clutching his own sword, Storm approached the bank and the Captain pulled his superior from the magically-created lake.

The group looked on as the mysterious burning plant sank into the depths of the tarn, sending a milky-white froth to the surface in its wake. Storm smiled at his troops in satisfaction, pleased another weapon of the gods had been destroyed with little danger or effort. A whirlpool began to form in the centre of the pond and like a drain, started to remove the water from the mountain-top. The rivulet which ran down the hill ceased and the farmers tending the fields in the town of Delug gazed up in confusion. This puzzlement quickly turned to rage, and snatching any available weapons, the populace began to voyage up the mountainside towards the company.

The Captain ordered his men to draw their blades and prepare for combat, knowing the peasants would be easy victims for his soldiers and enraged by the population's defiance of the guards of the Queen. Storm however halted this action and instead commanded the troops to mount their steeds, not willing to allow the taking of innocent lives, although knowing the farmers faced starvation as their paddy-fields dried up. He was not prepared to embarrass Sobranie by such meaningless bloodshed and create a reputation for her akin to her late father's.

The Captain glared briefly at his superior in annoyance, but nevertheless ordered his men to their horses. Storm glanced once down the mountain at the approaching army of serfs in regret, fearing he had only destroyed one evil to create another. But he knew Hemlock could not be allowed possession of the Water sword, and thus believed his actions just and true. Storm waved to the screaming peasants below in sympathy, before leaving the region and followed his company north-east towards their next destination and the third weapon of the gods.

*   *   *   *   *

It was the shattering of the door-frame that awoke Hemlock from his peaceful slumber. He was just in the process of curling his feet up to his chest in the comfort of the king-sized bed when the dark-elves entered the magnificent chamber. They halted momentarily to admire the overwhelming luxury of the room where pictures of battles and heroes past adorned the walls and four giant oak-chairs surrounded the bed.

"You had better have a good reason for this intrusion, elf," Hemlock snapped, throwing aside the heavy covers and stretching his legs, "I treasure my sleep, it is the only time my fevered mind is at rest."

Ucein sneered as he approached the bed and sat on one of the enormous chairs. "Perhaps your brain should never be at ease, for mine never is," the black sorcerer said as his colleagues crowded around him, "my dreams were of our common enemy and his destroying of the Water sword."

Hemlock left the warmth of the bed and stood to his feet, seemingly unabashed by his naked state. "You were witness to this action? I would not have believed such visions possible."

The elf scowled in reply. "My powers are far greater than yours," Ucein announced, "nothing magical takes place in this world without my notice, it was a small deed to foresee your mage-genocide spell and counteract it."

"If your abilities are so considerable, then tell me of this great Shield of Protection and its location," Hemlock retorted, picking up his discarded clothes and finally beginning to dress, shivering in the cold mountain air.

"The object is to be found in Betel," Ucein said, "the same town which hid the Night sword until its destruction. The ancient mages placed the shield in a deep well adjacent to the Alderman's residence, which the populace have used as a sewer for decades."

"And you expect me to search this hole?" Hemlock replied in disgust, "A stranger probing a shaft of excrement might be noticeable, even in a miserable town like Betel."

"The settlement with the elimination of the Night blade has undergone a major change," the sorcerer declared, "their celebrations will hide your passage for the populace will be too drunk to hinder your entry into the community."

The warlock gazed at the company of elves in distrust. "Would they not have searched this pit long ago for such a fabulous object?"

"Would you investigate a tunnel of human-waste on a hunch or vague suspicion?" Ucein retorted, "The shield lies untouched and patiently awaiting you."

"And what of the seven swords?" Hemlock inquired, "While I search for the shield, the Queen's soldiers will be swiftly destroying the blades in my absence."

"Our common enemy is eliminating the least powerful weapons first before moving on to the more dangerous ones," Ucein replied sharply, "we will let him have his minor victories and while he wastes his energies, you will attain possession of the Fire sword for yourself and the Time blade for myself."

"That instrument is the most awesome weapon ever created," Hemlock growled, "I have serious doubts about whether I can trust you with that sword and not destroy me."

The party of elves burst into laughter. "You flatter yourself with pretensions of grandeur and magical power," Ucein smiled, "I could kill you in an instant with the loss of only minor energy, I do not require the Time blade to take your pitiful life."

"Be careful who you threaten or insult," the warlock retorted in rage, "I have three thousand men-at-arms outside and dozens of dragons, at a single command your lives would be forfeited."

"The bandits surrounding this castle quake in fear at my presence and the reptiles would not dare harm such a powerful sorcerer as I," the dark-elf declared, "it would only take a moment for these servants of yours to change loyalties and follow my orders. I let you live only as long as it suits my purposes, you would do well to remember that, thief."

Hemlock did not reply, but glared instead at the group of elves in fury. He finished dressing and picking up a shortsword, headed for the door. He halted briefly to turn and sneer at the company who were chatting unceasingly, seemingly oblivious to his presence, before leaving the chamber.

The warlock left the castle in silence, still fuming at this indignation. The mercenaries sitting outside rose instantly at his arrival and saluted, but their new-found master passed through them without a word or glance. Hemlock approached the devastated town-gates and raised a hand to the sky.

The gathering of bandits and thieves watched on in speechless amazement and terror as a giant Silver-Dragon left the flying flock high above their heads and descended, its enormous claws reaching out for the ground. It swooped down over the ruins of the area and landed close to where the warlock stood. The reptile pulled in its massive wings and spiny-tail and lowered its colossal skull to the earth, thus allowing its rider to mount.

Hemlock climbed up onto the back of the huge beast and wrapped his legs around its neck. He glanced once more for a brief moment at the castle and his makeshift army of mercenaries, before thumping the dragon on the side and commanding it to take flight. The beast and rider rose into the sky and quickly left the district behind. Hemlock pointed south and the reptile obeyed, moving through the region swiftly; passing over the mountains in minutes, and taking its master to whatever destination or destiny he desired, or could not avoid.

CHAPTER THIRTY-THREE

It was the subtle shaking which frightened the horses that first altered Storm and the soldiers to the unstable area before them. The Captain glanced at his superior in anxiety, fearing their mission was gradually becoming more dangerous with each successive sword of the gods.

Storm sighed in reply. The guard's gaze spoke volumes in its silence, but the company knew that this weapon, the Land blade like all the others had to be destroyed. The party descended into the region, having to dismount and leave the horses behind. Storm smiled, this district was fortunately not inhabited and thus they would not have to encounter civilians. However, it made the task of locating the Land sword that much more difficult.

The group noticed upon entering the area the battered ruins of an ancient town, the populace long since gone. Not a single tree stood for miles around and a fierce breeze suddenly blew dust into their faces. It was this gale which further caused Storm concern, for the small notebook which Dryad had given him made no mention of the known location of the Wind blade of the gods. The magical grimoires stored in the library of Winterlending were tattered and torn, and the book regarding the Wind weapon had several pages missing. However, the old metallurgist had mentioned that the object was reputed to be in or around the same location as one of the other swords. This was an added bonus, not only were there no citizens present, but they could also destroy two weapons simultaneously and thus remove four blades so far from the potential clutches of Hemlock.

The company were two days journey north-east from Delug, their former destination and were comfortable in the knowledge that they had left the enraged population far behind. As the party entered the ruins of the town itself, they noticed the trembling under their feet increased and the maelstrom around their heads intensified.

Storm began to fear they might have to search for days amongst all the rubble of the former houses for the two swords. The Captain suggested he and his soldiers should continue the excavation of this region alone, while their superior moved on to the next destination and the Day instrument. But Storm was unwilling to split the company and needed to witness the elimination of each and every one of the magical weapons. However, the swordsman did not mention his own private reasons to remain, to confront Hemlock as the warlock possibly searched this area and personally dispose of him. He also knew the ten guards were no match for the necromancer and as their leader, owed it to the soldiers to return them safely to their families in the capital.

The men began to dig and sort through the various forms of litter and muck in pursuit of the blades. They knew each hour spent searching here brought Hemlock closer to the other swords and this dire knowledge increased their frantic labour. The Captain was the first to cry out in frustration at this seemingly pointless task as the weapons failed to materialise. Storm was rapidly beginning to agree with his second-in-command when something caught his attention. A hundred metres off in the distance was an open pit apparently created by the earthquakes which continued to rip through the district. Several deep cracks seemed to converge at this point and forged the dark hole, and as the soldiers observed, they could see dust and dirt being blown out of the fissure as if some great unseen force was driving the soil upwards.

The group discarded their spades in excitement and cautiously advancing on the chasm, gazed at its shaky edge into the deep abyss. The shaft descended into darkness, though it appeared wide enough to allow entrance for the men. Storm removed his backpack and any excess baggage before preparing to enter the pit.

"I would advise taking an escort on this occasion," the Captain declared, "previous incidents at Betel and Delug regarding the actual elimination of the magical instruments were less dangerous, this task appears substantially more perilous."

Storm was forced to agree. The destroying of the Night and Water blades seemed more straightforward than this particular assignment. The Land and Wind weapons appeared to be located deep underground, and the frequent quakes that rocked the area promised the constant threat of cave-ins which could seal their escape-route to the outside world. However, the very nature of this investigation excluded the majority of the company's participation for it was advisable few enter such a narrow fissure. Furthermore, if a cave-in was to occur deep within the bowels of the earth, the rest of the party could either formulate a rescue-plan, or continue on to the next destination and the Day sword of the gods.

As Storm and two guards prepared to enter, the remainder of the group gathered together and wrapping a thick rope around their waists for collective-support, handed the end-piece to their superior and fellow soldiers. Storm tied the cord around his own waist and as the company took up the strain, began his descent into the crumbling shaft. The Captain lit a torch using a segment of flint and handed the blazing fire-stick down to the swordsman. Storm accepted the gift with a groan of dissatisfaction, for he had wished they had brought lanterns on the voyage, for the power of the Wind instrument was sure to extinguish such a naked unprotected flame. Yet he did not blame the men for they were forced to leave the capital in a hurry and missing items were to be expected. The other two guards who awaited their turn glanced at the Captain in nervousness as a tremor shook the region and caused dirt to fall into the chasm. Storm who had barely descended ten feet cursed in annoyance as a river of soil fell down on his head and into his clothes. He gazed upwards in irritation before continuing his journey into the dark unknown.

Storm began to fear the pit was bottomless as he travelled nearly forty feet into the ground. However, he sighed in relief as his shoes suddenly touched level earth and yanking on the rope, silently commanded the two soldiers to follow their superior into the fissure. The guards both lit torches before gently lowering themselves into the black abyss, utterly dependent on the lifeline which their comrades held. Storm glanced above him and could only see the blazing firebrands flickering in the pitch darkness, the only indication that his back-up was approaching.

Storm reached out his hands, attempting to ascertain the width of the shaft. As he made a circle, he touched impassable rock all around him, bar one direction directly in front, leading deeper into the ground. Storm hoped the blades were nearby down this slender path, for a growing feeling of constriction and anxiety was gradually filling his mind and clouding his judgement, and he knew with dire certainty that he needed his full wits about him in this dangerous place.

The soldiers steadily approached, slowed by the burden of the fiery torches which they held in one hand, the other clasping firmly to their lifeline as they slid downwards into the blackness. Occasionally their extended fist would bash off a jutting stone and they cried out, yet still held on for they could neither allow the loss of the fire-sticks, nor risk bringing in the hand for fear of the flames severing the rope linking them to the outside world.

Finally they reached the bottom of the chasm and Storm was forced up against the rocky-wall in the narrow space. The swordsman cursed in frustration, his temper rising in the claustrophobic atmosphere of the tiny chamber. Storm briefly glared at the men in annoyance before ordering them to follow him down into the tunnel, the walls and ceiling barely five feet apart. The swordsman held one of the torches as he bent down in the dimly-lit darkness, his head nearly at the same level as his stomach. A mysterious gale suddenly blew up the shaft and nearly extinguished the lights, and the men halted in momentary confusion. They knew the path behind was likely the only exit and entrance, the fierce breeze assaulting them had to be created by the Wind blade and was therefore probably located nearby. Storm hoped this suspicion was correct for the tremors seemed to be increasing and he feared a cave-in at any moment. The sooner they destroyed the magical instruments, thought Storm, the quicker they could leave this terrible place.

The tunnel began to twist for approximately a hundred metres until they turned a corner and abruptly halted. Dimly glowing in the distance of the shaft at a rocky dead-end were the two swords; the Land and Wind weapons of the gods. As the small company approached, they noticed the instruments were criss-crossed together and firmly implanted in the stony-ground, barely revealing the handles and two inches of steel. It became apparent to Storm that these blades like the Night and Water weapons, were also steadfastly impaled into something solid and thus virtually un-removable. The ancient mages who hid the swords obviously intended they should never be retrieved and therefore the only method of ceasing their magical aura and halting the resulting disasters was the destruction of the instruments. Yet Storm knew Hemlock would discover a means of safely extracting the blades and thus harness their abilities. The only conclusion was to ensure the obliteration of each and every one of the seven weapons of the gods.

Storm drew his own sword and advanced on the two objects, though stopped upon seeing a nest of worms and maggots surrounding the hilt of the Land instrument as if feeding off its bizarre energy. The two soldiers held back, fearful to approach further, believing the elimination of the blades would unleash a great force and bring the unstable tunnel down on their heads. Storm glanced behind at them and sighed in agreement, his mind like the guards was also focused intensely on their perilous predicament and their possible deaths upon the destruction of the objects. The swordsman knew the slightest expulsion of energy from the weapons could shake the fragile shaft and seal their doom.

Storm crept alongside the magical instruments, clearly feeling the power being expended and directed down the tunnel. The strong gale seemed to be flowing out of the handle of the Wind sword, while simultaneously like the Land blade and the previous other two destroyed weapons of the gods, gave off a distinct heat signature, yet not enough to warm the fierce breeze being sent through the shaft.

Storm laid his dead torch on the ground before striking the Wind instrument just below the hilt and severed the jewelled handle, sending it into the nest of worms. He gazed briefly back at the soldiers in fear before staring at the walls of the tunnel, expecting a rush of energy to collapse the shaft. But no such force came. The gale instead within the cavern faded into a whisper before disappearing completely.

Storm smiled at his comrades as they began to laugh off their anxiety and nervousness. However, moments later to their dismay Storm felt the tremors increase and the walls of the cave started to shake apart, dirt and stones falling on their unprotected heads. The swordsman let out a groan of disbelief at his own stupidity. The two weapons had been linked all along, with the elimination of one, the other blade was now going into overload. The Land instrument was unleashing major quakes which would not only destroy the tunnel, but also most likely obliterate the entire region.

The two guards began to swiftly make their way back through the cavern towards the place of entry where lay the beginning of the rope and the relative safety of the outside world. Already they could hear their Captain and fellow companions cry down into the chasm in fright, fearing the district was ripping itself apart.

Storm figured if he was about to die, then he may as well eliminate the other weapon and seal this pit forever. The contents of the nest surrounding the Land sword was rapidly diminishing as the worms and maggots furiously burrowed into the ground, knowing the collapse of the shaft was imminent.

Storm struck the remaining blade just below the hilt and severed the ornamented handle, sending the warm metal to the floor. His two soldiers began to scream in terror down the tunnel at their superior to follow, uncaring whether their shouts might cause the cave to further disintegrate. Storm sheathed his own weapon and bending down, ran up the shaft to the impatient guards, one of whom was already scrambling up the chasm and towards the surface where awaited the rest of the company.

Storm ordered the other soldier to begin climbing which the man-at-arms obeyed instantly, too terrified to protest that his superior should go before him. His comrade high above had nearly reached the surface when a mighty tremor shook the pit and caused the walls to disintegrate, sending a shower of small rocks and earth down upon Storm. The swordsman glanced up to see the first guard lose his grip on the lifeline and fall, striking jutting stones on the way down. The second soldier swung and pushed himself up against the wall, knowing he too would fall if his companion managed to hit him as he descended. Storm considered catching the man-at-arms, but the force of such a drop would mean both their deaths, and so he moved slightly back down the tunnel and watched on helplessly as the guard struck the rocky-bottom of the chasm.

The swordsman slowly approached the soldier, knowing it was blatantly obvious that the man was dead and had probably broken practically every bone in his body. The cave upon its imminent collapse would cover his corpse and seal it from the outside world forever. Storm faintly heard the Captain above cry out in rage at the loss of one of his comrades, as the other guard reached the top in safety. Storm swiftly followed, hesitating briefly every few minutes as further quakes shook the pit and sent a flood of debris down the shaft. Eventually he reached the summit as the Captain extended a hand and pulled his superior from the opening of the abyss.

Storm wearily stood to his feet and glanced first at the Captain and then down into the fissure where lay the battered body of one of their own. The Land and Wind blades had been destroyed, but at a terrible price. The officer sighed in anger and regret, knowing the remaining weapons of the gods would be even more difficult to eliminate, and many more of his men might die before they saw the end of this mission. Storm and the company briefly saluted the valiant dead soldier of the Queen's Royal Army, before running for the horses. The tremors sent further cracks through the ruins of the former town and demolished what remained of the dilapidated houses. Storm gazed back to see the chasm collapse and the shaft which once hid the Land and Wind instruments disappear forever, a deluge of dirt and rock filling the unnatural tunnel.

By the time the party had reached their steeds and prepared to leave the region, the tremendous quakes had seemingly ceased and the district fell under an eerie silence. Storm mounted his horse and stared at the barren and ravaged area before him. With the exception of Betel, the destruction of each of the swords had inflicted serious damage to the regions, yet Storm knew his enemy could not be allowed possession of the magical items, otherwise the entire land might very well end up like this district. However, Storm was growing increasingly weary of this mission and the mysterious absence of Hemlock, and promised to himself if the necromancer did not make an appearance soon, then he would leave the elimination of the remainder of the weapons to the Captain and his men, and proceed on alone to Ferulas and somehow infiltrate the heavily-guarded ruins to finally dispose of the warlock.

Hemlock smiled, it seemed the dark-elf had been correct. The populace of Betel was too busy celebrating the revitalisation of their town to notice the arrival of strangers. The necromancer also knew the monarchy was furiously attempting to quell spreading rumours about his returning from 'the grave', though that was becoming increasingly more difficult to achieve after he had obliterated Ferulas and his rapid organising of an army there. The mercenaries and bandits gathering at his base of operations were already calling him 'The Black Ghost', because of his evil nature and seemingly miraculous defiance of death. But the only title Hemlock would be satisfied with was that of King or Emperor, all other designations were transient and therefore meaningless.

The warlock moved silently through the cheering crowds, uncaring of the people's apathy to his presence and drunken behaviour as they danced in the town-square. The residence of the Alderman came into sight and he pushed through the gathering towards the house of the politician. The building was unguarded, Betel having no army though it provided a substantial amount of weapons to the capital. Hemlock passed close to the structure, leaving the crowd behind. He briefly turned to sneer at the jovial population, before returning his full attention to the object adjacent to the large residence, the well hiding the fabled Shield of Protection from the outside world. Hemlock let out a cough of nausea, even several feet away he could distinguish the distinct smell of human-waste. He thought it bizarre the open sewer should be placed so closely to the ruler of a community, yet knew Betel during its long period of darkness and depression cared not for such civilised behaviour as proper hygiene, and frequently deposited the human-material from all the houses in the settlement into what was once their only source of water. The populace therefore came to depend completely on regular supplies of food and barrels of water from the city of Winterlending, and in their laziness and apathy never once stopped to consider why the capital never chastised or criticised such outrageous conduct.

Hemlock approached the well while removing a strip of cloth and a rock from his backpack. He wound the fabric around his mouth and nose, forcing back the urge to vomit at the pungent stench. He tied the end of a hundred-metre long rope around the black iron ore and hesitating to glance in every direction, threw the stone into the pit. It made a sickening plop as it entered and quickly began to sink as Hemlock smiled. Ucein had taught the warlock the method of extracting iron ore from black igneous rock and charging the crude metal to make it magnetic. The stone was one of the few meagre possessions the dark-elf had retained from Sulphur Mountain, his former home and hence valued the object highly. Hemlock let out a laugh as he wondered if the sorcerer would want the ore back after its travels through this well of shit.

The ruler of Ferulas watched as the rock fell deeper into the foul abyss and became concerned as the rope in his hands was reaching its end. Yet finally it appeared to touch the bottom and Hemlock sighed in satisfaction. He yanked the cord, hoping it had attracted the extra weight of the Shield of Protection, but in vain. Hemlock began to circle the well, slightly lifting and dropping the ore in silent desperation. As the minutes passed, the warlock started to growl in annoyance and impatience, knowing even the intoxicated citizens would notice this bizarre activity soon and question the motive for this strange investigation of the town-sewer. Hemlock feared Ucein had betrayed him like he always suspected he would, and had now taken charge of the dragons and the army at Ferulas. The thief knew his powers were inferior to that of the dark-elf, but believed a well-placed arrow in the back would finish even a mighty wizard like Ucein and his treacherous company of elves.

Hemlock groaned in frustration, out of the corner of his eye he could see three smiths approaching, curious at the intentions of this stranger in their town. Just then the warlock felt the iron ore become attracted to something heavy and started to pull furiously, dragging the smeared rope out of the well, uncaring as his hands became covered in the fiercely pungent fetor of human-faeces. If the weapon-smiths recognised the necromancer, they did not let it show. Perhaps the alcohol had given them false courage, Hemlock pondered, otherwise they likely would be hesitant to approach. However, the warlock was not about to allow this ignorance or foolish bravery stand in the way of claiming his prize, and then leaving this wretched region forthwith.

Eventually the start of the cord and rock came into sight and Hemlock cheered as a large round object covered in dark waste reached the surface. He removed the cloth from his face and frantically began to wipe the item, trembling with excitement. The fabled Shield of Protection was the single only magical armour reputed by legend to potentially exist, and now finally here it was in his grasp. As the excrement left the instrument, Hemlock could see various decorative symbols engraved on the metal and leaning over, detached the object from the ore. Replacing the magnetic stone into his backpack and removing what remained of the putrid waste from the shield and his hands, he turned to face the men who were now only mere feet away from the well.

The smiths drew to a halt upon witnessing the discovery of the magical item from the sewer and glanced first at the stranger and then at each other in confusion. One of the men suggested informing the Alderman of this mysterious activity, but his companions disagreed. A lone individual required not the attention of the ruling politician, they responded, they could sort out this matter personally without disturbing the Alderman from the celebrations. However, they swiftly regretted this hasty decision as a single command from the warlock released a fireball the size of Hemlock's fist from his outstretched hand, and struck one of the smiths in the chest which then promptly exited out through his back, sending a froth of charred flesh and blood onto the clothes and faces of his two comrades. The now terrified men began to flee, but a second and third fireball quickly followed and engulfed them, setting their bodies alight. The festival ceased as women and children screamed in shock and several citizens ran to douse the flames consuming their brethren as the two smiths fell to the ground. The Alderman gazed across and gasped in astonishment upon recognising Hemlock, and desperately fumbled in terror for the words to summon armed civilians to the scene. The necromancer saw the politician's face and smiled in reply, before swiftly leaving the town and headed for the wilderness where awaited the dragon and his transport to the locations of the remaining swords of the gods. Hemlock laughed as he held the shield high, now believing that victory and the crown would soon be within his grasp, as if fate itself had decreed that it was inevitable.

CHAPTER THIRTY-FOUR

The sweat was pouring off in rivulets from the drenched bodies of the company as they approached the town of Solaris. Storm and the soldiers had left the region of the destroyed Land and Wind weapons yesterday and had made good time to reach the settlement before them. The district was similar to that of the previous area in that it was also virtually barren of agriculture and vegetation, bar a few palm trees blowing in the light breeze. Of the meagre population resident in this town, only a few could be seen, lazing in the shade and drinking from barrels of ale, avoiding the perpetual heatwave. The intense temperature had transformed Solaris into a holiday-resort where recuperating troops and civilians came to enjoy the rainless weather. The incredible heat however had made all other activities bar stagnation virtually impossible, but the uniformless guards who watched the party approach preferred it that way. Their lives consisted of constant backbreaking labour, any opportunity to simply sit around and bask in the sun was not to be ignored.

Storm sighed in nervousness, if these same soldiers realised their intentions and the nature of their mission, then a form of mutiny might well occur. Once again, a swift departure upon the elimination of the Day instrument of the gods might be advisable.

Storm and the group cautiously entered the settlement, attempting to ascertain the location of the blade. Where the temperature was at its greatest, the swordsman believed, then that is where the weapon resided. They passed by the roofless houses where lazing troops observed their travelling companions in a mixture of curiosity and amusement, puzzled by the heavily-dressed nature of the guards and began to wonder if they were about to discard their uniforms and join them. But the party ignored them and continued through the town, following the likely source of the heatwave.

They entered the surrounding wilderness, the hooves of the horses causing resounding cracks in the dry brittle earth. The temperature was now oppressive and the soldiers were forced to dismount, fearing the collapse of the steeds. Several minutes later and some of the men also could not proceed further. The Captain ordered them to the shade of a nearby clump of palm-trees as the remainder of the company persevered on.

This section of the wasteland was utterly devoid of any life or any indication of the location of the Day instrument. Storm was now about to fall to his knees also, overcome by the sweltering weather. However, through the haze he heard the Captain roar in excitement and turned to the officer. The swordsman followed the guard's outstretched hand that pointed due north and smiled. What appeared to be a pool of water off in the distance caught their attention. Storm feared it was a mirage; a trick of the mind in the brilliant heat, but as they dragged themselves closer to the small lake it became apparent it was no illusion.

Storm wondered why the liquid had simply not evaporated or the populace of Solaris did not venture here for replenishment of their water-stocks. The reason for the lack of citizens quenching their thirst here became obvious as the group approached, for the pool was boiling, sending froth into the air and onto the surrounding bank. Storm figured the pond was being fed by an underground-stream and replaced what water quickly evaporated. The location of the Day weapon was easy to discover, for the handle of the magical object was sticking up out of the fluid in the very centre of the lake. It seemed the instrument was impaled in a large boulder which like several others nearby, jutted up out of the liquid.

"How are we to destroy the sword, if we cannot reach it?" inquired the Captain, wiping sweat from his forehead.

Storm glanced at the soldier in momentary concern, but then smiled. He unsheathed his own blade and retrieving from the officer's backpack the rope they used at the pit, wrapped the cord around the hilt of the weapon. The swordsman stood cautiously at the edge of the bank and holding his blade like a spear, threw the instrument at the Day sword. However, it missed and struck the rock below the magical item, resulting in a dreadful clang. Storm retracted his weapon from the bubbling froth by pulling on the rope and hurled his blade a second time. The Captain let out a cheer as his superior's sword struck the handle of the Day instrument a glancing blow. However, the strike did not appear sufficient to shatter the impaled object and so Storm removed his weapon from the lake, letting it lie on the bank for several minutes to cool down before he would try again.

Moments later however the Captain suddenly caught his leader's sleeve and pointed at the centre of the pool. The hilt of the Day blade seemed to sway and then fall off into the boiling fluid, the instrument having been severed three inches below the jewelled handle. The party roared in joy and approval as Storm sheathed his own sword in satisfaction. The oppressive heat hovering over the area appeared to be subsiding and the Captain waved to the other troops far off in the distance at the palm-trees that everything was now all right.

However, just then the water seemed to intensify its bubbling and a fountain of boiling liquid was sent high into the air. A wave of scalding-hot froth rose and fell on the embankment, catching two soldiers off guard. They were showered in a cascade of scorching-hot water and screamed in pain as they became drenched. Storm ran to their aid, but it was hopeless. The men fell to the ground and swiftly died with the shock, the Captain grateful for this fact as the soldiers would have been horrifically scarred and lived a long life of intense suffering.

They dragged the bodies from the scene and buried them at the outskirts to the town. Storm then decided that it was time to leave the district as the bubbling of the pond increased further, sending more waves onto the bank and into the wilderness.

The company retrieved their horses and returned to Solaris, as the lazing citizens were rising to their feet in confusion, perplexed by the change in weather and the approach of dark clouds heralding rain on the horizon. The group quickly left the settlement behind and headed north-east for the Lake of Pure Water and the Time blade, the most powerful and dangerous of all the seven swords of the gods. The Fire weapon only then remained, pondered the Captain, though he wondered if any of the company would survive this hazardous mission and return home to the capital.

*   *   *   *   *

It was approaching nightfall when the dragon neared the town of Combuse, passing high over the surrounding mountains and forest. Hemlock gazed down, admiring the countryside and the world he believed that would soon be his. The Shield of Protection lay strapped to his back and banged against his spine in the fierce wind.

The reptile descended and landed on the western edge of the woodland and on the outskirts of the nearby settlement, the populace not noticing the arrival of the enormous beast in the darkness. The warlock dismounted and leaving his magical transport behind, entered Combuse. The population of this small farming community appeared apathetic to the presence of this stranger in their midst and uncaring of his intentions and nature. They seemed more preoccupied with discussing the day's labour in the fields and the removal of lumber from the forest, both of which lay to the east and south of the town.

Eavesdropping on these banal conversations however was not without benefit, for Hemlock learned no produce or livestock lay to the west of the settlement, and the necromancer suspected that region held the location of the Fire sword.

Hemlock swiftly moved through the community, making for the western-exit and the wilderness. No citizens blocked or hindered his path and he quickly found himself out of the town and in a bizarre wasteland. A blackened ruin of charred earth and trees greeted his vision and as he watched in speechless amazement, a bright flame rose inexplicably up out of the ground and gushed into the air. It was followed by a second and third fiery discharge, creating firebrands out of nearby plants. Hemlock glanced behind and noticed the outer-wall of Combuse was dark with soot and several cracks ran across the stone from the intense heat of former fires. The populace had ignored this area in fear, and considered it unwise and unsafe to investigate the reason for such unnatural activity. Hemlock however knew the origin for this strange action, though pondered on how he could search such a dangerous region, for he could be incinerated at any moment.

The warlock removed the magical shield from his back and holding the instrument in front of him, proceeded cautiously into the unstable wasteland. The thief halted frequently in nervousness as fountains of flame shot into the air near him, yet they were too far for him to be singed. Hemlock was forced to thread slowly and carefully for the ground was littered with layers of burning fire-sticks. He ventured deeper into the blackened-wilderness, yet could see no sign of the Fire blade. Hemlock abruptly came upon a small mountain of dead branches, but thought nothing of it until something deep within the pile caught his eye. An object seemed to be shining through this heap of charred wood and in growing excitement, he began to brush aside the burned faggots until the distinct handle of a broadsword came into view. The steel of the blade appeared to be engraved with abstract symbols in a magical language Hemlock vaguely recognised and the hilt was studded with various types of jewels, including diamonds and emeralds.

The warlock fell to his knees before the weapon in a mixture of admiration and adoration, and started to feel a desire for this instrument the like of which he had not felt since first seeing the sword of Proteus in Karlaband. He reached out and touched the blade and found it was quite warm. Hemlock gently attempted to pull the item out of the ground, but in vain. It was firmly implanted in the earth amongst the nest of charred branches, and it became obvious that it would require more than mere physical strength to remove.

The thief kept his hand on the hilt of the weapon, and remembered the words Ucein had told him which would be needed to release the magical grip the ancient mages had applied on the seven swords to prevent their theft.

"Elohai Surgat Abrah Doea," the warlock growled and watched in amazement as the blade began to rise up out of the ground.

Hemlock grasped hold of the handle of the Fire instrument and pulled it free from the remaining earth, too impatient to wait for the weapon to remove itself fully from the nest. He ran his left hand down the smooth warm metal and laughed in satisfaction and triumph. Centuries had passed since any man had wielded a sword of the gods, and here was one of the most powerful of the seven blades in his possession.

Hemlock raised the weapon to the sky, relishing his victory. He caught sight of a lone willow tree in the distance, the branches drooping down to the ground. The plant appeared to be unharmed by the ravages of the region and the warlock pointed the Fire instrument in its direction. A fireball the size of his fist shot out of the tip of the blade and struck the tree, igniting it instantly. Bright golden flames burned high as the plant became engulfed and began to collapse to the earth.

Hemlock discarded his shortsword and sheathed the Fire weapon into a second scabbard that he had brought along. The thief left the devastated area and bypassing the community of Combuse by travelling around its outer-walls, soon found himself at the edge of the forest and the waiting dragon.

Hemlock mounted the reptile and ordered the beast to take flight, and proceed south-east towards the Lake of Pure Water where lay his next prize, the Time blade of the gods.

CHAPTER THIRTY-FIVE

A day's journey north-east from Solaris brought the company to their next destination, the Lake of Pure Water. Before the soldiers was the second last stage in their mission and they greeted this knowledge with a mixture of trepidation and relief. The Time sword would be the most difficult and dangerous to destroy. However, its location was not unknown and thus would require little searching. The notebook which Dryad had given Storm spoke of a cave on the western bank several feet below the surface of the water, and which led into a shaft where lay the weapon of the gods.

Storm groaned in disbelief at the incredible perpetuation of the ancient mages at placing the blades in bizarre locations, thus hindering their removal. The aura surrounding the Time instrument was far more intense than all the other swords, and its powers were clear to see. No vegetation grew in this region and no fish swam in the murky depths of the small pond. It however did not seem to affect the river that ran alongside the lake and continued southwards to the capital and the coast. Storm figured the infected liquid became distilled and rendered harmless by the river. The swordsman believed the name of the pool to be a contradiction, for long before the mere became polluted with the powers of the Time blade, nearby villages would come to drink from this freshwater pond to avail of the crisp pure fluid, but now the liquid was tainted and fouled with the rotting bones of fish which had inadvertently swum into the pool from the river. Storm believed the mere should be renamed the

Lake of Dead Water as he observed its lifeless murky depths.

The Captain informed his leader that a maximum of fifteen minutes was all that could be allowed before Storm would become affected by the aura of the Time weapon and begin to age a year with every passing minute. The swordsman discarded his excess baggage and upon entering the pond, started to shiver at the intense cold of the water.

The lake measured approximately two hundred feet in diameter and the surface was incredibly calm and placid. Storm waved to the party as he prepared to dive, his head sticking out of the icy liquid. The Captain smiled in reply, yet then abruptly frowned. Storm glanced at the officer in confusion, perplexed by the soldier's sudden anxiety. He then saw the reason for the man-at-arm's nervousness as an enormous creature descended from the heavens, its rider clinging to the beast's scaly-back.

Storm knew he was vulnerable, unable to defend himself as he bobbed about in the water. He could only watch on helpless as the dragon unleashed a massive fireball and ignited the entire area, incinerating the guards where they stood. He let out a scream of rage as the soldiers roared in a cacophony of pain before falling to the ground, their charred bodies rolling into the pond.

Storm dived beneath the surface of the pool to avoid the wave of flame which rushed across the lake, but soon dissipated as the magical reptile began to land. Storm knew he still had the element of surprise, for Hemlock was unaware of his presence and believed he had perished with the group of guards.

Storm quickly swam along the western bank and then dived, searching for the entrance to the underwater cave and the location of the Time instrument, determined to deny the warlock possession of the weapon.

Hemlock dismounted and stepped over the blackened corpses of the Captain and his men, pleased a few less soldiers of the Queen would be hindering his plans. He discarded the Fire blade and his backpack before entering the lake and disappeared from the outside world as the surface of the pond rose over his head.

Storm felt around in the pool, his vision distorted by the murkiness of the water and was becoming increasingly frustrated. He could not risk surfacing for fear of being discovered, and yet he was running out of air. He reached out his hands once more and in relief touched the entrance to the tunnel. The swordsman swiftly swam into the shaft and saw light ahead. Storm was beginning to feel his lungs bursting as he rose to the surface and found himself in a small cavern. The chamber measured barely eight feet in diameter with the ceiling ten feet distant. He was in a three foot diameter-length hole in the centre of the room, the only exit to the outside world. The single only source of light in the gloomy chamber was emanating from the Time instrument which was seemingly impaled into the rock-floor not two feet from the hole. It like all the other blades of the gods was similarly decorated with jewels and engraved in an ancient language beyond Storm's knowledge. But the swordsman was not concerned with deciphering the hidden meaning or the significance of such words, only the destruction of the magical weapon. Only the Fire instrument Storm knew remained, and the swordsman vowed that Hemlock would be deprived of that dangerous possession also.

Storm pulled himself free of the cold water and advanced on the blade. He drew his own weapon and prepared to strike at the impaled object when he suddenly felt a sharp pain at the back of his head and fell to his knees. Storm put a hand to his skull and felt a trickle of blood run down his neck. Nearby was a rock that had not been present moments before and the swordsman turned and smiled. Pulling himself from the hole was the warlock and it seemed he was unarmed. Storm let out a laugh of triumph. It appeared too good to be true, here was his arch-enemy with nowhere to run and weaponless. Storm could dispatch Hemlock at his leisure, and promised the thief's body would be battered and torn before he delivered the final death-blow.

However, it seemed the necromancer was unconcerned at his fragile predicament as he smiled at his opponent from another age and time. "Well sailor," Hemlock declared, "it appears you have beaten me to the prize."

"I have done worse," Storm replied with a laugh of satisfaction, "I have denied you of all the swords of the gods."

Hemlock grinned. "Not all sailor," he retorted sharply, "the Fire blade rests topside with my dragon, it has powers enough to lay waste to the world."

Storm sighed in dismay at one of the seven weapons eluding him, but he vowed the Time instrument; the most dangerous of all the swords would not reach the warlock's grasp. Storm turned and raised his blade towards the impaled item at his feet, but a shout from Hemlock halted this act.

"It would be most unwise to attempt to destroy my prize," the thief growled, "although I am without a sword, I am not weaponless."

Storm glanced back and saw Hemlock juggling a fireball in his right hand, the magical object bouncing up and down, ready to be thrown. The necromancer's flesh seemed unharmed by the intense heat of the ball of orange flame as it lit up the gloomy chamber. Storm replied by spitting at his enemy in contempt before swiftly side-stepping to his left and struck the Time blade. Hemlock let fly the fireball which struck Storm a glancing blow before it hit the wall, disintegrating with the impact. The flames had set Storm's jerkin-shoulder alight and he cried out in pain. He gazed down however and laughed in delight as the handle and top two inches of steel of the Time weapon lay severed on the rocky-chamber floor.

Hemlock summoned a second larger fireball and prepared to kill his opponent, when Storm side-stepped again and revealed the broken impaled blade at his feet. The warlock's jaw dropped open in shock and disbelief, and hesitated in eliminating the destroyer of his prizes. Storm realised saving his own life at this moment was more important than trying to kill Hemlock, especially since he would be unable to reach the necromancer before he dispatched the lethal ball of flame. There would be another opportunity to extract his vengeance.

Storm dived into the pool and heard the fireball explode at the surface of the water-hole behind him. As he swam through the shaft towards the main lake, he felt the liquid around him becoming turbulent as if some great unseen force was causing the pond to become violent. Storm supposed the dying powers of the Time instrument were behind this malady, and hoped it would not harm Hemlock, for he wanted that singular honour. He entered the main lake and rose to the surface, before returning his sword to its sheath at his waist.

The weather in the region was calm and without a breeze, yet the entire expanse of the mere was in wild turmoil as if an underwater volcano was erupting deep beneath the surface. Storm saw the dragon which was observing this strange behaviour of the pool intently, worried for its master's safety. The swordsman contemplated sneaking out of the pond and attempting the theft of the Fire weapon, but the reptile would spot him easily in such an open treeless area.

Storm turned instead to face Hemlock who was sure to surface at any moment. However, the fury of the lake increased and Storm found himself being drawn into the fast-flowing current of the neighbouring river. He cursed as the waterway carried him downstream and away from the pool. However, his present situation demanded his sole attention in keeping his head above water, and thus he had to forsake his ambitions of killing Hemlock. Storm saw the warlock leave the mere and consoled himself with the fact that at least the thief had survived and another chance would arise in which he could claim his revenge.

Storm let the current of the river carry him miles southwards before he eventually pulled himself from the waterway, and ventured on foot in the direction of the capital to report the near-success of his mission.

*   *   *   *   *

Hemlock arrived at Ferulas hours later to find a waiting dark-elf greeting him at the blackened town-gates.

"So you have returned without my prize," Ucein declared with obvious disappointment, "and also failed to dispatch our common enemy and acquire my ancient possession which he wields."

"The sailor was more resourceful than I previously gave him credit," Hemlock replied, yet then smiled, "but I have the Fire weapon of the gods which eluded him."

The thief unsheathed the magical instrument and held it high, the amassed gathering of bandits and mercenaries gasping in astonishment.

"The swordsman will retreat to the capital to inform the Queen of the Fire blade escaping his grasp," the elfin-sorcerer said firmly, "we should be prepared to move our forces southwards, for Sobranie will now consider an invasion of Ferulas to eliminate this threat."

"It will not be the monarch who starts this fight," Hemlock replied, "I plan to send dragons to our neighbouring settlements Solaris and Betel and obliterate them, forcing the Queen to declare full-scale war."

"That would be foolish," Ucein retorted, "we need time to gather an army of orcs and ogres from The Frozen Wastes and amass them some distance east of the capital to prepare an invasion of Winterlending. Sobranie will likewise need time to collect her forces, especially from Karlaband and the Army Barracks to counter this threat. We could catch her by surprise and take the capital within days."

Hemlock laughed. "The town Kilfish would notice such a colossal force travelling south-eastwards and report the movement to the Queen. Besides, she is sure to have spies watching us right now, therefore surprise is out of the question. We should get in an early strike and destroy weak targets like Solaris and Betel, robbing Sobranie of such possible extra armies. Furthermore, Betel is one of the major manufacturers and suppliers of weapons to the capital. The elimination of this settlement is a military necessity, we cannot allow this town to survive."

"Very well," the dark-elf agreed, "order the reptiles to lay waste to those two communities. I will travel to The frozen Wastes and establish an alliance with the orcs and ogres, they will listen to a mage like me and will be only too willing to escape their exile in the ice-lands, and inflict bloody retribution on their mortal enemies; the humans. Move the army of mercenaries and dragons to the plains north of the settlement Abe. You will be briefly hidden by the mountains to the west and south of the grasslands. Send the reptiles to the outskirts of the region and thus will deter the Queen discovering the true size of our small forces, and prevent your destruction until my return with our reinforcements."

Hemlock nodded in agreement and approached his makeshift army to order them to gather together their meagre belongings, before turning to summon two Gold-Dragons and commanding them to incinerate the neighbouring towns. He glanced once behind to see Ucein and his party of elves mount horseback and leave Ferulas for The Frozen Wastes, and Hemlock watched them depart with a mixture of regret and relief, for although he desperately required Ucein's support and advice, he also wished the dark-elf would never return.

CHAPTER THIRTY-SIX

Upon his arrival at the capital city Storm was greeted by a small body of heavily-armed guards at the gates. The swordsman noticed the entire settlement was crowded with soldiers, not just of the capital, but men-at-arms from Ledge, Tomilusk and Abe. He also recognised the crest of such towns as Hellsbreath, the Army Barracks, and to his surprise, Karlaband; an insignia he had not seen for centuries. The officers that passed him were of a high rank, including Commanders, Captains and Lieutenants. There seemed to be no guards of a lesser status than Sergeant wandering the streets of Winterlending, other than those normally assigned to the protection of the capital city. Storm's escort led him through the community until they reached the palace and a further ten men led him into the throne-room.

The usually near-empty chamber was dense with soldiers from far and wide who gathered around Sobranie in noisy chatter. The high-ranking officers all appeared to listen to Cairn closely, and a quick examination of the colourful badge on his chest followed by a brief conversation with a nearby Lieutenant explained the reason why. In Storm's absence, the former champion of the late King had been promoted from Captain of the Guard at Tomilusk to Commander of the entire Royal Army and the small Royal Navy. Next to the Queen, he was now the most powerful and influential person in the civilised world.

Upon recognising the approaching swordsman, Cairn dismissed the soldiers before he and Sobranie took him aside to a far corner of the room.

"It seems congratulations are in order," Storm declared with a smile, pointing to the orange and black-striped badge on his friend's chest.

Cairn smirked in reply, but then frowned in regret. "I wish the promotion had been in happier times," the Commander sighed, "how fared your mission?"

"I managed to destroy every blade bar the Fire sword," Storm replied, "I'm afraid that weapon now rests with the warlock."

Sobranie sighed in dismay. "That instrument is very dangerous," the Queen said, yet then smiled in relief, "but we are very pleased the other blades have been eliminated, especially the Time sword."

Storm gazed around the chamber in confusion before returning his attention to Cairn. "What has happened in my absence? Why are there men here from practically every town in the land?"

"We ferried these high-ranking officers by using the giant eagles of my father to reach the capital swiftly, for we had to know their loyalties quickly," Sobranie responded sharply, "Hemlock has forced me to declare war by attacking the settlements Solaris and Betel with his dragons. Fortunately Betel was not seriously damaged, for they immediately had the appropriate weapons necessary to fend off the fire-breathing reptile, unlike defenceless Solaris which has been completely obliterated. It is my fault for not earlier invading Ferulas and vanquishing this threat."

Cairn laid a hand on her shoulder in sympathy. "You would not have succeeded in destroying Ferulas, for the mountains would have hindered our entry while the dozens of dragons would have circled and annihilated us."

"That does not make it any easier to accept now that I am compelled to send a lot more men to their deaths," the Queen sighed in despair.

"But we now have a much greater force at our disposal with which we can defeat Hemlock," the Commander retorted, "every town in the land has sworn allegiance to the government. Even now the officers plan to depart for their homes and return forthwith with their armies, and amass this enormous gathering at Abe before meeting the warlock on the plains north of the settlement."

"Then the situation is firmly in our favour," Storm declared, "for we have a far greater force than Hemlock."

"Perhaps," Sobranie echoed, yet then frowned in dismay, "if it were not for the dark-elf and his powers of persuasion."

Storm stared at her in confusion before glancing at Cairn, and was surprised to see a look of nervousness on his face at her statement. The Queen gazed at the swordsman, realising he was unaware of such knowledge due to his absence from the capital.

"The individual I speak of is called Ucein, formally a member of the extinct High Council of elves," Sobranie announced, "he is probably the single most dangerous and intelligent person to have ever lived. His magical abilities and knowledge of military-strategy is without equal, and we know he has formed an alliance with Hemlock. Spies have reported the elfin-sorcerer is making for The Frozen Wastes where he will most likely establish a treaty with the races of orcs and ogres in exile there. Those despicable creatures respect only brute force or magick, therefore they will listen to Ucein and obey his orders. Fortunately the dark-elf abhors travelling by dragon and so will give us valuable time in which to gather our armies. We have no accurate information as to the size of these races, but fear the orcs and ogres may number upwards of two hundred thousand."

Storm gasped in shock. "Is there anything I can do to help?"

"I am sending Cairn to Cracas Island to meet my uncle King Aliped and his military-Commander Aphis to establish an alliance and add his large army to our own," the Queen replied and Cairn sighed in annoyance at having to meet Aphis again, "your voice would be constructive in such a delicate negotiation, and I would be pleased if you could travel there and bring that force to the capital forthwith."

Storm smiled. "It will be an honour to support such a treaty, especially if it helps to seal Hemlock's doom."

Sobranie briefly embraced the swordsman before returning to her advisers, and Cairn led Storm out of the palace and into the adjacent street. The Commander took his friend aside and stared at him fixedly in nervousness. Storm gazed at the master-warrior in confusion, not understanding the nature of the soldier's obvious distress.

"I have a confession to make, and it has been a long time coming," Cairn sighed solemnly and handed his friend his magical spear, "as regards the true ownership of this weapon and the sword at your side."

Storm stared at the Commander, believing a secret centuries old was finally about to be revealed, and it was a tale he feared would blacken the memories he possessed of Kassier, the man who had saved his life and gave him the blade.

"The dark-elf Ucein the Queen spoke of is the true and rightful creator of the two instruments," the master-warrior declared in anxiety and his head began to sink in guilt, "in my younger years I travelled to Sulphur Mountain to visit the grave of my grandfather. However, while there I discovered a magnificent spear forged by Ucein and a parchment containing a spell which would transfer ownership to me, thus allowing me to use the weapon and having it return to my grasp every time it was thrown. In a moment of weakness I stole the object and manuscript and fled from the mountain. I have used the instrument since to vanquish my enemies and win The Game every year, for no opponent can withstand or defend against the weapon."

Storm gazed at his friend in a mixture of anger and sympathy. He did not approve of the soldier's actions, but believed the guard had suffered enough guilt over the years since to pay for his crime. "How did you know the spear and my sword were a pair?"

"The parchment spoke of another instrument; a blade fashioned from the same magical metal," Cairn replied.

"Did you deliberately strike up a friendship with me in that tavern all that time ago to simply steal my sword?" Storm growled.

"No," the Commander retorted sharply, "I was curious about you and how you came to acquire the weapon, and was hoping you might sell the instrument."

Storm explained about Kassier and how the old smith had simply given the object away. Storm now began to realise that Kassier had most likely also stolen the blade, and sent him to Sulphur Mountain before the Battle of the Temples so Storm might inadvertently learn about the true origin of the instrument, for the old man had not the courage to confess his crime.

"Not even my fiancée Sotera knows of this," Cairn announced, "but I do not care anymore if everybody knows of the theft and my shameful past."

Storm smiled and embraced the soldier. "People in this city have committed far worse deeds," the swordsman said, "this will remain our secret, for we are now the possessors of these weapons, and it is probably far better Ucein never had the chance to use the items against us or the government."

Cairn nodded in agreement. "Come my friend, and let us prepare for our journey on a giant eagle to Cracas Island, and our fateful meeting with the King."

"Do you think Aliped will agree to a military-alliance?" Storm inquired, "He has never shown much love for Sobranie."

The Commander laughed in reply. "I believe I have an offer he cannot refuse to accept."

Storm glanced at his friend, perplexed. Yet he was confident of Cairn's ability and cunning methods of persuasion.

Storm gazed at the populace as they went about their daily business, seemingly unconcerned at the impending arrival of war. The swordsman hoped for their sake that the treaty on Cracas would be successful, and that it would be enough to save the world from Hemlock, and the devastation which he promised.

PART FOUR

CHAPTER THIRTY-SEVEN

The two travellers left Winterlending early in the morning and would arrive at the harbour-town Port on Cracas Island before nightfall. The giant eagle soared high above the mountains and the coast, bestowing a magnificent view for its occupants in the wicker-basket on its feathery-back.

Storm was witness to the devastation of Nez as they passed overhead from the tsunami created by the obliteration of Aren Island. Only a quarter of the population had survived the onslaught of the tidal-wave, Cairn declared, and those few hundred were now homeless. The settlement appeared to be under heavy construction with carpenters from nearby towns arriving daily to deal with the colossal workload. However, it would require dozens of generations to replace the depleted populace, and houses were being made that would not have occupants for years. Business in their own communities was currently lax and the bored carpenters therefore decided to now build dwellings for the future children of the survivors.

"It does not make sense," Storm said in confusion, "erecting houses for people not yet born."

"True," Cairn agreed, "but the residents of Nez are too eager to restore the former size and beauty of their town to care about such practicalities."

Storm shook his head in disbelief at such crassness, especially if Hemlock should win the war upon which he would destroy every settlement in the land. Business for the carpenters would not be so lax and they would likely be overwhelmed constructing homes for people very much alive.

The companions left the activity of Nez far behind and soon arrived at the town Port. They were greeted by a twenty-man escort of the King and led to a nearby tavern for the night. The following morning the travellers quickly found themselves on the road again in the direction of the city Blackgame; the capital of Cracas Island. Neither of the two friends were eager to return to the city, the site of the beginning of the annual combat-event The Game where many men had died and Aphis had threatened the two companions with death for defiance of the strict rules. As they approached, Storm noticed the community had changed little, bar the greater display of armed force at the gates which observed their entry with suspicion. The escort kept close to the travellers as if fearing they might attempt to escape their endearing company. The palace of King Aliped swiftly came into view and a further ten soldiers guarding the double-doors led the treaty-makers through the building and into the throne-room. The chamber was relatively sparse compared to its counterpart in the capital on the mainland. A rough forty-foot length rectangular oak-table lay in the very centre of the room with uncovered wooden chairs strewn around its perimeter. No tapestries lined the walls surrounding the only other piece of furniture, the throne of the ruling monarch of Cracas where sat King Aliped watching them approach with piercing green-eyes. Alongside him stood Aphis, the Commander of the army and tiny navy of the large island.

The motionless officer sneered at Cairn as he drew to a halt a mere twenty feet from the throne. "So our champion returns," Aphis smirked, "if one can call you that after you broke the rules of The Game upon faking your death."

"Perhaps I simply became tired of the monotony of always winning and allowed Storm to succeed," the master-warrior retorted, moving closer to Aphis, intent on intimidating him.

"You deserve to die on your knees for disgracing our great annual combat-festival," the Commander of Cracas snapped.

Cairn laughed. "The Game is a joke at best, a disgusting blood-sport for ghoulish spectators at worst," the delegate of the Queen declared, "you are the one who is in disgrace for organising such a carnival. You may be the Chief of the army on Cracas, but you would only be qualified to clean the sewer in the capital city Winterlending back on the mainland."

At this remark, Aphis drew his sword and launched at Cairn, intending to run him through. However, the master-warrior simply side-stepped out of the way and as the soldier passed, Cairn hit him squarely on the back with the flat of the blade of his spear, sending Aphis to the ground. The Commander of Cracas turned and glared up at Cairn in fury, and prepared to rise to his feet and launch a second attack. However, a shout from his monarch brought a halt to the fight.

"Enough," Aliped growled, "I am here to listen to terms of a possible military-alliance, not to entertain petty squabbles. Aphis, sheath your blade and return to my side."

The organiser of The Game sighed in anger, before rising and gradually moved back to the throne, yet he continued to stare at Cairn in silent rage.

The King turned to the master-warrior. "Explain the benefits of sending my entire army across the sea to their deaths," the monarch said, "what purpose does it serve to support my idealistic niece?"

"Your survival depends on this decision," Storm retorted, "Hemlock will not stop with the conquering of the mainland."

Cairn took a few steps closer to the throne, further annoying Aphis. "The Queen is prepared to offer you full independence of the mainland and its government."

"My brother always ignored me, especially in times of crisis;" Aliped snapped, "it was a form of independence which we enjoyed. However, we are a poor nation and the recent weather has devastated our agriculture, we therefore require substantial assistance."

"Sobranie will send without charge regular adequate supplies, and gold to supplement your economy," Cairn declared.

The Commander of Cracas said. "Then we will have to depend on the mainland for our survival, we will have no independence."

"You cannot have it completely both ways," Storm said flatly, "take it or leave it."

This statement surprised Cairn for the master-warrior was the chief negotiator, yet he smiled at this ultimatum for it was forcing the King into a corner from where he would have no choice but to move forward and accept the proposal.

Aliped glanced at Aphis in a mixture of anxiety and distrust, before turning back to the two emissaries. "Very well," the monarch sighed, "I accept the terms of the alliance."

Cairn promptly revealed a parchment containing the treaty which displayed the signature of the Queen and the seal of her office. King Aliped of Cracas Island leaned over and nervously added his name. Aphis grabbed a lit red-candle from the wall and holding it over the manuscript, allowed a few drips of wax to fall onto the paper. The monarch imprinted the seal on his large ring and let out a grunt of approval.

The organiser of The Game led the two travellers out of the palace and into the courtyard. "I will send thirty thousand soldiers by ship to the mainland in time for the battle," the guard announced, "but this army will be under my command."

"And you will take your orders from me," Cairn said sharply.

"I agree," Aphis sighed in resentment and indignation, before returning inside the palace.

The two companions mounted their steeds and the waiting escort began to lead them towards Port.

"That was a gamble you played back there," the master-warrior declared, "they could have rejected our offer."

"But it was a chance worth risking," Storm smirked, "besides, as you said in the capital Winterlending, they really did have no choice."

Cairn smiled at his friend in satisfaction, before they followed their escort out of the city Blackgame and soon found themselves in the harbour-town Port where intense activity greeted the two delegates. The quay was crowded with fishermen arguing a price with groups of soldiers planning to travel to the mainland for the war. The former Commander of Tomilusk realised it would require the entire Royal Navy of both Cracas and his own nation to transport such a tremendous force across the ocean. He only hoped the army would reach Abe in time for the battle, for they badly needed Aliped's troops for the war.

The travellers soon left the settlement of Port far behind and journeyed by the giant eagle back to Winterlending. Upon their arrival, they were informed by the skeleton-force guarding the capital city that the Queen and her soldiers had already left for Abe. The emissaries swiftly departed and a two-day voyage brought them to the gates of Abe, the town of the shield-maidens. They passed by thousands of men-at-arms making their way through the countryside, eager to spill their enemy's blood on the battlefield. However, this was a small body of guards compared to the enormous gathering surrounding the region of Abe.

Storm gasped in astonishment. A sea of armed soldiers and civilians filled his vision; he could not begin to estimate the magnitude of the army before him. Cairn drew up alongside the swordsman and grinned in pride, for these men were his to command.

"Behold my friend," the master-warrior declared aloud, "the greatest amassing of troops the world has ever seen!"

Storm sighed apprehensively in reply as they approached the crowded entrance to the town, and hoped the immense force would be enough to defeat Hemlock and his minions.

CHAPTER THIRTY-EIGHT

The gathering of guards let out a combined roar of approval as their leader entered the area. They seemed either unaware or uncaring of Storm's presence in their excitement to greet the Commander. Cairn dismounted and smiled as he shook the extended hands of eager young soldiers, inexperienced in the savagery of battle, yet prepared to lay down their lives for their country and Queen.

A personal escort of the monarch herself appeared and requested the two emissaries follow them into the settlement. The travellers left the cheering troops to their tasks of training and erecting of tents for the night. Storm had to practically barge his way through the dense crowds to reach the house of the ruling politician, the Alderwoman of Abe; the single only female leader bar Sobranie who was accepted by her fellow man to rule over them. Sotera was the Commander of her armed forces of shield-maidens, the only all-woman army in the history of the world.

The two delegates were escorted into the main-chamber which was filled to capacity with Captains and Lieutenants from nearly every town in the country, arguing battle-tactics and strategies. Cairn passed through them until he halted upon noticing a lone individual, standing apart from the gathering.

"Aphis," the master-warrior declared, "for once I am glad to see you, I hope you brought your forces with you."

The organiser of The Game said in reply. "Unfortunately I cannot say I am pleased to see you,

Commander," the guard retorted, "but yes, I have my army amassed outside of the town-gates. It required all five longships of our Royal Navy and all ten of yours, not to mention every fishing-boat and trawler in the civilised world to transport my men from Cracas to reach Abe through the river which runs adjacent to the settlement. I just hope all this trouble is worth it."

"Tomorrow you will find out on the battlefield," Cairn replied firmly, "and witness a war the like of which has never been seen."

The master-warrior's attention was drawn to his only superior as Sobranie approached. The Queen smiled briefly at Storm before ushering the two men into the inner-circle of high-ranking officers.

"Friends and comrades-in-arms," Sobranie announced, her voice echoing throughout the large room, silencing the chatter of the soldiers, "come the dawn we will march to the plains and confront the warlock in a battle whose result will determine the future of mankind. I am grateful to all of you for your loyalty and efficiency in swiftly bringing your armies to this town in time for the war, I am certain the outcome of this fight would have already been decided if any of you had not vowed your support."

The Queen moved to a huge rectangular oak-table that had been placed in the very centre of the chamber. Strewn upon its varnished surface were several maps of the land and a manuscript listing the size of the individual forces which had gathered for the battle.

"The largest army is from Cracas under the command of Aphis with a strength of thirty thousand," Sobranie declared and the organiser of The Game nodded in reply. "The Army Barracks has sent its full compliment of twenty-five thousand men with Karlaband delivering eighteen thousand to our cause. The capital itself has managed to find fifteen thousand, with Hellsbreath and Tomilusk offering eight thousand each. The smaller towns have sent varying amounts from Nez dispatching just two hundred men to Iron and Ledge delivering four thousand each. Abe itself has promised five thousand highly-trained shield-maidens to the war."

There was a collective cheer of approval and all the troops present began to shake hands in friendship and loyalty. The Queen smiled at this sign of solidarity and knew morale was high. Cairn moved alongside the monarch and with a shout ended the self-congratulations. The guards turned to their military-leader in respect, eager to hear the battle-plans.

"Our combined force is just over one hundred and twenty-three thousand, the majority of which is made up of civilians. The groups from Cracas, the Army Barracks and Hellsbreath are the only gatherings with no peasants in their ranks and all the men are on horseback. This should give us a great tactical advantage for Hemlock has no steeds, bar the stallions assigned to him personally and Ucein and his dark-elves," Cairn announced. "Spies which have observed the giant force travelling through the country have estimated the ogres to number approximately forty-five thousand, with the orcs measuring in the region of one hundred thousand."

The Captains and Lieutenants let out a groan of dismay and began chatting nervously about the difference in magnitude of their armies.

"Furthermore," the master-warrior added, "the warlock also has his highly-trained company of mercenaries who number about three thousand, and these bastards have old scores to settle with the government. However, I believe the odds weigh in our favour. Hemlock will be compelled to send the dragons home to their island, for despite Ucein's talent for *persuasion*, the ogres are terrified of the magical reptiles and will not fight in their presence. I also firmly believe the gathering of orcs will swiftly disperse and flee upon the deaths of Hemlock and the dark-elf Ucein, their assassinations are therefore our highest priority."

Storm smiled at this statement, vowing to be the one to carry out the killing of the necromancer, he was not too concerned with the fate of the elves.

Cairn turned towards the table. "The battle-strategy is simple and direct," the Commander said, "the orcs and ogres have no skill in archery, only the mercenaries do. That is an advantage the warlock will fear, for we have seventy thousand trained archers at our disposal. Unfortunately, the thick skin of Hemlock's inhuman races will be difficult to penetrate, and a dozen diamond-headed arrows might not be enough to dispatch even one orc," Cairn paused for breath before continuing. "After the archers have let fly their ammunition, we will send in the main force of horsemen with lances to disperse the necromancer's gathering before charging in with the rest of our army. In the confusion that will follow, Hemlock and Ucein will become separated from their personal bodyguards and opportunities to kill them will arise," the master-warrior added, "I have nothing further to say, except I wish you good luck and good hunting!"

Cairn then became involved in further conversation with the congregation of soldiers on more minor subjects as they crowded around him with eager questions. Storm seized the chance to leave the chamber and the settlement to be with his own thoughts. Sobranie noticed the swordsman depart and began to follow, her personal escort close behind, fearful for her safety in such dangerous times.

Storm left the busy activity of Abe and the many tents surrounding the town, and entered the wilderness; the outskirts of the region. The swordsman gazed at the mountains which hid the plains where resided the forces of his mortal enemy, and did not hear the Queen approach until she stood beside him. Her bodyguards lay a hundred metres behind, standing watch for any suspicious movements. A single shout from one of these troops, and a thousand men-at-arms would be at the scene within seconds.

"Concerned about tomorrow?" Sobranie inquired.

"Who would not be?" Storm sighed, "I fear for the lives of my friends."

"And what of your own life?" the monarch asked, "It is not necessary for you to fight, we both know Hemlock will not leave the battlefield alive."

Storm smiled in reply at her comment, yet then his face became cold and emotionless. "I owe it to my friends and my late wife to attend the war and personally finish the warlock."

"It is your obsession that drives you," Sobranie retorted sharply, "not any obligation to dead comrades and lovers," she said and laid a hand on his shoulder. "What of your former career before all this happened; before Hemlock killed Nereid?"

"Yes, I was a simple sailor once," Storm sighed in regret, "satisfied to sail the calm seas and fish, but that life is now long gone; I can never return to so passive an occupation."

"And what of us?" the Queen inquired, "Is there any chance for you and I when this battle is won? The opportunity to become King presents itself."

"Maybe," the swordsman replied, "or perhaps I am courting above my station."

"Nonsense," Sobranie responded, "you are the finest and noblest man I have ever met, and it is I who would be honoured to have you as my consort."

Storm smirked. "When this fight is over and Hemlock lies dead, I will owe no more to my friends, my wife, or my quest for vengeance," he said and turned to embrace the monarch, "my only obsession then will be to love you."

The Queen held him tight in her arms and they watched the sunset as the final rays of the day faded over the mountains, and she prayed her beloved swordsman would live to see another night.

*　　*　　*　　*　　*

The warlock watched the enormous army approach in astonishment, his black eyes gazing upon the largest body of dark-skinned monsters he had ever seen. The company of mercenaries instantly rose and snatched up weapons in fright, as the mortal enemies of all humans arrived on the plains. Hemlock turned and extended a raised hand towards the hired bandits, motioning for them to maintain their position and lower their swords.

Ucein and his seven elves were clearly visible upon horseback, and the sorcerer dismounted to greet Hemlock. "It was quite a struggle getting the bastards here," sighed the elf, "every near-deserted town we passed by proved to be an irresistible temptation for the orcs, I had to kill several thousand to keep them in line and focus their full attention on reaching the plains in time for the battle."

"I too was becoming anxious," the thief said, "the armies of the Queen have gathered at Abe, and the dragons circling above us at the outskirts of the plains were the only things preventing the bitch's forces from charging into us."

"They will wait for the dawn to march and confront us, knowing you will be compelled to send the fire-reptiles home," Ucein declared.

"I regret having to send the magical beasts back to their island," Hemlock growled, "they are a valuable asset."

"It is unavoidable," the dark-elf retorted sharply, "the ogres required heavy persuasion just to enter this area in the same company as the dragons. But you will not need the flying reptiles, for a body of forty-five thousand blood-thirsty battle-crazy ogres will frighten the wits out of the peasants of the Queen and decide the fate of the war. Sobranie's forces are composed primarily of untrained inexperienced farmers who will flee at the very sight of the ogres charging towards them."

"I have promised the mercenaries that they will be in the capital in four days," Hemlock said, "and the crown will be finally mine."

"The ogres and orcs have requested Karlaband as their new home," Ucein announced, "it is an offer we cannot refuse, we should be grateful the monsters have chosen a city on the other side of the world as their haven, and thus will leave us in peace."

"Tell me about the battle-plans," the warlock inquired and led the elves towards his tent in the centre of the encampment.

The gathering of bandits watched Ucein in distrust and suspicion, before staring fixedly at the races from the ice-lands in nervousness. The orcs and ogres glanced back and licked their lips in anticipation, eager to spill blood and feast on human bodies.

Inside the large marquee of the thief was a six-foot square table from Ferulas which was covered with a comprehensive detailed map of the land. They crowded around the waist-high piece of furniture and all turned to Ucein, eager to hear his advice.

"The strategy is simple, yet effective," the dark sorcerer declared aloud, "the three thousand mercenaries will unleash their arrows before the main force of orcs and ogres will enter the fray. The ogres are far stronger than any human and their strength will guarantee heavy casualties for the Queen's army. We unfortunately have little defence against her archers, we can only hope our gathering will push through quickly and surround them. The morale of our forces is high, whereas the many timid civilians of Sobranie's army will flee at the sight of such bloodshed and the fury of the orcs. I and my elves will remain apart of the main fray and circle around, intending to eliminate the Captains and Commanders, in particular their Chief Military-Leader Cairn and reclaim my spear."

Ucein turned to Hemlock. "I advise ordering the dragons home before retiring for the night," the elf said, "tomorrow promises to be long and tiring and I want your full attention on the battle."

The thief nodded in reply and left the tent. Ucein followed him out, intending to organise the sleeping-arrangements for the orcs and ogres, and keep them apart from the bandits.

"Why not send the fire-reptiles to attack Abe?" Hemlock inquired as he turned to the sorcerer.

"The town is too well defended," Ucein retorted, "I am not willing to sacrifice the lives of the dragons on such an obvious suicide-mission."

The thief frowned in confusion. "I always believed you had no respect or feelings of compassion for any living thing."

"Not usually," the elf replied, "but the flying reptiles are creatures of magick, like me."

Hemlock watched Ucein disappear into the night, amazed the sorcerer had some scruples, before raising his hands to the sky. The warlock let out a series of roars and smiled as the dragons heard his command, and circling once more in a sign of farewell, swiftly departed from the region and headed home for their island. The ogres sighed in relief as the reptiles vanished from sight and began to settle down for the night, polishing their crude blades for the following day.

Hemlock retired to his tent and bed, but sleep did not come easy. A vision of his long-dead brother Kava invaded his fevered mind, haunting his slumber. His sibling promised death the next day and an eternity in hell for Hemlock. Kava then began to laugh which rose into an insane cacophony that echoed through the warlock's head.

Ucein heard the thief's mumblings and distress as he passed near to the marquee and entered. He laid a hand on the necromancer's sweat-drenched forehead and read Hemlock's sleeping thoughts. The colour started to drain from the elf's face and he ran from the tent. His company of dark-brethren confronted their master at the entrance to the warlock's marquee and inquired as regards the sorcerer's anguish.

Ucein turned and pointed towards Hemlock's sleeping form. "I fear I have made a grave mistake in our choice of the thief as future leader of this land," the elf declared, "here is no master-magician, not even a mere common mage, but rather a simple foolish dabbler; a lunatic driven solely by greed and lust for power; power I believe he shall never find."

The group of elves left the tent behind and returned to the encampment of the orcs and ogres, to ponder their fate and the day ahead, and wondered if they would live to see the war's end.

CHAPTER THIRTY-NINE

Storm was awoken just before dawn by excited shouts from eager soldiers passing just outside his tent. He quickly dressed and snatching up his blade, left the small marquee behind and entered a busy gathering of activity. Guards from nearly every town and city in the world rushed past him, unaware of their superior as Cairn moved through them to greet Storm.

"Well, swordsman," the master-warrior declared, "it appears your long wait is finally over."

"Yes, my friend," Storm replied with a smile, "I promise Hemlock will not escape me this time, but what of Ucein? It is certain the dark-elf will be present and eager to reclaim his former possessions."

"And well he may try," Cairn retorted sharply, rubbing a hand down the ten-inch blade tip of the magnificent spear.

The two men mounted their steeds and waited several moments as the rest of the Commanders, including Aphis and Sotera crowded around them. The organiser of The Game glared briefly at Cairn, as if annoyed more being awoken so early in the day, rather than any other feelings of hostility he held for the master-warrior. The officers saluted as Sobranie and her personal escort appeared and approached them.

They began to depart from the settlement as the individual armies behind them swiftly filled into ranks and followed. The forces outside Abe were already prepared to march, dressed in full battle-armour and armed with an assortment of weapons, including swords, double-headed axes, lances and halberds.

The enormous body of men and shield-maidens gradually left the town behind and entered the outskirts of the plains where lay the battlefield. Cairn and Sotera started to nervously scan the skies for any indication of roaming dragons, but to their relief, the reptiles seemed to have vanished and returned home.

The vast army of Hemlock stood patiently, awaiting the arrival of the Queen and her forces. The mercenaries lay in front, ready with their bows while behind them the orcs and ogres unsheathed their giant broadswords and axes in anticipation of a war they had prayed to come for centuries.

Ucein gazed across the gathering which stretched in both directions and behind him as far as the eye could see. He turned to the thief who rode on horseback alongside him. "I care not for the fate of the monarch," the elf announced, "but the life of Cairn is mine to take, he and I have an old score to settle."

"And what of the swordsman; our common enemy?" the warlock inquired.

"Do what you want with his miserable carcass," Ucein replied flatly, "just bring me back my sword."

Hemlock nodded and they turned as the army of Sobranie began to come over the hillside. The mercenaries took a step back in momentary uneasiness at the sight of such a large body entering the arena. It took several minutes for the colossal company of the Queen to gather at the opposite side of the battlefield as Hemlock and his forces stood motionless. The Commanders moved to the front to observe the progress of the war and ferry orders into the fray to counteract the warlock's instructions.

The orcs and ogres started to cheer and roar in excitement and Ucein feared the temptation to prematurely charge would be too great for the black monsters from the ice-lands. But a glance from the master-elf forced the races to keep their ground and await the proper command.

The civilians from the towns stared at Cairn and their individual leaders in fright and the master-warrior feared the timid farmers would take flight and destroy the stability of the gathering and severely injure morale. Yet they managed to regain their composure and readied themselves for the fight. Storm glanced at Sobranie and she forced a smile in reply, worried for the swordsman's safety. She appeared unconcerned for her own life, even though the monarch was obviously the most sought-after prize for Hemlock, her death was absolutely necessary for the warlock to steal the crown and the rulership of the land.

After drawing blades, the two armies stood in motionless silence, both seemingly unwilling to give the order and unleash their massive forces. It was Cairn however who started the battle. He raised his spear high and seventy thousand archers moved to the front and readied their longbows. Storm watched the men as they left the main ranks of the company and a long line of archers filled his vision in both directions from east to west. They raised the bows to the sky and Hemlock let out a growl in reply, signalling for the hired-bandits to do likewise. However, before the mercenaries could unleash their weapons, a dense rain of diamond-headed arrows descended upon them and the warlock roared in rage as men fell all around him.

Five hundred bandits collapsed to the ground dead while two hundred ogres and three hundred orcs also fell to the wooden shafts. It seemed the thick skin of the ice-races had prevented heavier casualties, and Hemlock could see orcs with several arrows protruding from their dark bodies and yet quite prepared and able to carry on. A second shower quickly followed and a further eight hundred mercenaries died, their corpses littering the front of the army. Ucein groaned in frustration as Sobranie's archers appeared to have increased their accuracy and deadly-efficiency as four thousand more ogres fell alongside seven thousand orcs.

The inhuman races seemed to have lost their patience and surged forward, unwilling to allow the remaining seventeen hundred bandits the opportunity to let fly their wooden ammunition. The orcs and ogres wanted to inflict retaliation at a much closer level. The monsters charged up the hillside towards their enemy and Cairn ordered the horsemen to ride into them with lances.

Ten thousand armoured men on horseback left the main army and with a combined shout rode down the mountain. The master-warrior looked behind and sighed in dismay for the majority of their forces was now almost purely civilian, yet he smiled for the seventy thousand archers had discarded their longbows in favour of their swords and rejoined the main gathering. The horsemen smashed into the orcs, impaling them with the lowered lances, even their tough skin little defence against such savage blows. Hemlock responded by sending in the remainder of his army into the fray and Cairn was therefore compelled to order the charging of the footmen, the shield-maidens and the lightly-armed farmers and labourers.

Sobranie observed the troops leave their side and soon it was every man for himself on the furious battlefield. Both soldiers and orcs quickly found themselves knee-deep in blood and battered bodies as they struggled towards the opposite end of the plains and their opponents' leaders.

Cairn dismounted and turned to Storm. "It is time to personally enter the war, my friend," he declared, "and redden our weapons with the blood of our enemies."

"The Chief-Commander should not put his own life at risk," the monarch said sharply, "besides, I require your constant advice and support."

"The fight is now out of both your hands and Hemlock's, my Queen," the master-warrior retorted, "you can do nothing else but wait and watch, I on the other hand plan to participate in the greatest battle mankind has ever seen."

Storm nodded in agreement and also dismounted, much to the dismay of Sobranie and Sotera, fearful for the safety of the two comrades.

Aphis appeared alongside them and drew his sword. "May I join you?" the organiser of The Game inquired, "I would like to return to Cracas with some tales to tell."

Cairn nodded in approval and the three men left the monarch, the shield-maiden and the assortment of Commanders behind. The master-warrior was not short of available opponents, for his uniform identified him as an irresistible and much valued target for the ogres. It seemed they had forgotten Ucein's orders about ignoring Cairn, for the elf wanted the exclusive pleasure of taking the guard's life.

A quick flick of his wrist and the spear removed the head of one ogre, its bulbous skull rebounding off the grass. The two Commanders joined back-to-back to fend off attackers while Storm became separated as mercenaries took turns to launch at the lone swordsman. However, they soon discovered their expensive armour proved to be little defence against the magical blade as Storm easily cleaved through steel and flesh.

The swordsman began to make his way back to Cairn when a peculiar sight greeted his vision. A strange robed figure forced a path through the fray, followed closely behind by seven younger bizarre intruders on the plains. Storm gasped in shock as he recognised the face of a man he had not seen in centuries, and remembered the mysterious elf who had called out to him in Sulphur Mountain before the Battle of the Temples. He knew the individual could be no-one other than the dark sorcerer Ucein and he was swiftly approaching Cairn and Aphis.

Storm attempted to cry a warning to his friend above the noise of the war, but in vain. Dozens of orcs fighting soldiers separated him from the master-warrior and barred his path. The swordsman could only watch on helpless as Ucein grabbed a longbow off a nearby bandit, and notching an arrow, fired the shaft at Aphis. The wooden instrument penetrated the left eye of the Commander of Cracas and the guard cried out in pain before falling to the ground dead. Cairn turned and gasped in surprise upon recognising the dark-elf. A mere twenty metres was all that appeared to separate the two opponents and the master-warrior laughed at this threat before him.

"So, you have come for your possession," Cairn roared above the fury of the battle, "approach and reclaim it, if you dare!"

Ucein smiled in reply, but did not take a single step towards the Commander. Instead he gathered his seven elves to him, three at one side and four at the other and with a shout, the seven robed figures revealed loaded crossbows from beneath their black cloaks. Cairn stared at the dark sorcerer in apathy, as if not believing the elf would be so devious, or that he actually had the courage and audacity to kill him.

The master-warrior glanced at Storm across the plains as Ucein screamed and seven foot-long steel-tipped crossbolts entered the soldier's torso. The Commander gazed down in disbelief at the shafts protruding from his armour and fell to his knees. He did not hear Storm cry out in rage and anguish as the swordsman finally managed to force his way through to reach him, however moments too late to save his companion's life. Cairn found the energy to rise to his feet and with the last of his fading strength, let fly the magical spear across the grasslands. Ucein mumbled a few words and a translucent solid shield appeared in front of him, blocking the weapon's path. However, the spear easily penetrated the enchanted barrier and impaled the dark-elf through the stomach. It pierced his liver and on its exit, shattered his spine. A mouthful of black blood came to the sorcerer's lips as his party of elves crowded around their dying master in astonishment. Despite his considerable powers, Ucein swiftly dropped to the grass and died within seconds. The group in their absolute shock did not notice Storm's arrival until he stood before them. The swordsman ignored their feeble pleas for mercy and furiously hacked at them until a river of thick crimson blood ran from the spot, staining the plains. He left the smashed bodies behind and returned to Cairn who now lay on his side, unable to move. Storm was amazed the soldier still lived, though he knew his friend had mere minutes of life left.

"Tell Sotera I'm sorry," the Commander whispered through the pain, "she always said my foolish recklessness would be my undoing. Take the spear from Ucein's carcass and give it to her for our unborn child, perhaps when he attains adulthood he will use the weapon more wisely than I have done."

Tears came to Storm's eyes as he glanced around the battlefield and through the haze of combat, saw the shape of a shield-maiden fighting a clear path through to reach them. The swordsman returned his attention to his fallen comrade, but the master-warrior was already dead. Storm gently laid the guard's head on the muddy-grass before approaching the battered corpse of the dark-elf. He retrieved the spear and upon his return to Cairn's resting-place, found Sotera weeping at his side. Storm could find no words to comfort her, but simply placed the magical weapon into her hand and retold her fiancé's final message. The swordsman stared down at the peppered body of his friend in disbelief, not willing to acknowledge his companion was truly dead, and the fact that had he lived he would have soon been a father. Hemlock's cohorts had deprived Cairn of that family-life, just like the warlock had done for Storm when he murdered his wife and unborn child.

The swordsman left the shield-maiden to her grieving and returned to the main fray. He had only just begun to enter into combat with an axe-wielding orc when a great commotion to the north of the region ceased their fight. A bright golden-inferno consumed a substantial part of the plains and set the grass alight. Footmen from the ranks of the town Hellsbreath ran through the crowd, screaming in agony as they burst into flames. They fled past him, covered from head to foot in golden fire until mercifully they eventually collapsed and rapidly died.

Storm's opponent appeared equally confused until his human-leader who had just unleashed the lethal fireball stepped through the gathering and confronted the swordsman. The ogres and orcs drew back in respect and allowed entrance for the necromancer. A glance from Hemlock and his legions returned to fighting the soldiers, now ignoring their Chief.

Storm stared fixedly at the robed individual standing not ten feet from him in pure hatred. Hemlock sneered in reply and pointed at the object in Storm's hand.

"You have something I want, sailor," the warlock growled and drew the Fire sword from its scabbard, "and I mean to have it now Ucein is dead."

Storm glanced at the magnificent instrument in Hemlock's hand and the shield he held in the other in front of his chest. The blade was heavily decorated and inscribed like all the other weapons of the gods, but it was the waves of red flame that danced across the steel that caught the swordsman's attention. The fabled Shield of Protection seemed quite dull and uninteresting in comparison, yet Storm knew penetrating the magical metal would prove to be next to impossible. He just hoped his own enchanted weapon would be perhaps formidable enough to pierce the steel of the shield.

"Your friend the elf died like a coward," Storm said, "I am sure you will prove to be no different."

"I cared not for the fate of that arrogant bastard," Hemlock retorted, "you did me a service ending his life and his company of elves, I would have been forced to kill the dangerous sorcerer once the war had finished. I believe he had designs on the throne himself."

"The Queen would like to have you tried for high treason and publicly executed," Storm declared, "but I would not be bothered with such pointless acts of kindness which you don't deserve."

The warlock laughed in reply. "You still pursue me for the death of your bitch centuries ago in Karlaband," the thief growled in disbelief. "Excusing that, why would you wish to kill me? Without me, you are nothing. When history is written, you will only be remembered because of me."

"Perhaps," Storm replied sharply, "but I am certain history will record me in a far better light, and as the killer of the foulest monster to have ever been born."

"Then advance and try your best to take my life, sailor," the warlock said.

Storm launched forward and struck out at his mortal ancient enemy, but Hemlock calmly defended off the blow. The thief Storm remembered was a trained mercenary and swordsman before he began his quest for the throne of the land, and hence he would be difficult to defeat. Yet Storm was not about to allow this uncomfortable knowledge to discourage him from his task. He struck at the necromancer again, but with a smile Hemlock blocked the attack.

Around them the battle raged on with the orcs rapidly making ground and gradually beating the forces of the monarch back up the hillside towards the Commanders. Storm realised their only chance of victory was the death of their human leader and hope this act destroyed the morale of his legions from the ice-lands and shatter their will to continue fighting.

Hemlock appeared to slip and lose his balance in the mud and Storm seized this rare opportunity, striking out and meaning to behead his opponent. Too late he realised the thief had faked his fall and easily blocked the blow with the shield. Storm in his eagerness to end the combat had let himself open, and Hemlock swung the Fire sword around in an arc and hit Storm on his left side just above the pelvis. The blade cleaved through the weak chainmail and sliced into the soft flesh of his flank, nearly cutting Storm in half. A sense of feeling more of shock than actual pain filled his body and he collapsed onto his side. Hemlock took a few steps back, not willing to take a chance, even though his ancient opponent was obviously mortally injured.

Storm looked up and saw the warlock start to laugh in triumph, and in rage snatched up the sword of Ucein and holding the weapon like a spear, hurled the instrument at the thief. Hemlock in his moment of victory did not seem to notice what had happened until he glanced down and saw the blade had pierced the magical shield, his heavy chainmail and finally his chest. A quick examination proved the tip of the weapon had exited his back just below his left shoulder-bone, and he dropped the Fire sword to the ground in his absolute surprise. As if sensing its master's approaching demise, the enchanted instrument shattered upon contact with the ground, yet Hemlock did not notice. The warlock fell to his knees on the grass as if praying for his fading life. His hands went to his face in shock as he felt his eyes return to their natural colour, the blackness disappearing. The thief sensed whatever magical powers he possessed vanish, and a realisation that he was becoming a normal person; a *nobody* again dawned on Hemlock. He turned to Storm in fear and the swordsman smiled in reply in silent triumph. Hemlock retorted by briefly sneering before the life finally left him and he collapsed to the ground.

Storm in excruciating pain rose to his knees and approaching his fallen enemy, retrieved his blade from the thief's carcass. He fell back on his side as he felt his entire body become cold. Storm found it hard to focus on the orcs and troops around him as their faces became blurred. However, he gazed across the battlefield and grinned, for a female figure began to make her way through the fighting. Storm laughed in delight as the visage of Nereid came into view and he extended his arms for an embrace. However, as the person came closer he realised it was not his dead wife, but Sobranie, flanked by a dozen armed guards, protecting her passage.

The Queen knelt alongside her beloved swordsman and laid his head on her lap as the tears fell from her face. Storm managed to raise a hand and touch her right cheek before his arm fell and with a sigh, the life left his battered body. The monarch briefly hugged him before turning and ordering his corpse to be taken from the battlefield. She reached down and snatching up the blade of Ucein, approached Hemlock and with one swift blow, beheaded the thief. She held the dripping skull high by its long brown hair and the orcs and ogres around her screamed in anguish and fear before dropping their weapons and started to flee from the plains.

The act had a cascade effect as the entire army of monsters ran from the arena and into the surrounding countryside, eager to return to their homes in the ice-lands. The war had been won, but at a terrible price, for most of the Queen's forces lay dead or dying, in particular the lightly-armed civilians whose previous inexperience in combat had sealed their doom.

Sobranie left the battlefield and encountered Sotera, holding the spear of her fallen lover. Together the two women departed from the plains and began to travel in the direction of Abe, eager to leave the bloodshed and slaughtered bodies behind, while dreading the grief and loneliness which awaited them.

EPILOGUE

The Queen gazed across the barren wilderness from the battlements of the town Abe. Outside of the settlement, the hundreds of mass-burials went on, soldiers working day and night to remove the ravaged corpses of comrades and their inhuman murderers. The river that ran west of the town and near the battlefield was red with the blood of fallen warriors as it seeped down to the coast. Sobranie sighed in dismay, knowing it would take dozens of generations to restore the depleted population and former beauty of the land, and all for the sake of the madness of one man.

The monarch turned abruptly as Sotera drew up alongside her, brandishing the spear of her late fiancé.

"So much devastation," the Commander of the shield-maidens declared, "and for what? To remove a lunatic and his evil hordes from our world. Time will likely provide us with a new madman with whom we will have to wage war upon, and suffer another cataclysm of bloodshed."

"Who knows?" Sobranie retorted, "Perhaps only at the world's end when man no longer walks the land will we know peace."

Sotera rubbed her stomach in regret. "Because of Hemlock I have no father for my unborn child," the Commander announced, "all I can offer the baby is my love and Cairn's spear, and hope my child does not die on such a battlefield and as young as his or her father."

The Queen glanced at her friend's swollen belly in envy. "I don't even have the privilege of pregnancy to remember Storm by and therefore not even someone to whom I can give love;" Sobranie sighed as tears ran down her face and she turned once more to stare out at the ravaged land before her, "all I know is that I am doomed to a life of loneliness, and to rule a wasteland."